CONFRONTING
THE
DRAGON

Also by Mark Cheverton

Invasion of the Overworld
Battle for the Nether

Trouble in Zombie-Town
Jungle Temple Oracle
Last Stand on the Ocean Shore

Saving Crafter

MARK CHEVERTON

CONFRONTING THE DRAGON

A GAMEKNIGHT999 ADVENTURE

SIMON AND SCHUSTER

First published in Great Britain in 2015
by Simon & Schuster UK Ltd

A CBS company

Originally published in the USA in 2014 by Sky Pony Press

10 9 8 7 6 5 4 3 2 1

Simon & Schuster UK Ltd
1st Floor, 222 Gray's Inn Road
London WC1X 8HB

A CIP catalogue record for this book is available from the British Library

PB ISBN: 978-1-4711-5844-5
Ebook ISBN: 978-1-4711-4434-9

Printed and bound by CPI Group (UK) Ltd, Croydon, CR0 4YY

www.simonandschuster.co.uk

For those that suffer in silence

CHAPTER 1

THE LAST BATTLE

Gameknight999 floated through a silvery mist, a feeling of dread pulsing through every nerve. Something was about to happen . . . something bad, and somehow, he knew that he could not avoid the deadly consequences of what was about to transpire.

Gradually, the cloud started to clear, and he found himself on a large plateau atop a huge mountain of bedrock. As the silvery fog settled to the ground, figures started to emerge from behind its misty veil . . . NPCs, all of them armored and carrying weapons; they were the surviving defenders of Minecraft.

Sensing a presence next to him, Gameknight turned and found Crafter and Mason standing next to him. They talked quietly to each other, their faces grim with determination. They glanced out across the plateau to the vast plain that sat at the mountain's base. Something seemed to be moving through the shining fog that obscured the ground . . . angry things . . . hurtful things.

Does the mist mean this is a dream? *He thought.*

That shiny fog seemed to be in all of the strange dreams I've been having lately.

He couldn't explain it, but something inside told Gameknight he was looking at the future . . . that he was seeing his own future. And somehow, a feeling from within made him shake with fear as he realized the truth about what was going to happen.

He was about to witness his own death and the end of Minecraft.

Shuddering, he turned to look at his friends. Next to Mason, he found Hunter standing rigid and strong, enchanted bow in her hand, and now he knew for sure that this was a dream. She looked haggard and exhausted, almost translucent, but with a look of deadly anger in her eyes.

How could this be the future when Hunter had already been captured by Malacoda and Erebus on the last server? *Gameknight thought.* How was this possible?

Gameknight looked about the plateau, and found that it was covered with what looked like beacons, transparent glass cubes with light emitting blocks trapped within. He could see a whole field of beacons, hundreds of them, maybe thousands. But the curious thing was that they were all dark save for two. One shone bright, sending a brilliant beam of white light straight up into the sky. It was bigger than the rest, in fact it was massive, taller than any of the NPCs, its base surrounded by diamond blocks that also cast shafts of icy blue light up into the sky. It was so bright that its light felt blazing hot, as if anyone that touched the glowing beam would be vaporized instantly. All of the other beacons were normal sized, even though they looked tiny in comparison. Only one of these smaller beacons shone with light, its brilliant beam feeling just as hot and deadly as its larger companion.

What's going on here? *Gameknight thought.* What am I doing here? What's that beacon for? Is this the Last Battle for Minecraft?

Gameknight could see that everyone on top of the mountain had looks of fear and uncertainty painted on their faces. In front of them was a steep stairway that led from the plains below up to the flat mountaintop where they stood. It was the only way up to the plateau of beacons; the sides of the plateau were sheer and unscalable.

Gameknight watched as Mason peered down the sloping hill and surveyed the landscape. He then turned and focused his green eyes on him.

"They're coming," he said with a grim voice. "There must be five hundred monsters, maybe a thousand, right behind Erebus." He reached up with a blocky hand and stroked his neatly trimmed beard, his eyes scanning the faces of his warriors. "I fear there is no way for us to stop this horde. Minecraft is doomed."

Doomed?! *Gameknight thought.* If this is the future, does this mean we're going to lose the battle for Minecraft?!

He wanted to yell, tell them to not give up, but his voice would not respond. He felt trapped within his own body, unable to do anything other than be a spectator from behind these helpless eyes.

"Do not despair, User-that-is-not-a-user," Crafter said, his wise voice resonating across the mountaintop. "You did all that could be done. There is no shame in failing after doing your best."

"What are you talking about?" Hunter snapped, her voice sounding dreamlike and surreal to Gameknight. She had a transparent look to her, as if she were not completely there, her fate still uncertain. "If we lose, then we lose. There is nothing to be proud about."

Gameknight turned and looked at Crafter. The

young boy with the old eyes gazed up at him, a look of sadness across his face.

"I'm sorry we couldn't do more," Crafter said in a low voice, his words meant only for Gameknight. "You've seen the horde below. You know we cannot defeat Erebus and the monsters of the night this time. We have barely a hundred soldiers left. They cannot stop the approaching tide of destruction."

Crafter turned to look up at the massive beacon, the Source, and sighed.

"I guess there is nothing left to do other than fight and die," Crafter said as he drew his own blade.

Gameknight looked at the scene with an overwhelming sadness. If this is the future, does this mean I led everyone to this point, to failure? Is there really nothing left I can do? Why does my body, my entire being feel so . . . so . . . defeated? *He couldn't bear to witness the destruction of his friends . . . of Minecraft. He wanted to turn away, but he couldn't; he had no control over this body.*

I have to do something . . . I have to try to help them! *he thought.*

Gameknight could now hear the moaning of the monsters as they reached the foot of the stairway that led to the mountaintop. The clicking of spiders, wheezing of blazes, and wailing cries of the ghasts echoed across the strange landscape, making the defenders on the plateau all cringe.

"There is still something I must do," Gameknight said to all the NPCs.

NO! That's not me talking! *he yelled from within his mind, but his body would not answer.*

Moving on its own, his body put away his sword, then stepped up next to the beacon, the shaft of blazing light just inches from his face. He could feel the unbelievable heat from the beam, like all the heat in the Nether compressed into this glowing ray.

"Gameknight, what are you doing?" Crafter screamed.

What am I doing?! *Gameknight thought, panicking.* Am I going to jump into that beam? Why aren't I trying to save everyone?

"That's the coward's way," Hunter yelled. "Don't give up, fight with us . . . with me." There was a peculiar sadness now to her voice, her eyes pleading for him to abandon this path.

"No, this is something I must do," Gameknight's body said in a loud voice.

Looking at his friends, Gameknight saw disbelief on all their faces as they watched him move closer to the brilliant shaft of blazing death. Then, Mason stepped away from the other NPCs and stood next to Gameknight, a curious knowing smile on his face.

"No, not you too!" Hunter cried, disbelief in her voice.

"You will come to understand in time," Mason replied.

Then, moving to the other side of the beacon, Mason raised his sword up high, grasping the hilt with both hands. With all his might, he brought the sword straight down, plunging it into the ground. It sounded like a crack of thunder when it pierced the bedrock, causing the whole landscape to shake. Grasping the hilt firmly with one hand, he extended his other blocky hand to the User-that-is-not-a-user, his green eyes locked onto Gameknight's.

"For Minecraft," the big NPC said in a surprisingly soft and reassuring voice

"For Minecraft," he heard his body repeat, then stepped into the blazing hot shaft of light.

Is this the end?! *Gameknight thought.* This can't be how it all ends. If this is the future, then is there any hope . . . can the future be changed? What about . . .

And suddenly, everything went brilliantly bright as pain erupted throughout his body, then everything started to fade. But just before everything became completely black, he thought he could hear something . . . voices . . . hundreds of them, and one in particular that he hadn't heard for what seemed like forever. It was a familiar voice of a friend that he missed so deeply, and as the voice started to fill his mind, Gameknight999 almost started to smile. Then darkness claimed him.

CHAPTER 2

FOLLOWING THE TRAIL

Gameknight woke up abruptly, his mind swirling with confusion and his brain trying to comprehend what he'd just seen.

Was that just a dream, he thought, *or was it something else? It felt real, but different . . . like somehow he was looking into the future.*

He could still remember the look of resigned acceptance on all the NPC's faces as they stared down at the massive monster horde that was approaching. There was no way that small group of defenders could protect the Source from the invading army. They would surely lose and there was nothing that Gameknight999, the User-that-is-not-a-user, could do about it.

Shaking his head, he tried to push the images from his mind. But they just rattled around in his brain like little hammers, each one chipping away at his courage. Sighing, he sat up and glanced around the camp, looking or any evidence of that monster horde here. Fortunately, he only found NPCs; bakers, carpenters, farmers, tailors, diggers, builders . . . every facet of Minecraft society now pressed into armor, weapons lying nearby. They were all here for him, because he'd guilted them into coming to the Source. They'd failed to stop Erebus and Malacoda on the last server and had followed the massive horde of monsters to this server, to the Source. But they were grossly outnumbered and didn't know where to go or what to do. So instead of making a plan and doing something useful, they were just following the blackened and charred path left behind by the monster horde in hopes of learning what the terrible creatures were planning.

Gameknight stood and stretched, reaching high up into the sky then arching his back, knots and cramps slowly releasing after sleeping on the hard lumpy ground. Looking up at the dark sky, he could see the square face of the moon starting to dip toward the tree line; it would be dawn soon. A faint red hue shone from the lunar body, something that they'd all noticed as soon as they'd come to this threatened land, something to do with all the monsters that had invaded, staining the very fabric of Minecraft with their violent hateful presence.

I wonder if the sun and moon will ever go back to their original color, Gameknight thought.

Scanning the camp, he saw soldiers stretched out anywhere that was flat, their army camped in a gentle valley on the edge of a pine forest. Small piles of armor-covered bodies here, blanket-covered NPCs there; they were spread out all throughout the bowl. He could see torches planted around the campsite, partially to keep monsters from spawning nearby, but also to put the NPCs at ease. Darkness seemed to make those from the Overworld nervous, for they had all learned a long time ago when they were but innocent children, that nighttime was monster time.

Stepping carefully around the sleeping bodies, Gameknight reached the edge of the campsite and came upon Mason, the actual leader of the army, walking along their perimeter.

"User-that-is-not-a-user," the big NPC said as he stopped and put his fist to his chest in salute, "you should be resting."

"I can't sleep," he replied, "so I thought I might check the perimeter."

"You are a wise leader," Mason said, "always being cautious."

Leader . . . right, what a joke, Gameknight thought to himself.

The army looked up to Gameknight999, the User-that-is-not-a-user, but he was not their general. That was Mason. He had a sense of command about him that made anyone listening to him *want* to do what he said. His concern for his soldiers was only matched by his concern for the safety of Minecraft. Mason was the real commander of this NPC army, and Gameknight knew it. Whether he liked it or not, the User-that-is-not-a-user felt like he was just a symbol, a figurehead that was supposed to somehow save the day and make everything better again. The problem was . . . he didn't know what to do or what to say.

"There has been no activity," Mason said as he turned and looked about their surroundings. "No monsters sighted anywhere."

"Doesn't that seem a bit strange?" Gameknight asked.

"Maybe Malacoda and Erebus are collecting those that they find and are taking them with them, making their army even bigger."

Gameknight grunted and nodded.

"That makes sense," Gameknight replied.

Of course it made sense, he thought bitterly. *Everything that Mason says makes sense!*

"What are you doing up at this hour, Mason?"

"A good leader stands with his men and does what he asks his men to do," the big NPC replied, his green eyes sparkling in the moonlight. "If I did any less, then I'd just be an arrogant, spoiled general for whom the soldiers would not fight. They have to know that I will do anything they are asked to do."

"But what are you watching for?" Gameknight asked as he moved next to the big NPC. "Malacoda and his monsters are far away from here. They won't attack."

"Attack your enemy where he is unprepared and appear where you are not expected," Mason answered as if reciting something that he'd memorized.

That sounded familiar to Gameknight for some reason . . . curious.

"That's what I would do," the big NPC said, "so that's what I prepare for." He paused to scan the line of trees then continued. "Come, walk with me."

Gameknight walked next to him, trying to stand as tall as the big NPC, something that was difficult to do even if you were the same height as him. No matter how tall he was, Gameknight always felt small next to Mason.

As they walked, the pale crimson moon slowly dipped below the tree line, the eastern horizon starting to glow a deep red; it would be dawn soon. The camp was starting to awaken. Tired forms stood in the dim light of dawn, putting armor back on and picking up weapons. When they saw Gameknight the soldiers instantly cheered and snapped to attention, fist to chest.

"User-that-is-not-a-user will defeat the monsters," someone shouted.

"Gameknight999, the bravest Minecraft warrior ever," said another.

More statements of praise came from the soldiers as they walked around the camp. This had been happening ever since they had come to this server . . . to the Source. For some reason, the warriors in their army had come to the conclusion that Gameknight999 was some kind of great hero, brave and courageous, and without fear. They all thought he would save them, defeat the monsters of Minecraft, and make everything all better.

What a joke, he thought. *They don't realize that I would run away right now if I had someplace to run to.*

Gameknight knew he wasn't as brave as everyone thought he was. He hated being afraid, but Minecraft had slowly worn down his courage and chipped away at his resolve. He cringed whenever they came across a lone monster or maybe a scouting party, and the thought of battling these creatures turned his blood to ice. He had learned much about facing his fears on the last server, but it was still difficult, still something that he wrestled with.

Mason was another matter. He *was* the first to go to battle. If someone yelled out for help, Mason was the first to be there. If monsters were spotted, then he was the first one to stand before them. In every case, Mason did not shy away from confrontation. In fact, he charged toward any threats to protect the warriors in the army as if they were his own children . . . curious.

Suddenly, an alarm sounded. Someone was banging on an iron chest plate with the flat side of a sword, screaming out loud.

"Spider jockey . . . spider jockey!" cried the voice.

Mason sprinted off toward the voice, Gameknight trailing hesitantly four steps behind. They ran to a sentry on the edge of the camp, his chest plate in his hand still ringing with the blows.

"What is it?" Mason asked.

"I saw a spider-jockey over there," the sentry said, pointing out onto the rolling, grass covered hills.

Spider-jockeys were skeletons riding on the backs of gigantic spiders. They were fast, could cover a lot of ground in a day if the skeleton wore a helmet, and could climb; they were fearsome opponents. Malacoda had probably sent out these monsters to find them and report back their position. Gameknight knew that they could not let this spider jockey report to its masters . . . that would be a disaster. But uncertainty gnawed at his confidence.

What should I do? Gameknight thought to himself. *Should I ride out and fight it . . . I've fought one before back when Minecraft was just a game. But now . . . I'm still not sure what will happen if I die. There are no more servers I could move up to; this is the highest in the pyramid of server planes . . . the Source. Will I respawn, or die for real this time?*

Uncertainty and fear flooded through his mind, drowning his ability to think. He looked down at the ground . . . afraid.

I don't want to fight a spider-jockey . . . not now. What do I do . . . what do I do?

Mason turned and looked at Gameknight, waiting for some command or sense of leadership, but he had learned to not wait very long. Looking up from the ground, Gameknight looked up into Mason's bright green eyes, his own filled with uncertainty and fear. But before Gameknight could speak, thankfully, Mason gave out the orders.

"You four, get on your horses and get that

spider-jockey," Mason commanded to a group of warriors, is voice booming with confidence. "Make sure he doesn't report our position."

"Yes, sir," snapped the NPCs.

"Archers," Gameknight mumbled.

"What?" Mason asked.

"Archers . . . you'll want archers so that you don't have to get up close," the User-that-is-not-a-user said, his voice sounding uncertain.

Most skeletons carry a bow and arrow.

"Yes, of course," Mason boomed. "Take some archers with you as well. Surround them with the archers and only charge if you can't get them with arrows. No sense in taking any unnecessary risks. Now go!"

The soldiers ran through the camp, gathering weapons and armor. Within seconds, a squad of soldiers, some men, some women, were galloping out of the camp in the direction of the sighted monster.

"They'll get it," Mason said confidently.

Turning, he put his arm around another soldier and whispered something into the boxy ear. The soldier then took off in a hurry, gathering with him twenty other warriors, some of them putting away their swords and drawing a shovel from their inventory. Gameknight watched them run off away from the camp to a large hill that was nearby. On the top of the hill, they started placing blocks of dirt, one on top of the other, sculpting shapes that resembled people and horses. One of them placed a block of netherrack that had been brought from the Nether after the battle with Malacoda on the last server. Touching it with flint and steel, it instantly burst into flames, making the artificial figures on the hilltop easier to spot, especially at night.

"What are they doing over there?" Gameknight

asked.

"They are setting up a little diversion," Mason answered.

He moved to stand next to Gameknight and admired the soldier's work. He could see shapes standing around a campfire, horse-like shapes standing near the tree line, soldier-like shapes amidst the trees, prone shapes on the ground.

"All warfare is based upon deception," Mason said as if reciting some lesson from memory.

Gameknight was about to say something when he suddenly realized that his statement sounded familiar . . . very familiar, somehow.

I've heard that before, Gameknight thought. *I know it! But how could that be? We're in Minecraft, not in the physical world.*

Gameknight searched his memory, trying to identify where he'd heard that statement, but he couldn't figure it out, the pieces of that puzzle tumbling about in his mind, unclear and veiled with confusion.

"We must appear to be where we are not, so as to confuse the enemy," Mason added.

"That's a good idea," said a young voice standing right next to Gameknight.

Turning, he found Crafter standing next to him, his bright smile lighting the child-like face with hope. Gameknight had met Crafter on the first server when he'd first been pulled into Minecraft by his father's invention, the digitizer. On that server, Crafter had been an old man, grey haired and bent with age. After saving that server from Erebus, the King of the Endermen and his army of monsters, Crafter had respawned into the next server as a young boy. It was always shocking, and a bit unnerving, to see those wise old eyes on the young face, the years of experience glowing bright behind those majestic blues. But after the battles on the last server, the battles in the Nether, Gameknight had finally come to accept that this was the form of his friend now; a wise old crafter encapsulated within the body of this young boy. He was probably the best friend he had in his life . . . well except for his friend in the physical world, Shawny.

I wish Shawny was here to help us now.

"Help!" someone yelled.

Without thinking, Mason was on the run, his sword drawn, ready. Gameknight drew his own as well and scrambled after the big NPC with Crafter at his side, a group of warriors following on their heels. Gameknight could hear the grinding ring of swords being drawn from scabbards as the warriors behind him readied themselves for battle. Fear and uncertainty started to coil around Gameknight's courage like a mighty serpent, its scaly body filled with every possible *what-if* he could imagine. As he hesitantly followed Mason, he could feel that great serpent of fear slowly clench down on his courage, squeezing it to nothing. But since he knew he had no choice, he gripped his diamond sword tightly and ran on toward this new danger.

CHAPTER 3

BULLIES

Help," the voice yelled again.

They were getting closer.

Gameknight could tell that it was coming from over the next gentle rise. He sprinted forward, careful to not overtake Mason but still running fast enough to not look too scared. When they reached the crest of the hill, they found Stitcher standing on the rise, her bow in her hand, arrow notched. The gentle wind blowing across the hilltop pulled at the young girl's brilliant red hair, creating arcs of crimson that circled around her neck and face. Turning her head, she smiled at Gameknight as she pointed to the tree line, slowly lowering her bow.

"Next to the trees," the young girl said as she relaxed and put away her weapon.

Down at the bottom of the hill, they saw a young, lanky NPC standing at the foot of a tall birch tree. The white bark of the tree glowed a soft crimson as the warm red light of dawn bathed the landscape. Scanning the area, Gameknight looked for any monsters that could be attacking, but only saw a lone wolf sitting nearby, a red collar hanging around its neck; it had been tamed. Mason, also seeing that there were no threats, charged down the hill to the gangly youth as he sheathed his sword.

"What is going on here?" Mason asked, his booming voice resonating through the birch forest.

"Well . . . ahhh . . . they said it was a . . . a game," the boy stammered.

"What's your name son?" Crafter asked, now standing at Gameknight's side.

"My name is Herder . . . is Herder," the boy said, then his eyes found Gameknight999. "The User-that-is-not-a-user, you are my hero . . . hero. I can't wait to see . . . to see you destroy the monsters and save . . . save Minecraft. I want to be just like . . . just like you."

Stepping forward the boy placed his hand lightly on Gameknight's arm, his face lit with reverence. Embarrassed, the User-that-is-not-a-user took a step back and looked at the ground.

What a joke . . . I'm just a scared kid, he thought to

himself. *I'm not a hero.*

"Herder tends to the animals," Stitcher added as she put away her bow and came to stand next to Crafter. "He watches them at night and keeps them all together. Some of the warriors have been picking on him because he's smaller and younger and . . . different."

"My tools," Herder said, his voice sounding embarrassed . . . no, humiliated. "They're in the . . . the tree."

Everyone looked up. They could see a group of tools bobbing up and down on the treetop, moving as if floating on invisible ocean swells. At the base of the tree, Gameknight could see a square patch were the grass had been killed. Clearly the bullies had built a column of dirt to gain access to the treetop, then deposited the tools and came back down, removing most of the evidence of their prank.

Using some brown spotted blocks of netherrack, Gameknight constructed a set of stairs that led to the top of the tree. He'd been carrying these blocks since their last battle in the Nether. Images of that terrible conflict burst into his mind as he placed the netherrack on the ground. The NPC army had gone into the Nether to rescue Crafter from the clutches of Malacoda, the King of the Nether, and had hoped to stop his army of monsters. They'd failed. Being able to rescue Crafter—which they had done—was reason to celebrate, but Hunter, Gameknight's friend and Stitcher's sister, had been captured. He could still remember the look on her face as she slowly sank into the portal that led to this server, Malacoda's long, slithering tentacles wrapped around her lithe body. The terrible sadness in her eyes had told him to shoot his bow and kill her; death would have been preferable to being a prisoner. But Gameknight lacked the courage to take the shot . . . so he let his friend be taken by the monstrous King of the Nether, and that cowardly act haunted his every waking moment.

Even though they'd won the battle, the monsters had still been able to escape through the portal Malacoda had constructed. Gameknight and Stitcher had followed the army, not willing to give up on saving Hunter. Fortunately, the NPC army had agreed to follow them as well. And now they were in this strange land, looking for Malacoda and Erebus, the two kings, in hopes of stopping their assault on the Source.

Gameknight looked down at the netherrack block in his hand and could remember all the screaming in their last great battle . . . all the pain . . . all the terror. Families had been shattered and lives had been lost . . . and . . . Hunter . . . the memories made Gameknight shudder. Pulling his attention from the terrible memory, he placed the last block, completing the set of stairs. He then motioned to Herder to collect his belongings.

The young NPC sprinted up the stairs to the treetop and collected his belongings, then ran back down, a smile beaming up at Gameknight999.

"Thank . . . thank you User-that-is-not-a-user," Herder said, smiling.

Gameknight grunted, then pulled out his pickaxe and started to dig up the blocks he'd just placed.

"What happened here, Herder?" Crafter asked.

"Well, the others . . . others said they wanted to play a . . . a game with me," Hunter explained. "They said that it would make . . . make me one of them . . . them. I'd be like . . . like them, a warrior." The skinny boy turned to face Gameknight. "I can fight the monsters. I can use . . . can use my . . ."

"Son, you're too young to fight," Mason snapped. "Anyway, your job is to watch the herd. That's what you have to do. You aren't going to fight, you're too small."

"But . . ."

"No discussion!" Mason commanded.

Crafter put a calming hand on Mason's shoulder, then turned back to Herder.

"Herder, continue your story."

"Well . . . the warriors told me to drop all my . . . all my inventory. The test had to be done with no tools . . . tools. So I dropped . . . dropped everything and closed my eyes . . . my eyes and waited. I was so excited to finally be accepted . . . be accepted by them. I thought I would finally . . . finally have friends and be one of . . . them. But soon . . . I heard laughing." Herder's voice became softer, as if reliving the humiliation. "When I opened my . . . my eyes, the soldiers were gone. All my . . . all my tools were up in the . . . in the tree. I could see the warriors standing . . . standing on the top of that hill laughing . . . laughing at me."

Herder turned and faced Gameknight. For the first time, he noticed the boy's eyes; one was a pale green, the other a cold steel blue. They stood out against his tangled mop of dark black hair and seemed to bore straight into Gameknight's soul. It was as if Herder could somehow see into Gameknight and knew that the User-that-is-not-a-user had experienced this same thing many times as well: had his books put on top of the basketball hoop, his lunch on top of the lockers, his shoes on top of the door . . . Gameknight had experienced this same thing many times with the bullies of his school, and now it was being played out here, in Minecraft.

It made Gameknight999 angry . . . and sad.

Why can't the bullies just leave me . . . leave us alone? What kind of sick person takes joy at another's suffering?

And then Gameknight knew the answer to this question here in Minecraft. Erebus, he took joy in Gameknight's suffering and was probably taking joy in Hunter's suffering . . . if she was still alive. Erebus was Gameknight's bully here just like the warriors were Herder's.

By now, a group of soldiers had collected on the hilltop, many of them chuckling and pointing down at Herder. Gameknight could hear their comments as their words carried across through the cold morning air.

"Why does he talk that way," one of the soldiers whispered not very softly.

"I think he's touched in the head," answered another. "You know . . ."

"That's pig-boy," said another, pointing at Herder with his sword. "He tends the animals and sleeps with them. People say that he's crazy . . . or stupid . . . or both."

"HEY," Stitcher yelled, her anger beginning to overflow, "his name is Herder and he's not stupid. He's just different from you, that's all."

The soldiers laughed.

Stitcher moved up next to Gameknight and gave him a gentle shove forward as if expecting him to say something to the soldiers.

"What?" he asked.

"Aren't you going to say something?" the young girl growled.

Gameknight look up at the warriors on the hill, their smirking laughter directed at the lanky boy. It brought forth so many memories of being bullied himself: the ganging up, the innocent shoves, the casual stepped-on foot . . . And when Gameknight thought of all of the bullying he'd suffered in school, it brought back all of his doubts and insecurities. It made him want to just disappear. Suddenly a blocky elbow shoved him in the ribs, bringing him abruptly out of his daze.

"Well?" Stitcher whispered.

"Oh . . . yeah," Gameknight stammered. "Ahh . . . go check the perimeter for monsters."

The soldiers laughed again, tossed a few more derogatory grenades at the young boy, then moved off, doing as the User-that-is-not-a-user commanded.

Herder brought his eyes to the ground as Mason glared down at him. A nearby cow raised its head and moo'ed, drawing Herder's attention. Turning from the big NPC, Herder slowly moved to the cow, putting his hand on its large blocky head and stroking its nose, calming the beast. He then moved off into the darkness, the cow following obediently behind.

"I have to herd the . . . the animals," Herder muttered to himself as he moved off, apparently instantly recovered from the incident.

The whole incident brought back terrible memories for Gameknight999. The countless times the bullies had shoved him into a locker, or picked him up and put him in a trashcan, or shoved him into the girls' restroom . . . the many incidents bounced around in his mind like reoccurring nightmares. He hated the bullies at school. Just because Gameknight was smaller than the other kids, maybe a little different, it seemed to make it OK for those boys to pick on him. He hated them.

Why didn't I stop those soldiers from making fun of Herder? Gameknight thought.

Gameknight looked at Crafter, then Stitcher, avoiding their eyes and judging gazes. He sighed as he looked to the ground, ashamed. Herder's voice could be heard across the camp as he talked to the animals that he was herding together, pushing them toward the center of the campsite.

"Come on," Crafter said. "Let's get this army moving. They will need to see the User-that-is-not-a-user standing at the front being the tip of the spear."

Tip of the spear . . . ha, what a joke, he thought, but he knew the part he must play. Sighing, he ran toward the center of the camp, Stitcher already three paces in front of him. Her wild red hair streamed behind her like liquid flames as she ran, reminding Gameknight of her older sister, Hunter.

I hope you're still alive, Hunter, he thought to himself, then shivered as the guilt over not taking the shot that could have saved her, over not having saved his friend when he had the chance, crashed down on him . . . again.

CHAPTER 4

MALACODA

Erebus gazed about the beautiful landscape, tall green trees, rolling fields of lush grass, and distant majestic mountains . . . The scene made him sick. Underground was a proper place to live, in the shadows and hollows of caverns and tunnels, not in this pathetically colorful panorama. The view turned his stomach.

Looking away from the landscape, the King of the Endermen glanced at the vast army of monsters that followed. They were marching across this server, seeking allies that would help them in their quest to destroy the Source. Erebus smiled when he looked at the vast numbers of creatures that were following him. Soon they would all be his to command . . . but not now. Next to him floated a gigantic ghast, Malacoda, the King of the Nether and the commander of this army . . . temporarily. Its pale, bone-white flesh almost had a rosy glow in the light of sunrise. In this lighting, Erebus could clearly see the mottled scars that peppered the monster's skin, but the scars that resembled tears under those angry red eyes seemed the most vivid. "What are you looking at?" boomed Malacoda, his loud bombastic voice mixed with high-pitched cat-like sounds.

"Nothing," Erebus replied, pouring in every ounce of fake sincerity he could muster. "Just admiring your magnificence . . . sire."

The King of the Nether grunted and turned his gaze away from the dark red endermen.

Next to Malacoda was his general, one of the wither-skeletons. The dark bony creature rode on the back of a giant spider; a spider jockey, as they were called in Minecraft. It was similar to its Overworld cousins, a creature made just of bones, but the wither skeletons were shaded black, as if they'd just been pulled from the ashes of a long dead fire, versus the pale white of the Overworld skeletons. Most wither-skeletons carried a sword as their weapon of choice, but this one carried an enchanted bow, spoils taken from their captive. The monster turned its body around so that it faced backward, glaring at their NPC prisoner.

"Again, thank you, villager, for the nice bow," the wither-skeleton said with a scratchy clattery voice that sounded like a collection of bones scraping against each other, somehow creating tones that formed into words. "I appreciate you giving me permission to use this. I don't think I've ever killed an NPC with such a fine weapon. I look forward to putting an arrow into your sacred User-that-is-not-a-user. He's insignificant. It will be fitting for him to be killed by a weapon crafted and enhanced by his own friend; it's wonderfully ironic."

"Stop your blabbering," Erebus snapped. "I'm tired of hearing mindless prattle come from your bony mouth."

Erebus suddenly disappeared and teleported right next to the wither-skeleton general, and the spider on which he rode suddenly jerked sideways as it was startled by his sudden appearance. The abrupt move almost made the wither-skeleton fall from its black fuzzy back.

"Look at her," Erebus commanded to the skeleton.

He then reached up with his lanky arms, the dark red of his skin standing out against the skeleton's smoky black bones. Grabbing his head, he twisted it so that he was looking straight at their prisoner, Hunter. She was held by one of Malacoda's ghasts, the nine snakelike tentacles wrapped firmly around her body. The monster's pale cubic body floated off the ground, its baby-like face looking straight ahead. Like all ghasts its body was splattered with grey scars that were etched deep into its skin, the most prominent were those under their eyes. The tear-shaped scars stood out on its young and terrible face; permanent markings of a sadness and shame from long ago. The tear-like scars made Erebus chuckle, drawing a glance from Malacoda, the King of the Nether. Malacoda's glare made all the monsters nearby stand up a little taller, their faces grim with determination. This was Malacoda's army, and these were his warriors . . . for now.

Squeezing the skeleton's head just a little, Erebus continued.

"Look at the eyes of that NPC. You aren't scaring her or killing her spirit or weakening her will to live.

All your useless taunts are doing is filling her with more hatred."

Erebus let go of the skeleton's head, then teleported next to Hunter, a haze of purple particles surrounding him. He reached up and stroked her long curly red hair, his clammy black hand brushing against her cheek. Hunter tried to pull back, repulsed at his touch, a look of disgust on her face.

Erebus laughed, his characteristic enderman chuckle filling the air. It made Hunter cringe.

"You see, threats do not bother this NPC, nor does the threat of pain or death." Erebus turned to face the skeleton general and continued. "I know this creature, and I know what she fears. It is not pain or agony or threats."

"You know nothing, enderman," Hunter snapped, her rage bursting out of her.

"I know everything there is to know about you," Erebus said, "at least the important parts. And especially, I know what you truly fear."

"Yeah, and what is that, enderman?" Hunter snapped back.

"A cage."

Hunter's mouth fell open in shock as a single tear leaked from one eye.

Chuckling again, Erebus turned from her and looked at the wither-skeleton.

"You see, skeleton, if you want to destroy someone's spirit, you have to know what really makes them afraid. This NPC here fears a useless life and a meaningless death. She fears having time move on after she dies, and she will have left no mark on Minecraft. We've destroyed her village, her family, everyone that knew her, and now she's going to die in the company of us without ever making an impact on anyone or anything. It will be as if she never existed."

He cackled again and flashed Hunter an eerie toothy smile. "This NPC fears oblivion."

Hunter shuddered as another blocky tear slowly traced out a path on her dirty cheek and looked away from the dark monster.

"Now stop your chatter and go check the scouts on our perimeter," Erebus ordered.

"Not yet," thundered Malacoda's voice from the head of the column. "I am in command here, and I will tell my general what to do."

You are in command . . . for now, Erebus thought.

"Of course, your Kingliness," Erebus said.

The King of the Nether glared at the enderman, his tentacles twitching, then continued. "General, go check the perimeter and make sure all is secure—and stop your useless taunting of the prisoner."

"Yes, sire," snapped the general as he spun around and steered the spider out of formation and out towards their perimeter.

Erebus gave Hunter another smile, then teleported to the head of the column, instantly appearing next to Malacoda, startling the King of the Nether for just an instant.

"Don't teleport right next to me," Malacoda snapped, irritation in his voice. "I hate it when you do that."

"I'm sorry your most-worthiness, I didn't realize that," Erebus said, a wry smile on his dark face. Removing the smile, he turned to face the ghast. "Can you feel him?"

Malacoda closed his blood red eyes for a moment then opened them.

"No, I can't feel anything. Can you?"

"Yes, I can still feel the User-that-is-not-a-user, but just barely," Erebus replied, his screechy voice low, his words solely for Malacoda's ears. "This new server is strange. There are things going on here that we did not expect, starting with that." Erebus pointed up towards the pale red sun that had risen up over the horizon. "I saw it change from its normal yellow to the pale red as soon as we came through the portal from the Nether. Some of my zombies and skeletons started to burn because of their exposure to the sunlight as soon as we came through the portal, but then the flames went out as the sun turned red. What do you think did that?"

"Us," Malacoda said in a proud voice as if he understood this at all. "Our presence caused this server to change and stained the sun from its normal bright yellow to the now pale red. And soon, when we find the Source, we'll destroy it and cause all the server planes to change."

"You mean cause all the server planes to die."

"Of course," Malacoda answered. "What could be more perfect? Then we'll take the Gateway of Light into the physical world and show those pathetic users what fear really feels like when we destroy their world and take it for our own. A physical world ruled by the monsters of Minecraft . . . it's almost poetic."

It will be even more poetic when I destroy you and take over this rabble, Erebus thought to himself, his wry smile returning.

"What are you smiling at?" Malacoda asked.

"Oh nothing, just imagining what you described," Erebus lied.

Pausing for a moment, Erebus looked at the terrain ahead of them. The taiga biome spread about before them, with tall pine trees covering the landscape and stretching high up into the sky. Lush fields of grass filled in the space between the conifers, the rolling hills dotted with colorful flowers of red and yellow. The occasional fluffy white wolf poked its head from behind trees and bushes, their playful barks and howls filling the air; it was a terrible scene to behold.

How can these NPCs stand looking at this horrible place much less live in it? Erebus thought. *Give me a nice cave, dark and damp with maybe a flow of lava or two in it; now that would be beautiful.*

Turning to look behind them, Erebus could see their army following behind the two rulers, a vicious collection of monsters from the Overworld and the Nether all focused on one thing—to destroy Minecraft. A black, diseased-looking trail stretched off into the distance marking where the angry horde had passed, their vile distaste for all living things actually scarring the land. Erebus could see that the black trail extended out into the distance, but was slowly diminishing as the land gradually adjusted to the spiteful hate that was coming from these monsters. The scarred path was slowly fading to an ashen grey as they marched across Minecraft, their presence slowly becoming harder to find.

Good, Erebus thought.

He didn't want to give the User-that-is-not-a-user any way to track their army. Turning to look forward, Erebus scanned the oncoming tree line, a mountainous biome following after.

"So do you know where they are?" Erebus asked Malacoda, still keeping his voice low.

The King of the Nether glanced angrily down at Erebus, his tentacles twitching, waiting for something.

"Oh yeah . . . *Sire,* do you know where to find these creatures that call themselves shadow-crafters?"

"When we get near, I will know it as surely as I know myself," Malacoda answered, a forced sense of confidence in his voice.

"So in other words, no, you don't know where we are going."

An irritated cat-like sound came from the ghast as his eyes flared red, the tear-shaped scars under his eyes almost glowing as his anger blossomed.

"The shadow-crafters came to me while I was in the Land of Dreams," Malacoda said. "They said that they will help us with the destruction of Minecraft, and I believe them. I will find our new allies when I am ready to find them."

"I can find these shadow-crafters with my endermen quicker than just wandering around," Erebus boasted. "It will actually be a plan that has some hope of doing something useful, unlike this random walk we're on. That will shorten this trip and get us into the physical world faster."

A ball of fire started to flare within Malacoda's tentacles, his eyes now like two ruby lasers. Erebus knew he'd pushed this foolish ghast a little too far this time.

"Sire," Erebus added quickly, hoping to stem the tide of his anger, "it would be our pleasure to serve the great King of the Nether in this endeavor, as it was an incredible idea that the great Malacoda formulated. We can find the shadow-crafters and report back to you, if it is your will. The shadow-crafters know how to find the Source, and it will be our pleasure to locate them for you."

Looking meekly to the ground, Erebus could see the fireball within the mass of writhing tentacles slowly diminish, the orange glow from the burning sphere darkening until the light finally went out.

Malacoda stopped and floated upward into the air, out of arms reach. He then turned to glare down at the enderman. His eyes were bright red, burning with anger.

"Enderman, you take many risks," Malacoda boomed, his voice echoing across the landscape.

Turning, he looked at his massive column of monsters and then back to Erebus.

"I have decided that the endermen will find the shadow-crafters," Malacoda boomed, his voice resonating across the landscape. "Endermen . . . my endermen," he glanced down at Erebus and smiled, "go forth and find the shadow-crafters, then report back to ME." He emphasized the last part with a howling cat-like sound. "Do not return until they are found . . . now GO!"

Erebus looked across the army at the tall endermen that stood out above the rest of the monstrous horde and gave *his* endermen a nod. And in an instant, the dark creatures all disappeared, leaving behind a cloud of purple mist that faded quickly.

"Might I suggest," Erebus said with the necessary meekness to his voice, "that you send out a little surprise for the User-that-is-not-a-user. Let him know that he does not rule here."

Malacoda grunted and glanced at his spider-jockey general. The King of the Nether nodded to his general, then turned away facing toward the distant mountains again. The general moved to a collection of spider jockeys and spoke in a low bony voice to the monsters. The gigantic hairy spiders then peeled away from the column and headed to the rear, the pale white skeletons bobbing back and forth as the spiders shuffled off, bows drawn and arrows notched. The wither-skeleton watched his Overworld cousins head off toward their quarry, then returned back to his Malacoda's side.

"They will not return unless they have captured or destroyed User-that-is-not-a-user," the wither general reported.

The King of the Nether grunted as he watched the expendable warriors disappear over a hill, then turned and faced Erebus. The big ghast gave him a satisfied toothy grin as if he'd been the one to formulate the plan.

How long must I suffer this fool, Erebus thought as he glanced up at Malacoda. He was about to teleport away to look for these foolish shadow-crafters, whatever they were, when one of his endermen returned, materializing right next to him.

"Why have you returned?" bellowed Malacoda. "You were ordered to find our allies and not return until you have been successful. Why are you here?"

A ball of fire started to glow within the tangle of tentacles that hung beneath the King of the Nether.

"Sire, they have been found," the enderman reported in a screechy voice.

Erebus chuckled, drawing an angry glare from Malacoda as he extinguished the fireball.

"Where are they?" the ghast boomed.

"Ahead," the dark monster replied. "At the foot of that rocky peak ahead."

The enderman pointed with one of his long black arms at the mountain that loomed ahead, its tall jagged peak dwarfing the trees that stood at its base. The mountain had a peculiar, diseased look to it; nothing alive decorated its surface. There was no grass, no flowers . . . nothing. The only thing that stood out were the leafless shapes of trees that looked decrepit and dead, their empty branches extended out at crooked angles into the air.

"That mountain?" Malacoda asked.

The enderman nodded. "The strange shadow-crafter said for you to go to the mountain and into the large tunnel that is cut into the base."

"Just as I thought," the King of the Nether added.

Fool, Erebus though as he chuckled to himself.

"Where is the rest of your kind?" Malacoda asked

the enderman.

"They have teleported ahead to secure the area."

"Excellent," Malacoda replied. "At least there is one enderman here with some brains."

Erebus just smiled.

Malacoda turned and floated high up into the air, facing his army.

"Ahead is our destination," he boomed, his voice carrying across the landscape like thunder. "Soon our secret allies will add to our numbers until this army is the biggest force ever seen in Minecraft." The monsters cheered as they marched, many of them holding their weapons in the air. "And when we are ready, we will swoop down on the inhabitants of this server and destroy them, leaving the Source unprotected. Soon, brothers and sisters, the monsters of Minecraft will destroy the Source and then take over the physical world. The age of the monsters is about to begin and woe to those that resist us."

More cheers.

Moving closer to the ground, the King of the Nether floated near Erebus.

"Enderman, after we get a report from the spider-jockeys, I want you to send some of your Overworld monsters out to find and harass the User-that-is-not-a-user. Send some of my zombie-pigmen as well; we need some real warriors there. I want him to remember that we're still here . . . understood?"

Erebus nodded.

"Where is my zombie-pigman general," Malacoda bellowed.

A zombie-pigman clothed in golden armor stepped forward, a razor sharp sword in his outstretched hand. Both the blade and armor shimmered with magical power casting an iridescent blue glow on the surroundings. Erebus noticed that this monster was bigger and taller than the rest of the Nether creatures. He moved with a fluid grace that was unexpected for a zombie, his motions like that of a predatory cat; careful, measured, dangerous.

I need to watch this creature, Erebus thought. *He could be a threat.*

"General," Malacoda said. "Find my enemy and give him a message with that golden sword of yours that he will remember forever."

The zombie gave his commander an eerie, toothy smile, then grunted acknowledgement and moved back to his own troops.

Erebus then teleported to his own wither commanders. Quickly, he explained what Malacoda wanted, then returned to the King of the Nether's side.

"My warriors will do as you ask," Erebus said as he watched the monsters of the Overworld slowly peel away from the rest of the army.

"Excellent," he said softly, then raised his voice to his normal bombastic level. "Now, my friends, forward, double time, to our destiny."

The army surged forward toward the rocky peak, the sound of Malacoda's catlike cries of malicious joy filling the air.

CHAPTER 5

HERDER

The army slowly lumbered across the rolling, grass-covered hills like a mighty leviathan, the speed of the NPCs limited by the weakest and oldest. Frustration built up inside Gameknight as he yearned to move faster, for in battle, speed meant life, but he knew that they had no choice. Recently, when they'd faced Malacoda in his burning domain, battling for the Nether itself, it had been speed and stealth that had let them win the battle. Now, with this slow moving collection of warriors and civilians, they were neither fast nor inconspicuous. The only thing that kept his frustration in check was what he had learned since getting pulled into Minecraft—never leave someone behind. That was why they were here, not only to stop the monsters of the Overworld and the Nether, but to also save their friend who had been captured by their enemies, Malacoda and Erebus. He just hoped that Hunter still lived.

Looking down, Gameknight saw Stitcher, Hunter's sister, walking nearby. She was talking to an older woman, the gray hair of the adult standing out in stark contrast to Stitcher's glowing red curls. By the look of her clothing, the old woman must have been a weaver in her past life; the pale blue smock with the smoky green strip marking her past occupation. Now, she was likely serving as cook or seamstress for the army; everyone doing their part to help save Minecraft.

As he watched the pair, Gameknight caught Stitcher's eye. She gave him a warm smile and started to walk to him. Looking down from his mount, he felt bad that he was riding alone when all the other riders had a second and sometimes third passenger on their horses with them. But Mason and Crafter had insisted that the User-that-is-not-a-user ride alone.

"It would be inappropriate for someone as important as Gameknight999 to give someone else a ride," Crafter had said. "You must be seen by everyone as their leader riding confidently toward your foe. It will give the others courage . . . and hope."

Gameknight had tried to object, but Crafter was

as stubborn as he was wise.

"You look lost in thought," Stitcher said as she approached.

This brought Gameknight back to the present.

"Just thinking," he replied.

She smiled, and the warm glow about her face reminded him of his own sister. He missed her. Looking across the landscape, Gameknight reveled in the colorful scenery. The green rolling hills stood out against the blue sky. Colorful flowers dotted the green hills like candied sprinkles on scoops of emerald ice cream. Huge boxy clouds drifted overhead, always from east to west; that was how Gameknight could easily tell which direction they were heading. Even with the pale red sun adding a pinkish hue to everything, it was still beautiful. The white clouds and deep blue sky were like the frosting on this colorful cake, all the shades and hues adding up to a banquet of color that even the most serious person would appreciate. His sister would have loved to see this. With her love of art and color and creativity, she would have been at home here . . . and likely fast friends with Stitcher.

Though I'm glad you aren't here, li'l sis', he thought to himself.

He wouldn't want her to have to take up a sword and fight monsters to save her life. Gameknight would not allow that to happen . . . ever.

Turning to look back across their army, he caught sight of Herder. The strange little boy seemed to continually attract teasing and abuse from some of the warriors. Right now, the lanky youth was helping an old man with a bundle of wood, lifting the stack of blocks that had been dropped and putting it in his own inventory to lessen the old man's burden. Gameknight saw Herder smile as the thankful old man gave the boy a hug in gratitude for his help. The boy then moved to another NPC, this time a warrior that was struggling with too many blocks of wool. Without thought for himself, Herder offered to help, taking many stacks of the wool into his inventory so that the warrior would have an easier time.

Stitcher looked up at Gameknight999 and saw where he was looking and smiled, then looked back at the young boy. After being thanked again, Herder turned toward another that needed help. As he offered assistance to another stranger, his piercing voice could be heard cutting through the many shuffling feet.

"Gameknight will save . . . save us," said the voice.

Quickly, Gameknight turned away as he heard him approach.

"Herder, over here," Stitcher shouted.

"Shhh . . . what are you doing?" Gameknight said in a low voice, his words only meant for the young girl. "He'll hear you and come over here."

"Stitcher . . . Stitcher," the boy said excitedly.

Gameknight sighed.

"User-that-is-not-a-user," Herder exclaimed. "I found . . . found you."

"Yeah . . . ahhh . . . here I am."

"I was . . . I was looking for you," the boy said excitedly.

"Hurray," Gameknight said sarcastically.

Stitcher punched him in the leg and scowled at him.

Yep, just like my li'l sis'.

"Be nice," she snapped in a soft voice.

Even though Gameknight wished the boy didn't follow him around, he was an interesting character. With a knack for taming animals, Herder was a natural at his job, his name reflecting his purpose in Minecraft. He could seemingly tame any creature he came across and then be able to get them to do his bidding, but the task of herding all of the army's livestock was a huge undertaking. It was too much for just one boy; so Herder went out and found help. Combing the countryside at every opportunity, he befriended packs of wolves, taming them with skeleton bones. The pack helped him to control the animals and protect them at night; all of the wolves were completely devoted to the boy. Now he had twelve in the pack and it was growing every day.

At night, Herder slept with the animals; it seemed to calm them and keep the animals from wandering away. The warriors had taken to calling him Pig-boy because of this. Some called him Dog-boy because of the wolf-pack that seemed to almost always be nearby, while others just called him Animal. Herder tried to ignore them, but the more the warriors picked on him, the more he seemed to mutter and stammer.

"How is the herd?" Stitcher asked.

"The herd is good . . . is good," he answered.

Looking up at Gameknight he smiled, giving the User-that-is-not-a-user a big toothy grin. Some of the soldiers nearby saw the smile aimed at Gameknight and laughed, sending a few sarcastic comments his way. Stitcher turned and scowled at the NPCs but they continued to snicker; Gameknight said nothing. Turning her head angrily, she looked back at the young boy.

"Herder," she said softly so that others would not hear, "what happened last night with those soldiers taking your stuff and putting it up in the tree? Had that kind of thing happened before?"

Herder snatched a glance at the cluster of soldiers nearby. One of them waved and gave Herder a mean, threateningly toothy grin. Clearly they knew each other.

"Do you know him?" Gameknight asked.

"Wood Cutter was from my . . . my village," he answered, turning away from the bully and looking back at Stitcher.

He sighed as painful memories replayed themselves through his mind.

"Yes," Herder answered softly, "those kind . . . kind of things had happened . . . had happened before."

"Can you tell us about it?" she asked.

"Well . . . ahhh . . . some of the boys in our village were gonna play a . . . play a game of spleef, you know, knocking away blocks of snow from under another person . . . person. If you can knock away the blocks of snow from under the other players and be the last person . . . last person standing—you win. Well . . . ahhh . . . for the first time, I was invited to play." His voice sounded excited as if he were reliving the memory. "I was so excited . . . excited to be included. The other boys never . . . never ask me to . . . to play, and finally they did. I couldn't wait to be included . . . be included and finally have some . . . some friends. So we started . . . started the game, and I got another kid right away."

He turned and glanced up at Gameknight, a look of pride on the boy's face. "I made him fall through the . . . the snow and down to the . . . to the ground that was three blocks below, but then the other . . . other kids all started to gang up . . . gang up on me."

Herder paused to look at the collection of soldiers again, glancing quickly at Wood Cutter, then back to Gameknight and Stitcher. His voice took on a pained distant sound, like the memory was somehow hurting him again. "They chased me . . . chased me into a corner of the spleef arena they'd constructed, then . . . then closed in. I got two of them before they got . . . got me, but when they knocked the block of snow out from under me, I fell . . . I fell into a two-block deep hole lined with . . . ahhh . . . cobblestone. I was stuck . . . was stuck and the wooden shovel I had couldn't dig me out. I was trapped . . . trapped there. These kids, these bullies, all laughed . . . laughed and called me names."

Herder's unibrow became creased with anger as his voice filled with rage. "They called me Pig-boy for the first time and then a bunch of other . . . other names, then they just left me there all . . . all night. They piled blocks of snow around my head so that nobody would see me. I stood there all night long listening to the monsters . . . the monsters that were prowling about in the darkness. I could hear spiders and zombies walking near . . . nearby, but they couldn't see me. I was so . . . so scared. In the morning, my dad came to get . . . get me; one of them must have . . . must have told him where I was. The look of disappointment . . . disappointment on his face was worse . . . worse than being trapped there all night."

His voice took on an almost wounded sound. He paused to sniffle and wipe away a tear from his eye, then continued, his voice growing angry.

"'I told you, Herder, you shouldn't play with the other kids,' he said to me as he pulled me . . . pulled me out of the hole. 'Because you're different, they are going to do things to you like this. You need to stick with your animals . . . those you can trust. Stay away from the other kids.'

"I was so mad . . . mad at him, not because he was so disappointed in . . . in me, I always seemed to disappoint him. No, I was mad at . . . at him because I knew . . . knew he was right. But it wasn't fair . . . wasn't fair, I should be able to have friends, but instead . . . but instead all I had were my . . . my animals, my pigs and cows. So I punished my dad . . . my dad by not talking to him and giving him the silent treatment. I didn't talk to him . . . to him for the next two days, but tried to be as noisy . . . noisy as I could at home, dropping things and slamming doors. I took my anger . . . my anger out on him when really I was mad . . . was mad at myself for trying to fit in . . . in with the other kids instead of just staying alone. He always told me . . . told me that I was different from the . . . the other kids and that . . . that I shouldn't try to fit in, but I wanted to have some friends . . . some friends so bad and just be a normal . . . normal kid. So I punished my dad by ignoring him. But I never got the chance to . . . chance to apologize for being so angry with him. The mobs came . . . mobs came to our village on the third day. He was killed . . . killed by a . . . a blaze and I was . . . I was taken to the Nether fortress to work."

Herder sniffled as more tears started to dampen his square cheeks. He looked away so that his idol, the User-that-is-not-a-user, would not see. Gameknight turned away as well, giving the boy a little bit of privacy.

"What's wrong, pig-boy, got somethin' in your eye?" one of the warriors nearby shouted.

This brought the curious stares from many of the NPC warriors. Gameknight could hear chuckles and mocking whispers as blocky heads turned toward the boy.

A guttural growl came from Gameknight as if it had a life of its own. He could remember this kind of thing happening to him, the mocking, embarrassing comments from the bullies on the playground, the accidental shoves and tripping feet in the aisle ways. It made him angry, but also made him want to hide and disappear as he always did when these things were happening to him.

Bullies, why can't they think about how their actions make others feel? Gameknight thought, and then he remembered how he used to treat other users in Minecraft, back when he'd been a griefer. He'd been no better than these bullies; just another thug trying to make himself feel better at another's expense.

More chuckles and comments came to their ears. Clearly they were aimed at Herder and meant to be heard. This caused a burning flame of anger started to blossom within Gameknight. He hated unfair treatment . . . he hated bullies. And then he remembered something that Crafter had taught him on the last server. *"Accepting the idea that success is a real possibility, even though it may still be difficult to achieve, is the first step toward victory."* Accepting the possibility . . . that was the key. Maybe he could be successful at having the courage to stand up against these bullies; maybe he could help Herder, and in turn help himself. He just had to accept that it *was* possible. And then an idea suddenly popped into his head.

"Herder," Gameknight said softly, an angry tone to his voice. "Don't let them see you get sad. Don't give them the satisfaction . . . that's what they want." He paused for a moment, then whispered to the lanky boy. "Let's show these bullies how important you really are."

Herder looked up at Gameknight, a confused look on his face. Then Gameknight spoke in a loud, commanding voice, "Herder, come up here with me."

Extending his arm down, he opened his hand to pull the youth up onto the horse.

"What . . . what?" Herder said as he looked at the open hand, the stubby square fingers extended out wide, then looked up at Gameknight.

"I said you're riding up here with me, now take my hand."

Then Gameknight scowled down at the skinny lad.

"The User-that-is-not-a-user commands it!"

Herder looked again at the outstretched hand then back up to Gameknight.

"But I have to check the herd . . . I have to . . ."

"*We* will check the herd," Gameknight said, his voice firm. "Now get up here right now."

Herder gave him an apprehensive look, then smiled and took Gameknight's hand. Pulling him up sharply, Gameknight swung him onto his horse so that he was right behind him. A pair of long skinny arms then wrapped around Gameknight's chest as Herder held on, more for emotional support than for balance. Instantly, the snickering and comments stopped as the warriors were shocked at what had just happened.

"The User-that-is-not-a-user just . . ." one of the warriors said.

"The boy . . . he's riding with . . ."

"What's he doing?"

The warriors all uttered their disbelief at what had just happened, and somehow, Gameknight999 could feel his companion smile behind him, and it caused the smile to spread to him.

Maybe it was possible.

"The herd . . . the herd . . . I have to check the herd," the young boy said in Gameknight's ear.

"Fine," Gameknight said as he glanced down at Stitcher.

He found her giving him a huge smile the stretched around her flat face, bending around her boxy head, lighting up her face. She reached out and patted him on the leg, clearly proud of the User-that-is-not-a-user.

Yep, just like my li'l sis'.

Gameknight smiled back at her, then turned his head to speak to Herder.

"Ok, to the herd," he said as he guided his horse

out of formation and to the center of the column. As he rode away, Gameknight could hear Stitcher saying something to the old woman who had come up to her side.

"You see," Stitcher said, "the User-that-is-not-a-user can overcome anything, even what's inside us."

Turning to look at the young girl, Gameknight found her still smiling at him, her hand now clenched at her chest in salute.

CHAPTER 6

AMBUSH

The army's herd was massive. There were cows, pigs, and of course chickens. Gameknight smiled remembering some YouTuber that always called them spy-chickens. Herder had been gathering them as they traveled across this land, drawing more and more creatures with his calming touch. Surrounding the herd were his wolves. Each patrolled the perimeter of the herd, nipping at the heels of any animal that tried to go astray.

Herder walked amongst the animals with arms held out wide, trying to touch each one. The gentle brushing of his fingers seemed to calm those that were nervous or scared. After walking amongst the animals, he moved to the wolves, scratching each behind the ears and giving them a piece of meat to satisfy their hunger and renew the bond of friendship. Gameknight could see red hearts appear above each wolf as it was given the tasty morsel, the grin on Herder's face getting bigger with each reward. This lanky boy was truly meant for this task.

Just as Herder fed the last of the encircling wolves an alarm was sounded. Turning, Gameknight bolted for his horse, jumping into the saddle in a single fluid motion. Spinning his mount around, he faced Herder who was running toward him.

"No, stay with the animals," Gameknight said.

"But . . . but I could help," Herder stammered.

"I need you here, protecting the herd. That's more important . . . now stay here and do your job."

Herder looked down as if he'd some something wrong.

"Herder," Gameknight said in a loud voice so that others would hear. "I'm counting on you. We all need *you* to take care of the animals. No one can do it better."

Herder pulled his head up and looked back at Gameknight, a look of confidence and pride on his face.

"Take care of them. I know you won't fail."

Then the User-that-is-not-a-user turned and headed toward the alarm. Tapping his heels into the horse's side, he urged his mount forward, but slowly; he wasn't anxious to get to the battle too soon. The sound was coming from the side of their formation with only a few soldiers nearby. Most of their troop rode at the front and back of the army, but few on the side. Moving toward the sound, he quickly came upon Stitcher. She was running toward him, her bow in her hand. As he approached, she held up her free hand. Reaching down, Gameknight grabbed it and swung her into the saddle in front of him.

"Let's go," she snapped. "We need to get to the battle and help."

"I'm not sure they really need our help . . . ahhh . . . Mason probably already has . . ."

"Just quit your whining," she snapped. "Get this horse moving, NOW!"

Gameknight reeled from her ferocity and heeled the horse into action, sprinting forward.

"You're just like your sister, you know that?" Gameknight said, not sure if it was compliment.

"Just shut up and drive this thing," Stitcher replied, then turned her head and gave him a smile.

As they sprinted, they saw warriors running in all directions, swords drawn, unsure where to go. Part the cavalry was also moving, but in every direction all at once. The alarm sounded again, someone banging on a chest plate with the flat of a sword. This drew the soldiers in that general direction, but they were still unorganized.

But then someone shouted out in a loud clear voice.

"There's the User-that-is-not-a-user."

"Follow Gameknight999," shouted another.

"The monsters will be sorry when he gets to them," said a swordsman nearby, his fist clenched to his chest.

A cheer rang out as the warriors merged together behind Gameknight, their courage buoyed by just his presence. Stitcher turned her head and smiled at her friend, then spun back around, her hair flinging in a wide crimson arc that brushed across Gameknight's face.

"Hey . . . you did that on purpose," he complained with a smile.

"What me?" she replied.

Stitcher turned again to give him another warm smile, then spun her head around even quicker, splashing his face with more curls. And then Gameknight felt chills run down his spine as he began to hear the sounds of battle on the other side of a gentle rise. A familiar trepidation filled him as he imagined the terrible things that were happening to people out there. What kind of monsters would they be facing? Would it be blazes, or spiders, or zombies . . . ? His imagination formed every terrible image it could muster, quickly eroding his courage and making him want to flee. But he could not flee; he had Stitcher sitting right in front of him. She was his friend and he couldn't let her down. So against every instinct he had to run away and hide, he urged his horse forward.

As they reached the crest of the hill he saw the battle, and his blood turned cold. Spider-jockeys. There must have been at least fifty of them. The dark furry spiders were scurrying about, a bone white skeleton riding on their backs. Wicked black curved claws slashed out from the spiders, scraping against armor and gouging into flesh. The skeletons on their backs fired arrow after arrow at the small group of NPCs that were already surrounded. Gameknight could see Crafter and Mason at the center of the circle, both firing their own bows at the elusive monsters.

And then Stitcher's bow started to hum as Gameknight started to charge toward the fray. Without thinking, he drew his enchanted diamond sword and urged his horse into a sprint.

Speed . . . they needed speed. If he kept moving fast enough, maybe none of the spider jockeys would attack him.

Zip . . . an arrow sped past him, threading the space between his chest and Stitcher.

"Stitcher . . . to the left," Gameknight shouted.

He pointed at the skeleton that had fired the shot. But without realizing it, the warriors behind him took his gesture as a command and all charged at the skeleton. They knocked the bony creature from his mount, then fell upon skeleton and spider, slaying both quickly.

The NPCs then formed a wedge, with the cavalry on the outside, swordsmen and archers in the middle, as Mason had trained them. They smashed into the encircling monsters. The mounted warriors had their swords drawn and sliced into the bony monsters while the archers fired at the spiders, taking the mounts out from underneath them. Seeing an opening in the enemy lines, Gameknight charged forward, leaping his horse over a riderless spider, Stitcher sinking three arrows into its bulbous abdomen as they flew through the air. The dark creature disappeared in a flash, leaving behind tangles of spider web and glowing balls of XP.

Driving his mount forward, he moved through the surviving NPCs, maneuvering to Mason and Crafter.

"Are you two OK?" he asked, his voice shaking.

"Yes, but we need to—" Mason said but was interrupted when an arrow clanked off his armor.

Stitcher answered the arrow with three quick shots. Her arm was a fluid blur as she drew arrow from inventory, notched it, then loosed it at her target; she never missed. She was certainly Hunter's sister.

"We need to get some cover," Mason shouted over the sounds of battle. "The skeletons are tearing us to shreds."

Clank, another arrow bounced off his back.

Thrum . . . thrum . . . thrum . . . Stitcher silenced another attacker.

The chaos of the battle had Gameknight terrified.

What should we do . . . what should we do? he thought. *I'm so scared, I just want to dig a hole and hide.*

"Gameknight, what should we do?" Crafter asked, almost pleaded.

I want to dig a hole and hide, dig a hole and hide . . .

that's it!

"Dig holes," Gameknight said, imagining some kind of World War II movie with John Wayne and his men digging fox holes from which to fight. "Dig down one block and fight from there. Crouch between firing."

He then spun his horse around before they answered.

"Archers to the center," Gameknight yelled. "Swordsmen, dig a one block deep moat around our position, then wait for the spiders to get close and hack at their legs. Cavalry, follow me . . . FOR MINECRAFT!"

Speed . . . they needed speed, just like back in the Nether.

Leading the horsemen, Gameknight punched a hole through the enemy lines, then led the cavalry around the spider jockeys. Once they were outside of the battle lines, he looked back. He could see their men encircled by the spider jockeys, Crafter and Mason at the eye of the storm, but then he saw the NPC start to drop down as they dug their foxholes. Just then a roar came from the top of the hill; more of their NPC army had arrived . . . the rear guard. Now they completely outnumbered the attackers, but they did not flee. The skeletons kept on firing their deadly missiles as the spiders continued slashing at exposed flesh.

It was complete chaos . . . terrifying and real.

Clank . . . an arrow bounced off his diamond armor right near his neck.

That was close, he thought.

Thrum . . . thrum . . . thrum.

Panic and fear started to fill his mind.

I can't do this, I can't lead the battle . . . I'm just a kid.

Another arrow zipped by his head. It reminded him of the day in the cafeteria when a milk carton had narrowly missed his head. These spiders were like those bullies in the cafeteria. They were all out to get him.

I have to get out of here.

Picking a random direction, Gameknight started his horse galloping; unfortunately, in his panic, he didn't notice he was heading near the edge of the encircling monsters.

"Follow the User-that-is-not-a-user," Stitcher yelled as she held her bow up high.

Gameknight ignored the cheer that bubbled up behind him. He just wanted to run . . . get away . . . hide. He rode past the spider ring and started to head out onto the open plain that stretched out before them, but Stitcher grabbed one of the reins and pulled on it, steering the horse so that it circled the spiders.

"Cavalry, surround the spiders," Stitcher yelled. "Follow the User-that-is-not-a-user!" She then lowered her voice and spoke to Gameknight. "Ride around them in a circle . . . it will be OK."

Gameknight, numb with fear, did as instructed. A storm of uncertainty and panic raged within his mind. He felt like he was watching the battle from within a tornado, but then he tried to push back on the storm within his mind, push back on the bullies down there attacking his friends.

Maybe it is possible . . .

"Draw your sword and strike at the spiders," Gameknight yelled over his shoulder as he drew his diamond sword, his insides still shivering with fear.

Reaching out, he slashed at spiders as they passed. Just then, one of the massive creatures leapt up and swung its dark curved claws at Stitcher. Leaning forward, he shielded her with his body, feeling the wicked claws gouge his armor.

Nobody's gonna hurt her, he thought to himself.

"Don't worry li'l sis', I won't let them hurt you," Gameknight said, his voice now filled with anger. *Nobody's gonna hurt my li'l sis'.*

Driving his mount faster, he slashed at the spiders, his mind filled with an overwhelming rage. Crashing into the gigantic spiders, Gameknight's sword was a blur of iridescent blue as his enchanted diamond blade became a spinning whirlwind of death. The ferocity of his attacks startled the monsters, making them hesitate for an instant.

"Look, they're afraid of the User-that-is-not-a-user," the warriors yelled.

This drove the NPCs even harder. The cavalry rode into the spider jockeys as the swordsmen leapt out of their moat and ran straight into the monsters. The archers picked off the skeletons as the cavalry and swordsmen attacked the spiders. In an instant the battle shifted. The spider jockeys changed from the hunters to the hunted. They were attacked from all sides at once. The warriors ignored their fears and charged forward, smashing into the massive creatures, the presence of the User-that-is-not-a-user giving them strength and courage. And in minutes, the battle was over, the ground covered with spools of spider web and skeleton bones.

The warriors cheered, men and women slapping each other on the back, but Gameknight did not cheer. He noticed the piles of armor and tools here and there, remnants of NPC inventories; belongings left behind by the dead.

Sighing, the User-that-is-not-a-user rode back up to Mason and Crafter. Before they could congratulate him or each other, Gameknight raise his hand high in the air, fingers stretched out wide. Stitcher looked back at him, then glanced about at all the items on the ground. She too raised her hand up high, her tiny fingers held out wide. Gameknight and Stitcher then clenched their hands into fists, squeezing tight until their fingers hurt; the salute for the dead.

The other warriors saw this and stopped their cheering. Arms started to sprout up out of the cheering crowd, bringing the jubilation to a halt. Soon everyone had their hands raised up high, fists pointing up into the air.

"Let us not cheer too loudly, for there are many who cannot cheer with us," Gameknight said. "Let us instead remember those that fell today keeping their friends and neighbors safe . . . keeping Minecraft safe."

And then Gameknight lowered his head as he brought his clenched fist down, the rest of the army doing the same.

Dismounting from his horse, Gameknight walked up to Mason and Crafter.

"You two OK?" he asked.

They both nodded.

"You think this was Malacoda's army?" Gameknight asked.

"No," Mason answered. "He's just harassing us. These spider-jockeys were likely sent out to look for us and told not to return until we'd been destroyed."

"But how could they do that? Malacoda only sent fifty of them out after us. They couldn't destroy our whole army," Gameknight said.

"That's true, but it tells us a couple of things," Mason said as he walked up to a collection of skeleton bones and spider silk. "First, he doesn't know our numbers or he would have sent more. He probably thinks only the User-that-is-not-a-user went through the portal. His mistake was to assume that the NPCs would not go against their programming and follow you. He underestimated us . . . and you."

"And what's the second little tidbit of secret knowledge you've drawn from this?" Gameknight asked in a sarcastic voice.

"Something important that we must remember if we are to be victorious," Mason said, his voice sounding as if he were uttering some kind of universal truth. The soldiers around them all became deadly quiet, listening for what was next. "These spider-jockeys had no supplies with them so that they could return to their own kind. This was a one-way trip for them." He paused to let this sink in, then continued. "He commanded them to seek out the User-that-is-not-a-user and continue to hunt him until their deaths claimed them. He commanded them to fight until they could no longer draw breath. That is important to know."

"Why is that so important to know?" Gameknight challenged.

"Know your enemy and know yourself and you can fight a hundred battles without disaster," Mason said.

The sea of NPCs, the soldiers, and fathers, and mothers, and children all nodded their heads as they pondered this statement . . . all but Gameknight999.

I've heard that before! Gameknight thought. *Why does he keep saying things that I recognize . . . something from school? Yes, it was from his history teacher, Mr. Planck. But how could he . . . ?*

Just then one of their scouts yelled something as he came riding back, his mount sprinting across the rolling hills. Gameknight couldn't quite hear what he was saying, but excitement started to ripple through the troops as the rider approached. Slowing to a canter, the rider came near, then stopped and dismounted. Walking up to Gameknight and Mason, he looked at them both, unsure who to address first.

"Well?" Gameknight snapped. "What is it?"

"Take a minute to catch your breath," Mason asked, "then tell us what you saw."

The NPC leaned over, putting his hands on his blocky thighs as he tried to slow his breath. "I saw a village, over that way," the villager pointed in the direction where the last spider-jockey had fled. "We were chasing a spider-jockey that was trying to escape and finally caught him. Roofer got him with a long distance shot from his bow. It was a beautiful shot the way the arrow curved through the air and . . ."

"The village," Gameknight said, agitated, "tell us about the village."

"Oh yeah," he continued. "When we got to the hilltop where the monster had died to collect his inventory and XP we saw it in the distance on the shore of an ocean . . . off to the north. It's what we've been looking for . . . a village."

"Where are the rest of your men?" Mason asked. "Are they alright?"

"I sent them to the village to keep watch on it but not to enter. I wanted to make sure there are no monsters about. They'll come back if they see anything dangerous and take out any small mobs."

Mason stepped up and patted the man on the shoulder, his bright green eyes beaming. The characteristic huge smile that they'd come to expect was painted firmly on Mason's boxy face.

"You did a great job; a great job indeed," Mason said loud enough for all around to hear.

The NPC beamed with pride.

"What are we waiting for?" Gameknight said. "Let's get to the village."

"In a minute," Mason said to Gameknight then turned a group of NPCs. "Deploy scouts all around us. I want the army in a circular configuration, the cavalry to the outside, then a ring of swordsmen, then the archers. At the inside I want the old, the children, and the wounded." And then he spoke as if reciting something from memory. "Be prepared and you will never be defeated."

That's another one I've heard! Gameknight thought. *What is going on here!?*

"That's a good idea," Crafter said as he watched Mason's orders carried out as soon as they were uttered.

The army started to move out, the massive body of those on horseback moving slowly so that those on foot could keep up. Gameknight looked suspiciously at Mason's back as his horse walked slowly to the north toward the distant village.

CHAPTER 7
THE VILLAGE

The army clustered at the edge of the spruce forest on a tall hill, looking down on the village. It sat on a strip of sandy desert that lined a wide river, the watery flow cutting through the dry land as if some giant had dragged a heavy axe across the landscape. The cool blue river, from the vantage point of the hill on which they stood, looked to Gameknight as if it were forming the forbidden shape within Minecraft; the curve. Everything in Minecraft was boxy and square, but from far away and up high as they were now, the river formed beautiful gentle blue curves that snaked their way through the desert biome until the waterway disappeared in the distance.

On the bank of the river sat the village that had been spotted by the scouts. It looked like any other village in Minecraft; a group of wooden and stone buildings around the village's well, a tall cobblestone watchtower standing at the center. But in this village, Gameknight could see that there was no NPC at the top of the stone tower.

"You see," Gameknight said, "no watchman in the tower."

"Strange," Crafter said.

Every village in Minecraft had a watchman in that tower. It was always the villager with the best eyesight, named Watcher for their task. Watcher would scan the countryside, looking for monsters. If seen, they would sound the alarm and warn the NPCs to run to their homes, for a villager caught outside during a monster raid had no chance of survival. Here, for some reason, there was no Watcher.

"Let's see what's going on down there," Gameknight said, but Mason put a hand on his shoulder.

"Not quite yet," the big NPC said.

Turning, he spoke to one of his generals. "I want squads of cavalry sent out looking for monsters. They are not to engage the enemy, they are to return and report. I also want archers placed throughout this forest. If they see anything, they are to shoot arrows high up into the air so that they land down there next to the village. The enemy will not surprise us with our backs against that river. Understood?"

The warrior nodded and moved off, relaying Mason's orders.

"Are we ready now?" Gameknight asked, his voice sounding a bit agitated.

He turned to see Mason and Crafter both nodding

their heads. Just then Stitcher came running up with Herder at her side.

"We're going with you, Gameknight," Stitcher said.

Some of the warriors saw Herder approaching and muttered *Pig-boy* just loud enough for him to hear, but soft enough that it was difficult to tell who was talking. Stitcher spun and glared at the warriors nearby, causing chuckles to leak from downcast faces. Turning, Stitcher looked up at Gameknight, an angry scowl on her face. She wanted Gameknight to stand up for Herder and stop the abuse, but the User-that-is-not-a-user stayed quiet, silently glad that the abuse was not directed at him.

Why are there bullies everywhere? I hate them.

Just as Gameknight was about to say something, a howl echoed through the forest.

"Wolves," someone said, and a ripple of fear spread through the occupied forest.

A pack of wolves will usually leave the lone NPC alone, but if one of its members was attacked or struck by accident, then the entire pack will fall upon the attacker in defense. A lone individual stood little chance against an attacking wolf pack; that is why villagers fear them and avoid them, all except Herder. Hearing the howls, the lanky youth turned and looked into the dark forest, his eyes searching for the furry creatures.

"Wolves. There are wolves . . . wolves nearby."

"As it sounds . . . yes," Crafter said.

Herder stood for an instant and waited for the howl to sound again. It came from off to the left, a sorrowful howl from somewhere deep in the forest. Pulling out a skeleton bone from his inventory (he'd stocked up after the last battle), Herder sprinted off into the woods pursuing the howling sound. This brought more laughter from the warriors, but Herder ignored them, his mind completely focused on the wolves. Bumping into others as he ran through the army, he was completely focused on the sounds of the forest. He did not hear the hurtful comments that were levied at his back.

Stitcher sighed and gave Gameknight another angry scowl, then reached up and jumped up onto his horse, settling down in front of him, bow in her hand, arrow notched.

"OK, I'm ready now," the young girl said angrily. "Let's go."

Gameknight nodded, then led his horse forward, the rest of the army following behind. He could hear comments from the soldiers.

"The User-that-is-not-a-user leads us to the strange village . . . "

"He isn't afraid of a village on the Source server . . . "

"Gameknight999 has no fear . . ."

He hated this adulation. It was like they thought he was some kind of mythological hero going off to slay the giant or kill the dragon. He wasn't a hero, he was just a kid . . . a scared kid that couldn't run away when he had Stitcher right here. She was relying on him to save her sister, and he couldn't let her down. Then something Crafter had said to him echoed in his mind, *"Deeds do not make the hero . . . it's the fear they overcome that does."* He knew he had to stand up to his fear, but he still struggled. Then he looked at Stitcher's flowing hair; she reminded him so much of his own sister . . . his own li'l sis'. He would not let anything hurt them, either of them. And when Stitcher turned and gave him a confident smile, he knew that he could not fail, so onward he rode.

The army approached the village cautiously. Gameknight rode out front, being the point of the spear. If something were to happen, some group of monsters emerging from one of the homes, Gameknight and Stitcher would know it first. This knowledge made him shake ever so slightly. As they rode forward, Gameknight saw movement on his left and right. Large groups of soldiers had peeled off and were now clustered on their flanks. Mason had broken up their forces into three groups, and they were now approaching the mysterious village from all sides.

As they rode down the grassy hill, Gameknight could feel the temperature slowly rise. When they passed from the bright green grass of the cool Taiga biome to the sandy plane of the desert biome, he felt the temperature rise sharply, causing tiny little cubes of sweat to form on his forehead and flow down his cheeks.

Before him the desert stretched out down to the village and continued on the other side of the cool blue river, the sandy hills extending to the horizon. Tall pillars of cactus jutted up out of the sand, their sharp spines looking all to real from *within* Minecraft. Gameknight carefully navigated around these prickly columns, knowing that touching them would bring pain and loss of HP. As he closed the distance, he could see villagers moving about, but instead of carrying out tasks that would be expected, he saw then kneeling on the ground, or standing next to a building, or gently caressing a cactus . . . strange behavior for villagers.

Heading toward the closest villager, Gameknight steered his horse to an NPC that was standing near a house, his body facing the wooden wall as if he were talking to it. As he dismounted, Stitcher leapt down and drew back an arrow, scanning the narrow streets of the village for threats. Gameknight too felt uneasy and drew his shimmering sword, the iridescent light painting the villager and wooden wall he was facing with a purplish hue.

Crafter and Mason dismounted their horses and approached. Moving up to the villager cautiously, Mason reached out and pulled on the NPC's smock. Startled, the villager spun around and faced the big NPC and young boy, five hundred warriors all in armor, with weapons bristling in the sunlight staring down at him.

"I'm sorry, I didn't mean to scare you," Mason said as he looked into the calm face.

The NPC was average in height, not very tall, not very short, with tan skin and light hair. It looked to Gameknight like this NPC spent a lot of time in the sun, his skin almost leathery because of exposure to what used to be bright rays. His light blond hair almost glowed in the sunlight, but the most remarkable feature was his smock; it was black with a wide gray stripe running down the middle.

"A crafter," someone said.

"They all are," another murmured.

Gameknight turned to look at the other villagers that were moving about and noticed that they were all garbed in the traditional clothing of the village crafter, black smock with grey stripe. Stepping forward to peer down the street, he saw more movement, NPCs going about their duties, but these were also clothed as crafters. This was curious.

"What's going on here," Mason asked, his confident voice filling the air. "Where is your watchman in the tower? Where are your farmers and builders?"

The NPC looked at Mason, then scanned the faces of the warriors, then glanced down at Crafter. He instantly recognized his clothing.

"Ahhh, you are one of us," he said excitedly. "A new one? What is your object?"

"I don't know what you are talking about," Crafter said. "My name, of course, is Crafter. We are here to fight against the monsters that threaten Minecraft. What is your name and what is this place?"

"My name is Woodbrin. Of course I work the wood," Woodbrin said, the words chopped short as if being spat from a machine gun, fast and staccato. "Over there is Cactusbrin, and Sandbrin." The NPC pointed to two villagers, both with light hair and garbed in black. One of them was kneeling on the sand, moving his hands in a blur as if crafting something, the other was standing before a tall cactus, his hands doing the same. "We work the desert biome. And of course we work the villages too."

Crafter looked at Mason, confused. The big NPC was about to speak, and by the look of frustration on his face, Gameknight could tell that his question wasn't going to be very nice. Stepping forward, he put a calming hand on Mason's shoulder. Instantly, Woodbrin saw the letters floating above the User-that-is-not-a-user's head.

"A user," the villager stammered. "There can be no users here . . . it is forbidden."

"Look at his server thread," Crafter suggested.

Woodbrin looked upward and searched the sky, confused, and then the realization of who this was standing before him sank in. Lowering his eyes, he stared at Gameknight999, his mouth agape. He then looked at Crafter who smiled and nodded his small head.

"That's right . . . the Prophecy . . . the User-that-is-not-a-user has come, as has the time for the Last Battle," Crafter said in a reverent voice. "The Last Battle for Minecraft is here, and all existence hangs in the balance."

Woodbrin glanced up at the sun. Its stained red face

looked wounded as it moved toward its apex. Taking a deep breath, he looked back to Gameknight999.

"Then the war has finally come and the end draws near," Woodbrin said in a sad voice. "I hope you can be what we all need to you be, or all is lost."

And then it was Gameknight999 who started to shake.

CHAPTER 8

LIGHT-CRAFTERS

We're here to stop the monsters from getting to the Source," the User-that-is-not-a-user said, trying to make his voice sound confident and strong, like Mason . . . he didn't do a very good job.

"Monsters are here?" Woodbrin asked, his eyes glancing about, looking for threats. "Monsters from the Overworld?"

"And the Nether," Crafter answered.

"The Nether too?"

Crafter nodded.

"We followed them through a portal made of diamond crafting benches to this server, and now we are going to stop them from destroying the Source." Crafter paused as he stepped up next to Gameknight999. Reaching up, he put a small hand on his shoulder. "The User-that-is-not-a-user is going to stop the monster horde and save Minecraft."

A cheer rang out from the warriors that had moved closer to listen. Many cried out Gameknight's name, saying that he was the savior of Minecraft . . . the warrior that could not be defeated . . . the one that would save their homes and their families. He hated all this attention and praise.

I'm just a kid . . . a nobody.

Crafter raised his hands to silence the crowd, then continued.

"We need help finding the Source so that we can prepare for the Last Battle," Crafter said to Woodbrin. "But we need information and we need help. We do not understand this server. Can you tell us anything?"

"Well," Woodbrin began, using short clipped sentences, "this server is different. It is not the same as all the other server planes. Here there are no villagers. Just code crafters like me."

"Code crafters?" Mason asked, his green eyes focused straight down onto Woodbrin, the flecks of red in those eyes shining bright in the pale ruby light of the stained sun overhead.

"Yes . . . code crafters. As you can see from our clothing, we are all crafters," Woodbrin explained, the words spat out quickly as if trying to conserve words. "But we are not crafters like your friend here," gesturing to Crafter. "We do not craft items. We craft modifications to the code that runs Minecraft." He paused to let the information sink in for a moment, then continued with his hurried explanation. "My job is to work on the code that rules wooden blocks and planks. I work to improve the mechanics of the wood. The texture, look, feel, sound . . . everything. This way it will be more realistic for the users. That is my job. As with all NPCs, I am named for my job; Woodbrin."

"But what does *brin* mean?" Crafter asked.

"*Brin* is from the ancient language of our ancestors. It's from the original testificates in pre-alpha. *Brin* means light. I am a light-crafter. All of my comrades in this village are light-crafters."

Gameknight saw movement from the corner of his

eye and spun, his sword ready. He found Stitcher was already pointing her bow in that direction, but lowered it as they saw more of the code crafters approaching. They all had light colored hair and wore the traditional black smock, but each looked a little different, as with all villagers from within Minecraft. Their eyes were all brightly colored: blue, green, tan, hazel . . . a look of optimism on their tan faces.

"I'm Sandbrin," one of them with sandy blond hair said.

"And I'm Cowbrin," said another with flecks of black in his white hair.

"And I'm Stonebrin . . ."

"And I'm Waterbrin . . . "

"And I'm . . ." The names flowed forth as the code crafters stepped forward, each one named for the block they worked, each name ending in *brin.*

"We are code crafters for Minecraft," Woodbrin said proudly with a scratchy grainy voice. "But you must beware. We have dark counterparts that strive to undo what we do."

"What do you mean?" Mason asked, eyeing Woodbrin with suspicion.

"We are the light-crafters of the desert biome. There are also shadow-crafters as well," Woodbrin said, then lowered his voice. "These are also code crafters for the things that live in the shadows."

"You mean like . . ." Gameknight didn't want to complete his question, for he already knew the answer.

Woodbrin nodded.

"Yes . . . monsters. There are code crafters for the monsters as well."

"Code crafters for the monsters," Crafter said. "I don't understand."

"We have a Cowbrin and a Sheepbrin and a Horsebrin. But they have a Creeperbrine and a Zombiebrine and a Blazebrine," Woodbrin said in a quiet, tense voice. A hushed silence settled itself uneasily over the army as all the NPCs strained to hear what Woodbrin was saying, through none of them wanted to really hear it. "The shadow-crafter's job is to improve on the things that live in the shadows."

"The monsters of Minecraft," Gameknight said, his voice cracking with fear as imaginary visions of these terrible crafters floated through his mind.

"That's correct," Woodbrin said as he looked into Gameknight's scared eyes. "The shadow-crafters work for Minecraft as we do. They improve the monsters of Minecraft to help enhance the experience of the users."

"But those monsters kill," Gameknight snapped. "How is that good for Minecraft!"

"If we have NPCs born and none of them die, then eventually they will overpopulate everything and crash the servers," Woodbrin explained. "Things must be kept in balance."

"But they aren't in balance," Stitcher said, then pointed up at the sun that was high overhead. "That proves that it isn't in balance. These shadow-crafters are pushing things out of balance by making the monsters more vicious . . . stronger and angrier." She then paused as she wiped a tear from her eye. "They took my . . . sister!"

Gameknight moved next to Stitcher and put an arm around her narrow shoulders.

"Don't worry, we'll get her back," Gameknight said in a reassuring voice.

She looked up into Gameknight's face, her curly red hair spilling down her shoulders; she looked just like her sister. For an instant, Gameknight thought he *was* looking at Hunter.

"Do you promise?"

"What?" Gameknight asked.

"Do you promise to save Hunter," she asked, her voice now choked with emotion.

Gameknight sheathed his sword then wrapped both his arms around the young girl, squeezing her tight.

"I promise I won't let you down li'l sis'. We'll get her back."

And then Stitcher cried for the first time since coming to this land. The emotions that had been bottled up in the young girl ever since she'd witnessed her sister's abduction; it all poured forth like a torrent of sadness. Gameknight held her as she cried, her body shaking, but he would not let her go . . .

Finally, drained of emotion, Stitcher stopped crying and looked up at Gameknight. Her eyes were red and swollen, almost matching the color of her hair, but there was a look of peace now within her. The ever-present look of anger seemed reduced a little as she wiped the tears from her cheeks.

"Don't worry," Gameknight whispered in her ear. "We'll find her."

She nodded and then let go of the embrace.

"Why are the shadow-crafters doing this?" Mason asked.

"We don't know," Woodbrin answered. "For thousands of CPU cycles, the shadow-crafters and light-crafters have kept Minecraft in balance. But recently a new shadow-crafter arrived. He is strong and he is evil. This new crafter is driving all the shadow-crafters to push the system out of balance. We don't know why, but we can sense him."

"What is his name . . . what does he craft?" Crafter asked.

"We don't know. But whatever he is doing, it's not good for Minecraft."

"Can you help us to find the Source?" Mason asked, his voice sounding impatient.

"We cannot tell you where the Source is. But we know that you will need the two keys," Woodbrin explained.

"The two keys?" Gameknight asked, stepping away from Stitcher and moving to Crafter's side.

"Yes, there are two keys," Woodbrin answered. "They will lead you to the Source. We only know the location of the first key, but it will lead you to the second. And that one will lead you to the Source. The first key is the Iron Rose and it is well guarded; we are not certain of the second. You must get these, one at a time, in order to reach the Source."

"Can you tell us where to find the Iron Rose?" Gameknight asked, his voice now sounding impatient.

"I will not *tell* you. But I will *show* you," Woodbrin answered. "You may need some of us on your journey. We must move quickly. If the shadow-crafters get there before us; all will be lost." He paused for a moment, his deep brown eyes scanning the faces of all that were listening. "We cannot delay . . . it is time to go, now."

Gameknight nodded then looked down at Crafter, his bright blue eyes almost matching the majestic blue of the sky. He remembered something he told him on the last server and it brought forth an idea.

"Before we go, can you craft items for us?" Gameknight asked.

"We can only make the things that we improve," Woodbrin explained. "So I can only make wood. Sandbrin over then can only craft sand, Stonebrin can only . . ."

"I get it, I get it," Gameknight interrupted. "Do you have a Gunpowderbrin?"

A crafter with yellow hair and a blond unibrow

stepped forward. His smock was covered with gray powder that made it look as if he just stepped out of a dust bin. He shook himself and the dust fell to the ground and formed small gray piles.

"I am Gunpowderbrin," he said in an old gravelly voice.

"What is it you have in mind, User-that-is-not-a-user?" Crafter asked.

"We need sand and gunpowder . . . as much as we can carry."

"Why?" Mason asked.

Gameknight looked down at Crafter and smiled.

"It was something your Great-Uncle Weaver once said; 'Many problems with monsters can be solved with some creativity and . . .' You know."

Crafter smiled and nodded his head.

CHAPTER 9

HUNTER

The strange silvery mist circled around Gameknight like the coils of a gigantic snake. He just stood there watching the turbulent cloud move closer and closer, as if the snake were trying to crush him. Suddenly, he was completely immersed in the cloud, the shining mist feeling damp on his face and making his skin tingle.

A forest emerged through the mist, rising up through the haze as if it were growing in some kind of accelerated timeframe. Tall pine trees now stood before him, their branches reaching from the tree's peak to the forest floor. Some of the trees, however, looked devoid of all leaves, the branches bare and lifeless. Gameknight stared at the bald trees and wondered why Minecraft would spawn something that looked so sad and diseased.

As he spun around, the landscape took on a sort of watercolor-ish look, close shapes merging together into a colorful smear as he turned. And then the realization struck him: Gameknight999 was in the Land of Dreams. He remembered talking with Crafter about the Land of Dreams; it felt like that was a thousand years ago. They'd gone through so much since then. What had he called them . . . and then the word came to him: dream-walkers—people that could move through the Land of Dreams. That's what Gameknight was, a dream-walker.

The last thing he remembered before coming into the Land of Dreams was that the army was on the move. They'd left the village and were heading toward the first key, the Iron Rose. After marching all afternoon, the army had camped by the edge of the river, following it to where Woodbrin had said they would find the Bridge to Nowhere, whatever that meant. He remembered Crafter asking Woodbrin why someone would build a bridge to nowhere, it made no sense, but Woodbrin had said that he would understand when they reached it.

Gameknight had fallen asleep almost instantly when they had made camp, fatigue from the day's hard march having drawn him into a fitful sleep.

And now he was here, in the Land of Dreams.

He wasn't sure what it all meant, but he remembered the other times when he'd been with Erebus and Malacoda . . . and those had been painful times. He'd escaped those other dreams because of Crafter and Hunter, but Gameknight wasn't sure what would happen in this place, on this server.

Instead of just standing around and waiting for some monster to find him and try to kill him, Gameknight did what he did best—he hid. Moving behind a large bush, Gameknight crouched. Scanning the area, he looked for threats. The silvery mist still floated about and made it difficult to see, and this made him nervous. He liked seeing an enemy from far off so that he could drill it with his favorite weapon, his bow. Back on Crafter's server he had a great bow, with Punch II, Power IV, and Infinity, it was the greatest bow he'd ever made and enchanted, and it had been his favorite. He wished he had that bow with him now.

Suddenly the bow materialized in his hand, the shimmering weapon staining the silvery mist with a bluish hue. Reaching into his inventory, he drew an arrow and notched it into place. Drawing it back, he aimed the pointed end at an imaginary target. The feathers on the end of the arrow tickled his cheek as he drew it back and looked down the lethal shaft. Gameknight could hear the familiar hum that always seemed to resonate from the weapon as if he could hear the enchantment buzzing from within. This was definitely his bow.

Gameknight smiled. But how did that happen?

He just thought it and instantly the bow was in his blocky hand. No he didn't just think it, he wanted it with all his heart, and being so familiar with the weapon, it was easy to form an image of it in his mind.

Feeling more confident, Gameknight rose and moved from tree to tree, looking about this strange forest. He relaxed his pull on the arrow and let the bow go slack. Turning to look behind him, he was surprised to find a huge mountain. Strange he hadn't noticed it before.

It was not your normal looking mountain that he was used to seeing in Minecraft. No, this thing had a sinister look to it, with jagged peaks and leafless trees all over the steep faces. The mountain looked like something that had been in a terrible accident, distorted and damaged from the horrific forces that fell upon it. The surface of this mountain was completely devoid of life or anything that could be remotely considered beautiful. Everything about it looked dead; there were no grass covered dirt blocks on its surface, no flowers, no bushes. It was just covered with stone . . . cold lifeless stone.

Gameknight shivered. This mountain scared him all the way down to the bottom of his toes.

Scanning the forest, he thought about his sister. She loved playing Minecraft, always wanting to build colorful shapes that expressed her inner joy and love of art. And then there she was. He could see her Minecraft name floating above her head, Monet113, named after her favorite artist. She looked as if she were building something, using colorful blocks of wool, a look of unbridled joy on her face. But something about her did not look real. She had a transparent, silvery look about her, as if she was not really present in the Land of Dreams, but rather she was part of the landscape.

Behind her, Gameknight could see another shape . . . a user or NPC, he couldn't tell which. But this person did not have a joyful expression on their face like his sister. No, this one looked hateful and angry, as if all of Minecraft were his enemy. Gameknight999 wanted to look away from the vile creature, but something about its eyes made him continue to stare. The eyes . . . they were glowing bright white, making the silvery fog around him glow as well. But they were not just glowing with light; they were burning with loathing revulsion for everything around him.

What would make the eyes glow like that?

And then he was gone, disappearing into the mist,

his blazing eyes that last thing to fade away. But then suddenly there was a new presence next to him. Spinning, he drew back the arrow and aimed, ready to fire.

"Would you put that away," a familiar voice said. "You're being an idiot again,"

It was Hunter . . . IT WAS HUNTER!

"HUNTER!" Gameknight yelled, dropping his bow and enveloping her in a bone-crushing hug.

"Would you quiet down," Hunter whispered as she shoved him away, "and pick up your bow, you knucklehead. You don't go anywhere around here without a weapon . . . there are always monsters in the Land of Dreams."

She drew her own enchanted bow and notched an arrow.

"But you don't need a bow, you're just part of my dream," Gameknight said, confused.

A look of annoyance came over her face, her dark brown eyes almost glowing with anger.

"You don't understand anything," she snapped. "It's a wonder you users can do anything at all in Minecraft."

Something cracked in the forest, a stick being stepped on. Quickly, she crouched behind a tree, an arrow drawn back ready to fire. Another snap of a twig . . . it was getting closer.

"Get to cover, you fool," she chided as she motioned to a nearby tree.

Gameknight, confused at what was going on, did as instructed.

But this is just a dream . . . it's not real, he thought to himself. But then he remembered when Erebus had choked him, and when Malacoda had punched him in the head . . . those felt real, maybe this was too. Crouching, he too drew back an arrow and waited.

The sound of loud breathing started to drift through the forest, a heavy animal panting that was coupled with feet stepping on sticks and leaves . . . it was getting closer. A cracking sound off to the left . . . there was another one, and then another one farther out. Gameknight wasn't sure where to aim. Moving quickly, he sprinted to Hunter's side.

"What are they . . . zombies?" he asked.

"I don't know," she whispered, "but we're about to find out."

A snap sounded behind them, and then another and another. They were surrounded. Putting his back to hers, Gameknight watched behind them as Hunter watched the front.

The sounds were getting closer. Gameknight could hear the rasping, guttural breathing of the creatures, a thick sound that made him imagine an armored zombie . . . or maybe a spider. Drawing his arrow back, he aimed at the loudest of the sounds.

Just then something started to show through the silvery mist. It was small and yellow . . . no two things, small and yellow. They looked like they were floating off the ground, gleaming in the silvery light of the Land of Dreams. Another pair of yellow dots appeared in the air shining through the mist, and then another and another. Everywhere Gameknight looked he saw a pair of these glowing things. Drawing his arrow back, he aimed at the closest and readied for battle.

And then the thing stepped forward. A white fluffy head emerged from the mist with two canine yellow eyes staring at him; it was a wolf. More wolves stepped forward, their teeth bared, ready to fight, their backs arched, fur bristling with tension. Gameknight knew that wolves were like zombie-pigmen; if you attacked one, then all would attack. Picking the biggest to be first, he aimed his arrow at the creature's head, but was surprised when he felt Hunter relax behind him.

"Put down your weapon, Gameknight," Hunter whispered as she lowered her bow and stood up.

As soon as the wolves saw Hunter they relaxed a bit, their white fur lying flat against their muscular frames. Stepping forward with her bow lowered, she held out her hand to the largest of the wolves, palm down. Snarling teeth disappeared as the rest of the pack recognized Hunter and stepped forward, tails wagging. The animals brushed past him as they walked up to Hunter, rubbing their snow-white fur against her legs, wet noses being pressed against her hand.

"We meet again, my friends," she said to the wolves as she reached out and ran her stubby fingers through the thick fur.

"Hunter, what is all this about?" Gameknight said as he stepped forward, bow still in his hand, arrow still pulled back.

Instantly, the wolves turned and growled, their yellow canine eyes turning red and focused on the pointed tip of the arrow.

"Put that away," Hunter said softly, gesturing to the bow and arrow.

Releasing the tension on the string, Gameknight put away the weapon. This made the animals relax a bit, their eyes fading from red back to normal but still focused on him. He could see that their bodies were ready for action, legs bent, backs arched. They were like coiled springs ready to release their energy on him if he made the smallest wrong move.

"Wolf-friends," Hunter said, still keeping her voice low, "this is my friend, Gameknight999."

She stepped forward and put a hand on his shoulder, then grabbed his hand and held it out for the wolves to smell. The largest of the wolves stepped forward slowly, *its yellow eyes glued on Gameknight, then smelled his hand. After a minute of inspection, the big animal licked the User-that-is-not-a-user's right hand. The pack leader then stepped back and let each of the animals come forward cautiously to collect Gameknight's scent. Once they smelled him, every wolf looked up into his eyes, a look of surprise in their yellow eyes, then took two steps back and just stood there, staring at the User-that-is-not-a-user. It was like they'd never smelled anything like this before and didn't know what to do . . . or maybe they did.*

"What is it?" Gameknight asked. "Why are they just standing there?"

"It looks like they are confused." She answered.

"Maybe they never smelled a user before," Gameknight suggested.

"Or maybe they have never smelled a user that wasn't a user," Hunter said with a smile.

Gameknight just grunted his response back to her as he held out his hand for the rest of the pack to smell.

"So tell me about all this," Gameknight said as he looked about the Land of Dreams. "Can you tell me what happened to you?" And then his face turned a little pale. "Are you dead?"

"You're such an idiot," Hunter said. "This is the Land of Dreams, the place between being awake and being completely asleep. You're a dream-walker."

"You mean you're not dead and all this is still a dream?"

"Idiot . . ." she growled. "I'm a dream-walker as well."

"So you're not dead?"

"Of course not," she replied. "I'm still Malacoda's prisoner."

"You're not dead? Ahhh . . . I mean . . . you're not dead . . . you're not dead! I can't wait to tell Stitcher."

"Stitcher, my sister . . . she's here?"

"Yes, she followed you through the portal, as did the rest of the army," Gameknight explained. "We're going to stop the monsters and save the Source . . . and of course rescue you too."

"She's OK?"

"Of course she is," Gameknight answered. "Crafter and I are taking care of her. She's safe."

Gameknight could see the stress drain from her face as she processed this news; her sister was safe! Hunter sighed and smiled a huge joyous smile that lit her face, a small boxy tear leaking from one eye.

"Tell me what's going on with you, and what this place is," Gameknight asked.

"Well, Malacoda has me prisoner. They just stopped here at the foot of this jagged, dead-looking mountain." She looked up behind her at the crooked, jagged peak that rose up out of the mist. The twisted spire rose up at least a hundred blocks, made of bare stone, the trunks of leafless trees dotting its surface. "Once they found this mountain, they were met by a bunch of NPCs that were all dressed like crafters. But there was something not quite right about these NPCs. They looked evil somehow, evil and dark . . . I don't know. But I heard them say that they were . . ."

"Shadow-crafters," Gameknight interrupted.

"That's right, shadow-crafters, whatever that means."

"Did you get any names?" Gameknight asked.

"The one that came out to meet us was called Ghastbrine," Hunter explained.

"That means that he works on ghasts, making them stronger, faster . . . better," Gameknight explained. "That's what the light-crafters explained to us. These shadow-crafters work on things that live in the shadows. It could be stone, or lava . . . or it could be *monsters."*

"And these shadow-crafters are helping Malacoda and Erebus," Hunter said. "This is not good."

Gameknight paced about, lost in thought. Brushing past the wolves he walked out into the clearing, Hunter staying where she was behind the bushes and trees.

"Gameknight, there is something else," she said.

He stopped pacing and turned to face her across the clearing.

"I've seen the size of the monster army . . . it's massive . . . probably five hundred creatures, if not more," Hunter said, her voice filled with dread. "And they are collecting more monsters every day. The mobs of this land are flocking to Malacoda and Erebus, causing his ranks to swell bigger and bigger." She paused for a moment, her eyes suddenly looking sad. "I'm not sure you have enough warriors to stop them."

Gameknight nodded. He'd thought the very same thing since they'd left Malacoda's fortress in the Nether.

"I know you had the users help you on the Crafter's server," Hunter said. "But you don't have them here. I don't think users can even come here. You're all alone here."

"All alone," he said to himself, trying to find the pieces of the puzzle that lay before him. Just as the faintest of ideas started to emerge he heard a cackling sound that instantly turned his blood to ice.

"So, look what we have here, it's my old friend, Gameknight999," Erebus said in a high screechy voice as he stepped out of the mist and into the clearing, a collection of creepers behind him. "You come to me to surrender . . . isn't that nice."

Gameknight glanced at Hunter. She had crouched behind the trunk of a tree, her brown eyes filled with fear. She tried to say something to him, but he couldn't hear her. Then he realized that she was just mouthing the word, not saying it. After a couple of tries he understood what she was saying.

RUN.

And then she disappeared, the wolves dispersing into the mist, their soft paws moving soundlessly through the forest.

Turning toward his enemy, Gameknight pulled out his bow and notched an arrow.

"You think you can hurt me with that, fool," Erebus mocked. "You shoot and I teleport right next to you and crush you. Besides, I haven't come to kill you, User-that-is-not-a-user. I've only come to torture you a bit. It brings me joy to know that I can find you here in the Land of Dreams whenever I'm bored."

"I'm not afraid of you, enderman," Gameknight said, trying to fill his voice with as much confidence as he could muster.

Erebus just smiled.

"I see right through you, Gameknight999. I know what you fear and therefore I know your weaknesses. It is just a question of time until I find you and destroy you in person, now put down that bow and come take your punishment."

Gameknight drew the arrow back farther and aimed, pointing the arrow right at Erebus' head. He could feel the fear pounding through him with every heartbeat, but knew that he had to try to stand up to this demon . . . maybe it was possible.

"Your arrow cannot harm me, fool."

"Who says I'm aiming at you?" Gameknight said with a smile.

He released the arrow. It sliced through the air, whizzed past the dark red enderman and struck a creeper. Instantly the black and green spotted creature started to glow as the ignition process started.

"No . . . I command you . . . do not explode," Erebus

screamed, his voice getting higher and higher.

Another arrow streaked past the King of the Endermen and sank into the creeper's side, then another and another. Gameknight's bow hummed as he drove arrows into multiple creepers, starting the ignition process. The mottled green creatures started to hiss and glow as if lit by a bright white light from within as their bodies swelled.

"I COMMAND YOU . . ." Erebus screeched again, then teleported away just as the first creeper exploded.

The blast of the first explosion was followed quickly by three more. They sounded like cannon fire as the sound of the blasts echoed across the Land of Dreams, lighting the surroundings as if it were day. Once the smoke cleared, Erebus reappeared where he had been standing, his eyes burning bright red with rage.

"You have meddled in my plans for the last time," he screeched.

And then the King of the Endermen disappeared in a cloud of purple particles and reappeared right next to Gameknight.

Not knowing what to do, he just shouted, "Wake up! . . . Wake up! . . . Wake up!"

And as the silvery mist started to dissolve into darkness, Gameknight could hear Erebus's voice screeching a loud frustrated scream.

"I'M COMING FOR YOU USER-THAT-IS-NOT-A-USER. I'M COMING FOR YOU . . ."

Gameknight woke up screaming. Stitcher sat up next to him and placed her hands on his chest.

"It's alright . . . it's alright, Gameknight," she said. "You're with friends."

Herder then ran to his side, one of his wolves on his heels.

"Gameknight is . . . is OK," he stammered as the wolf came up to him and smelled his right hand, right on the spot the other wolf in the Land of Dreams had licked. The wolf seemed to recognize the smell and licked the same spot, then rubbed his head against Gameknight, calming the User-that-is-not-a-user.

Crafter and Mason came running, weapons drawn, unasked questions on their faces.

"What is it?" Mason asked. "Are we under attack?"

"Gameknight are you OK?" Crafter asked.

Looking around, Gameknight recognized where he was and relaxed. He then reached out and pulled Stitcher close. Ignoring questions from Mason and Crafter, Gameknight999 knelt next to Stitcher and whispered in her ear.

"She's alive."

CHAPTER 10

SURPRISE ATTACK

Stitcher sat next to Gameknight999 on the green grass and wept. The smile on her face became brighter and brighter each time she asked him to say it again.

"She's alive."

Stitcher smiled.

"Say it again," she asked.

"She's alive."

More tears of joy rolled down her blocky cheeks. Gameknight tried to contain his own happiness, but Stitcher's smile was contagious.

"What's going on here?" Mason asked, a scowl on his face.

"Ahhh . . . nothing," Stitcher replied, giggling with

joy.

"Gameknight?" Crafter asked.

"I'll explain later," he answered. "Right now, we'll let Stitcher enjoy this moment to herself."

Just then, the light-crafter Woodbrin walked up. He looked down at Gameknight with an intense look, his brown eyes and brown skin glowing in the morning light, but his unibrow furled and creased with worry.

"We must move," he said in his short staccato voice.

"What is it?" Crafter asked, his blue eyes focused on Woodbrin.

"They are on the move," Woodbrin said.

Just then two other light-crafters, Grassbrin and Dirtbrin, stepped forward.

"Grassbrin can feel it, isn't that right?" Woodbrin said.

They all looked at the heavyset Grassbrin, waiting for some response. His green eyes looked strained, his forehead creased as if he were in great pain. Gameknight could see small cubes of sweat beading on his forehead, some of them dripping off his blocky chin and landing on the ground.

"Yesss, I can feel themmm," Grassbrin said in his long melodic voice.

Gameknight liked Grassbrin's voice. Everything he said sounded almost like a song, the words all drawn out and connected together. But today, the song was sad and full of suffering.

"Theyyy hurt the grassss and they're movingggg fasssst."

Gameknight looked anxiously at Crafter, then scanned the area for Mason.

"We need to do something," Crafter said.

"Mason . . . where's Mason?" Gameknight asked.

"We don't need Mason," Stitcher said confidently.

"We need the User-that-is-not-a-user . . . we need you."

Gameknight stood up and glanced nervously around. He could feel the weight of responsibility sitting heavily on him. Monsters were coming and they needed a plan. Indecision flooded through him as thoughts of the oncoming horde filled his mind. Looking frantically about, he scanned the area for Mason. And then there he was, the broad NPC pushing his way through the troops, a grim look on his face. His thin beard looked dark in the ruby-stained light of morning, his green eyes glowing with intensity.

"What is going on?" Mason snapped.

"The monsters are on the move," Woodbrin blurted.

"Where are they now?" Mason asked.

"Close, verrrrrrry close," Grassbrin sang.

The big NPC glanced at Gameknight, clearly wanting him to take command, but the User-that-is-not-a-user just glanced at the ground.

I can't do this, he thought as he looked about the camp. *I can't solve this puzzle and be responsible for all these lives . . . I'm not a hero. I'm just a kid.*

The situation felt like all those days back in school when he could see the bullies coming, their abusive glares focused on him. Knowing that the bully was coming his way made it seem worse, the anticipation making the whole thing seem more terrible.

'Anticipation of a thing can be worse than the thing itself.' It was something his father had told him long ago, and those words echoed in his mind as if they had just been spoken. But he was feeling that familiar feeling again, the anticipation of something terrible about to happen, but this time the monsters felt like the bullies . . . or maybe it was his own fear of failure that was the bully? All he knew was that he couldn't be responsible for his friends getting hurt. He wasn't strong

enough to shoulder that responsibility. So instead of trying to solve this puzzle, trying to come up with some kind of brilliant defense that would save lives, he just disappeared within himself and stared at the wall of fear that had materialized around his courage, every monster he'd ever seen being just another brick in the wall. Lowering his head in shame, he stared down at his feet.

Stitcher sighed and put a reassuring hand on his shoulder, then looked up at Mason. The big NPC nodded then started barking out commands.

"Scouts, get out there and tell me where these monsters are at. I want two circles of scouts around the army. As soon as you see the monsters, fire an arrow toward the camp." As the scouts got to their horses and rode out, Mason turned to face the rest of the army. "I want the elderly and the wounded at the center of the camp. Put a ring of swordsmen around them, then a ring of archers on the outside. When we know where the monsters are, we'll redistribute and ready our defenses."

"I can . . . can help," said a young voice.

It was Herder.

Gameknight looked up and was about to say something when Mason replied.

"We need warriors right now, not kids," Mason snapped. "You need to take care of your animals and that's all. Now go and do your job."

The big NPC pointed toward the herd that was clustered near a copse of trees, a ring of white furry wolves running about the perimeter keeping the animals together.

"But I can . . . I can . . ."

"No! Go tend to your animals."

Herder looked crushed. Gameknight could tell that he desperately wanted to help . . . wanted to be accepted, but instead he was relegated again to the animals. Lowering his head, the young boy slumped back to the herd, his eyes downcast. Gameknight could hear chiding comments from some of the warriors and grew angry.

"Yeah Pig-boy, go back to your little animals and let the real men get to work . . ."

"We wouldn't want your stinking animals missing their daddy . . ."

"You smell so much like a pig that a creeper probably wouldn't even know you were an NPC . . ."

The comments bit into Gameknight's courage . . . he could hear the bullies coming down the hallway . . . he could feel the trashcan being lowered over his head . . . he could feel the walls of the locker digging into his skin as he was shoved in . . .

His anger started to boil over, but for some reason he stayed quiet. Looking across the camp, he could see Herder reaching his animals, the wolves always eager to see his return. Kneeling, the young boy lowered his head. It looked to Gameknight as if he were talking to the furry animals, but as he was about to point it out to Crafter, the wolves suddenly raced away in all directions, their furry bodies like little bolts of white lightning. They streaked way from the camp on noiseless paws, performing some task for Herder. It didn't make any sense.

Just then a small hand settled itself on his arm. Looking down, he saw Stitcher's deep brown eyes looking up at him.

"Come on, the people need to see you," she said, pulling on his arm.

She drew him toward his horse, then jumped up into the saddle. Looking down at Gameknight, she gave him an agitated look that said *get into the saddle or else*. Sighing, he jumped up onto the horse's back and grabbed the reins. Crafter suddenly rode up next to him with his sword drawn, a look of grim determination on his face.

"Are you ready for this again?" Crafter said.

Gameknight just shrugged.

He glanced around, looking for some place to hide, but they were within a forest biome, with a desert biome visible in the distance. He could see tall pine trees standing off to the left, and something about them nibbled at the back of his mind as if they were one of the pieces of the puzzle. But how could a bunch of trees be a solution to the monster army that was approaching?

Well, at least they will offer some cover, he thought to himself.

Turning his horse, he headed across the grass-covered landscape, the clusters of trees jutting up here and there.

"Where are you going?" Stitcher asked.

Gameknight said nothing, he just focused on riding the horse, squeezing every bit of speed from the animal.

"Gameknight, we don't know where the monsters are," Stitcher complained. "You can't just take off, you might be riding away from the battle!"

Gameknight said nothing—he just rode. They were now at least forty blocks from the rest of the army and still riding, but then a howl echoed through the air. Gameknight brought his horse to a halt and listened, ignoring Stitcher's complaints. It was a sorrowful howl that was filled with strength and pride, but then it was suddenly silenced, a painful yelp punctuating the end.

That was one of Herder's wolves, he thought. *Why was it howling?*

Then suddenly an arrow fell down from the sky

and landed in front of them.

"ARROW . . . OVER HERE," Stitcher yelled.

Gameknight could hear commotion behind him as the army started to move, shifting forces in their direction. Looking down at the arrow, Gameknight sighed. He could hear Mason bellowing out orders, archers here, swordsmen there.

"Hurry, move to your positions," the big NPC yelled. "Speed is the essence of war."

Why did that sound so familiar . . . something from school, from Mr. Planck's class . . . how can that be?

Shaking his head, Gameknight knew that he couldn't focus on these familiar sayings of Mason's. Right now, he needed to figure out how to not get killed and protect Stitcher at the same time.

Then something in what Mason said resonated within his mind. Turning his head, he glanced back at the army. They were set up in a standard formation, archers at the front, swordsmen behind, cavalry ready for a charge . . . textbook tactics. But Gameknight could somehow feel that it was all wrong, the pieces of the puzzle spinning around in his head.

His eyes darted to the light-crafters, specifically Grassbrin and the tall Treebrin that had appeared sometime during the night.

"Gameknight, we need to move . . . now," Stitcher yelled. "I can hear them coming."

Gameknight looked at the treeline to his left and then remembered when he had first met Hunter. He and Crafter were facing off against a bunch of zombies, and they'd used a narrow alleyway to keep from getting surrounded. He wished they had an alleyway here now.

"Gameknight, we have to . . ."

Stitcher's voice was lost amidst the puzzle pieces that were starting to click into place.

Moans began to filter through the air as the rattling of bones echoed across the landscape. They were coming . . . fast.

"GAMEKNIGHT!" Stitcher yelled. This time she caught his attention.

"What?" he answered as if coming out of a dream.

"You might want to move this horse before we get trampled by a monster horde."

Looking up, he saw the monster army approaching. Zombies, spiders, skeletons, and endermen were approaching; the monsters of the Overworld. Scanning the ranks, he saw no sign of his nemesis, Erebus, but he was sure that the King of the Endermen was out there, somewhere.

Wheeling his horse around, he rode back to his own ranks to the sound of warriors cheering.

And then the last pieces of the plan came together in his head like a clap of thunder that almost made him laugh out loud. Leaping off his horse, he sprinted toward Mason, then motioned for the light-crafters to come closer.

"I know what to do," Gameknight said, "but we don't have much time."

"We can all help," said a gravelly voice from behind him.

Turning, he found Woodbrin standing directly behind him, his deep brown eyes looking up at the User-that-is-not-a-user. Glancing over his shoulder, he could see the dark outlines of monsters approaching . . . lots of them.

"Here's what we're gonna do."

And Gameknight explained his risky plan. And as he said it out loud he started to shake with fear, realizing how this strategy was fraught with peril. They'd be walking the razor's edge, and any misstep would doom many to destruction . . . or worse.

CHAPTER 11
BATTLE

The spiders charged forward first. Their hairy black bodies swayed back and forth as they scuttled across the grassy plain. Moving in and out of the shadows cast by the tree line nearby, they were at times difficult to see. The archers aimed their pointed shafts and fired, but the big monsters were able to jump left to right and dodge the incoming projectiles. The spiders were stronger and more agile on this server, as if they'd been upgraded.

"They're too fast to hit," one of the archers yelled, frustration in his voice.

"Keep shooting," Gameknight yelled. "Just keep shooting."

Turning his head, the User-that-is-not-a-user glanced at the light-crafters. They looked terrified. Having never seen battle nor the charge of an angry mob of monsters, they were understandably consumed with fear.

"Grassbrin," Gameknight said, "now."

"Yessss," the light-crafter replied as he moved up to the front rank of archers.

"Let him though," Mason commanded. "Archers on the flanks, keep firing."

Grassbrin stepped forward and put his hand down onto the grassy blocks at his feet. Closing his eyes, the NPC breathed in deep then let the air out in a low hissing stream as he extended his crafting powers into the grass.

Nothing happened

"They're getting closer," someone yelled.

"Archers, shoot faster," Mason bellowed. "Swordsmen get ready to charge."

"No . . . not yet," Gameknight yelled. He then knelt next to Grassbrin and whispered in his ear. "You can do it."

The light-crafter nodded and took in an even bigger breath, his chest heaving, then let it out again in a slow stream. This time, Gameknight noticed the light-crafter's hands glowing a soft emerald color. The glow spread from his hand into the soil, then flowed across the grassy blocks like a surging tide. Where the glowing wave touched, grass blades started to sprout.

"Gameknight, the spiders are getting closer," Stitcher said. "We have to pull back."

"Not yet!"

And then the grass started to grow.

Long green blades stretched up from the blocks all across the field, becoming longer and longer. The spiders tried to push through the web of green blades, but the long grass started to get tangled in their black hairy legs. The dark monsters charged forward anyway, but as the strands grew longer their legs became ensnared in a mesh of green until they could no longer move.

The spiders were stopped.

"Now!" Gameknight yelled.

The swordsmen charged forward with their weapons drawn, a jubilant cheer coming from the army. They slashed at the helpless arachnids, reducing them to glowing balls of XP and spools of string in minutes.

"Trees . . . NOW!" Gameknight yelled.

A group of mounted soldiers rode forward. They were fully armored but held no weapons. As they rode, they placed seedlings in the ground, small trees planted in two rows. The warriors rode out until they started seeing skeleton arrows streak through the air and land nearby, then rode back quickly filling in the lines of seedlings with more baby trees.

As the riders returned, Gameknight could hear a screechy cackling sound that made him shiver.

Scanning the collection of monsters, he could see the tall creature off to the right. His dark red skin was the color of dried blood and stood out against the bone white skeletons and mottled green creepers. With blazing red eyes, the King of the Endermen glared across the battlefield at Gameknight.

"I see our friend is here," a voice said next to him.

It was Crafter.

Stitcher appeared next to Crafter, her bow in her hand, arrow notched.

"Who is that?" she asked, pointing at the blood red creature with her bow.

"That's one of the monsters that took your sister," Gameknight said, his voice shaking with fear.

She growled and said something under her breath. Gameknight could feel the anger and hatred flow from the young girl. She wanted to run out there and assault the creature, but knew it was foolish to attack an enderman by yourself out in the open; that would likely mean her death. Instead, she squared her shoulders and faced the monster horde that was preparing to charge.

"Treebrin . . . NOW!" Gameknight yelled.

The tall, lanky light-crafter stepped forward, his long arms swaying side to side as if being blown by some unseen breeze. Kneeling, he drove his hand deep into the soil. Grasping the roots of one seedling, he drew in a long breath, then slowly let it out. The ground around his wrists started to glow a deep brown as his code-crafting powers flowed from root to root. And in an instant, the trees sprouted to full grown spruces, forming a funnel shape that would draw the monsters together. A group of soldiers then pulled out blocks of dirt and hastily constructed a set of steps that led up to the leafy canopy, giving access to the tops of the trees.

"Does everyone have some little presents for the monsters?" Gameknight asked. Nodding blocky heads answered him back. "Then go, and keep your heads down."

A group of thirty soldiers surged forward, each wearing diamond armor, a striped black and red block in their hands. They ran up the steps to the treetops then spread out across the trees. At the same time, the monster horde charged forward.

"Quickly . . . get those blocks out there," Mason yelled. "Archers . . . supporting fire . . . NOW!"

A stream of arrows streaked through the air as the warriors climbed to the top of the trees. Having been placed close together, they were able to move from treetop to treetop without any risk of falling. Gameknight could see the soldiers hopping across the leafy canopy as the monster army surged forward between the two rows of trees. The moaning of the zombies filled the air as they shuffled forward, the clattering of bones added to the symphony of terror. Some of the skeletons tried to shoot at the warriors on the treetops, but the bushy trees offered excellent cover from their pointed barbs.

As they ran, they threw blocks of TNT on the ground before the charging horde. The striped blocks stood out in stark contrast within the thick grass; they were easy to see.

"MORE!" Gameknight shouted to those in the treetops.

The air had now become a blur of arrows flying through the air, some raining down upon the NPC warriors, others falling on the monster horde. Screams of pain echoed through the army as skeleton arrows found flesh. He knew people were dying behind him, but he had to wait until all the monsters were within the trap.

"Taunt the monsters!" Gameknight yelled.

The soldiers instantly responded, lobbing jeers and insults at the approaching horde. The taunts made the monsters growl and run a little faster. They could see the bouncing slimes spring faster through the air as the few remaining spiders sprinted forward, leading the charge. At the back of the horde, Gameknight could see zombie-pigmen charging forward, their golden swords shining bright under the light of the ruby sun overhead. One of the pigmen was nearly a head taller than the rest, his body covered with shining gold armor. This monster had a look of vile hatred on its half-pink/half-rotten face; this monster was dangerous.

An arrow zipped past Gameknight's ear and sank into some poor NPC behind him. Screams of pain sounded in his ear as two more arrows sped past him . . . then the screams stopped.

Another dead because of me, he thought, and anger started to bubble up from within.

"Almost there," Gameknight yelled. "Swordsmen, get ready."

"Gameknight . . . Gameknight, let me help . . . help," a stammering voice said from behind.

It was Herder.

"Not now," Mason snapped. "You were ordered to watch the animals. This is a place for men, not animal tenders. Now GO!"

"Almost there . . ."

More of the monsters entered the avenue of trees. There must have been at least a hundred of them . . . too many. If they broke through their front ranks, they would spread through their forces and kill hundreds.

This better work, Gameknight999 thought as ripples of fear started pushing the puzzle pieces apart within his mind.

More arrows zipped by, tearing into arms and chests. Screams of terror and pain filled his ears.

He started to imagine what *might* happen if his plan were a failure, all of the innocent lives that would be lost because of his failure.

No . . . concentrate! Focus on THE NOW, not on the WHAT-IF!

And then the last of the monsters entered the gauntlet of trees.

"NOW . . . FILL IN THE BACK!" Gameknight screamed.

The warriors all ran across the treetops and piled blocks of TNT at the entrance of the tree-lined field. Gameknight saw one of the warriors fall from the tree and land amidst a group of zombies. He disappeared in a flurry of dark zombie claws and then was gone. The other warriors ignored their fallen comrade and dropped their blocks at the tree-lined entrance. Gameknight then pulled out his enchanted bow and notched an arrow.

Aiming high up into the air, he loosed the arrow.

The flaming projectile streaked through the air like a meteor, its blazing tip being watched by all the NPCs. Magical flames clung to the tip of the arrow as it flew, the enchanted bow making the arrow a flaming projectile. Some of the monsters at the front of the horde slowed to watch it arc gracefully overhead. It was almost beautiful, the way the magical blue flames trailed off the barbed tip.

And then it landed amidst the twenty blocks of TNT behind the monsters.

As the blocks started to blink, Gameknight fired more flaming arrows at the striped blocks nestled within the long grass near the front of the approaching army.

The monsters at the head of the charge instantly saw what was happening and tried to turn around, but couldn't. The mass of monsters at their backs continued to push them forward toward the flashing blocks of death. A look of panic covered the rotten zombie and bony skeleton faces. But there was nothing the creatures could do but be pushed toward their fate.

And then the ground erupted with thunder.

Blocks of dirt flew into the air as the TNT detonated. The explosion caused a chain reaction, igniting more blocks. Creepers were triggered by the fiery blasts, adding their own explosive lives to the chaos. Those monsters near the back tried to run forward, away from the explosions, but then the TNT at the front ignited. The TNT turned into balls of fire as the explosions rippled through the monster horde. Now, fiery chain reactions rippled from both ends of the monster army, slowly making their way to the center as the explosive wave tore a great gash into the flesh of Minecraft.

Skeleton bones and gunpowder rained down from the sky as the last of the explosions lit up the landscape. Tiny slimes fell to the ground as the TNT crushed their parents again and again, dividing repeatedly until only the smallest slime remained.

"Now, swordsmen forward," Gameknight yelled, handing his enchanted bow to Stitcher and drawing his sword.

"FOR MINECRAFT!" he yelled.

Charging ahead, the User-that-is-not-a-user jumped into the massive crater that now sat between the two rows of trees. His mind was a blur of anger and revenge. He'd seen so many die today, innocent people that would rather be tending a field or building a house, but instead they were here on the battlefield, dying. Moving on autopilot, Gameknight swung his enchanted diamond blade in great deadly arcs. He cut down a surviving zombie, then slashed at a skeleton, then chopped at a spider. Spinning, he ducked an incoming arrow, then sprinted toward a skeleton that was notching another. Before he could get there, another warrior crashed into the monster, slashing at it with an iron sword. In an instant the creature was just a pile of bones.

"FOR MINECRAFT!" came a deafening battle cry from behind. It made the ground shake with its ferocity.

Looking behind him, he could see the entire army surging forward. A sea of angry faces ran forward, all of their intense eyes focused on the surviving monsters that struggled in the crater. They flowed past Gameknight like an unstoppable tide, falling on the monsters with reckless abandon. There were still a lot of them on the field of battle, but the NPCs now had numbers on their side.

And then the moans of the zombie-pigmen echoed across the landscape. Looking up, Gameknight could see a mass of the half-alive, half-dead creatures running down into the crater, their razor sharp golden swords held out before them. At the head of the charge was the large zombie-pigman commander. His shining sword swung in great arcs, tearing through iron armor as if it were not even there. Gameknight could see a purple sheen rippling across the blade and could tell that it was enchanted. Archers fired arrows at the creature, but they bounced harmlessly off his armor as an iridescent glow rippled across it as well.

The golden monster was tearing a mighty gash through their army, destroying all challengers that came before him. He was like an unstoppable force of nature.

I have to do something, Gameknight thought as he dodged under an incoming arrow. *The monster is going to kill countless NPCs. What do I do . . . what do I do?*

And then Mason was there. The big NPC charged into the monster horde, slashing through a group of skeletons and kicking zombies from his path. He headed straight for the monster, a wedge of NPCs at his back.

Gameknight could see ranks of archers moving out of the crater behind the zombie-pigmen that were following their leader, attacking them from behind. They had the monster horde surrounded!

And then the massive zombie-pigman general and Mason met. Their swords clashed together with the sound of thunder. Gameknight killed off the last of the stragglers that were nearby, then moved slowly toward the two battling giants. The pigman general swung his mighty golden blade down, hoping to hit Mason on the head, but the big NPC was too quick, and sprang to the side just in time. But instead of moving with the slow, plodding motion of a zombie, this monster general was fast. Springing upward, he spun around, reaching out with his golden sword, raking it across Mason's chest.

The big NPC flashed red.

Gameknight could see that this was a skilled warrior, the zombie moving with a unexpected grace. He had to get there to help Mason, but his feet seemed to plant themselves into the shattered ground.

Mason moved back, then readied his next attack.

"That all you have, zombie-pigman?" Mason taunted. "I've seen better from your Overworld cousins."

The monster gave off a moaning sound that was filled with anger and rage, then charged forward, its shimmering sword swinging wildly. Mason blocked the attack with his own sword, then spun and sliced at the monster's legs, scoring a hit that made the zombie flash red. The creature moaned then leapt forward, his blade held high overhead. He brought it down onto Mason's armored shoulder, making the big NPC flash red again.

Rolling away from the monster, Mason turned and faced the rotting creature.

"I used to think you zombie-pigmen were dangerous," Mason said as he smiled at the monster, "but I think the baby slimes of the Overworld are better fighters now."

Mason laughed at the zombie-pigman general, then turned and faced his own troops that were finishing off the last of the monsters on the battlefield.

"One more left, then all these failures will be erased from this land," the big NPC yelled, holding his sword up high. His troops cheered.

The zombie-pigman wailed and charged forward. Mason spun and dodged to the side as the golden sword came down, just grazing his arm. Spinning slowly, Mason attacked, but his strike was easily blocked. The zombie then stabbed forward, catching the NPC in the side.

He flashed red again.

Then the zombie-pigman charged forward, his sword moving in great sweeping arcs, smashing relentlessly down upon Mason.

Flash . . . red.

The zombie's sword then became a blur as he attacked with a speed that would have been thought impossible. His golden sword shot toward Mason again and again, pushing the big NPC back. Some of the warriors moved toward him to help, but Mason commanded them to hold their ground.

"This is my fight," Mason said to the army with a smile. "You boys just sit down and enjoy the show."

"You are near death, and yet you talk as if you are going to win," the zombie-pigman said in a moaning voice. "I may not survive this day, but I will surely kill you before I go."

Mason looked at the half-rotten face of the zombie and stared into the cold dead eyes, then smiled.

"Your death will be meaningless and insignificant, just like your entire race," Mason taunted. "You have infected this world long enough. The creator banished you to the Nether after the Joining because your kind are pathetic and useless. You are not worthy of my sword."

And then Mason did the unthinkable; he threw his iron sword to the ground.

The zombie-pigman screamed a moaning cry of rage and ran forward, his mind completely overwhelmed with crazed fury. And as he swung his golden sword toward Mason, the big NPC pulled out an enchanted diamond sword and parried the attack. Now it was Mason that moved faster than anyone thought possible. His shimmering diamond sword slashed at the rotten creature, slashing at his side, then cutting into his chest plate, then smashing his leggings. Mason spun and cut at his sword arm, then stabbed at his side.

The golden armor finally gave up the last measure of its strength and disappeared. Underneath, they could see the exposed ribs on one side, a healthy pink side on the other. Mason charged forward and slashed at the ribs, cutting into them with a ferocity that shocked the monster. The zombie-pigman tried to back up, but Mason charged forward faster than he could retreat, his shimmering diamond blade slashing down on the monster again and again until the flashes of red seemed almost constant.

The zombie's confidence and overwhelming hatred had now turned to fear as Mason chipped away at the monster's HP. And as the monster screamed a moaning sorrowful cry of rage and despair, Mason took his last bit of health. The zombie-pigman general disappeared with a pop.

The battle was over.

CHAPTER 12
AFTERMATH

The warriors cheered and chanted Mason's name. Gameknight ran down to stand next to the big NPC.

"What were you doing with that monster?" Gameknight asked. "It looked like you were playing with him."

"Appear weak when you are strong, and strong when you are weak," Mason quoted as if reading from some sacred tome. "Pretend inferiority to encourage his arrogance."

I've heard those before . . . I know it, Gameknight thought. *What is going on with him?*

"That monster was skilled with the blade and a deadly adversary," Mason continued. "If I had just charged forward and fought him as I normally do, he might have defeated me. So instead, I taunted him and let him think he was winning. An enemy certain of victory makes mistakes. And as I taunted him, he became angrier and angrier. As soon as he started to think with his emotions instead of his head, I knew I had him. An enraged opponent loses himself in the battle and stops thinking. Sometimes it's necessary to take some damage in order to trick one into making a mistake."

"That was a dangerous game," Gameknight commented.

"War is dangerous," Mason replied, "besides, I knew that if I was in any real trouble, the User-that-is-not-a-user would be there to help me . . . right?"

"Yeah . . . sure," Gameknight answered as he looked away, guilt showing on his face.

Warriors started flowing into the massive crater, slapping both Gameknight999 and Mason on the backs.

"That was glorious," someone shouted.

"The greatest battle ever," said another.

More soldiers cheered as they kicked at piles of skeleton bones and piles of gunpowder.

But then the celebration was silenced by a sad wail. It started out as just a whimper, but then grew in volume until it cut across the landscape like a hammer through crystal, smashing the jubilant celebration. Moving quickly to its source, Gameknight found an old woman kneeling on the ground, a pile of items floating in front of her . . . someone's inventory.

"My son . . . he's gone," she wailed.

He didn't know her name. She was just one of the many NPCs drawn into this conflict.

"He was my only child . . . and now he's . . . he's gone."

She wailed a mournful sad wail that brought a tear to those nearby.

Gameknight ran out of the crater and moved next to the mourning woman. Kneeling down next to her, he put his arm around her shaking shoulders, holding her tight. And he wept with her. He didn't know her son . . . didn't know her . . . but he knew her pain, and so he held on to her with all his strength until her tears subsided.

Standing, he helped the old woman up, then turned to face the army. Many of them were still patting each other on the back, smiles painted on the survivors . . . and something within Gameknight999 snapped.

"There is nothing good here . . . only sadness," Gameknight shouted.

He turned to look at the old woman. She was bending down and collecting her son's inventory, then stood and faced the User-that-is-not-a-user, tears still running down her cheeks. Wails of grief continued as she turned and headed away from the battlefield.

"Battle is not glorious . . . its terrible," Gameknight continued. "Wars do not make one great . . . they just hurt people. Violence is never a good solution, it only brings pain and loss. This is not something we should celebrate, it is something we should mourn, for we lost friends and family today."

"But we won," someone shouted.

"NO!" Gameknight pointed at the old woman. "We lost."

And then he put his hand up into the air, fingers spread wide.

We shouldn't feel good about destroying others, even if they are our enemy, he thought as he watched more hands rise into the air.

It reminded him of the bullies in his school . . . how they felt good about abusing him and others like him, and how he used to behave in Minecraft. He'd been a bully himself, taking out his feelings of frustration on those weaker than him . . . and he'd felt good about it. That was wrong.

Why couldn't I have helped the younger and weaker players, and felt good about that? Why did I need to hurt others back then? Helping would have made me feel just as good as hurting.

Slowly, he clenched his hand into a fist and squeezed it tight. All of his frustration was compacted into that fist, all of the anger focused at the monsters, the sadness for those lost, and maybe the guilt for how he used to be . . . a griefer, the King of the Griefers.

Helping others could have made me feel just as good as griefing.

Slowly, he lowered his hand and looked across the battlefield. All eyes were focused on the User-that-is-not-a-user.

"Gather everything you can find," Gameknight said in a calm voice. Wiping away the tears on his flat cheeks, he turned to those in the crater. "Pick up all the skeleton bones and give them to Herder. Collect any arrows you can find. We have to leave here before the next attack comes."

"Next attack?" Crafter asked. He was now standing next to his friend.

"Yes, the next attack. This was but the smallest slice of the army that faces us. Their forces are massive and still outnumber us. This attack was nothing but Erebus's frustration lashing out at us . . . at me. We will have to face fifty times more than this before this war is over." He looked down into the bottom of the crater at Mason. The big NPC was still surrounded by warriors, his diamond blade in his hand. "We have to get the keys as fast as we can before Malacoda and Erebus can catch us. We have to use speed and put ourselves in a position of strength."

"Those skilled in war bring the enemy to the field of battle and are not brought there by him," Mason quoted.

That's another saying that I know, Gameknight thought, looking at the big NPC with curiosity. *There is something about him that just doesn't add up.*

But before he could ask, Mason was barking orders to the army, sending scouts out to watch their flanks and deploying the troops. And as the army moved back along its path toward the Iron Rose, Gameknight thought he could see a dark figure standing atop a small hill. It looked like an NPC, short and squat, but its hair was jet black, which was unusual. And the eyes . . . the eyes . . . they seemed to glow with pure white hate, causing him to shiver as fear slithered its way down his spine.

CHAPTER 13

SHADOW-CRAFTERS

Malacoda's army of monsters approached the craggy, jagged mountain with trepidation. Their cold dark eyes all glanced up at the distorted peak that loomed over them as they approached. Every monster felt the danger of this place and had an urge to flee, but they knew that it would mean their deaths if they turned and fled, so onward they marched with their leaders, Malacoda and Erebus, out front.

"I don't like this," Malacoda said, his voice unusually quiet.

Erebus just grunted an affirming response. The enderman was ready to teleport away if something unexpected happened.

"Send our blazes forward," Erebus said in his screechy, high-pitched voice, "then send the wither skeletons out to the flanks."

"Yes, that sounds like a good idea," Malacoda said.

Turning, the King of the Nether glared down at his wither-skeleton general.

"Make it so," the ghast said.

The wither skeleton, still riding on the back of the giant spider, scurried away, dispensing the orders.

Erebus looked to his own withers, the three headed skeleton torsos floating nearby. These vile creatures had no legs, just the stubby protrusion of a spine that hovered close to the ground. Dark, curved rib bones wrapped around their shadowy bodies and connected to the spine at the back. Their three ash-colored heads swiveled about on their broad bony shoulders, looking in all directions at once. If they saw a threat, they would fire a stream of poisonous flaming skulls at their target and the resulting explosion would splash the deadly venom on those nearby as well. They were powerful fighters and served as Erebus's own generals.

Flicking silent signals with his dark fingers, he ordered the withers to spread out and watch for anything unusual. The dark nightmares floated silently off, their blackened half-bodies disappearing between trees.

As they neared the foot of the mountain, Erebus began to notice that lack of leaves on the trees. It was as if something had stripped the branches bare, making the tree look lifeless and diseased, casting a gloomy pall on the whole area.

Erebus cringed . . . *what could have done this*?

Soon, the enderman was able to see the base of the mountain. The area around the mountain had been cleared of plant life, the soil barren and dead. Erebus could see his endermen standing about forming a ring near the base of the mountain, their purple eyes glowing bright. When they saw their king, they all stood up straight and tall, a mist of purple particles orbiting each. Teleporting to them, Erebus appeared within their protective ring. Turning, he surveyed the clearing, then spun and looked up at the mountain that now stood before him. He could see a massive dark opening was carved into the foot of the mountain, a jagged outcropping sticking out over the entrance.

"All is safe, my king," said one of the endermen.

Erebus turned to him and nodded.

"You did well," the King of the Endermen replied. "Where are they?"

"They went into that tunnel. We were given a message for you and Malacoda."

"What is it?"

"We were told to tell both of you."

Erebus turned and looked at that idiot, Malacoda, floating high up over the treetops, approaching the clearing.

"Tell me now," Erebus commanded.

"But we were . . ."

"NOW!"

The enderman bowed and spoke the message. "You and Malacoda are to go into the entrance and meet them deep within the tunnels. He said that you are to keep going until you reach lava, then he will meet you there."

Erebus nodded, then teleported back to Malacoda's

side. When he materialized near the giant floating ghast, he noticed a stream of water flowing from a crack in the side of the mountain. The column of water fell from a height of at least twenty blocks until it landed in a wide pool on the ground. He'd have to remember that this was there so that he could avoid it; water was lethal to endermen.

Cautiously, they approached the massive tunnel entrance and stopped in front of the huge opening. Even though the endermen had the place secure, it still felt dangerous. Looking at the opening, it reminded Erebus of the yawning maw of some kind of gigantic beast waiting to devour its next foolish victim. Malacoda deployed his forces in a protective ring, making sure they would not be surprised by an attack from that annoying User-that-is-not-a-user. Gathering his forces, Malacoda posted zombie-skeletons out on the perimeter and then put a ring of blazes around the massive tunnel opening. He then deployed his own ghasts high up in the air, allowing them to see any approaching forces in the distance. Once he felt their position was secure, he turned and faced Erebus.

"The shadow-crafter instructed us to go into the tunnel," Erebus explained.

Malacoda slowly moved closer to the ground, suspicious.

"Station your Overworld monsters here," Malacoda commanded. "We'll go into the cave accompanied by my withers and a squad of blazes."

"What of the captive?" Erebus said, motioning to Hunter.

"We'll keep her here. My ghasts will keep her company." He then turned to the ghast that still had its clammy tentacles wrapped around her body. "Keep her safe until my return."

"As you command," replied the ghast as he floated up higher into the air, Hunter firmly in his grasp.

"Now, we enter the cave of our friends," Malacoda said, apprehension in his voice. "Enderman, I think you will go first."

The ghast chuckled a cat-like laugh.

Erebus grunted as he walked into the wide opening, ready to teleport away at a moment's notice. He could hear Malacoda following, his long tentacles dragging on the ground like limp snakes. Looking over his shoulder, he saw the King of the Nether's face; he looked nervous. Ghasts are always nervous in enclosed spaces; their primary defense of flight completely nullified in this cramped tunnel.

Erebus chucked a wry laugh.

"What's so funny, enderman?" Malacoda snapped.

"Ahhh . . . nothing . . . sire," he responded.

The tunnel sloped down quickly, plunging into the rocky depths. At first, Erebus could feel the temperature drop, but as they moved deeper and deeper into the passage, the temperature started to rise; they were getting near lava. It felt like home to the King of the Endermen. The smoky, lava-filled underground chambers of the Overworld were his domain and he knew them better than any other creature. But just as the tunnel leveled off, it opened into a massive chamber bigger than anything Erebus had ever seen, torches lighting the entrance.

They were shocked by what they saw. Villagers—or at least they looked like villagers—were everywhere, on ledges, in crevasses, in lava pools, hanging from the ceiling . . . everywhere. They looked like they were each crafting something different, but they had no crafting benches.

Erebus stared at the curious villagers as he stepped further into the chamber. He didn't feel the normal hatred or desire to kill as he usually felt around NPCs. These creatures were different somehow . . . they were not the enemy, they were friends, and that didn't make any sense. Just as he was about to ask Malacoda, one of the dark villagers approached their party.

"You finally arrived," the dark haired NPC said.

Erebus looked carefully at the newcomer. He had the normal bulbous nose of a villager, a dark unibrow stretching across his forehead, but there was something about this creature that made him different from every villager Erebus had ever destroyed. It was the eyes . . . they glowed ever so slightly as if lit from within.

"You are the one that spoke to me in the Land of Dreams?" Malacoda asked.

The villager nodded and stepped forward into the torchlight. His face was a pale, sickly green as were his arms. As he stepped further into the light, Erebus thought that this creature almost had the look of a zombie about him, minus the decaying body parts and outstretched arms. It was then that Erebus noticed his smock, black with a grey strip running down from neck to hem. This was a crafter! He then looked around and noticed that all of the NPCs were garbed the same way . . . they were all crafters; no, not just crafters . . . something else . . .

"Yes, I was sent to find you in the Land of Dreams," the NPC relied, his voice filled with a sorrowful moaning quality. "My name is Zombiebrine. I work the zombies."

"What?" Malacoda asked.

"We are the shadow-crafters of Minecraft," Zombiebrine explained. "We make upgrades and improvements on the items that live in the shadows. My specialty is zombies. Over there," he gestured to a shadow-crafter working on a creeper, "is Creeperbrine." The shadow crafter had a similar mottled look to his skin, a faint green tint on his face and arms. "Above us is Batbrine. Below is Lavabrine. All of us work to make the creatures of the shadows stronger and faster and more lethal. We strive to tip the balance of Minecraft in our favor."

"Why?" Erebus asked.

"Ahhh . . . what?" Zombiebrine moaned.

"Why do you tip the balance in favor of the creatures of the night?"

Zombiebrine looked confused, then turned and looked at a shadow-crafter that was watching them from a balcony carved high up into the cavern wall. Erebus, whose eyes were used to the darkness of underground caverns, spotted the shadow-crafter instantly. It wasn't hard; his eyes glowed bright white like evil little beacons, brighter than anything else in the chamber . . . even the lava and torches. Erebus could see that this creature had the look of command; this was the one that was in charge here. Zombiebrine looked nervously up at the watcher then turned back and glared at Erebus.

"It is our task and we do it because we are programmed to do it," Zombiebrine answered, beads of sweat forming on his face.

"And now," Zombiebrine continued, "we are programmed to help you with your venture. We will help you to destroy the Source."

"That's what we want to hear," Malacoda said as he slowly floated closer to Zombiebrine.

Glancing back up to the dark balcony, Erebus noticed that the bright-eyed shadow-crafter had disappeared.

That one with the blazing eyes was dangerous, very dangerous, he thought.

Looking back down at Zombiebrine, Erebus saw the shadow-crafter stop moving as if listening to something in the distance, then moved further into the circle of torchlight.

"I will show you how to find the Source," the shadow-crafter said, "but before we can do that, we must find the first key."

"The first key?" Malacoda ask, his blood red eyes still glancing about, looking into the shadows.

"Yes," Zombiebrine replied, his moaning voice echoing throughout the chamber, "the first key to the Source . . . the Iron Rose. That is where your path starts. After that, you will need the second key, and then you can go to the Source."

"Where is the second key?" Erebus asked.

"No one knows," Zombiebrine replied. "The first key will lead you to the second key, and then to the Source. But there is no time to waste. Come, follow me."

Zombiebrine walked past Malacoda and his wither guards, heading into the tunnel and back to the surface. Erebus looked up at Malacoda and shrugged, then turned and followed the shadow-crafter through the passageway, not waiting for the King of the Nether.

In a few minutes, Zombiebrine reached the huge entrance and emerged from the bowels of the mountain, a collection of wither-skeletons and the King of the Nether following close behind.

"The Iron Rose is in that direction," Zombiebrine said, pointing toward the north. "Come."

Erebus took two steps out of the tunnel, then it started to rain. The drops landed on Erebus' face and instantly made his flesh sizzle, causing small tendrils of smoke to rise from the fresh wound.

Water . . . I hate water, Erebus thought as the droplets burned his skin.

Gathering a mist of purple teleportation particles around him, he disappeared and reappeared inside the rocky tunnel, his skin still smoldering from the moisture. Malacoda slowly moved out of the tunnel and hovered in the air, allowing the rain to bounce harmlessly off his blotchy bone-white skin. Turning to face the enderman, the King of the Nether grinned an eerie smile, then gave off a cat-like laugh that echoed through the forest.

"What's wrong, enderman, don't like the rain?" Malacoda mocked.

Erebus said nothing, just glared back at the ghast.

Zombiebrine pushed past the monsters and stepped out in the rain. The shadow-crafter scowled as he looked up at the falling drops.

"Rain," he moaned. "I can't stand the rain!"

And then his face seemed to turn a sickly color of green as anger welled up within the shadow-crafter.

"I hate you Rainbrin," Zombiebrine yelled, then started walking to the north.

"General," Malacoda said to his wither-skeleton commander.

The dark skeleton rode his spider up to the ghast's side and looked up into his red eyes.

"You will take a portion of my army and retrieve for me this Iron Rose." He turned and gave Erebus a wry smile, then continued. "We will let our brothers from the Overworld lead this charge with a few of my blazes and zombie-pigmen with them, just to make sure they do not lose their resolve."

The King of the Nether cast his gaze across his army as the raindrops bounced harmlessly off his head. All of the endermen were huddled in the tunnel opening. This made Malacoda give off a booming laugh that sounded like thunder.

"Go my brother! Bring me back the Iron Rose and

destroy that annoying User-that-is-not-a-user. NOW GO!"

The wither-skeleton followed the shadow-crafter, his spider scurrying to catch up. The huge collection of monsters from the Overworld followed the dark spider jockey, their angry, hateful eyes looking out across the land for something to destroy.

Slowly moving closer to the ground, Malacoda faced his captive, Hunter.

"You, my dear, are going to stay with me for a while."

The ghast flicked one of his tentacles in the direction of one of the shadow-crafters that had just emerged from the tunnel.

"I have a little gift for you, something that I had made special just for you."

"You don't frighten me, ghast," Hunter spat.

"Yes, I'm sure." He then turned to the shadow-crafter. "Ironbrine, bring it forward."

The shadow-crafter walked forward, then pulled a large structure out of his inventory. It was a cage made of iron bars, the top of the cage still open.

"Drop her in," Malacoda commanded.

The ghast that held her floated up into the air over the cage, then released her suddenly. She fell into the cage, flashing red with damage when she landed. Before she could scramble out, Ironbrine sealed the cage with another layer of iron bars, trapping her within the cage. Grabbing the bars, Hunter shook them violently as if she could somehow break them apart.

Malacoda laughed as he watched her panic grow.

"Enjoy you new home, NPC," Malacoda said. "You'll be in it for quite a while."

The King of the Nether glared at his prisoner, then looked back at Erebus, a mischievous, knowing smile on the square, baby-like face.

Does he suspect me? Erebus thought, then glanced away.

The rain stopped falling, allowing the endermen to come out of their protective tunnel. This made Malacoda laugh again.

"Go endermen with your brothers, and do not return unless you are victorious," Malacoda commanded.

The dark creatures looked from the ghast to Erebus, uncertain what to do. The blood-red enderman nodded, signaling them to obey. A purple mist of particles enveloped each as they disappeared and teleported to the monster horde.

"Well?" Malacoda asked Erebus. "Do as your king commands."

Erebus scowled at the King of the Nether.

I'll do as you say . . . for now, Erebus thought. *But soon your time will be over and the King of the Endermen will rule.*

Drawing on his teleportation powers, Erebus disappeared to the sound of Malacoda's booming laugh.

CHAPTER 14

HERDER'S PRISON

The NPC camp lay quiet, nestled amongst the tall trees of the hilly birch forest biome. They had been following the river at the edge of the desert biome for two days now, marching day and night, and the soldiers were tired. Gameknight had suggested that they needed a good night's rest for tomorrow they would reach the First Key. Woodbrin had said something about the Bridge to Nowhere, but nobody really understood what he meant.

"Why would someone build a bridge to nowhere?" Stitcher had asked the light-crafter. "It would be a complete waste of effort and resources."

"That is what the bridge is called," Woodbrin had answered, his words always quick and staccato, his voice like the short, rapid beats of a drum. "It goes somewhere now . . . to the Iron Rose. But it is the name we have given the bridge."

Everyone was anxious to get to the first key, but were also a little afraid as well. Woodbrin had warned that there were sentinels guarding the Iron Rose, and they would not give it up easily. There would be danger . . . and this was what worried Gameknight999.

Shuddering, the User-that-is-not-a-user pushed the thought aside as he walked through their camp. The tall birch trees gave them excellent cover, making the army difficult to spot. Looking about the forest, he marveled at the majestic beauty of this biome. These birch trees were at least ten to twelve blocks high, the speckled white bark reaching all the way up to the dark green leaves. The heights of these trees made him feel safe for some reason, like the giant wooden creatures would somehow protect him if a horde of monsters attacked . . . not likely, yet still he felt comforted to be amongst these majestic giants.

The forest stretched out as far as the eye could see, with steep hills and narrow valleys in the distance; it was a spectacular landscape and would have been fun to explore . . . that is except for the threat of being attacked by terrible monsters. Nighttime still belonged to the monsters, even in this peaceful land. Looking up, he could see some of the guards standing on the treetops, their watchful eyes looking for threats. It had taken some effort to get them up there. Builders had to place blocks of wood around the trunk of one of the trees, forming a spiral staircase that reached high up into the leafy canopy. Once they reached the treetops, it was easy enough for them to jump from tree to tree, placing watchful eyes all throughout the forest.

As he walked through the camp, he could hear the snoring of sleeping men and women. Many of the soldiers had been too tired to even take off their armor and now lay on the ground in their iron cocoons, their bodies exhausted.

Just as Gameknight was about to head toward the river, he heard a rustling sound, like people running through the forest. He could hear leaves being crunched and sticks being broken under heavy-booted feet.

Is it an attack? he thought. *No, it sounds like people running, and zombies and skeletons can't run. It must be soldiers.*

Gameknight cautiously walked toward the sound, his enchanted diamond sword casting an iridescent blue glow on the white bark of the trees. As he approached, he started to hear someone whimpering . . . no . . . crying. Then there was a banging sound of wood on stone. Moving toward this new sound, Gameknight could hear the wooden tool groan and creak as the wood started to crack . . . and then a shattering sound echoed through the forest as the wooden tool gave up the last morsel of its existence against a rocky obstacle.

Then the sound of fists pounding on stone thudded through the air. Someone was trying to break a stone block with their hands.

Maybe someone is in trouble?

Hurrying his pace, Gameknight moved silently

through the forest toward the thumping sound. Then he heard steps off to his left as well as behind. Pressing his back to the speckled white bark of a tree, he crouched and peered into the forest.

Was this a trap? Are there other creatures out here with me?

Fear started to flicker through his mind as he peered into the dark forest, his eyes looking for the elusive shapes that his ears told him were out there. A dark shadow flitted around a tree trunk. He could see something in its hand but wasn't sure what it was . . . a weapon? And then another shape, this one taller than the last, moved through a bush, the slivers of moonlight that pierced the leafy ceiling not bright enough to illuminate the creature.

What's going on? Was that Erebus?

And then a voice pierced the forest. "Help."

It was first soft and feeble, almost afraid to be heard, but then it grew in volume . . . and in sadness.

"HELP!"

It was Herder.

Suddenly, Gameknight hear the scurrying of many feet behind him. Looking back, he saw small furry white things streak through the forest like tiny snowy missiles. They dodged around the trees with incredible speed, each heading straight for Herder. And in an instant Gameknight knew what they were . . . wolves . . . Herder's wolves. Running forward, Gameknight sprinted toward the sorrowful cries, following the quick animals.

In twenty paces, he entered a small clearing. A three block high structure of cobblestone sat in the middle of the clearing, a ring of red collared wolves standing around it, teeth bared. Mason, Crafter and three other soldiers stood before the protective canine ring, their weapons drawn. From within the stone structure, Herder's cries still resonated. When Gameknight entered the clearing, all eyes turned to him.

"Herder, it's Gameknight. I'm here and it's alright."

The cries for help stopped, but now the growls of the wolves filled the air.

"How do we get to him?" Crafter asked. "The wolves won't let us get close."

Mason took a step forward and was greeted by vicious growls.

Just then they could hear more footsteps behind them; more soldiers coming to help . . . or just watch. Gameknight could hear some of them snickering as they entered the clearing.

Suddenly, Stitcher was by his side.

"What happened?" she asked.

"I'm not sure," Gameknight answered. "We can't get close enough to dig him out."

"Let me try."

Stitcher put away her bow and slowly walked forward. Instantly she was greeted by angry growling that forced her back.

"Kill the dogs," someone yelled from behind.

"Yeah . . . kill them, that will teach Pig-boy to be messing around out here."

Gameknight ignored them and sheathed his sword. He then held out his hand, the one that had been licked by the wolf in the Land of Dreams and slowly walked forward. As with the others, he was greeted by angry growls.

"Gameknight . . . get back," Crafter said. "This is too dangerous. Those wolves could kill you."

Gameknight ignored his friend and continued moving forward. He could hear bows being pulled from inventories, their wooden frames creaking as arrows were notched and the strings pulled back. Holding his left hand in the air in hopes of stopping anyone from firing, he continued to move forward, his right hand still outstretched.

Moving a few steps closer, Gameknight looked into the red eyes of the closest wolf. It was not the pack leader, but still a big animal. If it attacked, he wouldn't have time to draw his weapon . . . he'd be helpless. Staring straight into the eyes of the wolf, he stepped even closer.

"It's OK, nobody is going to hurt you," Gameknight said in a calm voice.

The wolf growled.

"I'm a friend."

Another angry snarl, its ears pulled back low.

Reaching forward, Gameknight moved his hand toward the wolf. The animal snapped its teeth together then growled as the tasty hand grew near. But then the wolf sniffed the air. Its nose, being incredibly sensitive, smelled the air around Gameknight's hand, then moved forward and smelled the back of his hand. It stood still, frozen with indecision for what seemed to Gameknight like an eternity, and then the ears came back up as the wolf licked the User-that-is-not-a-user's hand, its eyes fading from red to their normal canine yellow. The other wolves, seeing this, all came to Gameknight and sniffed his hand, then licked it affectionately. Turning his head, Gameknight could see warriors lowering bows and sheathing swords.

"Quickly, get Herder out of there," Gameknight commanded as he patted the large pack leader on the head.

Three warriors quickly moved forward with iron picks. In seconds, the clobblestone was removed and an embarrassed Herder was free.

"What is going on here?" Mason asked, a stern look on his blocky face. He then lowered his voice.

"We're trying to hide from the monsters of this land. We can't have people yelling out for help. Why did you trap yourself in there?"

"Well . . . ahh . . . I didn't . . . I didn't . . . ahh . . . "

"Herder, did someone else do this to you?" Crafter asked.

The gangly boy nodded, ashamed.

"Who did this . . . who did this?" Mason demanded.

Crafter stepped up to Mason and put a calming hand on his shoulder, then turned to Herder.

"Can you tell us what happened?"

Herder looked at all the warriors in the clearing, then glanced at Gameknight999. There were still tearstains on his cheeks, his eyes red and blotchy. Stepping forward, Gameknight put a reassuring hand on the boy's shoulder and just nodded his head. Herder looked up at his idol and took a slow, calming breath, and then spoke.

"OK, OK . . . well, you see, some of the warriors said that I could . . . I could be one of them . . . you know . . . a warrior. But I had to pass . . . pass the test. They said I could only have . . . only have a wooden sword. I gave up all my tools and took . . . and took the sword, but then they put the blocks . . . the blocks around me." Herder explained, his gaze focused on a nearby cow that was grazing on some of the grass in the clearing.

"Who did this?" Mason barked.

"My fault . . . it was my fault," said the boy. "My dad was . . . was right. My fault."

"What's he talking about?" one of the warriors said.

"I think he's touched in the head," said another.

Gameknight could hear Stitcher growl like one of the wolves as she spun around and glared at the warriors.

Someone laughed.

"We do not have time for this," said a grainy voice from behind Gameknight.

Looking over his shoulder, he found Woodbrin standing right behind him, his brown eyes impatiently surveying the situation.

"It was my fault. I should have . . . should have just stayed with the . . . the animals, my dad was right," Herder stammered as he stepped forward to put his arm around the largest of the wolves, the pack leader. Kneeling, he patted the big animal warmly on the side then stood and turned to face Gameknight999. "That is my place, with the . . . with the animals. It's my fault that I'm . . . that I'm different."

"NO!" Stitcher snapped. "We are all different. That's what makes a community so special. Each of us has a different gift to offer that helps us all. Mine is this bow. Mason's is his leadership. Your gift is . . . ahh . . . "

"What she's saying," Crafter interrupted, "is that we're all special and we're all different. That's the way it is supposed to be." He raised his voice so that all in the clearing could hear. "And those that pulled this terrible prank, you must understand that you hurt the community by these actions. If we all help and accept one another, then we can all do great things together. But if you continue these actions, you will, in the end, isolate yourselves and not be trusted by anyone."

Someone laughed.

Gameknight turned toward the sound and found Wood Cutter staring at Herder, a mischievous smile on his square face. Instinctively, he took a step away from the bully, experience with the bullies in his own school making him want to just disappear. But then Stitcher was at his side, her bow in her hand. He could feel the anger boiling within her as she glared at Wood Cutter with a vengeance. Her anger, and strength, made Gameknight feel like a coward.

I'm afraid of these bullies and they aren't even doing anything to me, Gameknight thought. *And look at Stitcher. She isn't afraid of anyone or anything . . . just like Hunter.*

He wished he had just the tiniest morsel of her courage. But then, just for an instant, everything made sense.

"Herder, you need to just be you and stop trying to be someone else," Gameknight said softly as he turned to face the boy. "Don't change for these idiots . . . they are too short-sighted to appreciate you for who you are." He then stepped forward and put a hand on the young boy's shoulder. "Believe in yourself and accept that you are the best Herder that anyone can be. Do not diminish yourself for anyone!"

Herder nodded.

"We can solve this problem later," Mason boomed, his angry green eyes surveying everyone in the clearing. "Right now, we're breaking camp and heading for the Bridge to Nowhere. Everyone gather your things . . . we march."

And on his words, the soldiers snapped into action. All of the mocking laughter and name-calling was pushed aside as the warriors started to do their jobs.

Gameknight reached out and tussled Herder's hair, then leaned close to the boy.

"Go tend to your animals, Herder. Nobody can take care of them as well as you can."

Wiping the tears from his cheeks, he looked up at his idol and gave him a weak smile.

"Really?"

The User-that-is-not-a-user nodded and patted

the lanky boy on the shoulder.

"Go on, I'll be along soon to check on you," Gameknight said, then turned and found Stitcher standing right in front of him.

"You need to stop them from doing this to him," she said with an accusatory tone.

"What can I do?" Gameknight asked.

"You can speak up! You can make sure that he doesn't suffer alone. You can give him hope, like you do for the warriors in battle." She scowled as she tried to bring her anger into check. "Just be there for him, that's all I ask."

And then she spun around and headed to the camp to gather her things.

Gameknight999 sighed as he watched her leave, then headed for his own horse. He knew that she was right, but seeing Herder being picked on by the bullies brought back so many of his own painful memories from school. He wanted to be brave and he wanted to help Herder, but just thinking about bullying in real life made him want to hide and be invisible. He wasn't sure how to stand up against them. He sighed, then climbed up on his horse. Once everyone was ready, they moved out of the woods and back to the river that snaked its way along the edge of the desert biome.

As they moved across the sandy dunes, Gameknight could see a structure appear on the horizon. It was an elaborate stone structure that arced high up into the sky, disappearing into the boxy clouds, seemingly heading nowhere . . . and that was where they needed to go. And as he looked at the massive structure, Gameknight shuddered. What danger would be waiting for them on the other side of the Bridge to Nowhere?

CHAPTER 15

BRIDGE TO NOWHERE

As the army moved across the hot desert sand they cautiously approached the foot of the Bridge to Nowhere. The bridge stretched high up into the sky, curving upward in a graceful arc and penetrating the clouds until the end was lost from sight. It was the biggest thing Gameknight had ever seen . . . well, except for Malacoda's terrible fortress in the Nether. It was at least twenty blocks wide if not greater at the bottom, with a set of ornate steps that reached down to the desert floor. It curved upward making a graceful arc as it stretched over the rippling waters of the river that flowed through the desert biome. Great columns of stone brick stretched up from the sides of the curving bridge to support the lofty arched roof. Blue blocks of lapis and green emerald cubes decorated the brick pillars, the colors shining bright. Across the roof, Gameknight could see bright redstone blocks, but their color mixed with the stained sun made them look ominous and scary, as if they were blocks of blood.

Gameknight shuddered.

Leaping off his horse, he slowly climbed the steps that led up to the bridge, each step taken with trepidation. At the point where the stairs met the curving bridge, a wooden sign could be seen fixed to the first brick column. It was an item frame. Moving up close to it, Gameknight could see that it had a picture of a flower on it; a rose. But the rose lacked its deep red color. In fact, it appeared to have almost no color at all, as if the greens and reds had somehow been drained by the passage of time. Leaning closer to the frame, Gameknight noticed that the petals of the rose had a peculiar sheen to them, like they were polished and metallic.

The Iron Rose; we found it!

Reaching out, Gameknight brushed his hand across the Rose, trying to feel the metal flower. But instead of feeling hard metallic petals, he only felt air as his hand passed through the image.

"Well, can you take it?" one of the NPCs asked behind him.

Gameknight999 reached out again, and the same thing happened again. His hand passed through the flower as if it were made of air.

"No," Gameknight answered as he stepped back from the sign.

One of the other NPCs stepped up and tried. The same thing happened; blocky fingers meeting air.

"What does it mean?" someone asked.

"It is just a sign," Crafter said. "A marker to confirm that this is the correct path, but it is not the Iron Rose that we seek. We must follow the bridge. The Rose will be on the other side."

"But we don't know where this bridge will lead," Gameknight said, his voice shaking a bit.

"It will lead to the Iron Rose," Woodbrin said from behind the User-that-is-not-a-user.

The light-crafter had the uncanny ability to sneak up right behind him without ever being seen or heard. It unnerved Gameknight a little.

"All we know is that the Iron Rose will be on the other side," Mason said confidently. "We have to get this key before the monsters can reach it."

He turned and faced the army that stood at the foot of the bridge. The massive collection of NPCs stretched out across the sandy desert they had just crossed. All of them looked up at Mason, confidence and trust showing in their eyes.

"A small party of us will go across the bridge and bring back the Iron Rose," Mason explained. "Those that remain, I want to you fortify this end of the bridge and prepare for the enemy, in case they dare to challenge us here."

He paused for a moment to consider his words, then continued.

"He who is prudent and lies in wait for an enemy who is not, will be victorious," Mason said as if reading some kind of famous quote.

Gameknight glanced at Mason's blocky form, and for an instant their eyes met. A guilty look seemed to flash across Mason's face, as if he'd been caught with his hand in the cookie jar, then the big NPC looked away.

I remember that one, Gameknight thought. *It was on Mr. Planck's wall, next to the pencil sharpener. It was a saying from that Japanese general . . . what was his name . . . oh yeah—Sun Tzu. It's from his book, The Art of War . . . how can he know these things?*

"Prepare overlapping fields of fire for the archers, and spaces for the cavalry to charge out to meet the enemy," Mason continued, his eyes avoiding Gameknight's. "Build obstacles to stand behind, walls and columns. Be sure to . . . "

Gameknight mind drifted to the memory of that battle at Crafter's village when he and Shawny had faced off with Erebus for the first time. It seemed to be a million years ago. They could certainly use Shawny's tactical know-how right now . . . but then something his friend had said came back to him.

'A flood is coming, my friends,' Shawny had said. *'We cannot stand rigid against this flood for it will wash us away. Instead, we will redirect the flow to*

where we need it and where we are prepared.'

A flood is coming . . . redirect the flow . . . these words bounced around in his head, the pieces trying to find their place on the game board that now lay before him. And then he had it.

"Redirect the flow and have a little surprise waiting for them," Gameknight said aloud, then started to laugh.

Mason stopped his instructions to the troops and turned toward Gameknight, a look of confusion on his face.

"What?" the big NPC asked.

Gameknight looked up into his square green eyes. Placing a hand on his shoulder he smiled.

"I know what to do . . . something Shawny taught me back on Crafter's server," the User-that-is-not-a-user said.

"Redirect the flow?" Mason asked, clearly confused.

"That's right . . . redirect the flow."

Moving back down the steps, Gameknight knelt and explained his plan, drawing formations in the sand. Blocky faces nodded as the warriors muttered to each other, seeing the wisdom in Gameknight's plan.

Mason nodded as Gameknight explained his plan, a wry smile stretching across his large boxy head.

Once he'd finished, Mason stood and spoke with his powerful, commanding voice. "While you are building, some of you start mining. We need resources, and this is as good a place as any to start." Mason then glanced at Woodbrin for a moment, lost in thought, then continued. "Light-crafters, you will go with us across the bridge, in case we need your help."

"We cannot help you there," Woodbrin said, his voice creaking with tension, almost sounding like a board cracking with strain. "The light-crafters will stay here and help prepare for battle."

"Very well," Mason replied. "We will retrieve the Rose while the rest of you hold this end of the bridge." He then drew his sword and held it up high. "The monsters of Minecraft will have a painful surprise if they try to stop us here. FOR MINECRAFT!"

"FOR MINECRAFT!" the warriors answered, their weapons now held high up in the air.

But as the warriors cheered, Gameknight had the feeling that the monsters of Minecraft *would* challenge them here, and that there *would* be a great battle at the foot of this bridge. He could almost hear Erebus's cackling as the monsters swarmed forward, smashing against their defenses with reckless abandon. Images of what *might* happen started to spin through Gameknight's head, pushing aside his courage and causing him to shake with fear.

Will my plan work, or will it lead us to ruin? What if Erebus figures out my plan and gets around our defenses? What if . . .

But then something his father had once said started to echo faintly within his mind. And as the words grew louder, they pushed aside the imaginary failures and began to fill him with confidence.

Don't focus on what might happen, his father had said to him. *Let go of the what-ifs and focus on the now!*

The now . . . that's right, the now . . . I'll focus on the now and let the rest go.

Pushing aside the events that hadn't happened yet, he spun around and started climbing the gently rising bridge. Drawing his diamond sword, he pushed aside his fears and headed forward, toward the now.

"You see, the User-that-is-not-a-user is already heading for the Iron Rose," Mason shouted. "Nothing can stop us when we have Gameknight999 as the tip of our spear. His courage is an example to us all!"

The soldiers cheered.

Focus on the now.

A clattering sound filled his ears as Crafter rode up next to him, his small hand holding the line to a horse.

"Come on Gameknight, we ride," Crafter said.

Gameknight grabbed the reins and jumped up into the saddle. From this height, he thought he would be able to see over the curve of the bridge and see the opposite side, but it still arced up and away, the far end still a mystery.

Mason rode up next to them, a collection of twenty horsemen at his back.

"We're ready," Mason said in a firm voice. "Lead on, User-that-is-not-a-user. Lead us to the Iron Rose."

Before Gameknight could move, a hand grabbed his leg. Looking down, he found Stitcher looking up at him, Herder at her side.

"You aren't going anywhere without me," she said in the characteristic stern voice. "My place is at your side," she continued. "and until my sister comes back, it's my job to keep you from doing something stupid. I have to keep you safe, and that's what I'm gonna do."

Gameknight frowned down at her, but she just scowled back.

"You can leave me behind, but I will follow you," she snapped.

"Me too." It was Herder.

"Herder, your place is with the . . . " Gameknight said.

"My place is with you!" Herder said in a stern voice, his two color eyes glaring up at Gameknight. "You said believe in myself . . . myself. Well, I do. I know that I can . . . I can help, and I'm going with . . . with you."

Reaching up, he swung up into the saddle behind Gameknight.

Glancing to Crafter, Gameknight looked to his friend, hoping he would help.

Crafter only nodded and smiled.

"Come Stitcher," Crafter said, "you can ride with me. I think Gameknight's horse is kinda full."

The young girl laughed, then moved quickly to Crafter's horse. She swung upward into the saddle, her red hair flowed like a crimson wave, then landed deftly in front of him, her bow out, an arrow notched.

"Let's go," she said, then smiled at Gameknight.

It was a smile of victory.

CHAPTER 16

BRIDGE TO SOMEWHERE

They rode up the curving bridge for at least ten minutes. It had arched upward so high that the cool water of the river below was now completely out of sight. White blocky clouds started to drift across the tall pillars that supported the multicolored ceiling; the greens, reds, and blues getting muted by the floating mist.

Gameknight could tell by the pattern of stepped blocks that they were almost at the top of the bridge's arc; they would be heading down soon. But instead of finding the flat top of the bridge, he was shocked to find something else; a portal.

A huge purple rectangle of light bisected the bridge. It covered the entire pathway, with the edges of the portal built into the brick pillars that held up the colorful ceiling. Gameknight could see small purple teleportation particles moving about the portal's edge, floating out of the iridescent field then getting drawn back in.

Moving up close, Gameknight dismounted and moved to the edge of the bridge. Holding onto one of the brick pillars, he leaned out over the edge of the rocky structure. He could just see around the edge of the portal, and found nothing but open air. They could have built a pathway around the portal and bypassed it, but there was no place to go. Their only choice was to go through the portal or go back.

Grabbing his horse by the reins, Gameknight walked up to the portal, his horse pulling back a little.

"It's OK, boy," Gameknight said to his horse, patting it lightly on the head.

"Stroke him like this," Herder advised as he gently petted the horse on the bridge of his nose.

Gameknight did as instructed, and the horse seemed to calm down a little.

"We must go through," Mason said as he stepped off his horse.

"Gameknight and I will see what is on the other side, then come back and report," Crafter said as he stepped forward, the line to his horse firmly in one hand, his iron sword in the other.

"Herder, Stitcher, I need you to stay here," Gameknight said, his voice sounding almost as if he were pleading with them.

Crafter looked at Stitcher and nodded to the young girl, agreeing with the User-that-is-not-a-user.

"We may need to move fast, and it will be easier without extra passengers on the horses," Gameknight said, this time a little more confidently.

"OK, we'll stay," Stitcher said, "but not for long, so you better hurry up."

Crafter smiled at her, then turned and faced the portal. Moving up to the sparkling purple field, Crafter turned his head and looked directly at Gameknight999, then stepped through the portal with his horse in tow. He wavered for just an instant, then was gone.

Gameknight could feel all eyes on him; the soldiers waiting for the User-that-is-not-a-user to join his friend. Gripping his horse's lead firmly in his hand, he stepped up to the portal. He could feel the serpent of fear start to coil around his courage and squeeze his will, but he ignored his fear and stepped into the portal.

The purple wavering field filled his vision and made him slightly motion sick for an instant, then he was through. He was shocked that the blasting heat of the Nether didn't smash into him as it did on the last server. In fact it was fairly cool, almost comfortable . . .

Looking up, he found Crafter waiting nearby, already mounted on his horse.

"Thanks for joining me," the young NPC said, a smile on his face.

Gameknight wasn't sure if he was being sincere, or sarcastic.

"Let's get this done," he said as he swung back up onto his horse.

Turning he faced away from the portal. They could see the other half of the bridge stretching out before them, the gentle arc slowly bending back down to the ground. There were no threats nearby.

"Wait here," Gameknight said to Crafter as he rode down the pathway.

The bridge was identical curving down as it had been curving up. Digging his heels into his horse's flanks, he sprinted down the length of the bridge. Below him was water, a vast ocean that stretched out underneath the bridge, a sandy beach slowly coming into view. He could see stairs at the end of the bridge that led down to the beach, but instead of leading to a desert biome, it led to something that was completely pale, with sand everywhere across the ground. Instead of grainy sandstone or rocky hills, Gameknight saw only white. It wasn't snow; it was something else. Stretching out away from the bridge was a gravel path that led off between two tall spires, all white. Carved into the spires were the shapes of two NPCs, each one wearing billowing cloaks and robes. They both held a sword in one hand, the other hand held straight out as if commanding all those approaching to stop.

Looking across the landscape, Gameknight could see no threats, just the tall statues of the two stony kings guarding the entrance to who knows what. Spinning his mount around, he charged back up the bridge and back to Crafter.

"What is it?" the young NPC asked. "Are there monsters?"

"No, nothing," Gameknight answered. "Just the other half of the bridge."

Gameknight dismounted to catch his breath and allow his horse to rest.

"Bring the rest," he said to Crafter. "I'll wait here."

Crafter dismounted and grabbed the horse's reins. He then stepped through the portal, pulling the horse close behind. They disappeared in an instant, but within a minute Crafter returned, with Mason and their soldiers at his back.

Herder moved excitedly back to Gameknight's side, Stitcher already mounted on Crafter's horse.

"What is it that lies before us?" Mason asked as he mounted his horse.

"A strange land at the foot of the bridge," Gameknight answered, "but no monsters that I could see."

"This is good news," Mason said in a loud voice. "We've beaten the creatures of the night to the first key. Come on, let's go."

The warriors stormed down the bridge with Mason and Crafter at the head of the column, Gameknight taking up the rear. When they reached the bottom, the soldiers spread out, taking up defensive positions, all eyes scanning the terrain looking for threats.

Gameknight trotted his horse up to Crafter and Mason and stopped off to the side.

"Where now, User-that-is-not-a-user?" Mason asked.

Pointing along the gravel path, Gameknight kicked his horse forward, his shimmering diamond sword in his hand, Mason and Crafter following at his side. The path led him between the two massive statues, their flowing robes made out of sand stone, the outstretched arm formed from what looked like iron blocks. Gameknight and Herder both looked nervously up at the two figures as they rode between them, Gameknight hoping they would not come to life and squash them.

"Who do you think built these statues?" Gameknight said.

"The Creator built everything on this server," Crafter said as if reciting from some sacred tome. "This is his private server, where much of the development of Minecraft was done. Everything you see was formed by the Creator's hand."

Gameknight grunted.

"I wish he'd created a quicker way to find this stupid Rose," Gameknight replied, a disrespectful edge to his voice. This brought a grunt from both Crafter and Mason as they galloped forward, but drew a laugh from Stitcher.

The gravel pathway led past the two statues to a

high wall maybe eight blocks tall, a colossal mountain beyond that, all made of the shining white blocks. There was no plant life in sight, no trees, no grass, no flowers; just a sea of antiseptic cubes of white. Ahead, he could see a narrow opening in the wall just two blocks wide, the path leading straight for the gap. As they followed the gravel trail to the high wall, Gameknight reached out and tapped the pale blocks with his sword. They rang like a bell; a pure tone that resonated to the neighboring blocks, creating a harmony of sounds that filled the air.

"Iron blocks," Gameknight said as they passed through the narrow opening, the confines forcing them to ride single file. "Why would someone form these walls, and what looks like mountains ahead, out of iron blocks?"

As they passed through the tight passage, Gameknight could see the white mountain more clearly in the distance, its surface also shiny and smooth; more iron blocks. The gravel path quickly spilled them into an area that looked like an arena, with steep vertical walls surrounding a flat basin. The area must have been at least fifty blocks across from wall to wall, with a few gentle hills dotting the area. As with the area around the foot of the bridge, there were no blades of grass adorning the arena as would be expected in a rolling hills biome, nor a dusting of flowers. In fact, the landscape was almost completely barren. The only plant life visible in the arena-like area was the presence of vines growing down the sheer walls, their long green fingers stretching down across iron blocks.

At the center of the arena, they could see a hill maybe eight blocks high. The top of the hill was capped with a shimmering white glow, as if a bright white torch sat atop the peak.

"That must be the Rose," Crafter said, pointing to the hill. "Come on."

He was about to urge his horse forward when Mason reached out and grabbed his arm.

"Wait," Mason said as he turned his head to look back along their path. "The rest of you come here," he yelled.

A clattering of hooves filled the air as the rest of the warriors galloped to join them, the sound echoing off the iron walls.

"The rose stands on that hill," Mason said. "We're going to move cautiously and slowly towards it. Everyone dismount and draw your weapons."

The soldiers climbed down off their mounts quickly, drawing their swords to be ready for whatever was going to happen; yet nothing did. The arena stayed eerily quiet. No sound could be heard, not even the sound of the wind . . . nothing.

"Herder, you are to stay behind and hold on to the horses," Mason said. "The rest of you follow me."

Herder dismounted and took the leads from the other warriors. He had a look of disappointment on his face, but knew that he was the best person to do this job.

Mason stepped forward, still following the gravel trail, but it quickly ended, the speckled brown path disappearing at the edge of the arena, the ground ahead all iron. Glancing at the ground, Mason took a hesitant step off the pathway and onto the iron floor. Instantly, things began to rumble and shake. It looked to Gameknight as if the walls were coming alive as the vine-covered blocks started to move. Shapes began to emerge from the walls, bodies with short stout legs, broad shoulders, and long arms. Faces could be seen on the large heads as dark eyes opened and turned towards the intruders, thick unibrows creased with anger.

"Iron golems," Gameknight said as he gripped his sword tighter, fear rippling though him.

"Our village used to have one of these," one of the warriors said as he stepped forward.

Putting away his sword, he walked towards the closest of the metal giants.

"There's nothing to fear," he said. "Golems are friendly to NPCs. They used to protect our village from the mobs. They are our friends, watch."

The soldier walked straight up to the golem. There was no look of fear on the soldier's face, in fact he looked quite excited, as if he were about to be reunited with an old friend. But when he was within ten paces from the giant, a grumbling started to come from the metal goliath, a sound like the grinding of gears within an echo chamber. As it neared, the angry grating sound grew louder and louder.

The warrior stopped and held out his arms, as if expecting some kind of gift, waiting for the creature to take its final steps to him. When it reached the soldier, the iron golem threw up its arms in a quick motion, striking the warrior and throwing him up into the air. Gameknight could see the soldier flash bright red as he flew through the air. He landed on the ground with a thud, flashing red again, then disappeared, dead.

"What happened?" one of the soldiers cried.

"He's dead, the golem killed Carver . . . " said another.

"What are we going to do . . . "

"Let's get out of here . . ."

As they stood there looking at the pile of possessions float on the ground that used to belong to the dead warrior, more of the metal giants emerged from the walls. They lumbered slowly towards their party, the sound of grinding, creaking metal filling the air, their angry eyes focused on the NPCs . . . and Gameknight999.

CHAPTER 17

BATTLE WITH IRON

As the ground shook, more of the metal giants emerged from the walls, all of them heading straight for the NPCs. Their dark eyes seemed to glow somehow with hatred for these invaders, their unibrows creased with venomous rage.

"Here's the plan," Mason said quickly. "We charge in, grab the Rose, and then charge out. The User-that-is-not-a-user will lead us."

The warriors all retrieved their horses from Herder and mounted . . . all but Gameknight, the User-that-is-not-a-user lost in thought.

"Ready . . ." Mason boomed.

This plan is suicide, Gameknight thought. *Can I do this? I'm not sure if I'm smart enough. I'm certainly not strong enough to stand up to one of those golems. What if I can't do it? What if I fail?*

" . . . set," Mason continued.

And suddenly the pieces of the puzzle fell into place and the solution burst into his mind . . . a farm.

"I know what to do, I know what to do!" Gameknight suddenly exclaimed. "Everyone get off the iron blocks, quick."

The golems were getting closer.

Turning their horses the warriors all moved out of the arena and back to the gravel path. As soon as the last soldier moved off the iron blocks, the iron golems stopped their plodding advance and turned around. Lumbering back to the sheer walls that surrounded the arena, they sank back into their outlined recessions, their bodies melting into the metallic walls. This made the warriors pause, many of them cheering at the disappearance of the massive creatures. They lowered their weapons and looked towards the User-that-is-not-a-user.

"You see, one time I made a golem farm, to harvest their iron, and I . . ."

"You made what?" Crafter asked as he sheathed his sword.

"A golem farm to harvest their iron. You see . . ."

"You mean you killed . . . killed them for their iron?" Herder asked.

"Well . . . that was back when I used to be a . . . I mean I was only . . ." Gameknight paused as he hung his head in shame. "Yes, I killed them for their iron back in my griefing days, but I know how to stop them without having to fight them. I know how to get them out of the way without having to kill them . . . I know how to get the Iron Rose."

Nervous eyes glanced at the green vines that decorated the iron walls, each set of vines representing a golem ready to emerge and protect their prize, and there were lot of vines all around the arena. The warriors then brought their gazes back to Gameknight999.

"Then tell us what you need," Mason said quickly as he too sheathed his sword. Motioning to the rest of the soldiers, they too put away their weapons.

"All we need is water, lots of it," Gameknight999 explained. "Did anyone bring any buckets?"

A handful of soldiers stepped forward with buckets in their hands.

"Good. Go get water from the ocean at the foot of

the bridge, as much as you can carry," Gameknight commanded. "The rest of you, draw your picks, we have digging to do. There is no room for error, for we've seen what happens when you try to stand your ground against these monsters."

"Not monsters," Herder interjected.

"Yes, yes, not monsters," Gameknight agreed, "but deadly nonetheless. Now gather around so that I can explain what must be done . . ."

Gameknight explained his plan to the warriors, their blocky heads nodding as they listened. After he had finished, the User-that-is-not-a-user looked each soldier in the eyes and made sure everyone knew their task. When all were ready, they gathered at the edge of the gravel path, none of them stepping onto the iron floor of the arena . . . not yet.

"Is everyone ready?" Gameknight asked.

The warriors all nodded, a look of fear and uncertainty painted on their blocky faces.

"Ok then," Gameknight said as he jumped up onto his horse, Crafter doing the same. "Be sure you're ready when we get to you," he said to Mason who stood at his side. "Our lives are counting on it."

"We'll be ready," the big NPC replied, his green eyes glowing bright with anticipation.

"Now . . . FOR MINECRAFT!" Gameknight yelled as he kicked his horse into a gallop, Crafter right at his side.

As soon as their horses stepped onto the iron arena floor, the ground started to rumble as the golems again emerged from the vine-covered walls, their lumbering forms all converging on the two horsemen.

Mason and the rest of the warriors waited for a minute or two, allowing Gameknight and Crafter to draw the metal giants away from the entrance, then sprinted forward, pickaxes and buckets of water in their hands. Instantly, they started to carve out a large rectangle into the iron floor, their own iron picks ringing out as they dug into the metal floor, excavating a region six blocks wide by twelve blocks long.

As they dug, Gameknight and Crafter sprinted towards the glowing hill, all of the golems slowly moving towards them.

"Remember, we must move like we did on your server when we faced Erebus and his army," Gameknight explained. "Hit and run, like in Wing Commander."

"Wing Commander?" Crafter asked.

"Never mind, just make sure we keep all these golems chasing us and away from Mason and the others. We must keep them busy until Mason is ready."

"Well, it doesn't look like that's going to be a problem," Crafter said as he pointed off to the right.

Turning his head, Gameknight could see at least a dozen golems converging on them, their arms swinging upward violently. Off to the left, there were five more iron giants, a look of overwhelming rage on their metallic faces.

"Quickly, down the middle!" Gameknight shouted as he urged his horse forward.

They rode between the two groups of monsters, just staying out of arm's reach. After passing the groups, they spun around and rode towards the walls of the arena, Gameknight going to the left, Crafter to the right. Using every ounce of speed their horses possessed, they rode around the perimeter, drawing those at the center toward the walls, creating a large opening in the center again.

"Now!" Gameknight shouted.

They pivoted and headed straight toward each other, pulling the golems back to the center of the arena. Turning, Gameknight headed for the Rose as Crafter headed back to Mason, looking to draw a long golem back to the center of the arena and away from the vulnerable ground forces.

Riding up the gentle sloping hill, Gameknight sprinted to the center of the hill. As he passed the peak, he looked down and could see a solitary rose growing out of a block of iron, the metallic petals giving off a bright white glow that almost hurt his eyes. Looking away from the prize, he focused on the metal beasts that were closing on him from all around. He could see at least a dozen or more golems coming at him from the far side of the arena, their arms swinging wildly, another group approaching from the other direction. The grinding, grating metallic sounds of the lumbering giants filled the arena and reflected off the polished iron walls, making it sound as if there were more than he could see.

Spinning his horse, he abruptly changed direction, pulling them to the left. He charged straight at a cluster of them. The creatures seemed to wait for him, excited at the prospect of crushing this intruder, but at the last instant he veered away, a massive metallic fist flashing in front of his eyes, just missing his head.

Gameknight shuddered. He had just avoided death by mere inches.

That was too close, he thought.

Snapping the reins, he wheeled and headed for the opposite side of the arena, drawing more of the metal giants toward him. Looking off toward the entrance, he could see that Mason had the rectangular pit dug up and they were starting to fill it with water.

Good . . . it was time.

"Come on you metal giants," Gameknight yelled, "follow me, if you can." .

Drawing every ounce of speed from his stead,

Gameknight sprinted in a zigzag pattern, still drawing the golems together, but also moving them towards the entrance.

"Everyone get back to the entrance," he yelled as he approached the watery trap.

As he neared, Gameknight could see that water had been placed along one end of the rectangle. The water flowed down the length of the rectangle, only able to flow six blocks, then fell into a hole two blocks deep. Spinning in a tight circle, Gameknight let the golems get closer, then sprinted straight for the watery trap. Leaping into the flowing water, he sprinted across the rectangle, having to gallop at an angle to keep from being pulled into the deep end. Once he made it to the opposite side and jumped out of the watery trap, Gameknight turned his horse and watched. The golems headed straight toward him, their arms swinging wildly. The grinding sounds from the metal giants sounded like thunder as they echoed off the nearby walls, making Gameknight want to cover his ears, but instead he drew his sword with his free hand, the other on the reins.

The first group of golems stepped into the watery rectangle and were instantly pushed sideways by the current. Confusion quickly replaced rage on their faces as they were driven into the deep end by the watery flow, pushed into the two-block deep channel at the far end. Quickly, they found that they could not step out of the deep hole and were trapped.

A cheer rang out from behind Gameknight as the warriors saw the first victims of the trap. Just then, he was startled by the splashing form of Crafter galloping through the water trap, another cluster of golems on his heels. The iron titans splashed into the trap and were instantly pushed sideways by the current, slowly drawn into the deep end with their comrades.

The mighty creatures flailed their arms as they tried to escape the watery clutches of the current, but they were no match for the forces pushing on them; they were just too slow to escape.

A cheer rang out from the arena entrance as he dismounted. The warriors chanted Gameknight's name and held fist to chest in salute. As they cheered, the last few remaining golems lumbered toward Gameknight, each glaring at him with such venomous loathing that he bet they wished they could cut him down with those angry eyes. He'd never seen such a look of unbridled hatred except from him nemesis, Erebus. These creatures craved his death with every fiber of their being, and would gladly trade their lives for his.

In minutes, only one golem remained, but this lone survivor looked different from the rest, bigger and more dangerous. Instead of dark eyes, this one had bright yellow eyes as if made of gold. They sparkled in the rosy red light of the overhead pale crimson sun. In addition, the green vines that hung down the creature's left side and arm were also wrapped around its head. It looked to Gameknight as if it wore some kind of leafy crown, a majestic look of command on its angry face.

This must be the leader, the King of the Golems, Gameknight thought.

The creature stood at the edge of the water trap and glared at Gameknight. Drawing his bow, he fired arrows at the metal giant, one after another, but they bounced harmlessly off his metallic skin; the iron giant did not budge. Glancing down at the rectangle, the King of the Golems started to move around the side, walking around the trap instead of through.

Oh no, he's not going to fall for the trap, he thought. *I have to do something to make it angrier so that it will charge straight at me.*

And then Gameknight saw the glowing hill over the golem's shoulder.

Of course, the Iron Rose.

Leaping up onto his horse, Gameknight sprinted around the opposite end of the trap and headed straight toward the Rose. He could see the King of the Golems following him out of the corner of his eye.

I have to get to it and dig it up before that monster can reach me.

Digging his heels into his steed, Gameknight sprinted up the hill. When he reached to top, he leapt off his horse and landed on the ground with his iron pickaxe in his hand. Hammering away at the block under the Rose, he dug as fast as he could. The grinding, grating sound of the golem was getting louder.

"Get out of there," Stitcher yelled from the entrance. "He's coming!"

"Move, Gameknight," someone else yelled. "MOVE!"

Gameknight ignored the warning and focused on digging.

The iron block was stubborn, not wanting to give up its prize. Gameknight kept at it, even though he could now feel the ground shake with each lumbering footstep of the approaching giant.

"He's getting closer, get out of there!" someone yelled.

Driving his pick even harder, Gameknight could see cracks starting to form on the iron block, but they were also forming on his pick, his tool starting to lose its strength in the battle.

THUMP . . . THUMP . . .

The footsteps of the mighty giant were shaking the ground so hard that it was almost knocking Gameknight over. He wanted to look up, to see how close he was to death. But he knew that if he looked away, the battle would be lost and the iron block would win. Instead, he pushed harder on his pick, swinging it with every ounce of strength.

And then, *SNAP*, his pick shattered on his last swing . . . he'd lost. Out of pure instinct, Gameknight ducked just as a mighty iron fist wooshed past his head. As he stood, Gameknight looked down at the rose and was surprised to find the iron block had also shattered, leaving the rose floating there on the ground. Reaching down, he scooped it up and rolled to the side just as another iron-mailed fist move within inches of his head.

Standing, he sprinted for his horse. In a single, fluid motion, Gameknight jumped up onto his mount and headed back for the rectangular pool. A mechanical howl of rage echoed throughout the arena as the King of the Golems screamed. Following with all his speed, the iron giant chased after Gameknight, a look of overwhelming hatred painted on the metallic face.

When he reached the pool, Gameknight drove his horse right into the center, but instead of jumping to the other side, he stayed in the center, constantly pushing the horse up against the current. He was just able to hold his position as the golem approached. Reaching into his inventory, Gameknight pulled out the Iron Rose and held it high into the air. The petals glowed bright, casting an intense circle of light around the User-that-is-not-a-user, making him almost appear to glow as if lit from within. He could hear the trapped golems all scream in anger, but their chorus of rage was nothing compared to the Golem King. He bellowed a loud mechanical cry that made the very walls of the arena shake.

"You want this," Gameknight yelled at the

guardian. "Then come and get it."

The King of the Golems howled again. This time, it was so loud that many of the NPCs dropped their weapons and fell to the ground, shaking in fear.

"Return what you have stolen," the mechanical giant bellowed, his voice filled with the sounds of metallic gears.

"Yeah? COME AND GET IT!" Gameknight yelled back, moving a step closer to the edge of the pool.

This time, the golem leapt into the pool, his long arms swinging upward violently. Wheeling his horse at the last instant, Gameknight moved just out of the way, the long metal fist landing a glancing blow against his arm, almost making him drop the Rose. Pain shot down his shoulder and arm, but he did not let go of the prize. Urging his horse forward against the current, he headed for the opposite side. Leaping with all his might, Gameknight's horse jumped out of the watery trap and landed on the dry iron ground.

Another metallic howl came from the King of the Golems as the flowing water pushed him into the deep end of the pool, trapped.

I did it, Gameknight thought, *and even managed to not get killed. Yay, me!*

And then the mechanical howling stopped as all of the golems stopped their thrashing and turned to face the User-that-is-not-a-user, their king at the front.

"We will take back what is ours," the King of the Golems said, his voice sounding like distant thunder, "and nothing will stop us. We will appear when you least expect us and then the tides of battle will shift. We will take what is ours; whether you die as a result of it is up to you."

Gameknight shook slightly, as if the golem king's words were some kind of premonition, but then he was startled by the sound of cheers directly behind him. Spinning his horse, he found the warriors had surged forward to congratulate the User-that-is-not-a-user. Dismounting, Gameknight was greeted with pats on the back and shoulder as the soldiers all wanted to touch the one that had taken the Iron Rose. Holding it up high, he let the bright light from the silvery petals shine across the arena, forcing many to shield their eyes.

"Come on, we need to get back to the others and find the second key," Crafter said in a loud voice.

"Yes, the others," Gameknight agreed.

Jumping up onto his horse he started to ride back to the bridge, the clop of the horses' hooves all ringing on the iron blocks of the arena. But as they moved out of the arena and back onto the gravel pathway, a rhythmic sound echoed across the land. It was a ringing sound, like someone banging on a huge bell with a metal hammer, the gonging sound resonating pure through the air. Turning to look toward the noise, he saw Herder digging away at the iron blocks that surrounded the water trap. Spinning his mount around, Gameknight rode to the lanky youth.

"What are you doing?" the User-that-is-not-a-user yelled over the gonging sound.

"They are trapped . . . trapped. We cannot . . . cannot leave them trapped."

"What?" Gameknight asked as he dismounted.

Moving to the young boy's side, careful to avoid the swinging pickaxe, Gameknight put a reassuring hand on his shoulder, then reached over and grabbed the handle of the pick.

The banging sound stopped.

"Herder, what are you doing?"

The young boy lowered the pickaxe and turned to face his idol. Behind him, the thrashings of the iron golems could be heard, their iron fists struggling against the watery current and smashing against the edges of the trap. With each blow, the ground shook as the mighty giants tried to gain purchase on the edge of their liquid prison. Only the Golem King stood stationary, a cold hatred burning in his eyes for the one that had imprisoned his kind; Gameknight999.

"They are trapped," Herder said, "they can't get . . . can't get out."

"That's the whole idea."

"What is wrong?" a voice asked behind them.

Gameknight turned and found Crafter directly behind them, Stitcher at his side. Mason then walked up, a look of impatience on his square face.

"We must be going," the big NPC said in a deep voice that seemed to boom across the arena.

The iron golems in the water trap heard this booming voice and stopped their struggling. Their cold eyes all turned toward Mason and looked at the big NPC, the look of hatred that had been there an instant ago seemingly evaporated. Even the King of the Golems seemed at peace as he looked toward Mason, but then the hateful look returned as he turned his glare back to Gameknight999.

"Cannot leave them here . . . trapped," Herder said again, his voice now strained with emotion. "Like the spleefing . . . like the spleefing. This is not right, they must be . . . be freed."

Raising the iron pickaxe again, Herder continued his digging, slowly breaking iron blocks near the trap.

"You know what it's like to be trapped, don't you Herder?" Crafter said with a soft, reassuring voice. "But we must be going. We have to get to the last key."

The lanky youth ignored the question and kept on digging.

Pulling out her own pickaxe, Stitcher stepped forward and added her strength to the effort, slowly digging a channel that would allow escape for the metal giants. Sighing, Gameknight took out his own pickaxe and move forward to help. As soon as he stepped forward, the iron golems became agitated, their arms swinging about dangerously.

"They don't seem to like me very much," Gameknight said as he stepped back, putting his pick back into his inventory.

Patting the User-that-is-not-a-user on the shoulder, Mason stepped forward, a shining iron pickaxe in his hand. As he approached, the golems calmed and stopped swinging their massive fists.

"You best go back to the bridge, User-that-is-not-a-user," Mason said, glancing at Gameknight over his shoulder. "You still hold their Iron Rose. As soon as they are released, they will attack you. It would be best to be out of arm's reach when that happens."

"You think?" he replied. "Stitcher, come with me."

The young girl smiled, then put away her pickaxe and ran toward him, leaping gracefully into the air and landing on his mount, her red hair flying through the air like a sheet of flame.

Jumping up onto his horse, Gameknight sat behind her and rode to the gravel path that led to the bridge. Looking over his shoulder, he saw Mason release the last block with his pick, and step back quickly as the iron monsters slowly climbed out of the water trap. Instead of moving to the recessions in the walls of the arena and going back asleep, they all slowly walked straight toward the User-that-is-not-a-user and their Iron Rose.

Turning his mount, he rode for the bridge, the sound of the others quickly catching up. As Gameknight rode up the ornate stone bridge, he glanced over his shoulder. The iron golems slowly trudged out of the arena, the King of the Golems, with his crown of vines glowing bright in the rosy sunlight, glaring straight at him. The look of venomous hatred made Gameknight cringe.

CHAPTER 18
ONCE MORE UNTO THE BREACH

They rode through the portal with Gameknight at the head of the column, the Iron Rose pulsating from within his inventory as if somehow alive. He could feel it pulling on him, drawing him to the north, likely toward the second key.

Gameknight shuddered. He was sure that the second key would likely be just as dangerous as the first, if not more.

Stitcher craned her head, trying to look across the curving bridge.

"Can you see the army?" she asked.

"I think we're still too high, but we'll see them soon enough."

Urging his mount into a gallop, he headed down the curving path, the Iron Rose guiding him. Looking over his shoulder, Gameknight could see the rest of their squad coming through the portal, Crafter emerging from the purple mist with Herder's skinny frame looming behind him on his mount.

As he turned back, Gameknight felt a strange chill settle across his skin. It was as if someone had sprinkled small shards of ice across his skin, the sharp chilly points digging ever so subtly into his flesh.

Something's wrong, he thought.

Stitcher could feel him tense up and turned her head to look up at him.

"What is it?"

"I don't know," Gameknight answered, "but something is not right."

Kicking his horse into a sprint, he sped down the curving arch as his head swiveled from left to right, looking for threats.

The chill slithered its way down his spine. The feeling was familiar. He'd felt it in that dream of his basement, and in the swirling mist of the Land of Dreams countless times.

"He's here . . . I can feel it."

"Who's here?" Stitcher asked.

"He's here . . . he's here."

And as they neared the bottom of the bridge, he could see what he already knew was waiting for them. A huge wave of monsters was crashing against their defenses. Gameknight could tell that this was the smallest fraction of Malacoda's army. The majority of attackers were the monsters of the Overworld, with a few Nether-creatures amidst the horde. This was not an attack, it was a test . . . a very deadly test.

Ranks of giant spiders clashed with the defenders on an outer wall composed of cobblestone. Flashes from exploding creepers punctuated the scene as the stone wall was pierced in multiple locations, allowing the flood of monsters to flow forth.

A series of walls had been built in Gameknight's absence. The outermost had now been breached as monsters flowed through the gaps, falling on the NPCs too slow or unaware to run for their lives. Fortunately, the majority of the defenders had retreated when the wall was shattered . . . just as they had planned.

Now a second wall stood before the monsters, this one made of dirt and sand. Archers stood atop this earthen barrier, raining arrows down upon the approaching army, but their pointed barbs did little to slow their approach.

At the rear of the monster horde, Gameknight could see a huge group of endermen, their black skin standing out against the bright sand. At the back of this group was a tall shadowy creature that was the color of dried blood; a dark, dark red just a few shades above black, his menacing eyes glowing bright crimson. It was Erebus, his nemesis . . . his nightmare.

"Is that him?" Stitcher asked.

Gameknight nodded as a shiver ran down his spine.

"Maybe it's time we showed him that he should be fearing us," she said as she pulled her bow from her inventory and notched an arrow.

"No, put your bow away," Gameknight said.

Stitcher turned and looked at him, confused.

"Put it away," he said as they reached the end of the bridge.

She put away her bow as she looked up at him, her unibrow was creased with confusion. Gameknight reached into his inventory and pulled out his enchanted bow, the iridescent light from the sparkling weapon lighting up both their faces.

"Your sister gave this to me, but I think you could put it to better use."

He handed her the iridescent bow as waves of purple magic ran up and down its length. She looked down at the bow, then fitted an arrow into its string. Pulling the arrow back, she loosed it into the air. The flaming arrow streaked up into the blue sky, soaring off the bridge and landing in the river below. Turning back, she looked up at Gameknight and gave him a smile that lit up his very soul.

"She'll be glad to know that you have it," Gameknight said.

"You be sure to tell her when we rescue her," Stitcher replied. "We *are* going to rescue her . . . right?"

"Assuming we survive today . . . yes, we will go get your sister."

She gave him another huge smile then turned and scowled at the approaching army.

As the monster army approached the dirt wall a cloud of purple particles formed at their head. Suddenly, a wall of endermen appeared before the dirt barrier. Reaching out, the shadowy creatures grasped key blocks of dirt and sand, then teleported away, leaving behind a hole in the barricade. Returning, they continued to disassemble the barrier, teleporting back and forth. The defenders held their fire as the endermen slowly disassembled their battlement, not wanting to enrage them, allowing them to join the fighting. So they chose the only option open to them . . . retreat.

Sprinting back to the last wall, the defenders quickly positioned themselves as planned. The last wall was made of cobblestone on the left and right sides, but was composed of only sand in the middle. Tall towers dotted the last wall, their peaks bristling with archers. Swordsmen stood behind the walls with swords drawn as the cavalry stood ready for the last charge. Out in front of this sandy wall, the normal desert sand was replaced with blocks of dirt. From his position, Gameknight could see saplings planted here and there throughout the field of dirt, likely a little surprise from the light-crafters.

Having finally reached the bottom of the bridge,

Gameknight moved to a small mound of sand to watch the battle, Mason and Crafter at his side. They could see the monsters approaching the sandy mounds, with charged creepers at the front of the pack. The sparkling blue field about the green mottled beasts would cause the explosion to do twice the normal damage. Their sandy barrier would easily fall.

"Ready," Gameknight shouted.

All eyes shifted from the wall to the User-that-is-not-a-user.

"Let slip the dogs of war," he muttered to himself, then sat tall in the saddle.

"NOW!"

NPCs flipped levers that activated redstone circuits, triggering the pistons that sat under the tall mounds of sand. And in an instant, the sandy wall fell away into a hole in the ground revealing a line of TNT cannons. The long rectangular cobblestone structures, with the flowing water going down the center, suddenly came to life. Redstone torches were set to blocks of TNT and quickly the clear skies were alive with thunder.

At the same instant, Grassbrin and Treebrin asserted their light-crafting powers, causing huge oaks to sprout forth, obscuring the vision of the attacking horde, while long blades of grass slowly slithered across the battlefield, tangling feet and slowing the charge.

And then the cannons roared their welcome. Blocks of TNT exploded, flinging a blinking cube into the air. The ignited block of TNT fell amidst the monster horde that was trapped in the long grass and exploded, shaking the ground. A huge gash was torn into the ground as the explosion took with it dozens of monsters.

"FIRE . . . FIRE!" Gameknight yelled.

More cannons were lit and the air was suddenly filled with blinking red and black cubes. As they flew into the air, the cavalry readied for a charge.

"Once more unto the breach," Mason yelled. "CHARGE!"

The horsemen and horsewomen charged forward to take out the closest of the monsters. Swords rang out as they bounced off armored skeletons and clashed with zombie-pigmen blades. The fighting was terrible. Gameknight could see people that he knew disappear in a cloud of items as their HP was extinguished, only to be replaced by another warrior. There was no retreat for the NPCs, so they fought for their lives . . . and their family's lives . . . and for Minecraft.

They were turning the tide . . . the monsters were starting to pull back. But then a stray arrow fired from some defender hit one of the endermen. The dark monster started to shake as its eyes burned bright white. Then the other endermen started to shake as well as they all became enraged.

And in an instant, the battle turned again as the endermen joined the fray. The shadowy creatures teleported from place to place, attacking NPCs relentlessly, creating chaos wherever they appeared.

To make matters worse, the sound of thunder from the TNT cannons started to change. Instead of the booming hollow sound, it started to give off a metallic grinding sound, like metal surfaces scraping against each other. Turning his head, Gameknight's heart sank.

Iron golems.

They'd come through the portal and were now moving toward the NPCs. But surprisingly, the metal giants didn't seem to notice any of the defenders; they headed straight for Gameknight999.

The King of the Golems howled out a metallic

scream of rage that caused everyone to freeze mid-battle.

"I can't do this," Gameknight muttered. "There's no way to win."

"Don't worry," Stitcher said from in front of him, her bow singing as she fired on the monsters from his horse. "We can figure this out, just go and . . ."

He didn't hear her, all he could hear was his own fears screaming at him from within his soul . . . *you're just a kid . . . run . . . hide.*

And so that is what he did . . . run.

Digging his heels into his mount, Gameknight charged straight toward the attacking horde of monsters, streaking past zombies, creepers and spiders. As he sprinted, he saw Erebus staring at him in surprise; he just rode past as fast as he could, looking straight ahead.

Stitcher cheered as she looked back behind them. The iron golems were following their prize, the Iron Rose, and fell on the attacking monsters. The mighty creatures flung their arms up, throwing monsters high up into the air. When they landed on the ground, the monsters perished in a flurry of red flashes, leaving behind zombie flesh, spider thread, and gunpowder. The golems fell on the monsters in their way with a fury, the ancient feud between golems and monsters reignited and burning bright.

Moving from monster to monster, the metal giants stomped on those that were foolish enough to attack while flinging their arms into clusters of creatures, throwing bodies high into the air. In minutes, the attacking army was in full retreat, the few that survived seeking to get as far from this place as they could.

When Gameknight was far enough away, he turned and watched the melee. He could see Erebus across the battlefield, the dark creature's eyes burning bright red with hatred and malice. And then, in a cloud of purple mist, Erebus disappeared.

"Gameknight . . . we won," Stitcher said as she looked up into his eyes.

"What . . . what?"

"We won, look."

Gameknight turned his head away from where Erebus had been standing and looked back at the battlefield. He could see that all the monsters had fled to the south, the few stragglers being picked off by the cavalry. But now that the monsters were gone, the iron golems continued to pursue the User-that-is-not-a-user.

"Listen," he said to Stitcher, "I'm going to lead the golems away, then catch up with the army."

"What are you talking about?"

"The golems, they won't stop until they get the Iron Rose back. I'm going to lead them away to the south, maybe catch some of the monsters. Tell Mason to head north, that's where the next key is located. I'll catch up after I lead them away. Now go."

He gave her a shove, pushing her off the horse, then galloped away.

Landing on the ground in a crouch, she rolled once then sprang to her feet. She watched as Gameknight999 galloped away, then turned and started walking back to their army. The ground shook as the iron giants headed off to the south after Gameknight999, all except for the King of the Golems. The majestic leader stepped up to her and stopped, its crown of vines standing out dark against its forehead. Stitcher readied herself for his attack, but instead of swinging his mighty arms, he slowly raised one hand. Held within his massive fist was a single rose, its red color in bright contrast to his shining metal skin.

Carefully, she took the flower as she watched the golems continue their trek, following Gameknight's trail.

She put the flower to her nose and inhaled its perfumed scent, then looked up as the sound of approaching hooves reached her ears. A squad of cavalry was approaching with Mason and Crafter out front. Reaching up, she grabbed Crafter's hand and swung up into the saddle, then looked at the backs of the iron golems.

"Be safe, User-that-is-not-a-user, and come back soon," she said. "We cannot do this without you."

Looking down at her enchanted bow, she smiled and thought about her sister, then stared up at the craggy mountains that loomed in the distance.

"I'll find you somehow, sister," Stitcher said aloud to no one. She looked back in the direction Gameknight had ridden and sighed. "We'll find you . . . I promise."

CHAPTER 19

EREBUS

Erebus materialized near the foot of the craggy mountain. As the mist of purple teleportation particles cleared, he looked up at the stony peak. The narrow rocky spire stretched up high into the air, the neighboring peaks reaching up just as high in the background. They looked to Erebus like the clawed fingers on some kind of hand that had pierced up through the ground, the fingers bent and distorted as if in terrible pain.

They made him smile.

Looking about the landscape, he could see the large tunnel opening at the foot of one of the peaks. Sick, leafless trees dotted the area, their bald limbs stretching out in hopeless despair. At first, these contorted trees made him uneasy, but now he was starting to appreciate their anguished beauty. Off to the right, the King of the Endermen could see some trees with their leaves still attached. But as he watched, he saw the leaves on one start to wither and die on the brown braches, the leafy canopy slowly turning from a lush green to a sickly grey, then crumbling to ash. It made him smile.

As he walked toward the tunnel opening, Erebus saw one of the shadow-crafters approaching from the direction of the now dead tree. It was the one that never seemed to speak . . . just watched; the one with the bright glowing eyes. Zombiebrine had never told them this crafter's name, but seemed to silently defer to him as if he were the one really in charge . . . curious.

Erebus nodded to the shadow-crafter as he approached the tunnel opening. He noticed for the first time that this crafter lacked the typical bulbous nose and unibrow that he'd come to expect from the NPCs and shadow-crafters of Minecraft. In fact, this creature looked more like a user than an NPC. Glancing above his head, Erebus saw no letters floating above his dark hair, nor the server thread of a user. He was definitely part of this server, like Erebus and every monster and NPC, but he was something different . . . more than what appeared.

Interesting.

The shadow-crafter disappeared into the tunnel entrance. Erebus started to follow but stopped as the tunnel grew bright. Something aflame was approaching. Stopping in his tracks, Erebus waited as a stream of blazes emerged from the entrance followed by a group of wither-skeletons, their dark ashen bones lit with an orange-ish hue from the internal glow of the blazes. Following the dark skeletons was Malacoda himself. The King of the Nether floated high up into the air as soon as he cleared the tunnel entrance. A look of nervous unease seemed to leave his wrinkled brow as soon as he was high enough off the ground to be out of reach.

Following Malacoda came Zombiebrine and a few other shadow-crafters. Erebus could see the one with the glowing eyes standing back in the shadows of the tunnel, close enough to hear, but not close enough to be seen . . . except of course by the keen eyes of the King of the Endermen.

Off to the right of the entrance, Erebus noticed the iron cage was now sitting atop a pedestal of stone, his red-haired prize still trapped within. He gave her an evil toothy smile then turned and faced Malacoda.

"Where are your forces, enderman?" Malacoda asked.

"Most are destroyed. Some are approaching, but very few."

Erebus lowered his head as if showing respect, as he knew that Malacoda would be dangerous when he heard this news. Gathering his teleportation powers, he readied himself to leave in case the ghast struck out at him, but he found that he could not draw the purple particles to him; he could not teleport.

Looking up, he saw an evil grin painted on the baby-like face of the King of the Nether, his beady little eyes burning a bright red. The tips of the ghast's tentacles were glowing a soft orange, as if working some kind of magic.

"Going somewhere, Erebus?"

"Ahhh . . . no . . . I was just . . ."

"Stop your excuses," Malacoda boomed. "I still have use for you, that is why you still live. Now tell me what happened to that poor excuse of an army you commanded."

"It was the User-that-is-not-a-user," Erebus said. An angry scowl formed on his dark face when he mentioned the name of his enemy. "He has a large force of NPCs and they were ready for us. Somehow, they knew that we were coming. Their fortifications were adequate but not enough to stop us."

"Yet you still come before me in defeat. Why is that enderman?"

"He had iron golems . . . ahh . . . sire."

"What's this?" Zomiebrine asked as he stepped forward. "He commanded iron golems? What did they look like? Were they all identical, or did one wear a leafy crown?"

"Yes, one did look like you say, with a crown of vines and leaves around his head," Erebus explained.

Zombiebrine turned and looked back at the tunnel opening. Erebus could see with his keen enderman eyes that the shadow-crafter hiding in the shadows looked disturbed, his eyes burning brighter than normal. It looked like Zombiebrine was in silent communication to this creature, somehow. When their soundless conversation was completed, Zombiebrine turned back and faced Malacoda.

"They have the first key!" the green shadow-crafter explained. "The iron golems were the guardians of the Iron Rose, and the King of the Golems would never leave his post unless the Rose had been taken."

Malacoda glared down at Erebus as if this were his fault, somehow.

"They must have had some help," the King of the Endermen interjected. "The way they used the land to defeat our forces, growing trees in an instant and using grass to ensnare my spiders in the last battle . . . they must be getting help from someone."

"Why didn't I know of this?" Zombiebrine snapped.

He turned to glance back at the tunnel opening, then turned back to Erebus and Malacoda.

"They are being helped by the light-crafters," Zombiebrine explained.

Bringing his hands to his mouth, the shadow-crafter blew through his green-tinted fingers creating a high-pitched whistling sound that grated on everyone's ears. A rustling sound came from the tunnel as all of the shadow-crafters emerged from the dark passage.

"We must pursue the army of light and destroy them," Zombiebrine said. "They have the first key and must be destroyed. It is time to attack."

"No!" Erebus snapped.

All eyes turned to the tall enderman.

"We will let the User-that-is-not-a-user lead us to the second key. We'll let him battle the monsters that protect that key. And after he's unlocked the Source for us, then we will attack."

"You speak as if you are in command," Malacoda said, a violent edge to his voice.

Erebus gathered his teleportation power, but found, again, that this ability was, at the moment, out of reach. He could see the ends of Malacoda's tentacles glowing ever so slightly; that must be how he was extinguishing his teleportation powers. Looking up into Malacoda's hateful eyes, Erebus bowed and extended his long arms out from his sides in a flourish.

"I only seek to serve the King of the Nether," he screeched.

Malacoda looked down on Erebus and smiled.

"It is good that you know your place, enderman." Malacoda said. "But I have decided that we will follow the User-that-is-not-a-user, and destroy him when *I* am ready." Turning he looked down at his wither-skeletons. "Gather the troops, we leave as soon as possible."

"What of the prisoner?" one of the blazes asked, his voice filled with a mechanical wheezing sound.

"Our little pet will be kept here. My wither-skeletons will guard her and keep my prize safe."

"You are most wise," Erebus said meekly. "But perhaps it would be best to move her into the tunnels and surround her with lava so that escape is impossible."

"I don't need lava to keep my little pet safe," Malacoda snapped. "I will leave some of my wither-skeletons here to stand watch. They will not fail me as you have."

Malacoda glanced at his wither-skeleton general and nodded. The dark monster raised the shimmering bow he'd taken from Hunter in salute, then motioned to his other dark comrades. The ashen skeletons moved around the iron cage in which their prisoner sat, at least twenty of them, each with weapon drawn.

Standing, the King of the Endermen moved to one of his own endermen and spoke in a low voice.

"You are to stay and watch over the prisoner, but stay out of sight. Report to me if anything happens." Erebus said. "Do you understand?"

The enderman nodded, then stepped backward and disappeared amidst the leafless trees, his dark lanky form looking as lifeless as the bald tree limbs.

But then suddenly, Erebus could feel a tingling sensation across his body. It was as if he were getting stronger, somehow. Looking about the area, he saw nothing unusual, nor did anyone notice the changes that were occurring within his dark red body. But as he glanced into the tunnel entrance, he could see the shadow-crafter with the bright eyes working on something, his stubby hands a blur of crafting activity. Then his hands stopped and at the same time, the tingling stopped. The shadow-crafter looked up from the dark entrance and stared at the King of the Endermen, his eyes burning bright. And then he gave Erebus an evil smile, like he knew something that the enderman did not . . .

CHAPTER 20

DAYDREAMING

Gameknight daydreamed as he rode back toward the north. He was giving his horse a bit of a rest after that harrowing sprint from the iron golems and was now just relaxing a bit.

He'd led the metal giants across a narrow pathway that spanned a crevasse. He'd built the dirt pathway so that he could trap the golems on the other side and it had worked. They had followed him across the narrow pathway like mice, gigantic terrifying metallic mice, following a piece of cheese, but when they were on the other side of the deep crevasse, he'd doubled back, sprinted across the narrow pathway, then destroyed the dirt bridge with TNT, trapping the monsters on the other side. The crevasse had stretched as far as he could see in both directions; the golems would be trapped there . . . but for how long? Gameknight could still remember the furious glare the King of the Golems had given him, his dark eyes burning with hatred. The monster's metallic grinding voice still echoed in his head.

'*You will not escape our wrath,*' the King of the Golems had said from the other side of the crevasse, '*and nothing will stop us. We will take back what is ours; whether you die as a result of it is up to you.*'

He shuddered as the memory filled him with dread. Gameknight knew that the King of the Golems would never stop until he had the Iron Rose back.

As his horse walked, the rocking motion of the animal seemed to lull him into a waking *sleep*. Memories of *people* from his *past* surfaced from his subconscious . . . *his* parents . . . *his sister* . . . Shawny . . . the *Minecraft team* he used to be a member of, *Team Apocalypse* . . . until he griefed them and was kicked off. But as *his mind floated through* these memories like a dream, *a familiar voice started to tickle* the back of his mind. It was a *voice that he hadn't heard for what* seemed a long *time, the voice of his friend*, probably his only friend.

It was Shawny.

He was calling out to Gameknight, texting his name over and over again. It was like how Gameknight had contacted Shawny back in Crafter's village. The thought of that village made him sigh. He yearned for those simpler days, when it was just Minecraft, not this bigger-than-life battle he was facing. But as he was about to answer his friend the voice disappeared, replaced with another familiar one . . . Hunter.

A vision surfaced within Gameknight's mind, an image of Hunter trapped within an iron cage. She was shaking the bars and calling out his name as a collection of wither-skeletons looked on, all of them laughing a bony clattering laugh. Behind her, he could see a series of thin rocky spires, the jagged peaks stretching high up into the air. A silvery mist was wrapped around the peaks, its flowing tendrils slowly moving down the tall summits. The mountains were thin and crooked, like bent stone spires that had been distorted by something vile and full of malice. At the foot of one of these peaks, he could see a large cave opening, the darkness within the entrance filling him with dread.

Suddenly, Hunter stopped her screams and stared straight at Gameknight. A silvery mist seemed to surround her as the wither-skeletons seemed to fade away.

"User-that-is-not-a-user, you must come for me," she said in a calm voice as the iron bars slowly disappeared.

She was now floating in the air with the silver mist swirling about her in great turbulent currents. Her vibrant red hair was pulled along the silvery currents, making it look as if she had been enveloped in some kind of magical fiery aura. Her deep brown eyes stared straight into Gameknight's and he knew that she could also see him.

"It's time for you to be the User-that-is-not-the-user that was prophesized. Your time has come, but first you must rescue me. I know their plans. The army is walking into a trap. Erebus and Malacoda are planning to . . ."

Suddenly he was jolted out of the Land of Dreams. His horse started to gallop as a creeper came out from behind a tree and started to ignite. The explosion tore a great crater into the ground, but the speed of the horse had saved him.

"I have to save her before it's too late."

Digging his heels into his mount, he sprinted forward to the North. As he bolted across the landscape, he could see the trailing edge of the army start to come into view.

It was the rear guard.

They saw the lone figure approaching and reformed into a defensive formation, swordsmen at the front, archers behind. But as Gameknight neared, the warriors recognized him and cheered.

"The User-that-is-not-a-user has returned!"

As Gameknight rode through their formation to the front of the column, word of his arrival percolated ahead of him. By the time he'd reached the head of the column, the army had stopped.

Mason was already dismounted when he reached him. Stitcher sat in front of Crafter on his horse, her shimmering bow in her hand, arrow notched of course. Gameknight rode straight up to Mason and dismounted, then motioned to Crafter and Stitcher to join them.

"I see that the User-that-is-not-a-user has survived his trials with the golems and returned to us," Mason said. "I hope you didn't destroy all of the golems."

"They are all still safe," Gameknight answered. "I delayed them, but if we are not quick enough, they may yet surprise us."

He felt a pair of arms wrap themselves around his chest. Looking down he saw Stitcher looking up at him smiling.

"I knew you'd make it back," she said. "I told Crafter that you would . . ."

"We don't have time now," Gameknight interrupted. "Malacoda and Erebus are planning something, Mason. You are leading the army into a trap of some kind."

"A trap!" the big NPC said, drawing his sword in fluid practiced motion.

The sound of other swords being drawn rang out as nearby warriors saw Mason's reaction and prepared for battle.

"The trap is not here . . . at least that's what I think," Gameknight explained.

"Then where is this trap?" Crafter asked from

behind Stitcher. He too had his sword out.

"I don't know, but Hunter told me . . ."

"Hunter . . . you talked with my sister?"

"Yes. I spoke with her in the Land of Dreams. She overheard the monster's plans. We have to go save her . . . now!"

"Hold on," Mason said as he put away his sword. "You talked to Hunter in a dream and you want me to take the army to save her?"

"That's right," the User-that-is-not-a-user replied.

"And where is she?"

Gameknight was suddenly quiet. He wasn't sure where she was. Looking about the landscape, he didn't see anything that suggested where his friend was being kept, but then his eyes fell on five sharp peaks that stuck up out of the foliage in the distance. They were five narrow rocky mountains that bent this way and that as they climbed up into the sky. Closing his eyes, he could remember the look of those mountains in his dream, the distorted and diseased look about them, with the lifeless bald trees sprinkled across their surface. Opening his eyes, Gameknight drew his enchanted diamond sword and pointed toward the peaks.

"She is there," he said, his voice ringing with confidence, "and I'm going to go get her."

"Look . . . Gameknight . . . I understand that you feel guilty about Hunter being captured back at Malacoda's fortress in the Nether," Mason said. "But going off on a wild adventure, based on nothing more than a dream, will not bring her back. There is nothing more you can do."

"NO! I'm going to save her . . . alone if necessary, but I *will* save her."

"Not alone!" Stitcher snapped, her enchanted bow in her hand.

"You too?" Mason asked, exasperated.

Stitcher nodded.

Reaching into his inventory, Gameknight brought out the Iron Rose. It filled the area with white light as the metallic petals glowed with a purity that seemed to push back the red-stained light from the diseased sun. He then handed the Rose to Mason.

"You take it and follow its pull toward the second key," Gameknight said. "I'll save Hunter and return."

"How will you find us if you do not have the Rose?" Mason asked.

"I will lead . . . lead him back," said a stammering voice.

Herder stepped forward and stood next to Gameknight, standing tall.

"I can sense my animals from . . . from far away. They will lead . . . will lead us back to you."

Gameknight looked down at the lanky youth, reached out and patted him on the shoulder. He could hear the snickers and remarks leveled toward Herder. He slouched a bit and looked at the ground as the faceless bullies tortured him with their whispered insults. All he wanted to do was help his friend, and Gameknight respected that. Looking from Herder to Stitcher, the User-that-is-not-a-user squared his shoulders and stared back at Mason.

"We are three and we will save Hunter."

"Not three but four," Crafter said as he stepped forward and put an arm on Herder's shoulder. The skinny boy looked at Crafter and smiled, then looked back up at Gameknight, adulation for his hero in his eyes.

Holding up his hand with four fingers extended, Gameknight smiled at Mason.

"Apparently we are four," the User-that-is-not-a-user said.

"The Magnificent Four," Mason teased, then smiled.

But none of us are bald, Gameknight thought as his mind drifted back to an old movie. "We will return shortly with our friend and then we can take on Malacoda and Erebus."

Mason nodded and motioned to one of the nearby soldiers for horses. Fresh mounts were brought forward, one for each. As they mounted, Mason moved up next to Gameknight and spoke in a low voice, his words meant only for his ears.

"Be sure you keep in mind what the goal is here . . . to save Minecraft."

"Of course."

"Getting killed trying to save only one person serves no purpose."

"I won't leave anyone behind," Gameknight snapped. "Our devotion to our friends is what sets us apart from the monsters."

And the bullies, he thought.

"We will return, I promise."

"I'm going to hold you to that," Mason said, then gave him a huge, contagious smile that the big NPC was known for.

Gameknight smiled back, then pulled on the reins and headed for the craggy mountains in the distance, his three friends at his side.

CHAPTER 21

THE CRAGY MOUNTAINS

They rode toward the craggy mountains in silence, each rider urging as much speed as was possible from their mount without driving them to complete exhaustion. As they neared the tall peaks, Gameknight realized that the base of these mountains were massive, at least a hundred blocks across.

How can I tell which of the five has Hunter imprisoned at its base, and where around the perimeter will she be?

The task seemed almost impossible.

"Which mountain do we head for first?" Crafter asked.

Gameknight shrugged.

"I don't know. I've only seen her prison from up close. From far away everything looks the same."

"You know," Crafter added, "my great-aunt Baker once told me 'when you've lost your way, sometimes you just need to close your eyes and listen . . . to Minecraft and to yourself.'"

"Of course, close your eyes," Gameknight said as he led his horse to the base of a large oak tree, one of the tall mountainous peaks looming nearby

Dismounting, he quickly laid down on the grass.

"What are you doing?" Stitcher asked.

"I'm going to find Hunter," Gameknight replied. "All of you should dismount, I'm not sure how long this is going to take."

Adjusting his sword and armor, trying to get comfortable, he slowly closed his eyes. But the last thing he saw was Herder running off into the woods mumbling something. Sitting up quickly, he looked up at Crafter then back to the boy.

"Herder, where are you going?" Gameknight asked.

"More friends . . . need more friends," he answered, then turned and disappeared between the leaf-covered branches of the thick trees.

"Is he coming back?" Gameknight asked.

"Of course," Stitcher replied.

"How do you know that?"

"Because he would never abandon you," Stitcher explained. "You're like a father to him. He respects you and looks up to you, and wants nothing but your approval . . . don't you see it? Everything he does, he does to please you. You are his family now, just like Hunter is mine. Herder and I are much alike; we never give up on family."

These thoughts spun around in his mind . . . *like his father . . . but I'm just a kid. I can't think of him as my son . . . that's just wrong . . . OK, maybe a little brother, like my sister, only a boy.* Sighing, feeling the weight of more responsibility sitting heavily on his soul, he closed his eyes and tried to go to sleep. Of course, with Herder leaving, and Stitcher and Crafter staring down at him, and the scary mountain looming overhead . . . it was hard to rest. But he closed his eyes and reached out with his mind toward that Land of Dreams . . . *and suddenly, he was there.*

The silvery mist swirled about him. Drawing his sword he moved carefully through the fog. This was Erebus's land just as much as it was his, and he had to be careful. Reaching out with his mind, he felt for Hunter, her tenacious courage, her will to live . . . and then there she was.

Gameknight stood at the edge of a strange forest, with trees that lacked any foliage, their branches bare. It gave the trees a tortured, diseased look that made Gameknight not want to touch their smooth lifeless bark. Peering around one of the trunks, he could see Hunter inside an iron cage that was mounted on top of a pillar of stone. A dozen wither-skeletons stood guard around her, maybe more, each with a vile look of hatred on their bony faces. The massive tunnel opening stood dark and menacing next to her prison, a jagged outcropping jutting out from the mountainside some distance above. Off to the left, Gameknight could see a waterfall spilling out of an opening in the side of the mountain, the water falling at least twenty blocks before it hit the ground, filling a large pool.

Looking around him, he could see more of the leafless, sickly-looking trees around the area. That was how he would find her.

"Wake up . . . wake up . . . wake up."

Gameknight opened his eyes and smiled.

"You found her?" Stitcher asked.

Gameknight smiled and nodded his head.

The young girl wrapped her arms around the User-that-is-not-a-user's chest and squeezed, crushing him a little and making him thankful that he had on a full set of diamond armor. Releasing the hug, she looked up into his eyes.

"Which way?"

Looking up at the five peaks, he could see that each had a few trees sprinkled on their faces, but the nearest of the mountains showed only leafless trunks.

"That one," Gameknight said.

"Then let's go," Stitcher replied.

"But what of Herder?" Crafter asked and he brought all the horses forward.

"He'll have to catch up," Gameknight answered as he leapt up onto his horse. "I'm sure he'll be able to find us. I have faith in him. Now come on, let's get going. We need to reach Hunter before nightfall."

The three friends headed toward the mountain. As they rode, Gameknight looked into the woods, hoping to see Herder running toward them, but he saw nothing. Occasionally he heard the howls of wolves . . . lots of them, but no Herder.

Sighing, he rode on, hoping this was the right thing to do.

CHAPTER 22

THE ATTACK OF THE WOLVES

ameknight led the way, guiding his horse along the edge of the forest, the mountain now looming over them like a mighty claw reaching up into the sky. They could see the base of the mountain but its perimeter was vast, and without Gameknight's vision in the Land of Dreams they would have needed to search the entire area for days.

Moving as quietly as possible, the User-that-is-not-a-user looked for the telltale sign that they were getting closer.

And then he saw it.

It was a lifeless, sickly looking tree with all of its branches bare. Moving up close to it, Gameknight could see small piles of ashes on the ground, as if the leaves had been somehow burned away. Crafter, looking down at the ashes, then put his hand reverently on the tree and felt its knobby trunk. As he caressed the bark, Gameknight could see a tear trickle down his young cheek, his old wise eyes filled with anger.

"What kind of creature could do this to an innocent tree?" Crafter growled.

"You mean this isn't natural?" Gameknight asked.

"No," the young boy snapped. "This was done intentionally, out of malice and hatred." He looked away from the tree and glared at Gameknight999.

"We have to find this creature and destroy him before he can do any more harm to Minecraft."

"How about we save Minecraft first," Gameknight replied, "then we can find your tree killer."

"He didn't kill the trees," Crafter spat. "He wounded them. He tore away their ability to grow and left them to suffer a painful useless life. Nothing will grow on this spot, even if we cut this tree down. This creature has wounded Minecraft itself and must be caught."

"Like the User-that-is-not-a-user said," Stitcher interrupted, "let's save Minecraft first, and to do that we need to find my sister."

Gameknight dismounted and tied his reins to the bare tree branch. He then motioned the others to do the same.

"We go on foot from here," he whispered. "Stealth is more important right now than speed, and the sound of the horses may give us away."

The other two nodded and dismounted, tying the horses to the bare tree branch. Drawing his sword, Gameknight moved cautiously forward, making sure to avoid any of the fallen branches or dry leaves on the ground. As he walked, he thought of the Land of Dreams and what it looked like around Hunter's cage. He could remember the lifeless trees all around, but he also remembered something else . . . a waterfall high up on the mountainside.

Gameknight stopped for a moment and closed his eyes and listened.

"What's wrong?" Crafter asked, his eyes darting about looking for threats.

Gameknight raised his hand to silence his friend and tilted his blocky head slightly to the side. Reaching out with all his senses, he listened to the grinding, strained music of Minecraft. He could hear the clucks of some chickens nearby . . . then the moos of a cow . . . then the howling of some wolves . . . then . . .

He found it, the sound of falling water.

Opening his eyes, he pointed off to the left. "It's that way," he whispered.

Gameknight crouched and moved slowly ahead. Stitcher and Crafter both noticed the letters floating above Gameknight's head dim significantly when he crouched and followed directly behind them, their weapons held at the ready. As they wended their way through the forest, the sound of the waterfall became louder, but so did the clattering sound of sticks being rattled together.

Skeletons . . .

Gameknight turned and looked at Crafter, nodding at the sound.

"You hear them?" he whispered.

"Yes, I do."

"Sounds like a lot of them," the User-that-is-not-a-user said.

"We need a plan," Crafter suggested.

"Let's get closer first and have a peek, then we'll make a plan."

Crafter nodded and continued forward. The three companions stepped cautiously through the woods, moving from tree to tree to keep from being seen. The iridescent glow from Gameknight's sword and Stitcher's bow cast a subtle blue glow around them. He wondered if the glow would give them away. Sheathing his sword, he motioned for Stitcher to also put away her enchanted bow. With the magical weapons hidden in their inventory, the trio blended into the trees, the rosy light from the sun filtering between what remained of the leafy canopy and casting confusing patches of light on their bodies.

As they neared the clattering sounds of the skeletons, Gameknight noticed that more of the trees had that sickly, bare appearance—small piles of gray ashes everywhere. Crafter touched the bark of each tree reverently as he passed, muttering something under his breath as the angry scowl on his face grew more intense.

Pausing for a moment, Gameknight999 put his back against a leafless tree and listened, Stitcher and Crafter doing the same. They could hear the skeletons clearly now, their guttural, clattering speech hard to understand. It sounded as if they were over the next hill. Crouching again, Gameknight moved cautiously up the incline, motioning his companions to stay where they were. Hiding behind a large, leafless oak, he glanced around the trunk. Beyond the hilltop, he could see the large opening in the side of the mountain, the rocky outcropping high above. In the distance, he could see the tall waterfall, its watery column falling along a shear face until it splashed down into a large pool. This was the place.

Moving to the next tree, he was able to get a better view of the area. A clearing stretched out in front of the dark tunnel entrance, with a group of wither-skeletons milling about. Off to the side of the entrance, Gameknight could see Hunter trapped in an iron cage, the enclosure standing atop three blocks of cobblestone, but then Gameknight's heart sank. He could see the wither-skeletons clearly now. There must have been at least twenty wither-skeletons down there, each of them armed with an iron sword and one with an enchanted bow.

How can we fight twenty of these monsters with only three of us?

He needed to get her cage open and a bow in her hands. That would give them four attackers to fight the skeletons, and knowing Hunter, she probably counted as two warriors. And then he remembered a saying that was on the wall in Mr. Planck's classroom, one of Sun Tzu's quotes from *The Art of War:* "In the midst of chaos, there is also opportunity." That's what they required, chaos . . . a diversion. They needed something to pull the skeletons away so that someone could release Hunter and get a bow in her hands.

Walking quietly back down to the hill, he moved to Crafter's side, then motioned for Stitcher to come near.

"I saw Hunter . . . she's there."

Stitcher's face brightened with excitement and hope.

"But there are at least twenty wither-skeletons guarding her."

The glow in her eyes faded a bit.

"What we need is a diversion," Gameknight continued, "to draw the skeletons off so that we can open the cage she's trapped in. But the problem is that we'll have to . . ."

Suddenly, the forest erupted with the sound of wolves, the howling animals sounding angry . . . and hungry. Gameknight could tell that they were still far away, but getting closer and moving fast.

"Wolves?" Stitcher asked. "What do we do?"

An angry pack of wolves was a terrible thing to fight. They attacked from all sides, their gnashing jaws tearing at their enemy with merciless efficiency. And right now, it sounded as if the pack were heading directly for them.

"Quickly, behind me," Gameknight said as he drew his diamond sword. "Get back to back."

Stitcher and Crafter moved behind the User-that-is-not-a-user and drew their weapons, getting ready for battle.

And then they heard it, the sound of feet running through the forest, twigs breaking, dried leaves crackling. Like an approaching storm, the sounds of running paws grew more intense as they neared. The howls became louder but were now accompanied by the sound of angry growls . . . these animals were mad, really mad.

Small cubes of sweat formed on Gameknight's brow as he gripped his sword and turned to face the oncoming threat. He could remember trying to fight a pack of wolves once, back when Minecraft had just been a game. It had not ended well. And now he had to face off against a pack again. Turning, he glanced at Crafter and Stitcher and smiled, hoping to raise their spirits a little. They both had terrified looks on their faces, both knowing the likely outcome when fighting off against an entire pack of wolves.

And then the wolves were on them.

Huge, furry white creatures were running straight at them. Gameknight could tell they were enraged; their eyes glowed bright red. He could see in the distance that the pack must have been at least thirty strong if not more; they had no chance of surviving an attack like that. Each had a colored collar around their necks, but Gameknight couldn't make any sense of that; fear and panic was ruling his mind. Gripping his sword firmly, he readied for the first set of snapping jaws.

And then the massive pack of wolves streaked by.

They were like little white bullets as they shot past them, weaving around the leafless trees. The wolves ran up the hill and then plunged down the other side like an unstoppable white wave

As the last of the wolves passed, Stitcher cried out. "It's Herder!"

Gameknight snapped his head around and saw Herder sprinting after the last of the wolves.

"Hi Gameknight," the lanky boy said as he ran

past, a huge grin on his face.

"What?" Gameknight was confused.

"Come on, they're attacking the skeletons!" Crafter yelled as he streaked up the hill.

Still in shock, Gameknight sprinted up the hill and then stopped at the crest. What he saw stunned him. The clearing was bedlam; white wolves were battling with the ashen wither-skeletons. Sharp teeth were snapping at dark bones as iron swords tore into furry flesh.

"Come on, we need to help," Stitcher yelled.

"No, free your sister," Gameknight yelled as he tossed her a diamond pickaxe.

Stitcher caught the tool in the air and ran toward the iron cage as Gameknight followed her. Running into the battle, Gameknight swung his enchanted sword with every ounce of strength he had. Ducking under an iron blade, he slashed at a skeleton, then spun and blocked an attack with his diamond sword. Rolling under another iron blade, Gameknight took out the legs from an attacker as he turned and skewered another dark bony monster.

Looking over his shoulder, he could see Crafter locked in a deadly dance with one of the monsters, the tall skeleton driving his friend back, but then there were two wolves attacking the dark beast, snapping legs and crunching arms. The monster disappeared in a cloud of bones and XP balls. The skeletons were slowly losing the battle, but there were still many alive, and it only takes one to kill you.

Dashing forward, he grabbed the sword arm of another skeleton just as it was about to bring it down on a wounded wolf. Tearing the sword from its bony grip, he shoved the monster to the ground as two other wolves fell on it, consuming its HP in seconds.

Clank!

An arrow bounced off his diamond armor, pushing him back three steps. He'd been shot at by a bow . . . an enchanted bow.

Turning, he looked across the battlefield to see a wither-skeleton holding an enchanted bow, an arrow notched and aimed right at him. The skeleton released the arrow. Gameknight could see the arrow spiral through the air as it headed straight toward him. It was like watching a movie in slow motion. The approaching arrow transfixed him; his mind seemingly paralyzed by the experience. And then suddenly he was knocked off his feet, Herder on top of him. He could hear the arrow zip past his ear as he tumbled to the ground. Looking up at the skeleton, Gameknight could see the dark monster notch another arrow and aim it at Gameknight's head. He'd lost his helmet and sword in the tumble; he was defenseless. The wither-skeleton gave him a bony smile as he drew the arrow back, the pointed barb aimed right at the User-that-is-not-a-user's head. But just before he could fire, an arrow pierced the monster's side, causing his aim to waver. The skeleton released the arrow just as another shaft hit the monster in the chest.

"You don't shoot arrows at my friends!" Hunter screamed. "And I definitely did not give you permission to use my bow!"

The skeleton's arrow sank into the ground next to Gameknight as Hunter's projectiles struck the monster in the chest again . . . and again . . . and again. The dark monster disappeared in a puff of bones and coal.

"Now that's what I'm talkin' about!" Hunter exclaimed.

She then dashed to Gameknight as the wolves destroyed the last of the wither-skeletons.

"You OK?" Hunter asked as she reached out and

helped him up.

Gameknight nodded, then turned and looked for Herder. He found him on the ground with an arrow in his side. Extending a blocky hand, Gameknight reached down and help the youth up to his feet.

"Are you OK?" Gameknight asked.

Herder touched the arrow protruding from his side and winced, then gave him a huge grin.

"I told you . . . told you I needed more friends . . . friends," Herder stammered.

"Well, you certainly brought the right ones," Gameknight replied, slapping him on the back and making him wince again.

"It's a good thing you found a pack of wolves and not a herd of pigs," Crafter added as he approached, a huge grin on his young face.

This made Gameknight laugh for the first time in . . . who knows how long. The image of a herd of pigs coming to Hunter's rescue caused him to chuckle.

And then Stitcher came running forward and dove into her sister's arms. Hunter instantly dropped the bow and wrapped her arms around her younger sister and hugged her as tears streamed down her cheeks. They stood there, unmoving, as they held onto each other, each grateful for the other's safety.

"I was so terrified when I saw that monstrous ghast take you back in the Nether," Stitcher whispered into Hunter's ear. "I cried out to you, but I was too far away. When I finally made it out of the fortress . . . you were gone."

"You were there . . . where?"

"I was taken captive after they . . . after they destroyed our village," Stitcher explained, cries of joy punctuated with a moment of sadness. "Mom and Dad . . ."

"Yeah . . . I know . . . they're gone."

And now Stitcher and Hunter were both crying again, this time joy replaced with sadness as the realization that their parents were gone sank in and became real. Their family had been shattered by Malacoda's evil plans and now they only had each other. This realization made them hold on a little longer until finally Stitcher released her hug and looked up at her big sister.

"I made Gameknight999 promise that he'd come save you," Stitcher said as she wiped the tears from her eyes, then smiled at the User-that-is-not-a-user. "And here we are."

"Well, I have to say that I am glad that he kept his promise," Hunter replied, smiling at Gameknight. "But who is this new person? I don't think I know you."

As she reached out to shake Herder's hand, she saw the arrow sticking out of his side.

"Oh no, you're hurt," she said to Herder.

"It's . . . it's nothing," Herder answered. "I've had . . . I've had worse."

"You're such a liar, Herder," Stitcher snapped. "Are you telling me that you've had worse than being shot by a wither-skeleton?"

The lanky boy looked away guiltily, shuffling his feet.

"That's what I thought," Stitcher said. "But you did great, Herder. Without your wolves, I don't know how we would have saved my sister. Thank you."

She gave him a kiss on the cheek, then a big hug.

The skinny boy's face turned red as he looked away, embarrassed. Just then, Hunter grabbed the shaft of the arrow and yanked it out of his side. Herder yelled in pain and surprise. A chorus of growls suddenly sounded in the clearing as the twenty or so surviving wolves started to slowly approach Hunter.

Moving quickly, Herder stepped in front of the pack with his arms outstretched.

"These are Herder's friends," the boy said. "You must treat them like you would treat me."

The red eyes slowly faded to yellow as the animals calmed down and relaxed.

"We have to go, now!" Hunter said. "I know what Malacoda is planning and we have to hurry."

"What is it?" Crafter asked.

"I'll explain on the way. I hope you brought horses, for speed is our only ally now."

"They're over that way," Gameknight said, pointing toward them with his shimmering sword.

"Then let's get going," Hunter snapped.

The party sprinted through the woods, the herd of wolves running with them toward their mounts. But none of them saw the dark enderman watching the entire battle from the top of the rocky outcropping that looked down on the clearing. The shadowy monster watched the group run through the trees until they were out of sight, then a mist of purple particles enveloped the creature as he teleported to his King . . . Erebus.

CHAPTER 23

MALACODA'S PLAN

After the enderman delivered the news of Hunter's escape, Malacoda screamed in rage, his booming voice echoing across the plain. The cat-like screams and blood-curdling cries made all the monsters nearby bring their clawed hands to their ears to block out the terrible noise.

Erebus stood his ground and did not move, but had been careful to be out of arm's reach when the bad news was delivered. He'd seen the speed at which Malacoda could strike with those nine tentacles and he didn't want to be his next victim.

"What do you mean she's gone!" Malacoda bellowed.

"*He* took her." Erebus answered, his voice screeching with nervousness.

"*He* . . . you mean that . . ."

"Yes, the User-that-is-not-a-user took your prisoner from your wither-skeletons. Do you remember back in your Nether fortress, when I told you that this Gameknight999 can do the unexpected at the most inconvenient of times?"

Malacoda just grunted and looked away.

"Well, that's what he did here," Erebus said. "He stopped his pursuit of the second key to the Source to save this one NPC."

"But it makes no sense," Malacoda boomed as he floated up higher into the air, his eyes burning bright red. "Why would he divert his entire army just to save one NPC?"

"He didn't have his entire army," Erebus answered with a wry smile. "There were only four of them in the battle."

The enderman next to Erebus muttered something to his King.

"Ahh yes, and a pack of wolves," he added.

"Four warriors and some dogs defeated my wither-skeletons?" Malacoda asked, disbelief and rage painted across his mottled face. The tear-like scars under his eyes were beginning to glow bright with his rage.

"Oh . . . and did I fail to mention that Gameknight999 was the only user amongst the four, the others were NPC kids."

"WHAT!"

Erebus smiled.

Malacoda was beyond insane with rage. Floating down to a nearby blaze, he reached out with lightning speed and slammed his nine tentacles into the fiery body. The punches sounded like bolts of lightning, the doomed creature's HP being extinguished in seconds, leaving behind only a few glow rods to mark the flaming monster's existence.

"How could you let this happen?" Malacoda screamed down at Erebus.

The enderman stepped forward and spoke in a low voice, only meant for the King of the Nether's ears.

"If you recall . . . your greatness . . . I recommended moving the prisoner down into the tunnels to have her surrounded by lava." Erebus paused, then stepped back to make sure he was again out of arm's reach, then spoke so that others could hear. "The User-that-is-not-a-user mocks all the monsters of the Overworld and the Nether with this insult. But we will have our revenge on him soon enough."

"I want revenge, now! I want him destroyed, NOW!" boomed Malacoda. "We will move to attack these NPCs from the Overworld and destroy them at once."

"No," Erebus said quickly, taking another step back.

"What did you say?" Malacoda growled, his cat-like voice filled with anger.

"That would be a mistake . . . your supreme kingliness." Erebus stepped closer again, risking the ghast's wrath, but lowered his voice for only the King's ears. "We should let those foolish NPCs lead us to the second key, then let them battle whatever guards it. After they capture that key for us, then we will take our revenge." Erebus then moved back a step or two and raised his screechy voice so that all could hear. "We will steal the keys to the Source from these insignificant NPCs and then the Source will be ours for the taking . . . and the destroying."

Erebus teleported to the top of a small hill that placed him at the same level as Malacoda. Glancing across the army of monsters, he held his long black arms out wide.

"Brothers and sisters, victory is nearly in our grasp. These NPCs are too few to stand against us. We will be like an unstoppable storm, and crash down on them so violently that they will wish their creator, Notch, had never bothered to write them into Minecraft's code."

The monsters cheered.

Erebus turned his head and looked at Malacoda. The King of the Nether looked agitated, his anger growing. He knew that he still had to be careful . . . for now.

Smiling, the King of the Endermen continued. "The King of the Nether will lead all of us to the greatest battle that has ever been seen. . . the Last Battle for Minecraft. And after we are victorious here, we will go to the physical world where we will take over EVERYTHING!"

Another cheer came from the monsters.

"But we must be patient and wait until the time is right," he added as Malacoda's burning eyes glared down on him. "All hail Malacoda, King of the Nether!"

Erebus extended a long dark arm towards the floating ghast, then raised his dark fists up into the air. The monsters cheered again, their moans and wails echoing across the landscape. Looking down on the army, Erebus could see the cold dead eyes of the monsters looking up at Malacoda, their faces filled with violent expectation, but many were also looking up toward him. Glancing out of the corner of his eye, he looked at Malacoda. The ghast was smiling at this momentary adulation and sucked up every moment of it, his eyes sparkling with self-satisfaction.

The fool.

Soon, they would be his soldiers and he'd be free of this idiot ghast. *Malacoda, your days are numbered,* he thought as he raised a dark fist up high and cheered. As he thought about his plan to eliminate the fool, a wry knowing smile crept across the King of the Endermen's dark face.

CHAPTER 24
SHAWNY

They rode hard, heading to the north-west toward Mason and the army. Gameknight rode out front, setting the grueling pace with Herder at his side, a furry white protective ring always surrounding the party. Stitcher, having refused to leave Hunter's side, rode with her on one horse, the two of them talking continuously—recounting everything that had happened since their village had been attacked. And Crafter, with his bright blue eyes scanning the horizon for monsters, brought up the rear.

Sometime in the afternoon, they crossed over from the tall hilly forest biome to the unusual and dry savannah biome. The strange, flat-topped acacia trees dotted the flat landscape with their gray-green leaves, looking unhealthy in the reddish hue of

Minecraft's sun. Their disjointed, angular trunks and grayish bark looked almost alien-like compared to the tall majestic oaks and lush, green pines of the forest biome. Gameknight liked this flat terrain, though; he could see monsters coming from far away. They saw the occasional zombie or spider approach across the savannah, their bodies cutting through the tall yellow-tinted grass like sharks through ocean waves, but Hunter made quick work of them with her bow; the monsters never getting close enough to make anyone draw their sword.

Riding through the rest of the day and all through the night, they made good time. Near dawn, Gameknight saw the sun start to brighten the horizon over his shoulder off to the east. As with most users and NPCs, he was glad to see the sun rising, for the night belonged to the monsters, but they had seen few during their trek back toward Mason.

As the landscape started to brighten, Gameknight turned to Crafter and smiled.

"I've always like the sunrise," he said to his young friend who was now riding up front.

"I know, me too," Crafter replied as he smiled and turned his head toward the rising square sun. "My great-great uncle Taylor used to say 'sunrises are Notch's salute to those that survived the night. It is a rebirth, where all the sins of the night are washed away by the luminous yellow face of the sun.'"

But then his smile quickly faded to a scowl.

Gameknight could feel the tension in his friend and looked off to the east. The sun was its normal deep red on the horizon, but as it climbed into the sky, the face of the sun kept its stained discoloration. It cast a deep crimson tint across the landscape, shading everything with a dark rosy hue as if the entire day were sunrise.

"It's getting worse," Crafter said.

"Those vile shadow-crafters," Hunter said. "They are the ones doing this to Minecraft."

"But why?" Gameknight asked as he urged his horse to go a little faster.

"They never said," Hunter replied. "The green one, Zombiebrine, did most of the talking, but from what I could tell he wasn't the one in charge. There was another, with bright glowing eyes . . . that one was in charge, though he never spoke."

"I think we should assume that these shadow-crafters are helping the monsters of Minecraft," Stitcher said from in front of Hunter. "After all, we have the light-crafters on our side . . . it's reasonable to assume that they will have the shadow-crafters."

Gameknight nodded and urged his horse forward a little faster. Looking around the landscape, he saw few living creatures in this biome with the exception of horses; they seemed to spawn naturally in the savannah. He was always nervous of the unexpected monster popping up out of a hole or tunnel entrance to surprise them. But today he felt unusually at ease. Likely this was due to the ring of wolves that encircled them; the pack obediently following Herder's commands—protect. If a spider or creeper were to suddenly appear, the wolves would quickly take care of them, allowing Gameknight to relax a little as he swayed back and forth in the saddle.

As they rode, the rocking motion of the horse nudged him gently toward sleep, and his eyelids started to get heavy. He was tired from the battle to free his friend and from riding all night, but he knew that they couldn't stop; they had to get back to the army before they reached the second key. And so as he rode, he slowly drifted into that place between wakefulness and sleep . . . into the Land of Dreams.

A swirling silvery fog seemed to rise up out of the ground, making it appear as if his horse were walking on a cloud. The billowing mist slowly covered the tall grass and bushes, leaving only the tops of the flat acacia trees sticking up out of the vapor. Sitting on his tall horse, Gameknight's head rode just above the silvery veil, the rest of his body feeling cold and damp. To his left and right, he could see his companions on their horses, but they had a transparent look to them, like they weren't fully there.

He was alone in the Land of Dreams.

Looking around, he scanned the horizon for monsters, not wanting to get surprised here in this silvery landscape. There were no other creatures around . . . he was truly alone. But then Gameknight thought he heard something. Looking behind him, he saw nothing. He was sure he'd heard something.

"Gamekni . . ."

There it was again, but this time a little louder and off to the right. Pulling on the reins, he veered to the right, looking for the source. A landscape of tall grasses and strange trees stared back at him. He was alone.

"Gameknight . . ."

It was behind him. Spinning, he turned toward the sound, his diamond sword drawn.

Nothing.

Snapping the reins, he urged his horse back to a canter as he caught up with his friends. He must be going crazy, because this time he thought it sounded like . . .

"Gameknight999, are you out there?"

Shawny . . . it sounded like Shawny, his friend, his only friend in the physical world. He'd helped Gameknight save Crafter's server what seemed like a thousand years ago. But how could it be . . .

"Gameknight999, are you out there!"

Focusing all his Minecraft skill, he concentrated on his computer in his basement. Imagining his hands on the keyboard, he pushed his thoughts and his mind toward the keys. Carefully, slowly, he imagined his fingers pushing on the keys.

"S . . . H . . . A . . . W . . . N . . . Y"

"Gameknight, is that you? OMG . . . we've been looking for you. Everyone has been . . ."

It was Shawny. Hearing his voice was wonderful, if you could call it hearing. It was as if the sound was coming from the silvery mist, but also from within his mind. When he closed his eyes, Gameknight thought he could also see the letters in his head, like he was reading the text on his computer screen.

"Shawny, it is really you or am I just dreaming this?"

"Of course it's me. I'm so glad you aren't dead, you know, after that last battle and all. Where are you . . . what's happened?"

Gameknight looked around at the silvery mist that swirled about him and smiled. He'd found Shawny . . . HE'D FOUND SHAWNY! He was so happy . . . and relieved. Maybe he could help.

"You remember Crafter sacrificing himself in the battle with Erebus and the monsters of the Overworld?" Gameknight said.

"Sure."

"And you remember when I set off all that TNT and kinda got blown to bits?"

"Of course I remember that. All Users have heard of that by now."

"Well, obviously, we didn't die. We moved up to the next server plane and are still battling to save Minecraft."

"We?" Shawny asked. "What do you mean we? Is Crafter still alive?"

"Yes, Crafter is still alive, but he's a boy now . . . he respawned in the body of a young NPC."

"Minecraft can do strange things," Shawny said.

Gameknight nodded his head and grunted an affirmation.

"So what's going on now?" Shawny asked.

"Well, we battled Erebus and Malacoda on the last server, but couldn't stop them."

"Erebus is still alive?!" Shawny snapped.

"Yep, and his new ghast friend, Malacoda, is even more terrifying," Gameknight explained.

"You certainly have a way with people," Shawny said, laughing. "So where are you now?"

"We followed Erebus and Malacoda and their army of monsters to this server that holds the Source."

"You mean you're at the Source? What's it like? What does it look like? Can I see it? What's your IP?"

"Slow down, Shawny, this is complicated. First of all, we don't know where the Source is; we're looking for it now. Secondly, Erebus and Malacoda are also looking for it, and they have a lot more monsters than we have NPCs, so we're in pretty big trouble here. I could use an expert strategist like you." Gameknight paused to look at his surroundings. He could see his transparent friends trudging along on their mounts, Herder's wolves completely hidden within the silvery mist. Satisfied there were no monsters near, he continued. "Tell me, where are you and what of the other users?"

"Well, we are in Crafter's village. You can tell him that all his people are safe. And the other . . ."

"We?" Gameknight asked. "What do you mean by we?"

"All the users, they're here with me."

"What? I don't understand. All the users are there?"

"Of course," Shawny said with a laugh. "All of

the users heard of your sacrifice. Believe it or not, Gameknight999 is a hero." Shawny laughed again. "And besides, Crafter's server is the only one still online. We can no longer get to any other Minecraft server. So if someone wants to play Minecraft, they have to come here. And besides, we aren't really playing, we're preparing."

"For what?" Gameknight asked.

"The War," Shawny answered. "We've been seeing all the Minecraft servers disappear. It was the only explanation for what's been going on."

"You were able to get the other users to help?" Gameknight asked. "You know, with all my past griefing, I'm not the most popular Minecrafter out there."

"Are you kidding? After that stunt you did with the TNT and blowing up all those monsters like that . . . you're a hero. Everyone wants to help the great Gameknight999."

"What?"

"Yep, believe it or not, everyone WANTS to help you. So we're here at Crafter's village getting ready for the Last Battle. We're all hoping that we can be a part of it and help to save Minecraft."

"I can't guarantee that I can get all of you here to this server," Gameknight explained, "but if I can, I will. We will certainly need your help against the massive army of monsters we're facing."

"What do you need us to do?"

Gameknight thought about it and tried to imagine the Last Battle, but the pieces of this puzzle had not materialized within his head yet. He didn't know what the battlefield would look like, or how the armies would be positioned, or . . . There were too many unknowns, too many what-ifs. He knew they would have problems with all these monsters, but he couldn't think of the solution. But then something Crafter had said popped into his mind and made him smile as one of the pieces of the puzzle clicked into place.

"Here's what I need . . ."

And Gameknight laid out the first part of his plan for the Last Battle for Minecraft.

CHAPTER 25

JUST BE

Gameknight emerged from the Land of Dreams to the sound of laughter. Looking around, he found Stitcher looking at him with a gigantic smile on her face.

"Are you back amongst us again?" she asks.

"What?"

"You've been mumbling some strange things," Crafter explained as he moved his horse up next to Gameknight's.

"Mumbling?" he asked, confused.

"You were in the Land of Dreams, right?" Hunter asked.

Gameknight nodded.

"You traveled through the Land of Dreams while awake," she explained with an almost reverent tone to her voice. "Gameknight999, you are now a full-fledged dream-walker, as I am, as my grandmother, Healer, was, and as her grandfather, Wood-cutter was. It is a rare thing to be a dream-walker; few even know of the ability."

"It sounds like being a dream-walker runs in your family," Gameknight asked. "Is Stitcher a dream-walker?"

Hunter reached up and patted her young sister on the shoulder and shook her head. "No, it is very rare to have more than one in a family with the gift. This has been my burden to bear since I was young, and is now my duty to make sure that the Land of Dreams is safe. For if you are killed in the Land of Dreams, you die for real. It is the duty of the dream-walkers to look out for the accidental visitors to the Land and make sure they are safe . . . as I did when you first dreamed of Erebus in your family's home."

"What?" Gameknight asked.

"You remember . . . you dreamed that you were back in the physical world, and the monsters of the Overworld invaded your home," Hunter explained. "You battled with Erebus while I fought with his monsters on the floor above. It was a magnificent battle. My bowstring hummed almost constantly as I took care of zombies, spiders, and creepers. But when I ran out of arrows, I left the Land of Dreams and went back to the waking world where I woke you up by knocking you out of your bed. Do you remember?"

He nodded. It had happened that first night after they first met Hunter in her village. Reaching up, Gameknight rubbed his neck where Erebus had choked him, though the skin had now healed.

"So what do I do with this dream-walking ability?" Gameknight asked.

"You protect those that are in the Land of Dreams . . . it is your responsibility."

Gameknight nodded again, considering this new information. Just as he was about to speak, Herder's voice echoed across the savannah.

"The army . . . the army, they're here."

Looking up, Gameknight could see Herder ahead of them. He had wanted to ride up front to look for the army. Now waving his long skinny arms over his head, Herder was shouting at the top of his lungs, his wolves all howling with excitement. Riding back to the party, he galloped up to Gameknight's side.

"The army is just over the next . . . the next hill. It looks like they are resting . . . resting for the moment. We can . . . we can catch up with them."

Gameknight looked up and could see the sun nearing the horizon, the square blocky face seeming to get redder and redder. Wanting to be back within the safety of the army, he urged his horse into a gallop.

"Come on, let's get to the army before dark," Gameknight said to the rest of the party.

They reached the encampment just as the last edge of the sun's crimson face dipped below the horizon, lighting the savannah with a deep red that seemed to last only moments before darkness enveloped the landscape. They were greeted with cheers as they rode through the camp, the warriors all calling out Gameknight's name as if he were some kind of mythical hero.

"Gameknight999 is here! Beware monsters . . ."

"The User-that-is-not-a-user will lead us to victory . . ."

"Our leader has returned . . ."

The accolades still made Gameknight feel uncomfortable and fake. He wasn't the real leader here, Mason was. That big NPC was a natural leader, with the confidence and decisive sense of command that made the other warriors feel safe and secure. But Gameknight, he was just a cowardly kid, afraid of what *might* happen if he made the wrong decision or did the wrong thing. And now that they were back and he could see all the people that were expecting him to keep them safe, the overwhelming weight of responsibility . . .

"User-that-is-not-a-user!" boomed a voice.

Turning, Gameknight found Mason striding toward them. Stopping his horse, he dismounted, the rest of their party doing the same.

"I see you have returned with a guest," Mason said with a huge smile. "Welcome back, Hunter."

"No thanks to you, I understand," Hunter snapped.

"We had to focus on finding the last key to the Source," the big NPC replied. "But everyone is glad to see your return. Many people look up to you. Your skill with the bow has become legendary while you've been absent."

"Whatever," she snapped as she turned and stormed away, Stitcher right on her heels.

"You all should get something to eat before we head out," Mason explained.

"Head out to where?" Crafter asked.

"There is a stronghold ahead, deep underground," Mason explained. "This is where the Iron Rose has been leading us." Reaching into his inventory, Mason pulled out the metallic flower and held it out to Gameknight. Its brilliant glowing petals lit up the area as if they were standing in the middle of a blazing supernova. "You should be the one carrying this. Here, take it."

Gameknight reached out and took it from Mason's blocky hand. As soon as he wrapped his own fingers around the stem, he could feel it vibrating as if it were alive. Closing his eyes, Gameknight's mind was filled with a distant rumbling, like waves of thunder rolling across the landscape. As he put it into his inventory, he could feel the Iron Rose pulling him off to the North, toward the stronghold that lay hidden underground.

"I want to see where this key is leading us," Gameknight said as he reached for the reins of his horse.

"I will show you the way," Mason said.

"No, I need to go on my own," Gameknight answered as he climbed up onto his horse.

Mason gave him a look of concern then nodded and stepped aside.

"Get some food, Crafter," Gameknight said. "You too, Herder."

"I can . . . I can go with you."

"No, I'm going alone. Besides, you need to see to your herd and make sure all the animals are OK. You have a responsibility and people are counting on you."

Herder nodded and knelt to whisper something into one of his wolf's ears. Then he ran toward the herd, his furry companions in tow.

"I'll be back shortly," Gameknight said to Mason. "Make sure the army is ready to move. We can't stay out in the open for very long. We make an attractive target for Erebus and Malacoda."

Gameknight moved next to the NPC and lowered his voice.

"Hunter heard their plans. They plan on having us lead them to the second key, then they will strike after we have defeated whatever guards it."

"Then we had better get the key quickly and get to the Source," Mason replied, then moved off, issuing commands to his troops.

Gameknight headed out of the camp in the direction the Iron Rose was guiding him. He could feel its strong pull from within his inventory; there was no question which way to go. As he left the camp, Hunter suddenly joined him atop her horse. In addition, a cluster of wolves ran with him, the furry animals clearly sent by Herder.

Gameknight looked down at the wolves and smiled, then turned and glared at Hunter.

"I wanted to go alone . . . to think."

"Too bad. I'm not gonna let you do anything stupid

after you just rescued me, so you might as well get used to my company. Now where are we going?"

"I wanted to see what awaits us at the second key. Mason said that it was in a stronghold, so I wanted to see it."

"This sounds like a *great* idea," she said sarcastically, rolling her eyes.

Gameknight just grunted in reply and rode in the direction the Iron Rose commanded, a group of wolves encircling them. After about ten minutes, they came upon a hole in the ground lit with torches. A squad of archers stood nearby; guards likely placed there by Mason. They all stood tall when they saw Gameknight approach, bringing fist to chest in salute, but eyed the wolves warily. Hunter looked at their snappy salutes, then glanced at Gameknight and laughed.

"Shut up," the User-that-is-not-a-user whispered to his friend, then smiled. "I've come to look at the stronghold," Gameknight said to the archers as he dismounted, Hunter doing the same. "Has anyone been inside?"

"No, User-that-is-not-a-user," one of the archers answered. "Mason marked out the entrance with torches, then had us stand guard until his return."

One of the archers looked down at the wolves and laughed, then said something to a comrade causing the other to laugh as well and look toward Gameknight.

"What is it?" Gameknight asked the soldier. "What are you saying?"

"I was just saying that Pig-boy apparently sent a few of his best friends with you," the archer explained. "That was *so* thoughtful of him." The warriors giggled and made funny faces in an attempt to impersonate Herder.

Gameknight growled under his breath and tried to ignore the NPCs, but the comment still made him mad. Glaring down at the soldier, he dismounted and approached the entrance. It was just an innocuous hole in the ground, with steps leading downward. Putting his foot on the first stair, he paused and looked around. All eyes were focused on him, expecting some kind of heroic act or statement from the User-that-is-not-a-user. Gameknight could guess what was down there in the stronghold and the thought of that made him shudder.

Moving down the steps, he could hear Hunter directly behind him, her confident steps easing his trepidation a bit. They went down maybe thirty steps until they reached the stronghold. It was built, as most of them are, out of cobblestone, with the rare mossy cobblestone blocks here and there. It had the kind of smell you'd expect from something that was ancient and rare, like some kind of treasure that had been sealed away for centuries. It was an odor that spoke of ancient structures with equally ancient secrets held within its shadowy corridors, but that still wasn't right. Gameknight inhaled deeply and tried to understand the aroma, but it was deceptive and always changing. Shaking his head to drive away the distraction, he continued forward.

The stronghold was like a maze of passageways, with some tunnels leading to dead ends while others turned around back on themselves, making a confusing loop. Finally finding a long passage, he moved past a chest that held a few bobbles, nothing very important. Continuing on, they came upon something that looked like jail cells. These were enclosures with iron bars across the front and a door rigged to a button on the outside of the cell. Gameknight never really understood why there were always jails within strongholds, but it was something that he'd come to learn was always true.

Knowing there would be nothing inside, he moved past the jail cells and continued down the main hallway. Torches dotted the walls occasionally, splashing out a circle of light that pushed back the darkness, but they did not illuminate everything. There were still rooms that lay cloaked in darkness. These Gameknight avoided, just putting a single block of dirt in the doorway to keep anything within from getting out.

Continuing on through the twisting passages, they soon came upon a library. It was awesome to see; racks and racks of books lining each wall, with tall bookcases through the center of the room as well. Stepping up to the shelves, Gameknight found that he could read the letters on the spine, something that he could never do when he'd just been playing the game for fun. In the past, the books had been written in the strange, cryptic letters of the Standard Galactic Alphabet, the strange characters illegible. But now, these letters seemed to hold some meaning to him.

Reaching out, he pulled two books off the shelf and blew off the dust from their covers. One was titled *The Great Zombie Invasion,* while the other just said *The Joining.* He wanted to sit and read through these, to really learn the history of Minecraft, but he knew that they didn't have time.

"Hunter, you ever read any books like these?" Gameknight asked.

She shook her head, completely uninterested in the vast collection of knowledge that sat on these ancient shelves. Putting the books back, they walked through the library and came out the other side into a long, dusty hallway. Down each side were iron doors, each leading to a different part of the stronghold. As they moved from room to room, Gameknight could feel the Iron Rose vibrating stronger and stronger. It was as if it could feel that the second key was near and it couldn't wait to be united with its kin. They were close. Drawing his sword, Gameknight moved cautiously forward.

Eventually, the duo reached the deepest part of the stronghold. It felt like something ancient and evil had been locked up there for a long long time, and this was where the Iron Rose had led them. Casting a furtive glance at Hunter, he moved through a long corridor, past another ornate chest, to the last room. As soon as he stepped through the doorway, Gameknight's heart sank. He knew instantly what stood before them.

A pool of lava three blocks wide by three blocks long sat on the floor. The heat from the lava brought back terrible memories of that last great battle with Malacoda and his Nether-creatures. A set of stairs led up to a second level of blocks that were positioned in a ring, two blocks above the lava. These blocks, set in groups of three, had a strange look to them. The center of each block had a dark empty opening, as if waiting for something to be placed inside. With a greenish color to them and a smattering of pale yellow lines across their face, they almost seemed like something from an alien world.

"What is it?" Hunter asked.

Gameknight sighed.

Suddenly, there was a sort of scraping, sliding sound, as if something had just slithered out from some cramped space. A silverfish scurried out from the back of the chamber, the small creature taking a quick-paced meandering path. The prickly spines on its back reflected the light from the lava, making it look as if it were aflame with some kind of magical power. Its long, segmented tail dragged behind the creature as it scurried about the room, making a sliding sound that echoed in the stone room, making him look for more.

Drawing his sword, Gameknight came down the steps. He knew he had to kill it quickly, for wounded silverfish would call to their brethren, drawing more of the little creatures from their hidden blocks. This could create a swarm of the little monsters, all of them attacking any NPC or user within sight. And surviving a swarm of silverfish was not easy. Gripping the hilt firmly, he readied his charge, but before he could attack, Hunter fired two quick shots into the little creature, making it flash red, then flip over and disappear.

"Nice shot," Gameknight said. Shooting a silverfish was extremely difficult.

Hunter only smiled as she notched another arrow.

Glancing at the steps that led to the landing above the pool of lava, Gameknight could see where the disgusting little creature had come from: a monster spawner. A small, single block sized metal cage sat at the top of the steps, sparks and ash flying from it as something unrecognizable rotated within its center. Stepping up to it with his pickaxe in his hand, Gameknight shattered the spawner with six blows, the final blow coming just before the next silverfish was to emerge.

Looking down from the steps, he saw a chest in the corner of the portal chamber. Moving down to it, he opened the ancient wooden box. A cloud of dust formed as the rusty hinges creaked and groaned, making him cough and turn his face away. But when he looked back, Gameknight found twelve strange greenish orbs. They looked like a dozen alien eyes staring up at him.

Reaching into the dusty box, he collected them all, then turned and went back up the stairs and stood before the strange blocks.

"What are they?" Hunter asked, but Gameknight did not answer, he only sighed.

He knew exactly what these were, and the realization of what was next filled him with dread.

Carefully, he placed one of the greenish orbs in each block's dark opening, the alien eyes changing to a square shape as they settled. When the last orb was placed, a portal activated, filling the room with a strange green light. Looking down, Gameknight could see that this portal did not have the characteristic purplish look like the doorways that led to the Nether. No, this one was different. It was filled with stars, as if it were looking into the deep dark recesses of outer space.

"Gameknight . . . what is it?"

Stepping down from the portal, he turned and glanced at Hunter. A look of terrified defeat was painted across his face.

I can't do this, he thought.

He could feel the monster on the other side of that portal and was terrified. It would pursue him, wanting to attack him, torture him, destroy him. It would be after him like all those bullies were at school, the strong attacking the weak.

Why can't I be courageous?

"You OK?" Hunter asked.

Gameknight sighed and shrugged. He could feel the Iron Rose pulling him toward the portal, and the thought of this filled him with terror.

"I can't do this Hunter, I'm not the leader they want me to be . . . I never was."

"What do you mean, you led us to victory at Malacoda's fortress."

"That was different. This portal leads to something terrible and it wants to get me."

"Oh, Gameknight, you don't know . . ."

"I do know. I can feel it, and I'm scared. I'm always scared . . . the monsters here in Minecraft make me think of the bullies from school . . . I can't seem to let go of my fear."

Hunter sighed and looked sympathetically at him.

"All of these fears you hold on to so tightly, they mask your true self," Hunter explained. "They keep you from being you . . . the real Gameknight999 . . . the real User-that-is-not-a-user. And until you learn to deal with these fears, you can never be the person you were destined to be." She put her enchanted bow back into her inventory and placed a blocky hand on his shoulder. "You don't know how great you can be, how much you can help others, how good of a friend you can be, because all of this fear and uncertainty is making you doubt yourself."

Gameknight sighed and lowered his gaze to the ground, then nodded.

"I wanted to stand up for the other kids being bullied . . . for Herder, but I was always afraid. I think of how terrible it would feel if the bullies stopped teasing Herder and decided to tease me instead, and so even though I knew it was wrong, I didn't say anything. I would just hide from my fears."

"Just like you're doing here, in Minecraft. You're hiding the true leader that you could be because of this fear. I see it when the warriors tease Herder. I see you look away, pretend not to notice, because you are afraid."

Gameknight nodded, shame filling his soul. He felt bad for all those other kids he could have stood with instead of hiding in the shadows . . . and Herder. His fear had kept him from being a good friend and he knew he had do better.

"What if I'm not strong enough to carry this battle

through to the end?" Gameknight asked. "What if I can't hold on tight enough when everything is on the brink of destruction? What if at the critical moment, when all eyes are on me and everyone is counting on me to be strong, I chicken out and run away? What if . . ."

Hunter gave out an exasperated growl.

"Gameknight!" she shouted, her voice echoing off the walls.

He turned and looked at his friend. She stood tall before him, her brilliant red hair glowing bright in the light from the portal. He could see the confidence and pride in her posture, her sense that she knew her purpose here in Minecraft and wasn't afraid of anything.

Why can't I be strong like her?

He knew that Hunter could see the indecision and fear that was still on his blocky face.

"Gameknight, you know what to do, you always know what to do, you just don't realize it ahead of time." She moved a step closer and lowered her voice. "Just do what you do best."

"And what's that?" Gameknight asked. "What can I do that's better than anyone else?"

"You can be Gameknight999! You can *be* the best Gameknight999 there is . . . just *be* the puzzle solver . . . just *be* the warrior . . . just *be* the leader . . . just *be* the griefer. Just be all those things and do them the best that you can. Fight with everything you have and grief Malacoda's and Erebus's army like you've never griefed before." She paused to let the words sink in, then lowered her voice. "Just be."

Stepping up to the portal, she peered down into the emptiness of the star-filled void. "Now, are you going to tell me what that thing is?"

He sighed and tried to sound confident and strong,

but he did a poor job of it. "It's a portal to The End."

"The End? What's that?"

"It's something just for users . . . and endermen . . . and a dragon, the most terrifying dragon you could ever imagine. That has to be where the second key to the Source is at, so that's where we have to go."

She stood silent for a moment, considering this information, then said with a shrug, "Well, I've never killed a dragon before . . . sounds like fun."

Hunter laughed and slapped Gameknight on the back. She then turned and faced the portal, her enchanted bow now in her hand, arrow notched. As they stood there, they could hear Mason and a group of warriors coming through the stronghold, all of them ready to follow the User-that-is-not-a-user into battle once again. But Gameknight did not think about the army, or The End, or the dragon, he just thought about Hunter's advice, letting her words roll around in his mind.

Just be . . . maybe I CAN do that!

CHAPTER 26

HERDER'S DECISION

Mason stormed into the portal room with his sword drawn, Crafter at his side, both ready for battle. Gameknight raised a hand to tell them there was no danger as he sheathed his own weapon.

"We're OK," Gameknight said as a handful of warriors moved into the room behind them, their iron armor clanking together as they squeezed through the doorway. Amidst the sea of iron-clad bodies, he could see Herder peeking into the room from the back of the crowd, a look of complete terror on his face, Stitcher standing at his side.

"There's no danger," Gameknight said softly. "Everyone can put away their weapons."

Crafter stepped forward and stood at Gameknight's side. He looked up at the steps that led to the ender portal, the walls bathed in a greenish-yellow light.

"Where's the rest of the army?" Gameknight asked Mason.

"They're waiting up above at the entrance," the big NPC said, pointing up to the ceiling with a blocky finger. "They await your command, User-that-is-not-a-user. We came down here to make sure you were not in any danger."

Gameknight nodded to Mason and smiled.

In any danger . . . what a joke . . . you have no idea what terrible danger awaits us!

"What is this place?" Crafter asked.

"I think we should talk outside of the portal room," Woodbrin said. Everyone was shocked to see him. The light-crafter had entered the room so silently, snaking his way effortlessly between armored warriors; it was almost as if he'd just materialized there. "Come, to the meeting hall."

"Meeting hall?" Crafter asked.

Gameknight shrugged.

The light-crafter turned and pushed his way through the collection of soldiers that filled the doorway, leaving everyone to watch his back. He walked confidently through the passages leading them to the meeting hall, knowing exactly which tunnel to take, his stride confident and strong as if he owned the place.

They moved out of the portal chamber and followed

Woodbrin through the maze of passages back to a large central chamber. They had to move quickly to keep up with the quick-paced steps of the light-crafter. After finally going up a flight of decaying and cracked stone stairs, they reached their destination; the meeting hall. Gameknight instantly recognized the tall pillar at the center of the room. It was adorned with torches placed at the top on all sides. They cast a warm yellow illumination throughout the chamber that pushed back the shadows; light always made Gameknight feel safer in Minecraft.

Mason and his dozen warriors entered the room with Crafter and Stitcher following behind. They spread out through the chamber, glancing down the connecting passages with weapons drawn, looking for threats. Off to the side, he could see Herder standing in a shadowy corner, a look of fear still painted on his face.

"What is this place?" Crafter asked. "I don't remember any NPCs ever building a place such as this?"

"Strongholds were not built by NPCs," Woodbrin explained. "These are from an ancient age. These were built before the time of wars and conflicts. Even before *The Joining*." He said the words with reverence as if everyone knew what he meant. Some of the NPCs looked at each other, confused, not knowing what the strange light-crafter was talking about. "Back in the ancient days strongholds were a place of learning. NPCs came together to talk about ideas, to debate, to learn."

"Then why are there jail cells?" Hunter asked. "Doesn't sound like a very friendly place to come to for a little light reading."

One of the warriors laughed, but was silenced by Woodbrin's angry glare.

"Yes, it is true there are jail cells here," Woodbrin continued. "It started around the time of the *Great Shame*. People started doing things for themselves. They stopped helping others. Crimes were committed." His short, choppy sentences echoed through the chamber like machine gun fire. "The criminals were brought to strongholds for judgment. If necessary, they were imprisoned."

"Sounds like a nice place," Hunter added.

More laughter. More glares from Woodbrin.

"After the *Great Shame* and *The Joining*," the light-crafter continued, "the cells and the strongholds were no longer needed. As you can see, they fell into disrepair."

Gameknight looked around the room and saw cobwebs in the corners, blocks missing here and there. This was a structure that was slowly falling apart and being reclaimed by the landscape of Minecraft, and that's when he realized what the smell was down here. It was not the aroma of ancient mysteries or hidden secrets. It was the odor of decay; the scent of a forgotten age. Looking up, he found Woodbrin staring at the User-that-is-not-a-user.

"You've been in a stronghold before, yes?"

"Yes," Gameknight answered.

"Then you know what lies beyond the portal chamber."

Gameknight nodded his head and sighed.

"What is it?" Crafter asked. "What lies on the other side of that strange portal?"

"A dragon!" Hunter shouted.

The warriors gasped.

"Gameknight, is this true?" Crafter asked.

"Yes, it's called the Ender Dragon, and it only exists in a land called The End. It must be the guardian of the second key to the Source, and I can guess what the second key is." He paused and waited to make sure everyone was listening, all eyes on him, then continued. "The second key is the Ender Dragon's egg. Is that right, Woodbrin?"

The light-crafter nodded his head.

"We have to go to The End, and battle the Ender Dragon so that we can take its egg," Gameknight explained. "That is the next challenge we must face in order to get to the Source."

"We don't understand," Crafter said, his voice cutting through the tense silence. "What is *The End*? We've never heard of this."

"It is a place only for users, not NPCs." Gameknight explained. "I have been there many times in my adventures as a user, and sometimes I survived the Ender Dragon, and other times I did not." A gasp came from the warriors. "The Ender Dragon is the fiercest creature in Minecraft, and The End is the strangest place you will ever see. This challenge will test our courage and our resolve. But we must overcome this obstacle if we are to get to the Source and protect it from Malacoda and his monstrous horde."

Looking about the room, Gameknight999 gazed into the eyes of every individual. He saw looks of excitement, hope, uncertainty, confusion . . . every emotion possible was held within those eyes, but most of all, he saw uncertainty and fear.

"I will tell you, honestly, I'm terrified to go back to The End. When I'd gone there as a user, I had every enchantment I could get, had the best weapons that I could steal from others, and had every software hack I could download, and still sometimes I failed to defeat that flying monster." The memories of those countless battles played back through his mind in an instant. Those massive claws reaching out at him, the ferocious toothy mouth snapping at him . . . and those eyes . . .

those terrible purple eyes . . . he realized that he was shaking and stopped to take a deep calming breath. "But we have no choice. We must go to The End and face the Ender Dragon, for good or ill. I don't know how we'll defeat this beast, but we have to try or all will be lost."

"But you make it sound impossible," someone shouted from the crowd.

"No, I didn't say it was impossible, I said that I'd tried many times and sometimes I was successful."

"How many times were you successful?" a high-pitched voice asked.

Gameknight paused and looked to see who asked the question. He found Stitcher looking up at him, her bow in her hand. There was a look of grim determination in her eyes, as if she were daring the Ender Dragon to come stand before her so that she could smite it.

"Once," he answered sheepishly. "I was only able to defeat it once without cheating."

This caused a burst of questions, some directed at Gameknight999, some directed at others. The meeting hall just about exploded in confusion as Gameknight's confession chiseled away at the strength and courage of the warriors.

"Why should we do this thing?" someone shouted.

"You were only able to defeat it once!" someone accused.

"How can we do this and survive?" another asked.

"We are doomed . . ."

Gameknight let them rant and rave, throwing their accusations at him, fear and uncertainty filling their minds and eroding their courage. He let them argue and debate, then raised his hands for silence.

"I know why I was unsuccessful all those times, and I know why I was finally able to defeat the Dragon."

"Why, User-that-is-not-a-user?" Crafter asked. "Tell us what you learned after all those battles with the Ender Dragon."

"I was defeated because I went to The End alone, by myself."

"Why would you go alone if you knew the danger?" Stitcher asked.

"Because I was Gameknight999, the King of the Griefers. And because of who I was, I had no friends and nobody to stand at my side and help me. I tried to defeat the Ender Dragon on my own because that's all I had."

"But what about the time you succeeded?" she asked.

"I finally made a friend, Shawny, and he was willing to stand at my side even thought I mistreated him from time to time." He paused as the memory of his friend filled his mind, making him smile. "I was able to . . . I mean, *we* were able to defeat the Ender Dragon because we worked together and helped each other. That is the secret to fighting the Ender Dragon." He paused and drew his sword, then pointed it across the sea of faces. "Look around you . . . are you alone? No! Is there someone that will help you and back you up? Yes!" He waited as the NPCs all looked at those standing next to them, then brought their gazes back up to him. "I tell you this. I'm scared, but we have to go to The End to battle the Ender Dragon. We *must* defeat that creature to save Minecraft."

And my family.

"I don't know how this battle will end." He glanced down at Hunter, then looked back at the sea of faces. "But all I can promise is that I will be the best User-that-is-not-a-user that I can be and will use my last ounce of strength defending Minecraft. I am as afraid as all of you are, but we must . . . "

"No . . . no . . . no," Herder stammered.

Gameknight turned and faced the young boy. He could see Herder was shaking almost uncontrollably, his dark hair flying about ever so slightly.

"Herder, what's wrong?"

"Dangerous . . . dangerous," Herder said, voice crackling with fear. "I need . . . need more. The dark portal to The End is dangerous . . . is dangerous. More . . . more . . . "

Gameknight moved to his side and spoke to him in a low voice. "What are you talking about? Look at me."

Reaching out, he pulled the young face toward him. Herder looked terrified, on the verge of panic, his eyes filled with a look of crazed insanity.

"I can feel it," Herder whispered, his voice cracking with fear. "The dragon . . . I can . . . I can feel . . . feel it . . . and what lies beyond." He put his hands to the sides of his head, then moved them to cover his eyes pressing them tight.

"It's OK, Herder, we're safe here," he said, but Herder was lost in panic and could not hear. Putting away his sword, Gameknight reached up and grabbed his head with both hands and turned it so that he could look straight into Herder's dual color eyes.

"The dragon . . . more . . . more . . ." Herder stammered. He sounded as if he were out of his mind.

"Herder, calm down. It will be all right, we'll fight this battle together. You can stay to the rear where it will be safe." Gameknight said.

Herder's eyes slowly focused on Gameknight and the shaking slowly started to subside.

"Yeah, Pig-boy, you won't be much help there anyway," someone said within the chamber.

Gameknight turned his head a glared at the

warriors, daring the individual to speak again, but said nothing. Turning back to Herder, he spoke in a soft voice, only meant for the young boy's ears.

"Herder, you can stay by my side the whole time. I'll keep you safe. Together, we can survive the battle. Do you understand?"

"The dark portal . . . dark portal . . . dangerous," Herder said, his voice sounding as if he were some kind of oracle predicting the future. "The dragon is bad . . . bad. Need more . . . more. Herder can help. Herder knows what to . . . what to do."

And before Gameknight could say anything, Herder turned and sprinted out of the meeting hall and headed for the surface.

"Herder . . . wait!"

Following in pursuit, Gameknight ran after the boy, pushing through the armor-clad bodies in the meeting hall, but his own bulky armor was making it difficult to keep up with the nimble youth.

"Where's the User-that-is-not-a-user going?" someone asked.

"Is he running away?"

"What's happening?"

"Where's he going?"

Gameknight ran through the corridors. He could feel the NPCs' confusion and fear. He felt that he had to catch Herder and figure out what was wrong. Something inside told him that this was important; somehow Herder was critical to their success.

As he ran, he could hear footsteps behind him, lots of them. Glancing over his shoulder, he saw Mason and Stitcher following him, their weapons in their hands, a look of uncertainty and confusion on their faces. Behind them were the rest of the NPCs, their lumbering forms pressed together in the narrow passages.

"Stay there, don't follow," he shouted, but nobody could hear him over the thunderous echoes of the many footsteps and clanking of armor that filled the passage.

Ignoring his pursuers, he ran on in hopes of catching Herder, who seemed to know exactly which way to go to escape the stronghold, moving from one corridor to the next without hesitation. Eventually, he led Gameknight back to the long flight of stairs that extended up to the surface. Herder was already halfway up the steps when Gameknight just reached the bottom.

"HERDER . . . STOP!" he yelled.

"Bad . . . dangerous . . . more . . ."

He couldn't hear his last words because of the echoing footsteps.

"Can't go . . . get . . ."

"Herder, wait!"

Bolting up the stairs, he chased the young NPC until he reached the entrance to the stronghold. Pausing to catch his breath, he stood and watched as Herder sprinted into the savannah, heading straight toward the hilly forest in the distance, his pack of furry white companions running at his side.

CHAPTER 27

THE ENDER PORTAL

That's right, Pig-boy, run away," one of the archers yelled at Herder's back.

Gameknight cringed.

"SHUT UP!" Stitcher shouted as she exited the

stairway.

She shot toward the warrior that had made the comment and stood directly in front of him, glaring up into his eyes. Sheepishly, he looked down at the ground and took a few steps back. Hunter came out of the entrance and moved next to her sister. Putting a hand on her shoulder, she pulled Stitcher back and moved to Gameknight's side.

Looking down at the young girl, he tried to give her a smile.

"Where is the boy going? Why is he running away?" Mason asked as he stepped out of the tunnel.

"I don't know," Gameknight answered, "I don't understand what's happening." He then sighed as he looked out across the savannah and watched as Herder's small form finally disappeared from sight.

"Maybe his courage finally gave out on him, and running away was the only avenue left to him," Crafter suggested as he stood next to his friend, panting to catch his breath.

"No . . . he isn't running away," Gameknight said meekly.

"What do you mean?" Mason asked. "Look . . . he's run away, literally. The boy is gone, he abandoned us."

A flurry of angry comments burst from the soldiers, accusations of cowardice . . . of failure . . . of being a traitor. Every vile and abusive name that could be lobbed at Herder's back was cast forth.

"You're wrong," Gameknight said. "I don't know what he's doing, but he's not abandoning us, it's not in his nature. Whatever he's doing, it's to help us."

Nobody listened to the User-that-is-not-a-user, his voice and conviction about Herder sounded weak.

Maybe he had run away, he thought. *NO, he wouldn't do that. He wouldn't leave his friends. But*

*then why? I should stand up for him, shout out his
innocence, but they hate him so much . . . are so angry.
How can I change all their minds, I'm just one kid, one
voice . . . but I need to at least try. He's my friend, and
he would do that for me.*

"He is doing the best he can . . . being the best
Herder that he can be, and we need to trust him,"
Gameknight said. "He didn't fail us when we rescued
Hunter . . . he won't fail us now . . . I think . . . I hope."
Nobody listened to him, his voice too uncertain, too
timid.

"He's abandoned us in our hour of need," Mason
bellowed. "We will need every able body to deal with
that dragon down there, and even that skinny boy
could have helped . . . I'm done with him."

"Do not be so quick to give up on him, Mason,"
Crafter said. "Herder may yet still surprise us. Have
faith and understand that what he's going through
seems important to him at this moment. We must be
true friends to him and help him wherever we can."

Gameknight looked at Crafter and nodded, but
still felt uncertain.

Herder . . . what are you doing?

Turning, Gameknight took a couple steps back
towards the entrance to the stronghold, then stopped
in front of Mason. "Tell us, User-that-is-not-a-user,
what is the plan?" Mason asked.

He glanced around at the collection of NPCs that
were standing near the stronghold entrance. There
were strong warriors here in all shapes and sizes,
men, women, the young, and the old. Looking across
the sea of faces, he could see butchers, bakers, and
torch-makers. There were farmers standing next to
wood cutters, diggers next to boat makers, farmers
next to hunters. Every aspect of Minecraft life was here
standing before him, with all of their dark eyes focused

directly on him, looking at him as if he were going to tell them some great plan that would save them all and make everything better.

I don't know if I can do this. I'm so tired, I can barely think. The Ender Dragon . . . it's so big, so vicious, so . . .

And then he thought of something that he realized he had known all along: the only way he could get past all this fear was to confront it. And that would start with the dragon.

Then the sound of murmuring voices around him trickled to his ears. Glancing about the army, Gameknight saw hopeful eyes all staring up at him, their very survival dependent on the User-that-is-not-a-user. But within each pair of eyes, he saw a look of determination in their square pupils, and a sense of togetherness on their faces. This was not just an army, it was a community, no, a family, with each person willing help another with anything they needed.

He wasn't alone, and that was the key.

He could confront his fear as long as he wasn't alone and had others with him, their faith in him adding to his courage and strength. Closing his eyes, Gameknight999 imagined himself confronting the Ender Dragon and staring straight into its evil purple eyes, his friends at his side.

I refuse to give up, Dragon, he thought to himself. *I refuse to give up to my fears!*

And surprisingly, he felt himself stand up a little straighter. It wasn't that Gameknight was now unafraid, no . . . he was still terrified of the dragon's razor sharp claws. Only a fool wouldn't be afraid of that beast. Rather, he didn't feel like he was trapped by his fear. His willingness to stand up to it, with his friends at his side, had somehow allowed Gameknight to be himself.

And then Hunter's words flooded through his mind like a tidal wave, pushing aside the remaining uncertainty and fear.

Just be . . . just be.

Gameknight took a calming breath and thought of all the times he had visited The End. He could see in his mind the dragon's claws reaching out toward him. It smashed everything he had ever built there, destroying every kind of block except for bedrock, obsidian, and end-stone. And the endermen, the many, many endermen that populated The End, they'd be relentless in their attacks. How could it be done?

And then one of the pieces of the puzzle clicked into place . . . the Ender Crystals . . . yes, maybe that would work. Why didn't he think of that before?

But how would we get down . . . of course, that's guaranteed to work. What about . . . yes, that might work, but only if . . . and then the pieces of the puzzle started swirling through his mind, clicking into place . . . .

As the plan solidified within his mind, he realized it was very risky. They'd be walking on a razor's edge, and the slightest nudge would push them off into the abyss. If any one piece failed, then the whole strategy would crumble . . . and many would die. But there was something missing . . . something to do with Herder. He didn't have all the answers yet, and he wasn't sure if he could really do this.

But he was Gameknight999 . . . he had to try.

Opening his eyes, he glanced about at the community that surrounded him, their eyes filled with hope. "Ok, here's what we're going to do. First of all, we're going to need buckets of water . . . lots of them. Second, we'll need . . ."

And Gameknight999 explained his plan for the battle with the Ender Dragon.

As the NPCs were collecting everything they needed from the Overworld, Gameknight waited impatiently by the stronghold entrance. As he stood there, he relived all those other battles in The End. On those countless trips to face the Ender Dragon, Gameknight had felt no fear because he knew he would feel no pain; it had just been a game.

This time it was different.

Closing his eyes, Gameknight imagined the gigantic, razor sharp claws of the dragon ripping through the iron armor of these warriors like it was paper and shuddered. Many would die and there was nothing he could do about it.

Just be.

He pushed aside the thoughts of what might happen and just focused on *the now*, as his father had taught him.

Many of the NPCs had now returned with their supplies and waited around the entrance, most of them afraid to venture into the alien stronghold. They milled nervously about, all of them tense and scared, talking amongst themselves. He could hear many of them questioning why "pig-boy" had run away.

I hate that name, Gameknight thought to himself. *I should have said something about that . . . should have stopped them from calling him that name long ago, somehow.*

Funny how brave and strong he felt after the one being picked on had already been abused and was gone. It reminded him too much of school, of the bullies abusing him, calling him names, taking his hat . . . all the little things that on the surface looked insignificant, like a game, but when put all together made the victim feel afraid to be seen, like they're less important, less of a person than the bullies.

I hate bullies . . . hate how they make me feel about myself.

More of the NPCs arrived with the remaining supplies. They were almost ready.

I should have said something . . . should have told others about the teasing and bullying so that Herder didn't have to feel so alone.

More voices started to fill the Overworld, more comments about the cowardly "pig-boy" running home to his mommy. Anger surged within Gameknight. He heard Hunter say something to the warriors, but his rage made her words unintelligible.

I hate bullies! Listen to them, they still pick on him even after he's gone.

"HIS NAME IS HERDER," Gameknight shouted to everyone . . . to no one . . . to himself. His voice echoed across the landscape as if David himself were challenging Goliath of Gath. He turned and faced the NPCs, anger erupting within him like an unstoppable volcano. "His name is Herder and he is MY FRIEND! He doesn't deserve your ridicule. He's done nothing to any of you to warrant your abuse other than help anyone that ever needed help. And I tell you all now, right now, that I accept Herder for who he is, even if he's different from me. Herder is my friend!"

Gameknight's voice sounded like thunder. All mumbles and comments instantly ceased as the eyes of the army were instantly drawn to the User-that-is-not-a-user. He turned and glared at those near him, then placed a block of cobblestone on the ground and stood on it so that he could glare at everyone. A look of rage and fury was painted on his blocky face.

"He is my friend and his name is Herder, not Pig-boy. He doesn't deserve your abuse or mistreatment.

He's always the first to volunteer to fight, the first to offer to help another." He glanced at Hunter, then continued. "In fact, if it hadn't been for Herder, we would probably have failed in saving Hunter. We were successful because of him. You all patted us on the back when we returned, but none of you said a thing to Herder. You should be ashamed."

I should be ashamed.

"The monsters of Minecraft have bullied all of you at one time or another. You all know how it feels, yet you can still do it to one of your own." Gameknight paused as he moved his gaze across the crowd. "The whole reason why we're fighting to save Minecraft is because we've had enough of the bullies like Erebus and Malacoda. Just because they are stronger than us, it doesn't give them the right to do whatever they want. We won't stand by and let the monsters do this to us anymore . . . and yet you all stand by while Herder is bullied . . . I did too." Gameknight lowered his eyes to the ground for a moment as a look of shame covered his face. "We all let Herder suffer alone and that was wrong. We all had the chance to stand with him and let him know that he had friends, but we did nothing." Sighing, he looked up again, a renewed look of determination on his face. "He is the best of us and deserves to be treated better, even in his absence. And if you can't accept that, then you should just go back and not follow me to The End."

Silence enveloped the landscape as he slowly stepped off the block. He could see shamed blocky faces lowered, eyes fixed to the ground while others glanced at each other, uncertain what to do. Stitcher said something to him, but he did not hear, he just turned and stormed down the stairway into the shadowy depths of the stronghold. He didn't care if anyone followed. He'd try this alone if he had to, even though he'd probably fail, but he would not stand for people abusing the weak or the different or the innocent.

Gameknight could hear his own footsteps echoing through the stairway as he descended. It sounded like the banging of a drum, one lonely drum. He despised how Herder had been treated by everyone, especially himself. It reminded him too much of how he himself had been treated back home in school. *That really makes me mad*! And he hated being here, in Minecraft, always afraid for his life, afraid to lead, afraid to fail, always terrified . . . always feeling like a coward.

Another drum joined the symphony, and then another and another. He could tell that people were talking to him, but he couldn't hear through his rage. He just stormed forward, heading for the portal room. The drumming footsteps became indistinguishable as more people followed Gameknight, the echoes now sounding like continuous thunder. When he reached the bottom of the stairs and started through the wide passages, he looked to his side. His stout friend Crafter was there, his sword in his hand. On his other side were Hunter and Stitcher, both with their enchanted bows held ready, arrows notched. Looks of grim determination were painted on their faces as they strode through the hallway. He knew that they were ready to go to battle with the User-that-is-not-a-user, and that they would give their lives, if necessary, to protect him and to protect Minecraft. Glancing over his shoulder, Gameknight saw that more people were walking with him now. Soldiers big and small were following him through the stronghold, weapons drawn, faces showing the same determination that his friends were showing. They were following their leader, the User-that-is-not-a-user, and they were prepared to do what was necessary and pay whatever price was asked of them to protect their friends and protect Minecraft.

He would not let the Ender Dragon bully him, just like he would not let Malacoda or Erbus do that to him again.

"I am Gameknight999, the User-that-is-not-a-user," he shouted aloud, not caring who heard, "and I will be afraid NO MORE!" A cheer rang out behind him that was so loud it made his ears hurt. "I will not stand aside when I see people mistreated, and I will not stand aside when I see Minecraft threatened." More cheers, this time even louder. "I am the User-that-is-not-a-user, and I stand for everyone, the small, the big, the brave, and the afraid. I will not let the monsters of the night threaten your world or mine!"

Gameknight entered the glowing portal room. Stopping at the top of the steps, he turned and faced the army . . . his army.

"I am going to The End to destroy the Ender Dragon and take the Dragon Egg. Then I'm going to the Source. Malacoda and Erebus will likely follow us and their army is massive, but I will not be deterred. I'm going to stop this war and stop the monsters forever. It may require my last breath and the last sliver of my life, but I don't care. I'm tired of being afraid of them, tired of being afraid to stand up for what's right. This is the end of all that and right now is the start of a new day. Follow me if you wish, but know that The End will test the last thread of your courage, and then it will only get worse when we get to the Source. But make no mistake—we *will* save Minecraft."

He then turned toward the portal and drew his enchanted sword.

"Come on Dragon . . . let's dance!"

And Gameknight stepped into the Ender Portal and disappeared from sight.

CHAPTER 28

THE CRAFTING
OF EREBUS

The blaze pushed through the collection of monsters until he stood before his king, Malacoda.

"Sire, the NPC army is gone," the flaming creature said, a mechanical wheezing sound accompanying each word.

"What?"

"They are gone," the monster explained. "We saw them moving about the land, collecting things. As you instructed, we hid so as to not be seen, but when we came back out of hiding, they were gone. But we did see one of them, a child, running away."

Some of the monsters laughed at that, many of them suggesting that the cowardly NPC was afraid of the King of the Nether. Malacoda raised a tentacle to silence the rabble.

"They likely went into that tunnel that leads underground," Erebus said in his usual screechy voice. "They're heading for the second key."

"Of course they are," Malacoda confirmed, "just as I expected."

Erebus chuckled. *This fool expected nothing.*

Malacoda glared toward Erebus, then back at his blaze.

"Are there any left on the surface?"

"No, Sire, they are all gone."

"Then we should attack now!" Malacoda boomed. "They won't be expecting us. We'll crush them and then we'll . . ."

"No!" Erebus screeched.

Malacoda turned and glared at the enderman, and ball of orange fire starting to blossom within the ghast's tentacles.

"Ahh, I mean . . . that might not be the best choice . . . sire," Erebus said quickly. "We should let the NPC army defeat the next guardian for us. Let them take the second key and unlock the Source for us.

"But they will be expecting that," Malacoda objected.

"Look around you. They cannot possibly defeat this army. It is the largest collection of monsters ever assembled. We are an unstoppable force that will crash down upon them like a ferocious storm. They can do nothing, and this time, Gameknight999 does not have his precious users to help him. They are cornered and trapped, and will soon be destroyed."

Malacoda floated up off the ground, lost in thought. While he considered his options, Erebus glanced about at their army. They were hungry for battle and wanted to destroy all those NPCs, but more importantly, they wanted to get to the Source and destroy it. This army of Overworld and Nether monsters thirsted to be free from the confines of Minecraft; they wanted the freedom of the physical world. Looking across the sea of creatures, his eyes fell upon the shadow-crafters. They were all clustered together, discussing something, their mutterings unintelligible over the moans of the zombies, clicking of the spiders, and mechanical wheezes of the blazes. Teleporting to a new position amid a cluster of magma-cubes, Erebus could see that the strange shadow-crafter with the glowing eyes was at the center of the group. He was crafting something, but Erebus could not tell what. It looked to be a dark thing that was being created, but Zombiebrine's green body blocked most of the shape. As he watched, Erebus started to feel a strange tingling all over his body, like something within him was being magnified, but he couldn't quite figure out what. And then he noticed purple teleportation particles starting to form around him . . . but he hadn't called on his powers . . . what was going on? Looking back at the shadow-crafters, he saw the one with glowing eyes suddenly stop his crafting. At the same time, the tingling sensation stopped and the teleportation mist disappeared. He was about to turn away when the shadow-crafter suddenly stood up and looked straight at Erebus, eyes blazing bright.

"One side's hero is the other side's villain," the strange shadow-crafter said with a scratchy voice.

"What?" Erebus asked, but it was too late, the mysterious shadow-crafter was gone.

He just silently disappeared, no teleportation particles, no popping sound as if his HP was consumed. The bright-eyed shadow-crafter just stopped being there. Looking around, Erebus scanned the area and could not find the creature . . . Turning back, he could see the other shadow-crafters looking at him with strange mischievous smiles painted on their blocky faces. Zombiebrine nodded to Erebus as if they had some kind of understanding, then turned and walked back to Malacoda. Looking to the floating monstrosity, Erebus could see that the fool was starting to give orders.

I better get back there and make sure that idiot doesn't do something stupid.

Reaching for his teleportation powers, he suddenly materialized in front of the King of the Nether. He didn't even notice the teleportation particles form, if they had at all . . . interesting.

Malacoda looked down at the enderman.

"I have decided that we will wait until the NPCs have acquired the second key," Malacoda boomed. "Then we will crush them at the footsteps of the Source itself."

"What a brilliant plan, your kingliness," Erebus mocked.

Malacoda glared down at him with an angry scowl.

I'll be done with this fool soon, he thought as he carefully reached for his teleportation ability. But this time, Erebus could feel more power there, as if it had been amplified, somehow. He could feel the difference and knew that this changed everything.

Yes, I'll definitely be done with this idiot soon, and then I will be the King of all the monsters . . . and Minecraft, and the physical world will soon be mine.

And Erebus chuckled his eerie, creepy enderman laugh as he smiled up at Malacoda.

CHAPTER 29

THE END

Gameknight999 materialized into a strange landscape of pale yellow blocks and tall dark pillars. But landscape was not quite the right word. He knew that this was actually a huge island, all made from the beige end stone blocks, the whole thing just floating in a dark emptiness that extended out in all directions; no features around the island . . . no stars, just the void.

Looking down, Gameknight could see that he had materialized on an obsidian platform that was five blocks by five blocks in size. And fortunately for him, the obsidian platform was actually on the island and not floating in open space; that was a lucky break.

Moving to the edge of the platform, he surveyed his surroundings. A hill maybe ten to twelve blocks high stood before him, blocking off his view of the area. Peeking up from far behind the hill, Gameknight could see the top of obsidian pillars, their summits capped with flame. Leaping off the platform he fell two blocks and landed on the end stone, his sword ready. Seeing that there were no threats nearby, he sheathed his blade and moved quickly up a gentle rise. Gazing across The End, he could see the dark forms of endermen dotting the pale yellow island, the shadowy creatures teleporting from place to place as they wandered about. There must have been a least a hundred of the terrifying monsters on the floating island, some collected in tight groups while others were spread out, their smaller dark cousins, endermites, always scurrying about nearby. As he surveyed the landscape, he could hear the others materializing behind him, the army slowly flowing from the underground stronghold and into this strange and frightening land. Feeling a presence next to him, he turned and found Crafter at his side.

"Welcome to The End," Gameknight said as he patted his friend on the shoulder.

Crafter looked at the landscape and shuddered.

"Look at all the endermen . . . they're everywhere."

Gameknight turned from his friend and looked across The End. From the top of the hill he could see the landscape of The End without obstruction. Endermen were indeed everywhere, but the thing that drew Gameknight's attention was the shadowy towers. Tall, dark obsidian pillars jutted up into the air all across the landscape like towering sentinels standing guard over the landscape. From experience, Gameknight knew that there would be about twenty of them, though he could only see six from this position. Atop each was a purple crystal that floated within a ring of fire, smoke and ash rising up into the dark, empty sky. The flames licking up around the purple crystals had a beautiful look to them, and made Gameknight think of the birthday candles on his last Minecraft birthday cake. He smiled. These purple crystals were the Ender-crystals and the secret of the Ender Dragon's strength.

They would be their first targets.

Turning, Gameknight walked down the hill and faced the army.

"Friends, the Dragon hasn't seen us yet, but he will soon," Gameknight said. "You cannot stand up against this demon, no matter how strong you think you are. If you try to stand and fight it, you might be able to do some damage. But then it will just fly up to the Ender-crystals atop those obsidian pillars and be healed. Our first challenge is not to fight the Dragon . . . it's to destroy those crystals.

"Archers, form a ring around the pillars and shoot the crystals. One shot will cause them to explode. They must be destroyed as quickly as possible. Swordsmen, guard the archers. Dig a channel three blocks wide and fill it with water. Archers, stand in the water. That will protect you from the endermen. Remember, if you see the dragon coming at you . . . run. Don't stand there and try to fight with it, unless you've given up all hope and want your days to end. Now let's go."

Drawing his sword, he turned toward the nearest pillar and ran.

"FOR MINECRAFT!" he yelled.

"FOR MINECRAFT!" the huge army bellowed as they followed him into the battle for The End.

They flowed across the landscape like an unstoppable flood. All of the endermen nearby stopped their senseless wandering and turned toward the invaders, their eyes glowing bright in the dim light of The End. Some of the dark creatures started to approach the army, their devilish curiosity drawing them near.

The first group of archers reached the nearest pillar and started firing. It was hard to get the range correct. The arrows fell short at first, embedding into the side of the obsidian pillar.

"Higher, aim higher," Gameknight yelled as he sped by, heading for the next tower. "Archers, spread out and get to all the Ender-crystals, quickly. Warriors, protect them."

And then one of the arrows made contact with the Ender-crystals. An explosion resonated throughout The End as the purple block exploded. A cheer erupted from the NPC army, but was cut short by a bellow of rage that sounded across the landscape . . . the dragon now knew they were here.

"Here he comes!" someone shouted.

Looking up, Gameknight could see faint movements in the sky. But it was hard to see clearly what it was, its body obscured by the smoke and ash that drifted up from the Crystals. And then he saw them . . . those terrible purple eyes blazing with hatred.

With a mighty roar, the dragon soared overhead, its terrible eyes glaring down at the intruders. As it flew by, Gameknight could see its long spiked tail trailing behind its winged body like a giant black snake. The grey spikes that ran down its length gleamed in the gloomy light of The End, the razor sharp tips sparkling ever so slightly. He knew that the touch of those spikes likely meant death and he shuddered.

Then the great monster banked, turning in a huge arc, its wings extended out. He could see the clawed tips of those wings and knew there was danger there as well. But then the monster straightened and soared over the army again. This time, Gameknight999 was able to look straight into the hateful eyes of the beast. It roared, opening its fanged mouth wide. He could see a purple glow come from deep within the monster; the strange lavender fire that glowed behind those eyes also burned inside its body. Suddenly, it snapped its jaws shut. The fangs crashed together like a mighty steel vise.

As it passed, the monster kept its terrifying gaze on Gameknight999. The reptilian head stayed focused on the User-that-is-not-a-user as it passed, its grey horns sparkling with sharp death.

Giving off another mighty roar as it passed, the horrific creature flew off into the darkness, likely getting ready for its first attack.

Gameknight shuddered, then tore his eyes from where the beast had flown. Gathering his courage, he ran to the next pillar. He could see Hunter and Stitcher firing their enchanted arrows at the next Ender-crystal. The pointed shafts streaked through the air like flaming missiles, embedding into the side of the pillar. Readjusting their aim, they fired again. The glowing projectiles arced through the air and struck the crystal, causing the top of the pillar to erupt in flame, the blast echoing across The End; another one destroyed.

Turning, he saw another group of archers laying siege to one of the towers, a ring of swordsmen on guard. Woodbrin was there planting blocks of dirt on the ground followed by Grassbrin who was leaving behind entangling grass. They were protecting one of their flanks, the swordsmen protecting the other. Just then, an enderman chuckled right behind one of the warriors. The swordsman spun and swung his sword, striking the enderman in the chest.

"Oh no," Gameknight heard the NPC say.

This enraged the dark creature, making its eyes glow bright white. It then stepped back from the NPC and screeched at the top of its lungs. The shrieking sound cut across The End like a blade through flesh, causing many of the NPCs to drop their weapons and cover their ears. The endermen all throughout The End start to quiver and shake, their eyes burning bright white with hatred; they were becoming enraged. Turning back to the NPC, the enderman struck out with its blunt fists, smashing into the NPC relentlessly until only the pile of his inventory marked his presence.

"It's started," Gameknight muttered to himself as he saw the endermen horde teleporting toward the army. "The endermen are attacking! GET READY!"

"Gameknight, get down!" Hunter yelled.

He dove to the ground just as four razor sharp talons narrowly missed his head. Rolling to his side, he stood up sprinting, running toward a group of archers that were being attacked by endermen. Looking up into the sky, he could see Hunter's arrows streaking toward the dragon, striking it in the side. The monster ignored the hits and flew near one of the Ender-crystals. When it was near enough, a sparkling beam of purple energy lanced out from the crystal, healing the dragon in an instant. The monster then turned gracefully in the air and dove toward a group of archers.

"RUN!" Gameknight yelled, but he was too far away.

The dragon fell upon the unsuspecting warriors,

flying through the group with its claws extended. The monster tore through their armor as if it were paper, reducing their number by half in mere seconds. As the dragon flew away, endermen teleported near the surviving archers and attacked with a ferocity that Gameknight had never seen before. The black nightmares teleported right next to the archers and hammered away at them with their dark fists, destroying the survivors. Gameknight watched the slaughter and felt responsible for every death.

They came here because of me, and I couldn't protect them . . . I'm nothing.

But then a voice echoed within his mind, bringing him strength . . . *just be.*

No, I won't feel sorry for myself, I'm Gameknight999, the User-that-is-not-a-user, and I refuse to give up.

"Swordsmen, put water around the archers," he yelled. "Protect the archers."

An enderman appeared right next to Gameknight. Spinning, he attacked the creature, slashing at it with all his strength. He landed two strong hits before it teleported away. Spinning in a circle, he saw where the monster had gone and charged at it. When he was within arm's length, he ducked under the dark fists that came toward him and slashed at it again and again until it teleported away. Finding where it reappeared, he charged at his dark adversary again, slashing at it as he passed, then charged again and again until its HP was consumed, leaving behind a purple sphere on the ground.

"Swordsmen, attack the endermen on the run," Gameknight yelled. "Don't stand still . . . hit and run, hit and run. Archers, keep after those Ender-crystals!"

A chuckle sounded to his left, spinning, he charged at another enderman, but as he neared, he saw the dragon swooping in from the right. When it neared, he dove to the ground and rolled away from the dark, sparkling claws.

More explosions sounded across the landscape as the archers, protected by water, started destroying more and more of the Ender-crystals. Looking up into the sky, he could see that the dragon was getting angrier, its purple eyes burning brighter and brighter. It dove down toward a company of swordsmen that were attacking a group of endermen. The dark creatures teleported away from the battle just as the dragon's claws raked through the NPC ranks. The warriors didn't stand a chance, their iron armor just not strong enough. Sighing, Gameknight felt sad, but knew he didn't have time to stop and give the salute for the dead. Right now, he needed to do that which he did best . . . grief.

Sprinting toward a group of endermen that were trying to reach a squad of archers, Gameknight attacked their dark backs as he ran by. When they turned to confront their attacker, he curved around and attacked their other side just as more Ender-crystals exploded. The endermen all turned toward the User-that-is-not-a-user and slowly advanced as he backed away.

"Attack their backs!" Gameknight yelled to the archers.

Suddenly, a wave of arrows fell down upon the shadowy creatures. When they turned to face their new attacker, Gameknight999 charged, carving great arcs of destruction with his shimmering diamond blade. More endermen disappeared, leaving behind purple ender-pearls. The monsters that survived his attack teleported far away, trying to escape blade and arrow; retreating from this small section of the battle.

The archers cheered, but were suddenly silenced when the Ender Dragon swooped down and destroyed them all with its mighty claws.

"Nooooo!" Gameknight yelled as he ducked under one of its shadowy wings.

The dragon continued to wreak havoc amongst those on the ground, tearing into squads of swordsmen as archers pumped arrows into the flying beast. But with every volley of arrows, the monster would fly high up into the air and find an ender-crystal. They could do little about the dragon until those crystals were destroyed. Turning, he suddenly found Hunter and Stitcher at his side.

"There are only two crystals left, but they are too high; our bows cannot reach them," Hunter explained.

"Where?"

Hunter pointed with her enchanted bow toward the opposite side of the floating island of end stone. He could see two wide, tall obsidian pillars in the distance, their tops glowing with a purple iridescent light. Sprinting in that direction, Gameknight put aside his sword and drew his shovel.

"Protect me," he said over his shoulder as he started to dig up the pale end stone.

Digging as fast as he could, he collected maybe twenty blocks of the pale yellow stone. They broke as easy as snow, though they felt heavy in his inventory. Putting away his shovel, he continued his sprint towards the last two crystals.

"Stitcher, have the archers all move to the opposite side of The End and attack the dragon when it gets near. You need to keep it busy for a while. Create a diversion." *In the midst of chaos, there is opportunity,* Gameknight thought; one of Mr. Planck's sayings on his wall. "Put down lots of water to protect them from the endermen. Hunter, you're with me."

Stitcher turned and ran off in the other direction, shouting at the top of her lungs. In seconds, he could hear Mason bellowing out his commands, the big NPC taking command of the rest of the army.

"What is your plan?" Hunter asked.

Gameknight looked at the two massive pillars of obsidian that they were approaching and thought about the situation, trying to put the pieces of the puzzle together. The two pillars were right next to each other, almost touching. One was taller then the other; that's where he needed to start . . . but how? Then he remembered the first spider he had to battle after being drawn into Minecraft and it gave him an idea.

"Here's what I want you to do," Gameknight said and then explained his plan.

When they reached the base of the obsidian pillars, Hunter kept running while Gameknight stared to build his own pillar of end stone. He jumped straight up as he placed his blocks, moving higher and higher into the air.

If the dragon catches me up here, I'm dead, he thought to himself. *Nobody could survive a fall from this height.*

"I hope you'll be ready, Hunter," he said aloud to no one.

Scanning the sky, he could see Stitcher's flaming arrow streaking up into the air at some unseen target. That must be the dragon.

He had to be quick.

Placing his blocks faster, he kept moving upward, the top of the impossibly high pillar getting closer and closer. The glow from the burning Ender-crystal was getting brighter as he neared the top, lighting the obsidian peak with an eerie glow. He was almost there, but he had to be faster. Placing the blocks as quickly as he could, Gameknight continued to move upward, but then . . . he ran out of end stone.

Oh no!

The Dragon destroyed any blocks it touched with the exception of obsidian, bedrock and end stone. Using anything else would be risky, but he had no choice. Reaching into his inventory, he pulled out a stack of cobblestone and continued his climb. If the dragon caught him now, he might survive the sharp talons raking across his diamond armor, but it would completely destroy the cobble he was placing. And that would likely mean falling to his death. He had to hurry.

Gameknight's hands were a blur as he placed the gray blocks of cobble one after another, jumping up into the air with practiced skill. Almost there . . . five more blocks. *I hope they can keep that dragon busy.* Three more. He went faster, jump-block . . . jump-block . . . jump-block.

And then he was at the top. Looking over the edge of the pillar, Gameknight shuddered as he realized how far up he was. This pillar was probably thirty blocks high if not more. A fall from this height would be impossible to survive; he had to be careful.

Turning back from the edge, he gazed in wonder at what he saw. Before him stood the Ender-crystal; a purple cube bathed in flame suspended above a block of bedrock. Around the Crystal was a strange metallic-looking frame that was impossibly complex, no . . . two frames each rotating about the crystal as if gravity didn't apply to them. On the faces of the Crystal, Gameknight could see complex writing, strange symbols that were difficult to read but he had seen before; probably letters from the standard galactic alphabet . . . some strange reference put in the game by Notch. As he looked at it, Gameknight could appreciate the beauty of the thing. It was a shame what he had to do.

Gripping his sword, he smashed the Ender-crystal. It exploded with a blast of heat and smoke, pushing him back a little, his diamond chest plate and leggings cracking but still holding. At the same instant, he could hear the dragon roar from the other side of The End. Far below, he could hear Hunter yell something, but he was just too far away to understand her words.

Moving to the edge of the pillar, he looked at the neighboring column. It was maybe four or five blocks shorter than the one he was on, and likely six blocks away. Pulling out his cobblestone, he thought about how to build a bridge from one pillar to the other, but then he heard a shout from the ground.

"D . . ."

He couldn't quite hear Hunter's words, but out of instinct, he dove to the ground, just as four sharp talons dug into his diamond armor. Pain radiated up his arm. Rolling to his side, he looked up as the dragon flew in a great curving arc, then lined up on him again, getting ready for the next pass. It dove straight down at him, its purple eyes blazing with hatred, white fangs shining bright within the monster's terrifying mouth. This was it, the moment just before his death. Gathering as much courage as he could, he stared at the approaching monster, a look of determination on his face. But then, at the last instant, a flaming arrow streaked through the air and hit the dragon in the chest, and then another and another. The monster stopped its dive and turned, flying away from Hunter and her deadly missiles.

It will need healing, Gameknight thought.

Standing, he looked at the last Ender-crystal. Moving to the opposite side of the pillar, he sprinted toward the edge and jumped with all his might. As he flew through the air, he could see the small form of Hunter on the ground, her red hair hanging around her shoulders as she looked up at him, a look of disbelief on her face. He landed with a thud, taking a little more damage, but that didn't matter right now. Pulling out his sword, he moved next to the last Ender-crystal and waited.

"Break it . . . quick, it's coming," Hunter shouted from the ground.

Gameknight waited.

"Break it before the crystal heals the dragon!"

He waited as fear started to ripple up his spine.

In the distance, Gameknight could hear the roar of the beast, and turned so that he could see the terrible monster.

"HURRY . . . BREAK THE CRYSTAL!" Hunter screamed.

But still Gameknight waited.

It was approaching low across the landscape of The End, keeping well out of range from Hunter's bow. As it neared, a beam of iridescent light lanced out from the Ender-crystal and shot straight for the dragon.

This was his chance.

Gripping his sword firmly, he brought it down on the Ender-crystal. It detonated as before, showering him with heat and smoke, but this time he heard the dragon roar in pain. The exploding crystal had damaged the dragon as well.

Turning in a circle, he looked for the monster and saw two purple specks turning toward him. The monster roared and accelerated right toward him, its dark claws outstretched, mouth open ready to devour his enemy. He had taken more damage from that last explosion; he wasn't sure if he could survive those claws tearing into him.

Taking a step backward, Gameknight moved near the edge of the pillar. He had nowhere to run.

Sheathing his sword, he moved to the very edge, his feet feeling the emptiness that was so precariously near. Turning, he stared up at the monster, terror filling his very soul.

"I hope you're ready, Hunter," he said aloud to no one.

The dragon roared as it turned, then tucked its wings into its side and dove straight toward his prey. It streaked down like a shadowy missile, like an unstoppable storm . . . like death. And as the dragon reached out with its sharp claws, Gameknight999 stepped backward and fell off the towering pillar.

CHAPTER 30

THE DESOLATION OF THE ENDER DRAGON

Time seemed to slow as Gameknight fell. He could see Hunter staring up at him, a look of shock and terror on her face. Turning his head, he found Stitcher and Crafter running to his aid. And as the wind blasted his face, he thought about his sister and the birthday card she'd made for him a few weeks ago. It had a childishly hand-drawn picture of him holding his sister's hand as they walked across pink rolling fields, gigantic purple and blue flowers dotting the landscape. She loved to paint and draw; some day he was sure she'd be a great artist . . . if she got the chance.

Everyone had some way of making their mark in life. For some of Gameknight's teachers, like Mr.

Planck, it was probably through their impact on their students. For his parents, their legacy was their children. But for the bullies that abused the smaller and weaker . . . what mark did they leave? The only people remembering them were their victims, and they remember their tormentors as pathetic and weak; cowards afraid to be themselves.

For Gameknight, he had been that bully within Minecraft a lifetime ago. But now, he wanted to change the mark he would leave behind. He wanted to be remembered as the person who did what was right, not what was easy or convenient. He wanted to be remembered as the person who stood up against the monsters, the creatures that made everyone afraid of the night. These thoughts all flowed through his mind as he fell. He didn't bother to look down to see what was approaching, for it made no difference. Either he would survive this fall, or he wouldn't. He just hoped he'd done enough to change his mark, and looked out at his new friends and hoped they would be OK.

And then suddenly there was a loud splash and Gameknight was standing knee deep in water.

I survived . . . I SURVIVED! he thought to himself.

Hunter had followed the plan and put the pool right where he'd needed it. Gameknight looked around at the pool and realized that it had only the smallest amount of water in it . . . just enough to cushion his fall. Looking up at the pillar from which he'd just fallen, Gameknight realized how lucky he'd been, and how narrowly he'd just avoided death. He shook just the slightest bit as the realization hit him full force.

I fell that far and just barely made it into this pool. I was lucky. He could remember his father telling him once, 'Sometimes, luck is just the effect of careful planning and hard work.' Well, whatever it was that landed him in this pool, he was glad . . .

"I just barely got the pool filled in time," Hunter said, holding an empty bucket. "Good thing I paid attention to your plan." She smiled and patted him on the back.

He winced as he stepped out of the pool. Just then, Stitcher and Crafter made it to their position, both winded from the long sprint. Drawing her bow, Stitcher scanned the sky, looking for the Ender Dragon.

"It's out there," she said. "I can feel it."

"Come on, we have to get to the rest of the army," Gameknight said as he drew his sword. "Now is our chance. The dragon can no longer recharge its HP. It's vulnerable. Come on!"

Gameknight took off sprinting toward the center of The End, not waiting for the others to respond. In the distance, he could see Mason running toward him, the entire army on his heels. As he closed the distance, he heard the dragon roar. Pulling out his shovel, he stopped running, and quickly dug straight down, something he would normally not do in Minecraft, but the circumstance demanded it. Digging down four blocks, Gameknight crouched as low as possible. Looking up, he saw four sharp claws pass through the end stone and narrowly miss his head; the dragon had misjudged the depth.

Climbing quickly out of the hole, he continued to run toward the army, his sword back in his hand. In seconds, he was met by cheering as the army closed about him, Mason at his side.

"We are glad to see that you're still alive, User-that-is-not-a-user," Mason said as he looked skyward for the flying monster.

"I'm pretty glad to still be alive too," he responded, drawing a wave of laughter from those nearby.

"What is your plan?" the big NPC asked.

"Quickly, form groups, archers in the center, swordsmen to the outside. The archers are the only ones that can stop the Ender Dragon, they must be protected from the endermen . . . and the dragon. Now, when we . . ."

"Incoming!" Hunter yelled.

The dragon dove down toward the army.

"Everyone SCATTER!" Gameknight screamed.

The warriors ran in every direction at once, causing the collection of NPCs to spread out. The claws of the Ender Dragon reached out and grabbed at soldiers, tearing into iron armor like it wasn't there, rending HP to nothing. In seconds, piles of items floated on the ground where NPCs had once stood.

More dead because of me! Gameknight thought.

"Form groups . . . NOW!" the User-that-is-not-a-user screamed.

The warriors formed prickling islands of iron, with the swordsmen facing outward, pushing back against the flood of endermen that were approaching. The archers at the center fired their deadly pointed shafts at the dragon as it passed, the flying nightmare looking for the Ender Crystals that no longer existed.

Gameknight ran across the battlefield, striking out at endermen at every opportunity. Off to the right, he could see Stitcher and Hunter running toward the dragon, Mason and Crafter at their sides. Turning, he sprinted toward his friends, cleaving through the dark endermen as he passed. As he neared, he could hear Hunter's and Stitcher's bow strings humming a nearly constant tune as they fired at the passing dragon, then turned their weapons on the approaching endermen. Mason sprinted ahead of the duo, his mighty blade carving arcs of destruction through the shadowy monsters, Crafter at his side.

Across the pale landscape, Gameknight saw the

dragon swoop down on a collection of archers and swordsmen, the flying beast flashing red as it smashed down on the NPCs. Villagers just disappeared as it flew through the company, leaving behind piles of items and vacant looks on those that just barely survived.

This dragon is tearing us to bits, he thought as he watched the carnage. *No more . . . NO MORE.*

"It's time we attack!" he yelled.

Sprinting to the remaining warriors, he had them form up into two columns with a wide space in between.

"Everyone crouch and wait," Gameknight shouted. He then turned to Hunter and Stitcher who had followed him. "I'll bring the dragon to you, Hunter. Be ready. When I hit him, he'll stop flying for a moment, then all the archers must charge forward and shoot as many arrows as they can, as quickly as they can. You got it?"

Before she could reply, Gameknight streaked away. He knew that the monster was still stalking him, and it was out there somewhere.

"Where are you dragon?" he screamed. "Come and get me."

Sprinting across The End, Gameknight scanned the dark sky for those burning eyes. He knew they were there . . . somewhere, and then he saw the purple flash. In the distance, Gameknight thought he saw something that triggered a memory from a dream . . . no from the Land of Dreams. It was the hateful creature with the glowing eyes; not an NPC and not a user . . . he was something else. The creature was just standing there and watching, unafraid of endermen or dragon, his eyes burning bright with hatred.

What was he?

A roar sounded from high up in the air. Tearing his eyes from those vile glowing eyes, Gameknight slowly moved backward toward the archers, watching the dragon approach. He had to time this just right. When he was right in between the two columns of warriors, he stopped running and stood his ground.

"I'm not afraid of you," he screamed at the flying beast, "and I won't let you hurt my friends anymore. The line is drawn here," he scratched a line on the face of the end stone, "AND YOU CAN GO NO FURTHER!"

The Ender Dragon bellowed out a great roar and swooped straight for the User-that-is-not-a-user. And then suddenly, Gameknight charged forward. Leaping high up into the air, he swung his shimmering blade and drove it into one of the monster's wings, cutting in deep. Stunned by the ferocity of Gameknight's attack, the monster just hovered in the air for a second.

"NOW!"

Suddenly, a hundred archers stood up and filled the dark sky with arrows. The sharp points dug into the dragon's flesh, making the beast scream out in pain. Beating its wings with all its might, it flew up into the air, out of range.

"Get ready, it will be back," Mason shouted as he directed the swordsmen toward attacking endermen, protecting the archer's backs.

"I see it," shouted Stitcher. "The dragon is over there."

Gameknight looked in the direction the young girl was pointing and could see the pair of purple eyes watching him with cautious discretion.

"I think it's afraid," Hunter said. "It's staying out of range."

"That's not good, we have to destroy that thing," Gameknight said.

Stepping up onto a small hill, he turned and faced the dragon. He could see those blazing eyes looking at him through the darkness as it circled around, looking for the Ender Crystals that no longer existed.

"Come on back, I'm right here!" Gameknight shouted. "I destroyed your Ender Crystals, all of them. What are you going to do about that, you flying worm?"

The dragon seemed to hesitate and hover in the air as it listened to Gameknight999's taunts, then turned its long scaled neck and looked back at him, its eyes like intense purple lasers. When he saw the eyes glare down at him, Gameknight threw his sword to the ground.

"What's wrong . . . you afraid of me?"

He then took off his helmet and threw that to the ground, then removed his diamond chest plate and tossed it aside as if the dragon could do nothing to him.

"COME ON YOU WORTHLESS CREATURE," the User-that-is-not-a-user screamed with all his strength. He held his arms out wide as if wanting to give the dragon a warm embrace and closed his eyes. "LET'S DANCE!"

The dragon let out a roar that made the very fabric of The End shake. The flying monstrosity turned and headed straight for Gameknight, but when it was within range, Hunter and Stitcher were suddenly at his side firing their enchanted projectiles at the monster. *Thrumm . . . thrumm . . . thrumm.* Their bows sang out as the arrows streaked toward their target. And then more arrows streaked out overhead as additional archers came forward, Bakers, Weavers, Diggers, Runners, Farmers . . . an entire community of people stepping forward to take their lives back. And as the massive wave of arrows fell down on the Ender Dragon, it roared one more time. This time it was not the angry, hateful sound it had been bellowing since the NPCs had invaded its land. Now it sounded mournful and sad, as if the dragon knew what was about to happen and was overcome with grief. Then the monster started to glow purple and white. Shafts of light shot out from the impaled body, filling The End with probably the first taste of bright light it had ever seen. The endermen all moved away as the dragon glowed brighter and brighter. The shafts of light stretched out in all directions, piercing the empty sky, and then suddenly the dragon exploded and was gone.

The Ender Dragon was dead.

CHAPTER 31

THE SECOND KEY

The army let out a great, joyous cheer.

With the death of the dragon, the endermen all seemed to have had enough of battle. Teleporting to the far side of The End, they disappeared in a cloud of purple mist. The warriors breathed a sigh of relief, sheathed their weapons and cheered again. They screamed at the top of their lungs, yelling in celebration for Gameknight999, for the User-that-is-not-a-user, for Minecraft. The NPCs were jubilant over their victory. But Gameknight did not cheer. Instead, he looked about the battlefield and saw hundreds of piles of items sprawled across the pale yellow landscape as well as the purple spheres dropped by the enemy; the markers for the dead. Looking at the survivors, they had easily lost half their number if not more.

This battle had cost them dearly.

Reaching up to the dark sky, Gameknight raised his hand, fingers spread wide. The NPCs saw this and instantly stopped cheering. Raising their hands in kind, they all gave the salute for the dead, squeezing their fists tightly over their heads as they remembered those dear to them that no longer drew breath. This was a great victory, but a sad day at the same time.

Lowering his hand, Gameknight wiped a tear from his face as he looked across the sea of faces. Reaching down, he retrieved his armor and sword, then turned to face Hunter and Stitcher.

"Thank you for being there for me," he said.

"What else were we gonna do?" Hunter answered. "We weren't gonna let you have all the fun."

"Hunter!" Stitcher chided.

Her older sister just shrugged and smiled.

Below the exploded dragon now stood another portal, a three block tall spire of bedrock surrounded by more blocks of the dark, impenetrable stone. The whole thing floated six blocks in the air, and gave off little puffs of ash and smoke as if it were aflame. Sitting atop the spire was a black egg, small facets of purple sprinkled across its surface.

Hunter gasped.

"It's beautiful," Stitcher said as she gazed up at the second key to the Source.

One of the soldiers pulled out a stack of cobblestone and built steps up to the mysterious structure. Putting away the blocks, he moved up close to the edge of the portal and reached up to take the egg.

"Stop!" Gameknight shouted.

The warrior froze.

"We must be very careful. The Dragon's Egg will teleport away when picked up. This must be done just right."

Walking up the steps, Gameknight moved around

the rim of the portal and next to the warrior. The portal at his feet had the same twinkling look as the Ender Portal in the stronghold. A sea of stars stared up at him, some blue, some gray, some white. As he moved around the edge, he could see the stars shift as if he were viewing some kind of three-dimensional projection.

Glancing up at the Egg, he knew that they had to do this carefully, or this entire battle would have to be replayed again, and he wasn't sure if their army was up for that. He'd been here many times before, trying to take the Egg only to have it disappear and reappear somewhere else in The End. Then he remembered a video he'd seen of someone using a piston to collect the egg. Looking up at the pedestal on which it sat, he considered all the pieces of the puzzle, then glanced down at the portal that was spread out at his feet, the stars sparkling a welcome invitation.

If the Egg falls into that portal then we will have lost, he thought.

"Cover the portal with cobblestone," he said to the warrior.

The NPC looked at him, confused.

"DO IT!"

This snapped the villager into motion. Putting away his bow, the NPC pulled out a stack of cobblestone and started to carefully cover the portal.

They would only get one shot and they had to hurry. Gameknight figured that Malacoda and Erebus would be here soon, and the King of the Endermen might be able to teleport with the Egg and take it if they failed here. They had to do this right and do it quickly.

Pulling out his own cobblestone, he helped with the cover, sealing away the starry portal from sight. As he worked, Crafter pushed his way through the crowd and ascended the steps. By the time Gameknight was done, the portal was completely covered with grey blocks of cobble, the puffs of smoke from the portal now contained within its sparkling depths. Gameknight moved out on the new surface, making room for his friend.

"What is it you are doing?" Crafter asked.

"We have to harvest the Ender Dragon Egg very carefully. We can't touch it unless it drops as an item."

Moving to the edge of the portal, Gameknight looked down at the soldiers below. Mason was standing next to Hunter, his bright green eyes looking up at him.

"I need some redstone powder and an iron ingot. Does anybody have . . . "

Before he could complete the sentence, the items were tossed up to him.

"Crafter, do you have your crafting bench?"

"Of course, what kind of crafter would I be if I didn't have a crafting bench?"

"Great," Gameknight said. "I need you to make a piston, quickly."

He glanced over to where the army had materialized into The End, expecting to see a massive army of monsters appear any second.

"OK, here you go," Crafter said as he handed the piston over to him.

"I need some blocks of cobblestone right here next to the egg."

The warrior moved next to Gameknight and placed two blocks on top of each other, right next to the bedrock spire.

"That's enough," Gameknight commanded.

Moving to the other side, he placed the piston so that its face was pointing toward the egg.

"Red stone torch," he shouted.

Crafter pulled one out and handed it to Gameknight.

"Put it on the piston."

Crafter moved to the piston and stuck the redstone torch into its side. Instantly, the piston activated, its flat surface suddenly extending outward, knocking the dragon egg off the bedrock pedestal and into Gameknight's hands. A cheer erupted below, the army shouting out in jubilation. Gameknight looked down at their faces and saw a look that he hadn't seen for a long time; hope.

"OK, let's uncover the portal and get to the Source," Gameknight commanded.

They broke away the stone cover and were surprised that the portal had changed from a star-filled night sky to one of complete darkness. Gameknight looked down into the portal and could see something in its depths. It looked like a beacon of some kind. He could just barely make out the streak of light that was stretching up into a dark sky. As his eyes became adjusted to the darkness, he could see the surroundings being lit by this beacon. There were other, smaller beacons near this large bright one, but the other beacons were dark, giving off no light . . . nothing. What did this mean? Gameknight suddenly knew that this was what he'd come here to protect. He was looking at the Source.

Suddenly a screechy cackling filled the air. Looking up, Gameknight saw Malacoda materialize into existence, Erebus at his side.

They were here.

"Quickly, everyone through the portal," Gameknight said. He then leapt into the portal and slowly dissolved from sight. The last thing he saw from The End was the glowing red eyes of his enemy, Erebus, an eerie toothy smile on his sinister face.

CHAPTER 32

THE CLASH OF KINGS

Erebus and Malacoda stood on the small hill of end stone that sat in front of the obsidian platform. They looked across The End and could see the army of NPCs standing around an island of bedrock, a tall spire sticking out of the middle.

"That's probably the portal to the Source," screeched Erebus.

He could see that annoying User-that-is-not-a-user standing on the edge of the island, staring back at them for an instant, then disappearing into the portal.

"We should attack them now!" boomed Malacoda. Turning, he looked back at the obsidian platform and a curious look came over his face. "Where is my army?"

"What? Are you missing your precious monsters?" Erebus cackled. "My withers hold the other side of the portal. They are keeping everyone out until I command that they may follow."

"Then tell them to come quickly, I command it. We can catch the User-that-is-not-a-user," Malacoda said.

"You fool. You still think that you are in command?" Malacoda whirled to face Erebus.

"Your days are over, Malacoda. It is now the time of the endermen."

Erebus gathered his teleportation power, causing a cloud of purple particles to dance about him.

"You cannot teleport, I forbid it," Malacoda boomed. "Remember when we first met, I stopped you from teleporting and running from me, and I will do it now." The ends of Malacoda's tentacles glowed slightly. "Kneel before me, your king, or be destroyed."

Erebus only glared back at the ghast and smiled. Malacoda bellowed with rage and formed a glowing ball of fire within the writhing tentacles.

"I've grown tired of you, enderman."

The burning sphere of death streaked toward Erebus, but at the last instant Erebus teleported away and appeared right next to the King of the Nether.

"You no longer control my teleportation powers, idiot," Erebus screeched. "I've been updated and no longer need to suffer your foolishness any longer."

He then gave off a high-pitched screech that made Malacoda cringe. It echoed all across The End, making all the endermen stop and turn toward their king. In an instant, all of the Endermen across the pale yellow land materialized right next to Erebus. Flicking one of his long, dark arms, he had three endermen move to Malacoda's side and wrap their long black arms around him, pinning him to the ground. The King of the Nether struggled to escape the endermen's grasp, but more came forward and wrapped their arms around the ghast, holding him tight. Then they picked him up and brought him near the edge of the floating island, where the end stone stopped and the massive dark void began. Erebus looked over the edge of the floating island and down into the darkness. It looked endless. Erebus knew that if one fell far enough they would eventually reach the end of the Minecraft universe, and at that point all entities died. That was where he was going to send the King of the Nether.

"Throw him over," Erebus screeched. "Make sure he does not return."

The endermen teleported out into open space with the King of the Nether held in their clammy grasp.

Malacoda tried to hover upward, but more of the endermen piled onto the ghast, making the collection heavier and heavier. They finally started to fall as more of the shadowy monsters joined the mass of bodies.

"You can't do this . . . I'm the King of the Nether," Malacoda bellowed.

"We aren't in the Nether anymore, fool," Erebus screeched. "Goodbye Malacoda, enjoy oblivion."

The enderman cackled his maniacal laugh as the screaming ghast slowly fell down into the void. As he descended, Erebus could see Malacoda's burning red eyes, his jagged mouth screaming out in anger and terror. And as he watched, the two red pinpoints of light became dimmer . . . and dimmer . . . and dimmer, until they winked out.

The King of the Nether was gone.

The endermen that fell with the ghast suddenly materialized, their dark skin smoking from contact with the end of the universe, but still able to teleport back and survive.

"And so ends the reign of Malacoda," Erebus said, then cackled the loudest enderman laugh ever heard in Minecraft.

"My plans are almost complete." He turned to one of the dark endermen standing nearby. "Go back and tell my wither generals to send them through. It is time for the monsters of Minecraft to fulfill their destiny."

The creature disappeared in a cloud of purple particles, then instantly, a group of three-headed withers materialized on the obsidian platform followed by a massive flood of monsters, enough to destroy any army that stood in their way.

Erebus smiled as he watched *his* army come through the Ender Portal and flow out upon the landscape of The End. But then his eyes fell on the shadow-crafter. His glowing white eyes made Erebus feel uneasy. There was something about this creature that he didn't like. It wasn't the sense of evil that always seemed to be circling the creature . . . no, that part he liked. It was something else. In the back of Erebus's mind, he had the feeling that this dark creature, the leader of all the other shadow-crafters, had some other plan in mind, and Erebus had not been able to figure it out. And because of this, he didn't trust this creature. He wouldn't even give his name . . . and that he definitely did not trust.

What had he said? Erebus thought, and then the scratchy words floated through his memory. *'One side's hero is the other side's villain.'*

"What do you craft?" Erebus said in a low voice to no one as he eyed the suspicious creature.

I have to keep my eye on that one, and the other shadow-crafters, he thought. *I don't trust any of them.*

But first, it was time to destroy Minecraft and that annoying User-that-is-not-a-user.

"Monsters . . . to the Source," Erebus screeched as he walked toward the bedrock portal, where Gameknight and the warriors of Minecraft had just disappeared. "I'm finally coming for you, User-that-is-not-a-user," the King of the Endermen shrieked. "And you don't have those annoying users to help you this time."

And Erebus cackled another of his spine-tingling laughs that echoed across the very fabric of Minecraft.

CHAPTER 33
THE SOURCE

Gameknight999 materialized in another strange land. The sky had the same look to it as in The End, a hazy, dark covering that blotted out the stars and left him feeling as if he were stuck in some kind of void. But instead of finding the pale yellow end stone that made up The End, here everything was bedrock. There were no obsidian towers, no ender crystals, no dragon . . . just a featureless sea of bedrock. The dark blocks stretched out in all directions and disappeared in the distance where they met the starless dark sky. The darkness of this land was oppressive, and felt as if it sucked away all his courage.

Turning to survey the landscape, Gameknight saw a thin shaft of light stretching up into the sky; the Source. And in this sea of dark stone and black sky, the Source felt like a beacon of hope. He could see it stretching up into the sky from the top of a huge mountain, the detail of the mighty peak hidden by distance.

"This way . . . and hurry," Gameknight shouted as he headed toward the beacon.

Sprinting forward, he headed straight for the shining beacon, moving across the featureless landscape as fast as he could. This was the thing they'd come to protect and they had to get to it and prepare before Malacoda and his monsters arrived.

It was hard to judge the size of the mountain due to the lack of trees or structures with which to compare it, but as he closed the distance, Gameknight was amazed at the size of the thing. It must have been at least three hundred blocks across at the base, and maybe two hundred to the top. The size of the mountainous structure would have easily dwarfed Malacoda's Nether fortress. This was the biggest thing Gameknight had ever seen in Minecraft.

Stopping for a moment to catch his breath, he surveyed the bedrock mount, looking for a way up. The sides were nearly vertical. Many places were a two or three-block jump. And with it being made from bedrock, there was no way to carve steps.

Then, off to the left, he noticed a shape near the foot of the mountain. It looked like a giant triangle had been built out of bedrock, the top of the triangle disappearing into the side of the mountain. Running toward it, he realized that it was a set of steps that climbed upward to the summit.

"OVER HERE!" he shouted to the footsteps he heard behind him.

Turning, he sprinted toward the gigantic stairway. As he ran, Gameknight glanced over his shoulder. He could see the entire army spread out into a long line of men, women, and kids, all heading straight for him. They had looks of wonder and grim determination on the faces, as if this were the most amazing place in the world . . . and the most terrible.

Every one of them knew what was going to happen here, and that thought filled all with dread.

When he finally reached the foot of the stairs, Gameknight paused. The steps climbed upward, forming a massive incline that halfway up started to cut into the mountain. As it carved the straight path into the body of the mountain, it left sheer walls on either side, vertical sides that none could climb except maybe the giant spiders. Gameknight could see that the stairway must have been at least thirty blocks across; too wide to defend. They needed a place where they could make their stand and he knew that the NPCs were completely outnumbered.

"We have to find a place where we can defend the Source," Gameknight yelled to his friends. "Hurry, to the top of the hill." Gameknight sprinted forward trying to reach the brilliant shaft of light that was lancing upward from the mountaintop. As he climbed higher and higher, the massive beacon started to become more visible. He could see that it was not just one shaft of light stretching up into the sky but many, all forming what looked from far away to be a single, brilliant column of light that extended up into the featureless sky.

"We're almost to the top," he yelled as he ran even harder.

When he finally reached the summit, Gameknight gaped in wonder at what he saw. Not a single massive beacon; in fact, it was nine beacons all right next to each other, their diamond centers all aglow. The cluster was mounted on top of a pyramid of diamond blocks three layers high.

Herder would have liked to see this, he thought, then sighed.

The light from the beacons was nearly impossible to look at. Gameknight had to shade his eyes, and when he blocked out the blazing light, he was surprised to notice a field of beacons behind the Source that seemed to stretch out forever. Moving carefully around the massive diamond pyramid, he looked across the mountaintop. It wasn't really a mountain at all, but a gigantic plateau that was completely flat and covered with individual beacons, each spaced four blocks apart. But the strange thing was, all of the individual beacons were dark save one. The darkness of the beacons looked sad, like an entire world of lives had been lost for each.

He looked back at the army that was now reaching the top of the mountain, but the size of the plateau made him realize how few there were. When he'd started this journey, it seemed that there had been so many NPCs willing to fight against the shadow of evil that was spreading across Minecraft, but now, looking at those that remained, it seemed so few.

They'd lost so many.

And then he thought back to all the battles they'd faced: Crafter's village against Erebus's monsters of the Overworld, the users in the chamber of lava, the failed battle in the Nether where Crafter had been saved and Hunter captured, the battle for the Iron Rose, and finally the battle for the Ender Dragon's Egg.

All of these battles had led them here, to the Last Battle for Minecraft, the battle for the Source. All of those previous battles had destroyed lives and taken loved ones from families. They had chipped away at their army until only a hundred or so defenders remained. How many monsters would they have to face? Could they even do this?

Hearing sounds behind him, he spun around quickly. Crafter was standing in front of the tall pyramid of diamond blocks, his mouth agape, a look of shock and awe on his face.

"It's beautiful," he said as his blue eyes grew wider.

And then Hunter was at his side. She too was overwhelmed by what she saw. They could all feel the power in that burning shaft of light and knew that this *was* the Source, the heart of Minecraft. If the monsters made it up here and destroyed this, then all of Minecraft would cease to exist. Moving up close to the Source, Gameknight stepped up one level, standing on one of the diamond blocks. Holding his hand in front of his eyes to shield them from the unbelievable glare, he tried to look into the shaft of light. He could see something flowing in the beam, moving in long strings. And then he realized what it was: 1's and 0's moving through the Source; the computer code spreading out to all the other servers.

"Be careful," Woodbrin said. "That is the pure data stream. No one in Minecraft can touch the data stream and survive. It will disassemble you and send you out as individual bits to all the servers it's connected to." He stepped up next to User-that-is-not-a-user and pulled out a block of wood. Flashing him a wry smile, Woodbrin tossed the block of wood into the shaft of light. Instantly, the block vaporized into 1's and 0's that streaked away. "Nothing survives the data stream. To touch the beam is to commit suicide."

"What of the other beacons?" Gameknight asked.

"Extinguished by the monsters of Minecraft," answered Woodbrin in his staccato voice.

Looking across the field of beacons, he could see one still lit.

"And that one?"

"That is the server that you saved," Woodbrin answered.

Crafter's server!

Gameknight nodded and stepped back from the Source only to bump into Hunter. Turning, he was shocked at how bright and vibrant her red hair was in the white light. It was beautiful, and for a moment, all of the worries that nagged his soul, the fears that were ready to devour him, the responsibility for all of these lives both within Minecraft and in the physical world . . . all of these concerns seemed to momentarily evaporate when he looked into Hunter's eyes. And then Mason shoved his way through the collection of soldiers that now stood on the hill top, his booming voice echoing across the plateau.

"User-that-is-not-a-user, what are your commands?" Mason boomed.

Gameknight looked at the plateau that would soon become a battlefield and looked for a solution. He could feel the puzzle pieces tumbling around in his head, but he couldn't see them. And then one clicked into place, one of the pieces of the solution that would allow them to survive this battle and save Minecraft, but Gameknight couldn't quite understand it. Closing his eyes, he concentrated on that piece, but all he saw was a small shaft of light. And then an ethereal voice echoed through the darkest recesses of his mind. It was a familiar voice, a comforting voice, a confident voice.

G...A...M...E...K...

He couldn't quite figure out what it was saying. Concentrating harder, he focused his attention on the voice.

G...A...M...E...K...N...I...G...

Suddenly, one of the NPCs screamed. Snapping his eyes open, Gameknight moved to the sound. One of the warriors was pointing out across the bedrock plain toward the portal. Turning in that direction, Gameknight could see the obsidian platform on which they had materialized glowing a bright purple as monsters flowed onto the bedrock landscape. A grumbling sound came from his left. Turning, he found Mason standing at his side, sword drawn, an angry sort of growling sound coming from the big NPC.

Monsters streamed out of the portal and headed straight for the mountaintop, toward the Source. It was like watching an endless flood of blazes, zombies, spiders, ghasts, magma-cubes, slimes . . . every kind of monster in Minecraft was moving onto this island. The flow of monsters seemed endless.

"They're coming," Mason said with a grim voice. "There must be five hundred monsters, maybe even a thousand, right behind Erebus." He reached up with a blocky hand and stroked his neatly trimmed beard, his eyes scanning the faces of his warriors. "I fear there is no way for us to stop that horde." His voice then turned sad, as if he were talking about the death of a dear friend. "Minecraft is doomed."

Gameknight sighed.

"Do not despair, User-that-is-not-a-user," Crafter said, his aged voice resonating across the mountaintop. "You did all that could be done. There is no shame in failing after doing your best."

"What are you talking about?" Hunter snapped, her voice filled with anger. "If we lose, then we lose. There is nothing to be proud about. If we lose this battle, then everything is lost . . . all the lives across the multitude of server planes, everything! I will not accept that we are defeated, not until we are all dead."

She fitted an arrow to her bow and moved to stand at the top of the sloping hill, putting herself between the field of beacons and the approaching horde. Mason moved to stand at her side, his diamond sword shining bright. The surviving soldiers on the plateau then moved behind their commander, each drawing sword or bow, ready for their own personal Last Battle.

Gameknight turned and looked at Crafter. The young boy with the old eyes looked up at him, a look of sadness across his face.

"I'm sorry we couldn't do more," Crafter said in a low voice, his words meant only for Gameknight. "You've seen the horde below. You know we cannot defeat Erebus and the monsters of the night this time. We have barely a hundred soldiers left. They cannot stop the approaching tide of destruction."

Crafter turned to look up at the massive beacon, the Source, and sighed.

"I guess there is nothing left to do other than fight and die," Crafter said as he drew his own blade.

Gameknight looked at the scene with an overwhelming sadness. Had he led them to this point, to failure? Was there really nothing left to do?

He couldn't bear to witness the destruction of his friends . . . of Minecraft.

This all seemed like déjà vu, like he'd seen this before. And then suddenly remembered, he'd had this dream those many weeks ago. He'd seen this event through the Land of Dreams, and he'd seen the outcome . . . his cowardice . . . his failure.

He could now hear the moaning of the monsters as they approached, the clicking of spiders, wheezing of blazes, and wailing cries of the ghasts.

NO, he would not let it end this way. He was the User-that-is-not-a-user and he didn't come here to be defeated!

Closing his eyes, he focused on the pieces of the puzzle again. And the distant, ethereal voice was there again, but it was clearer, he could almost recognize it.

GAMEKNIGHT999 ARE YOU THERE?

Suddenly he recognized the voice; Shawny. And then the pieces of the puzzle clicked into place.

Moving quickly to the lone beacon that still stretched up into the sky, Gameknight stood next to Crafter's server.

"There is still one thing to do," Gameknight said to all the NPCs.

Putting away his sword, the Use-that-is-not-a-user stepped up right up next to the beacon, the shaft of blazing light just inches from his face. He could feel the unbelievable blast of energy from the beam, like all the heat from the Nether all compressed into this glowing ray. Small square beads of sweat instantly formed on his face.

He was afraid. The terrible energy in this beam of light made his entire being shake as the serpent of fear that lay within his soul slowly awakened.

"Gameknight, what are you doing?" Crafter screamed.

"That's suicide . . . the coward's way," Hunter yelled. "Don't give up, fight with us . . . with me." There was a peculiar sadness now to her voice, her eyes pleading for him to abandon this path.

"This is still something I must do," Gameknight999 said in a loud voice.

Looking at his friends, he saw disbelief on all their faces. They had all heard what Woodbrin had said about touching the searing pillar of light, that nothing could survive that encounter, but Gameknight knew, despite the overwhelming sense of fear and panic that was filling his mind, that he had to follow this through. As he moved closer to the brilliant shaft of blazing death, Mason stepped away from the other NPCs and stood next to Gameknight, a curious knowing smile on his face.

"No, not you too," Hunter cried, disbelief in her voice.

"You will come to understand in time," Mason replied with a sad voice.

Moving to the other side of the beacon, Mason grasped his sword with both hands, tip pointing down, and plunged it into the ground. It sounded like a crack of thunder when it pierced the bedrock and sank deep into the dark block, causing the whole landscape to shake. Holding onto the hilt with one blocky hand, he then extended his other to the User-that-is-not-a-user, his green eyes locked onto Gameknight's.

"You have to believe in yourself with all your strength in order to do something truly amazing," Mason said in a low voice, almost a whisper. "To create something from nothing, from just an idea in your imagination, takes strength and courage, but more importantly, it takes an unwavering belief that you can accomplish anything no matter how difficult." He paused to look back at the warriors, the look of disbelief still painted on their faces. Turning back to Gameknight, he leaned down and spoke in an even lower voice. "And when you find yourself at your limits, and you feel like you can't take anymore, you need to just hold on to your courage and squeeze it tight. You need to wrap your arms around the very fabric of your being and REFUSE to let go, because only in giving up is there failure." The big NPC patted Gameknight999 on the shoulder. "Now, let's make a bridge."

Mason stood up straight and gripped the hilt of his sword firmly, then spoke in a surprisingly soft and reassuring voice.

"For Minecraft."

"For Minecraft," the User-that-is-not-a-user answered as he grasped Mason's hand, then stepped into the blazing hot shaft of light.

All at once, everything went intensely bright as pain erupted throughout his entire body. It felt like every nerve was aflame and his body was being consumed by pure energy. He could see 1's and 0's zooming past him in the blaze of the beacon as his own body started to dissolve, but something that Mason had said still echoed in his mind.

Believe . . . I have to believe that I can do this!

Gathering his courage, he pushed aside the serpent of fear that circled his soul and stood up straight, refusing the yield. Feeling the grip of Mason's hand in his buoyed his strength; for some reason, he felt that link was critical and he could not let go or all would be lost. Gripping his hand firmly, Gameknight999 wrapped his arm around his chest and held onto his body . . . his courage . . . his soul, and he refused to let go. Part of him tried to dissolve into individual bits, tiny 1's and 0's, but the force of his will was too great. He had to refuse to fail. And then an image of his sister popped into his mind. She was sitting on her bed playing with her stuffed animals, defenseless, and he refused to let her go. He thought about his friends on the mountaintop, about Crafter, about Hunter and Stitcher, and refused to let them go. He thought about all the lives throughout Minecraft, about the new crafter, Digger, about Fisher, and refused to let them go. He thought about all the people in both worlds that were relying on him at this very moment, and refused to let any of them go. Pulling himself together with all his strength he grasped the shaft of light using every bit of his courage and anger and rage and hope . . . and squeezed.

And then he started to hear voices, hundreds of voices. They were chanting his name, cheering for Gameknight999. Blocky faces started to float through the beacon, then boxy bodies formed as hundreds and hundreds of individuals passed through him.

He'd formed a bridge. No, he *was* the bridge.

Holding on with all of his strength, he let these shapes flow through him until the last traces of his strength seemed to evaporate, and then he held on for a little more until the last of them had passed. Finally, when he could hold on no more, Gameknight released his grip on the beacon and fell as darkness claimed him.

CHAPTER 34

FRIENDS

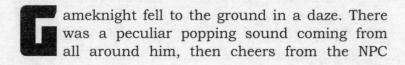ameknight fell to the ground in a daze. There was a peculiar popping sound coming from all around him, then cheers from the NPC

army. Looking across the plateau, he saw hundreds and hundreds of users materializing into existence, their names glowing over their heads, server threads stretching high up into the sky. Glancing to the nearest, he found his friend, Shawny, looking down at him, his black ninja skin glowing bright in the light of the Source.

"Hi Gameknight," Shawny said playfully. "Been doing anything interesting lately?"

He reached down and patted Gameknight firmly on the shoulder which brought a smile to his face for the first time in what seemed like an eternity. Reaching down, his friend helped him to his feet.

Looking about the plateau, he saw users he knew . . . like his old building team, Team Apocalypse: Nanozine, UltraFire9000, Gustobot2000, David769101, and ScottishRHere. Gameknight smiled. He'd spent a lot of time in Minecraft with them . . . that was, until he'd griefed some of them. He also saw Phaser_98 and King_Creeperkiller. They saw Gameknight and jumped up and down in the air. Closer to him, he saw a user named Wormican jumping up and down as well; it was one of the few ways that a user could show emotion with their Minecraft characters.

"Shawny, here's the situation," Gameknight said quickly. "There's an army of monsters . . ."

"I think I can see them."

Shawny pointed down at the approaching horde. They had stopped halfway up the inclined pathway, apparently shocked by the sudden appearance of the user army. Looking down the wide pathway, Gameknight could see a mass of zombies at the head of the column; cannon fodder, likely considered expendable. Following the zombies was a sea of giant spiders, their razor sharp claws tapping on the bedrock impatiently, their mandibles clicking together anxiously. It sounded like a million castanets being used at the same time, their clicking and echoing off the bedrock. The sides of the inclined pathway were lined with blazes, their flaming bodies pressed up against the walls, lighting up the edges of the army with angry flame, balls of fire ready for throwing. Behind these were more monsters from the Nether intermixed with others from the Overworld. It was truly the largest collection of monsters ever seen in Minecraft.

As Gameknight999 gazed down at the monstrous army, he started to hear commotion on the plateau. Looking up, he saw users running in all directions, building structures on either side of the stairway.

"Build them here and here and here, just like we practiced," a voice yelled.

Following the voice, he found Shawny striding across the plateau giving orders to the users, then directing the NPCs as well.

"We need a wall here with openings to shoot through, and raised platforms here and here," Shawny explained to a collection of warriors. "Quickly now, the monsters won't stay confused for long." He then turned and headed to the edges of the pathway. "Artillery . . . I want artillery along this edge, and archers behind them. Let's go . . . move, move, move!"

Mason moved to Gameknight's side.

"Are you OK?" the big NPC asked.

"Yeah, but I'm not sure if I'd have survived without holding on to you. Somehow, you kept me anchored to Minecraft. Thank you."

Mason nodded his blocky head, a wry smile on his blocky face.

"But . . . there's something I don't understand," Gameknight said as he looked up into Mason's bright green eyes. "Why didn't your hand dissolve into bits . . . it was in the beacon with me. It should have decomposed like that block Woodbrin threw into the Source."

Mason shrugged and gave him a mischievous smile. "Minecraft does what it wants to do, sometimes."

"GAMEKNIGHT!" Shawny shouted.

He sprinted to his friend.

"What?"

"Something's happening down there with the monsters."

Gameknight looked over the sheer wall that extended down to the wide stairs. He could see the monsters looking up at all the users, confused about what to do. But then, a dark form materialized at the back of the army, a tall creature that was colored dark red, just a shade above black. He had eyes that blazed with red intensity as if lit from within by a million burning candles. He had such an expression of vile hatred on his face for those on the plateau that it almost hurt to look at him.

It was Erebus.

The King of the Endermen scowled up at the defenders, scanning their faces until he found Gameknight. His eyes then flared brighter and brighter as he glared at the User-that-is-not-a-user.

Gameknight shuddered.

"Is that who I think it is?" Shawny asked from across the plateau. He was positioning the NPC archers so that they would have overlapping fields of fire.

Gameknight nodded.

"It seems like you've really patched things up with him," Shawny said sarcastically. "Congratulations." He laughed, then went back to positioning his defenders.

"They're moving," one of the users shouted.

Gameknight thought it might have been Disko42, the redstone master.

Turning back to the monster horde, Gameknight could see Erebus teleporting throughout his army, striking out at those that did not move forward. He was like a streaking bolt of black lightning, moving from place to place at impossible speeds. Screeching out threats, he pushed his army up the steps and toward the users and NPCs.

As they moved closer, Gameknight noticed that Malacoda was missing. There were still ghasts amongst the monsters, but the huge King of the Nether seemed to be absent. Also, there were no endermen except for Erebus. Something must have happened with the monster army.

Good, Gameknight thought. *Fewer monsters is always a good thing.*

As the horde moved forward, NPC archers high up on the sheer cliffs started firing. Waves of arrows fell down upon the zombies as they shuffled forward, their clawed hands extended before them, moans filling the air. Many fell under the pointed rain, but still more shuffled forward. But then the blazes started firing back with quick three-shot volleys. A flaming wave of burning spheres streaked through the air and fell on those not quick enough to step back from the ledge after firing their arrows. Painful cries filled the air as HP was consumed by flame.

"USERS . . . DRAW YOUR BOWS!" Shawny yelled.

As one, the users all pulled out their bows and the mountain top was suddenly shaded with cobalt blue light. Every one of the bows sparkled, iridescent with enchantments. Clearly, they had been busy while they waited for Gameknight to bring them to the Source.

"FIRE!"

The sky lit up as hundreds of flaming arrows flew

through the air and rained down upon the monster horde. The pointed barbs wreaked havoc on the monsters. Then the massive collection of skeletons returned fire. Their arrows streaked up toward the defenders, three hundred skeletal arrows tearing into armor and exposed flesh.

Erebus suddenly shouted an ear-piercing screech, and as one, the monsters charged forward. Spiders and blazes moved past the slow-moving zombies and charged up the steps.

"Fire at will," Shawny yelled. "TNT cannons open fire."

As if synchronized, groups of TNT cannons detonated, firing blinking black and red striped cubes into the heart of the monster army. The flashing blocks fell amongst the attacking monsters and detonated. They carved devastating holes in the monstrous horde, but were quickly filled in by new monsters. The concussive blasts continued as the TNT cannons did what damage they could, but there were just too many monsters and they were getting closer to the top of the stairway.

"First company, draw swords!"

A hundred users put away their bows and drew enchanted swords. They lined the sides of the stairway, knowing that the spiders would try to climb the sheer wall when they had a chance. More fireballs streaked through the air, smashing users and NPCs alike, some of them coming from the blazes, but other coming from above, from ghasts.

"NPC ARCHERS," Mason yelled, "TAKE OUT THE GHASTS."

And as Gameknight had taught them while battling Malacoda in the Nether, groups of six archers fired on the ghasts, each squad aiming for the same monster. They were still far away, but many of the arrows hit home. Slowly, they were pushing the ghasts back, the floating monsters choosing to move out of range rather than be pierced by a half-dozen arrows. That was OK. If they were too far away to be hit with arrows, they were also too far away to launch their fireballs. Once the ghasts had retreated, the archers focused their fire on the blazes, but there were so many of the fiery creatures that their arrows were having little effect.

The clicking of spiders could now be heard as their multiple red eyes peered over the top of the sheer wall. Gameknight drew his own diamond sword and leapt forward. Standing shoulder to shoulder with the users, Gameknight slashed at the monsters, his razor sharp blade tearing into spider bodies with a vengeance. Next to him was Kuwagata498, someone he was sure he'd griefed in some past battle. But that was the past. Right now, Gameknight was a killing machine, slashing at every spider that dared threaten any user or NPC, watching Kuwagata489's back whenever he could. As he fought, he saw PaulSeerSr firing his bow at the blazes that were now getting closer. Next to him, HoneyDon't and Zefus were adding their own arrows to the defense, Lamadia and InTheLittleBush guarding them with their shimmering swords. The warriors slashed at the monsters and fired their bows, but the horde was just too great and the defenders were slowly being pushed back.

"Everyone to the walls!" Shawny yelled.

Archers put away their bows and drew their swords. NPCs stood next to users as they fought back the eight-legged monsters. But as they fought off the spiders, zombies and creepers moved forward. The creepers charged up to the massive wall that had been erected across the stairway. Warriors fired through holes left in the walls, trying to push back the mottled green monsters, but again, there were just too many of them. The creepers hissed and swelled, then detonated against the cobblestone wall, tearing it to bits.

Gameknight could hear the monster roar as the first ranks of zombies move up onto the plateau. One of the users jumped right in front of them and swung his blade in great arcs. His name, Imparfa, shone bright against the dark green of the zombies, but he was completely outnumbered and taking damage. Flashing red with each set of gouging claws that racked across his armor, Gameknight could tell that he would not last long. But then, Mason was at his side, his own mighty blade carving through the zombie bodies with skilled precision. Running toward the battle line, Gameknight jumped into the fray, spinning with his diamond sword outstretched, landing blows on multiple monsters. Next to him, he could hear Hunter's bow singing a nearly constant tune, *thrummm, thrummm, thrummm,* the bow string a constant blur.

"PULL BACK, PULL BACK," Shawny yelled as he stepped up the stairs and stood on the plateau next to Gameknight.

"We need some kind of miracle, Gameknight," Shawny said to his friend. "There are just too many of them."

"I know, but if we . . ."

He stopped talking when the ground shook as if it was struck by a giant's hammer. And then it shook again and again. Looking to foot of the stairs, Gameknight could see a group of silvery giants lumbering across the bedrock plain, their heavy feet thundering with every step. Surrounding the metallic giants were white furry animals, hundreds of them, each with a red collar around their neck. And at the head of this new group Gameknight could see the lanky form of Herder, an angry, determined look on his face.

"HERDER!" Gameknight yelled, holding his sword up high. "YEAH!!!"

Ignoring the call, Herder directed his massive pack of wolves to fall on the monsters, followed by the huge iron golems. The metallic giants threw their arms up as they waded through the monster army, throwing multiple bodies into the air. The wolves attacked en masse, biting and tearing with their sharp white fangs as they tore through the back ranks of the monster horde.

The monsters were unsure what to do. The attack at their rear was devastating. Many of the monsters moved to the back to protect their rear, easing the attack at the column's front.

"Now's the time," Gameknight yelled. "Attack . . . FOR MINECRAFT!"

"FOR MINECRAFT!" the defenders yelled as they charged into the monster army.

The terrified moans and screams of the monsters filled the air as the defenders fell onto them from both ends. NPCs and users squeezed together so that they could get their swords at the monsters. Gameknight found himself at the front of the charge. A spider sprang forward to his right, attacking Slamacalf. Gameknight's sword swept up into the monster's bloated body, then kicked it back so that Slamacalf could finish it off. He was then pulled backward, off his feet just in time to see a fireball streak past his head. Turning, he found Stitcher behind him, her hand still on his shoulder.

"Thanks," Gameknight said.

"You're . . ." before she could finish, she fitted an arrow to her bow and fired at an approaching zombie-pigman, the arrow finishing off the monster's HP.

Standing up, she ran to the battle line, her enchanted bow humming the tune of war.

Gameknight stood and could now see the state of the battle. The monsters were sandwiched between two attacking forces. The iron golems were carving great paths of destruction through the enemy, the fireballs and skeleton arrows bouncing harmlessly off their iron skin. The metal giants were moving forward through the mass of monster bodies, an unstoppable force moving up the great stairs toward something . . . toward Gameknight999. The wolves were tearing at arms and legs, the animals too fast for the monsters to hit.

"I think we might just win this thing," a voice said to Gameknight's left.

Turning, he found SkyKid standing there, his dark sunglasses hiding the blazing intensity in his eyes.

"Don't say that, you might jinx the battle and . . ."

Suddenly, goose bumps started to form on Gameknight's skin as a cackling laugh sounded across the battlefield. It was Erebus's laugh, but it was somehow different, more confident. The King of the Endermen laughed louder than Gameknight had ever heard and his skin crawled from the evil, maniacal joy in his screeching snickers.

Stepping back from the battle, he looked down at the foot of the mighty stairway. A purple mist had covered the bottom of the stairs and extended out across the bedrock plain, the evil fog writhing with movement from within. He couldn't see anything in the mist for it was too thick, but as the teleportation particles started to evaporate something slowly became visible through the haze. At first they looked like small white dots, but as the lavender fog cleared, the dots gradually transformed into blazing white eyes; endermen . . . hundreds of them. In an instant, the plain was littered with hundreds of the tall shadowy monsters, each looking enraged and ready for battle. Erebus must have somehow brought all the endermen from the last servers as well as those in The End, and they were ready for battle.

They were doomed.

CHAPTER 35

THE LAST BATTLE FOR MINECRAFT

Gameknight sheathed his sword and slowly moved up the stairs, away from the battle. When he reached to top, he turned and looked down at the futile battle.

"What are you doing?" Hunter said as she ran up to him.

"It's over . . . can't you see it? We failed."

"As long as we can draw breath, there is a chance. Now come back to the battle."

Gameknight just sighed and looked at the ground. The endermen would eventually destroy the iron golems, giving the monsters the breathing room to overrun their defenses and destroy the Source. Then they'd go into the physical world . . . his world. They'd probably come out right in his basement, just like his dream.

He thought about his little sister.

I failed you li'l sis . . . I'm sorry.

"The monsters are rallying around Erebus and his dark creatures." It was Stitcher's voice cutting through the self-pity. "The endermen are encouraging the others, making them fight harder. We have to stop them somehow."

Stitcher's words triggered Gameknight into thought. The pieces of the puzzle started tumbling around in his head; a solution was out there, somewhere.

The monsters fight because they have hope, Gameknight thought. *And they have hope because of their leader.*

Gameknight remembered the looks from all the NPCs that night before the Battle for the Nether. They all stood with him because they believed in him, because his presence gave them hope. That's what he had to take from the monsters, their hope.

But how?

The puzzle pieces started to tumble even louder, filling his head with thunder. There was a solution here. He just had to see it. And as he looked down at Stitcher's sweat covered face, the pieces clicked into place.

"I know what to do," Gameknight said. "Hunter, Stitcher, come with me."

He turned and ran across the plateau, disappearing into the sea of dark beacons. Finding a place far from the battle lines, he stopped and turned to face his friends.

"What are you doing? The battle is over there," Hunter complained.

"No, it's not," Gameknight answered. "The battle is not with those monsters, it's with Erebus. I can break the back of that army and destroy their will to fight, but you have to do exactly as I say."

And then Gameknight999 explained his plan. As he described what he intended to do, fear rippled through his soul. Images of what might happen flashed through his mind, but instead of focusing on the *what-if's*, he concentrated on *the now*, but he was still filled with trepidation and uncertainty. And then something that Crafter had said to him long ago, echoed through his mind.

It's not the deed that makes the hero; it's how they overcome their fear. Crafter's voice echoed in his head, making him feel . . . stronger, somehow.

I'm going to overcome my fears.

Looking up into Hunter's square face, he could see the worry in her eyes. He knew how dangerous this was, as did she, but this was their only hope.

And then the User-that-is-not-a-user lay back on the ground and went to sleep.

A silvery mist flowed across the battlefield, wrapping the combatants in its delicate embrace. Gameknight sat up and could see Hunter and Stitcher standing over him, both of them with their enchanted bows in hand, arrows notched. They had a transparent appearance, as if they were not completely there; not part of the Land of Dreams. Standing, he walked to the top of the stairs and looked down at the terrible battle that was raging before him. The monsters and defenders had the same transparent look as they fought on the steep stairway.

Walking down the steps, Gameknight moved harmlessly past zombies and spiders as he headed toward his objective. He could see him in the distance, a vile, eerie smile painted on the creature's face. A shiver ran down his spine as he thought about his task, but he knew he had no choice; he had to do this to protect his friends and family.

Gathering his courage, he moved toward his enemy. Walking carefully down the steps, he wove a path around monsters and defenders, snaking his way through the battlefield. When no path existed, he just walked through them, his solid form passing through the transparent shadowy bodies as if they were made of smoke; he was in the Land of Dreams, and anything was possible. Stepping through a group of giant spiders, he carefully approached his foe. Suddenly, Erebus turned toward the User-that-is-not-a-user. As he moved closer, the King of the Endermen moved his head as if he were tracking the dream-walker, his burning red eyes focused on Gameknight.

It made him shudder.

Finally, when he was within ten blocks, he stopped and faced the dark monster. The silvery mist floated about Erebus's transparent body, curling around his long legs, making it look like he was floating. The red glare from his eyes gave the fog a faint reddish hue as if the swirling clouds were hiding the flames of some smoldering fire.

And then suddenly the enderman solidified. He was fully present in the Land of Dreams and glaring at Gameknight999.

"So, User-that-is-not-a-user, you have finally built up the courage to face me," Erebus said in a screechy voice. "Excellent." He cackled a spine-tingling laugh that made Gameknight cringe. "I will enjoy destroying you with my own hands."

"We shall see, enderman," Gameknight replied. "We shall see."

Slowly drawing his enchanted diamond sword, he held it out before him. This only made Erebus laugh. Then he did something that stopped the enderman's cackling. Gameknight threw his sword onto the ground. He then pulled out his axe and threw that to the ground, and then his shovel . . . anything that could be used as a weapon, he discarded. Standing before Erebus, User-that-is-not-a-user squared his jaw and glared defiantly at the King of the Endermen. It was well known in Minecraft that to stare directly at an enderman was to invite their rage, but Gameknight didn't care. He was tired of being afraid of Erebus and his monsters from the Overworld.

I hate this. I'm done being the victim, *he thought.* I just want to be me.

It was time to face his nightmare and push it back into the shadows.

"I'm not afraid of you anymore, Erebus," Gameknight said as he stared at the monster. "I won't back down and I won't run away."

"Then you invite your own doom," the enderman screeched.

"Yeah?" he said, a confident, defiant look on his face. "Let's dance."

Erebus charged toward Gameknight, but the User-that-is-not-a-user stood his ground and did not move. His sword floated on the ground at his feet, but he made no move to pick up the weapon. Instead he just glared at the approaching enderman, a look of confident disdain on his face. Erebus reached him in four large strides and attacked. Dark fists hammered into Gameknight but he made no attempt to defend himself. He could feel his diamond armor buckle under the assault, but he still stood his ground. Fear filled his mind as the dark fists slammed into him, but he had to endure . . . for his friends.

I believe that I can do it, *he thought to himself.* I am strong enough.

His helmet shattered and disappeared, unable to stand up against Erebus' rage. The dark creature turned his blows to Gameknight's legs, the long dark legs raining damage all along the User-that-is-a-user's diamond leggings. He could hear them crack and started to shake as shadows of fear began to fill Gameknight's mind. And then his leggings shattered.

I believe that I can do it, *he thought to himself.* I *am* strong enough. I *am* brave enough.

Erebus continued to hammer away at him, his relentless attacks striking him all over. The dark fists and feet were a blur to Gameknight, the speed of the attacks impossible to follow. The serpent of fear that hid deep within Gameknight started to coil around his soul, its sharp fangs getting ready to strike at his courage. SNAP . . . his diamond boots shattered, leaving him almost defenseless.

The serpent of fear struck, stabbing at Gameknight's courage, making him doubt his worth, making him question whether he was good enough or not. But no, he would not yield.

I believe that I can do it, *he thought to himself.* I *am* strong enough. I *am* brave enough. I AM GAMEKNIGHT999!

Gameknight looked at the ground at his shattered diamond armor, then looked up and glared at the monster, daring him to continue. Erebus stopped the flurry of punches and stepped back to look at his victim.

"What are you doing?" Erebus screamed.

"You cannot defeat me," Gameknight said, "because I've finally realized what my real strength is and it is something you will never understand."

"What . . . what is it you know that I do not?" the King of the Endermen screeched. "I know everything about Minecraft and the Land of Dreams. I know all there is to know about the Prophecies and about the Nether and about The End. I understand every facet of Minecraft."

"But you are unable to understand where real strength comes from."

"And where does your mythical strength come from, Loser-that-is-a-loser?" Erebus snapped back.

"You hurt others to make yourself feel better, to

make you feel like you're in control, but all it does is separate you from real friends and real relationships. You pick on those smaller than you, the weak, the fearful, and it shows your cowardice. Those around you don't respect you, for they too see your cowardice. They don't really like you. They think you are pathetic and weak, but are just too afraid to say anything. They're just glad that you haven't turned on them . . . yet. You are nothing. You are alone in your pathetic life and you don't even know it." Gameknight paused to let his words make Erebus even angrier, then continued. "My strength . . . it comes from my friends that I've made by helping others. That is something you'll never understand because you are just a bully, a pathetic lonely bully and for that I pity you."

"You pity me . . . EREBUS, THE KING OF THE ENDERMEN," the monster screamed.

The dark creature then screeched a high pitched sound and charged again, attacking the User-that-is-not-a-user with a flurry of punches and kicks . . . and again, Gameknight stood his ground. The more he did nothing, the angrier Erebus became until he was out of control.

SNAP . . . his chest plate shattered.

The blows were now landing on Gameknight's flesh. Pain radiated through his body, but still, he held his ground. And as Gameknight's HP dropped, he started to laugh, driving Erebus into a frenzy. And just when his attacker was completely overcome with rage, Gameknight leapt forward and wrapped his arms around the monster, holding the clammy dark body against his. Extending his thoughts into the Land of Dreams, he imagined his arms getting longer, curling around the King of the Endermen like coils of steel. Gameknight's arms wrapped around Erebus again and again pinning his long black arms to his side until the creature was trapped, unable to escape and to Erebus's surprise unable to teleport away.

"Hunter . . . NOW . . . WATER!" he screamed, his voice resonating throughout the Land of Dreams.

Hunter suddenly appeared floating above the Enderman, a bucket of water in her hands. She poured the cool liquid on top of them both, then dropped the bucket and poured another. Erebus flashed red as the water hit his skin. The liquid caused tendrils of smoke to rise from his dark body; water being one of the few things that can harm endermen. Suddenly, Stitcher was at Hunter's side, pouring her own water on top of the monster, a huge smile on her face as Erebus flashed red even faster. Erebus struggled, trying to get out of Gameknight's grasp, but he was unable. The User-that-is-not-a-user held on tight and allowed the water to flow over both of them. He could see panic fill Erebus' eyes as his HP fell lower and lower.

"You know why I am destined to win and you lose, Erebus?" Gameknight asked as he moved closer to the monster's terrified face. "Because I have learned to believe in myself and believe in my friends. I will do anything to help them and they will do anything to help me." Splash, another bucket of water . . . flash . . . flash . . . flash . . . "I just had to wait until you were overwhelmed with anger and hatred for you to forget that this is just a dream . . . but as you know, if you die in the Land of Dreams you also die in Minecraft." Splash . . . flash . . . flash . . . flash. "And today is your day to die. I won't let you hurt my friends anymore." The look of rage in Erebus' eyes suddenly turned to fear, then panic. The dark monster struggled to escape Gameknight's grasp, then started to whimper and beg, but the User-that-is-not-a-user held on with all his strength.

"Erebus . . . game over."

And with that, the enderman flashed one more time and then disappeared, dropping a bluish sphere on the ground.

Erebus, the King of the Endermen, was dead.

CHAPTER 36

GOING HOME

Gameknight sat up, Hunter and Stitcher at his side. Standing, he ran to the top of the stairs and looked down on the battle. The endermen had seen the defeat of their leader and their courage was now wavering.

I have to get the monsters to stop.

Reaching into his inventory, he found the strange, bluish sphere. It had a strange look to it, like it was some kind of blue pearl, but there was something at the center. Looking closely, Gameknight found what looked like a blood red eye staring back.

This was Erebus's ender pearl.

Holding it up high over his head, he walked through the battlefield. Monsters saw the ender pearl in the hand of the User-that-is-not-a-user and instantly stopped fighting and looked frantically around for their leader. A look of panic spread across the monster faces as Gameknight999 walked toward the battle lines. The endermen were the first to retreat. Initially only a few disappeared in a cloud of teleportation particles, but them more and more of them teleported away, the dark creatures disappearing in a cloud of purple mist and reappearing near the portal on the far side of bedrock plain. The zombie-pigmen and their Overworld cousins, all of them, followed them, pushing past NPCs ad users as they ran for the portal that would take them away from here.

Now Gameknight could feel a collection of warriors behind him, NPCs and users all walking slowly down the steps, every one of them ready to jump to the User-that-is-not-a-user's defense. A spider charged at him, but Hunter's and Stitcher's arrows plunged into the fuzzy body before it could get close enough. That convinced the other eight-legged monsters to retreat, turning and scurrying down the steps. Soon, all of the monsters were in full retreat, moving as fast as they could to the portal and away for the one that had destroyed their leader. Looking behind him, Gameknight smiled at those that were following him, many of them starting to cheer. The monsters of the Overworld and the Nether all retreated from the User-that-is-not-a-user.

But then thunder started to fill the air as the stairs shook. Turning around, he was suddenly face to face with the Golem King, his dark eyes glaring down at Gameknight999. Reaching into his inventory, he withdrew the Iron Rose and held it out to the metal giant, fully expecting to be squashed by his massive iron fists. But instead of attacking, the King of the Golems took the rose, turned, and headed back to the portal.

As he watched the metallic creatures lumber away, he saw Herder approach, the survivors of his wolf pack walking protectively around him. Running to him, Gameknight leapt forward and gave Herder a giant hug.

"I'm so glad you're OK," Gameknight said. Looking about at the pack of wolves, he reached out and patted the lanky youth on the shoulder. "You saved us with your wolf pack and the golems. We would have never survived without you."

Herder blushed, his blocky head turning a warm shade of pink.

"As I said back at the stronghold," Gameknight said as he addressed the warriors. "This is my friend and his name is Herder!"

The warriors cheered and all moved forward to pat the boy on the shoulder and pet the wolves.

"I thought you were running away, Herder. I'm sorry."

"It's OK. I was just doing what I knew I had to do, so that I could help you and help Minecraft," the boy said. "When I came back to the stronghold, I found the Golem King there with his followers. He liked me because of all my wolves and agreed to help me destroy the monsters."

"Herder, only you could have convinced the King of the Golems to help us," Crafter said as he approached the young boy. "Without you being you, we would have been lost. I think I can speak for everyone here, we don't want you to be anything other than Herder, for you are the best Herder there can ever be."

A cheer rang out across the army as the NPCs started chanting Herder's name.

Crafter then moved to Gameknight's side. "You notice anything?" Crafter asked his friend.

"What?"

"He isn't stuttering," the young NPC with the old wise eyes said. "I think Herder not only found this wondrous pack of wolves while he was away, I think he truly found himself as well."

Gameknight turned and looked down at the boy and was greeted by a gigantic smile on the boxy face.

"I've decided to be who I am; Herder, the keeper of animals, and I'm going to be the best Herder that I can be. People will have to accept that, because I'm not going to change just to fit in. I can fit in by being me."

"You are wise beyond your age, Herder," Stitcher said as she stepped forward to give the boy a hug. "I think you can teach us all a lot."

Herder beamed.

Gameknight smiled and put his arm around the boy. The wolves howled as Herder turned and hugged his friend.

"Come, to the Source," Woodbrin said as he pushed past Gameknight and ran up the steps.

The army followed the strange light-crafter up the stairs, everyone running to keep up with Woodbrin. When he reached the top of the stairs, Gameknight found the light-crafter standing in front of the Source, his eyes filled with wonder as he looked up and followed the shaft of brilliant light up into the air. Gameknight moved to Woodbrin's side and looked at him.

"How are these NPCs supposed to get back home?" Gameknight asked.

Woodbrin tore his gaze from the Source and looked up at Gameknight999.

"They will ride their server beacons back to their servers." He pointed out to the field of dark beacons. "You must light them."

"What?" asked Hunter.

"The User-that-is-not-a-user must light the beacons, so that all can get back home," Woodbrin explained.

"How do I do that?" Gameknight asked.

"Put the Dragon's Egg in the Source and hold it there," Woodbrin answered. "Minecraft will do the rest."

Hunter moved to Gameknight's side and looked up at him.

"Are you strong enough after that battle with

Erebus?" she asked. "Can you do this thing?"

Gameknight looked into her dark brown eyes and tried to give her a reassuring smile . . . he didn't do a very good job.

"I must survive. Look around, there is no food, no water. These NPCs cannot survive here; they have to get back to their servers, to their homes. I have to do this."

Turning from his friend, he stepped up the diamond blocks and stood before the blazing shaft of light. Pulling the Dragon's Egg out of his inventory, he held it forward and slowly moved into the Source. As first, his skin started to tingle, but then the sensation turned to needles poking him lightly all over his body, then it changed from needles to fire. It felt as if he were aflame, burning him from the outside but also from within.

"I can do this," he said aloud, gathering every bit of strength he still possessed.

Taking another step forward, he extended his arms into the brilliant pillar of light. It was so bright that he couldn't see anything, but he could *feel* where he had to place the egg. Moving a little farther into the shaft of light, he reached out and placed the egg into the central beam.

Suddenly, there was a great flash and he was thrown backward, the Dragon's Egg slipping from his grasp. Flying through the air, Gameknight crashed into a group of users, the force of his impact knocking Pips, Shin and SgtSprinkles from their feet. His whole body tingled as if he'd just been electrocuted. Looking down, he expected to see his arms scarred and burned, but they were pristine and square.

A pair of large hands reached down and pulled him to his feet. Looking up, he was greeted by Mason's bright green eyes, a huge smile painted on his face.

"Look what you have done," the big NPC said.

Gameknight looked up at the Source and could see the Ender Dragon's Egg floating in the Source. Shafts of light were reflecting off its faceted surface, hundreds of them, and spreading out across the plateau. Each beam of light was aimed at one of the dark beacons. When they struck the dark cube, it suddenly burst alight as if a switch were thrown. Now, as he looked across the mountain top, instead of a sea of dark blocks, Gameknight saw each beacon lit, their shafts of light reaching high up into the air. It reminded him of the cornfields near his school, the cornstalks standing tall and proud just before harvest. It reminded him of home.

Gameknight sighed.

"All of the server planes are reconnected to the Source," the light-crafter said, a look of pride and joy on his strange face. Turning, he looked at Gameknight and smiled, his eyes glowing a warm brown as if lit by some kind of light from within. "The User-that-is-not-a-user has fulfilled the Prophecy. Minecraft is safe!"

A great cheer rang out across the mountaintop, the warriors and users all holding up their swords and bows. Gameknight smiled as he looked at the sea of jubilant faces, but then saw a pile of weapons and items on the ground, the inventory of some poor lost soul. This was the place were some NPC had paid the ultimate price and had died protecting Minecraft. Wiping a tear from his eye, Gameknight slowly raised his hand in the air, fingers spread wide, then he looked at the survivors of this terrible battle, his face grim. Slowly the cheering stopped as more hands sprouted into the air, blocky fingers spreading apart like the pedals of a blocky flower. Everyone raised their hands, then clenched it into a tight fist, eyes cast down to the ground as they thought about friends and family, spouses and children, neighbors and strangers . . . all the people that had been lost in this terrible war, and they squeezed those fists until their knuckles ached. Gameknight looked up from the ground and slowly lowered his hand, the solemn salute for the dead complete.

But then suddenly, a purple circle of light materialized on the mountain top; a portal was forming. The purple field crackled and hissed as it formed, drawing everyone's attention. Then NPCs started running out of the portal. No, they weren't NPCs but shadow-crafters, their dark hair and dark eyes marking them for their station. He could see one that was colored like a zombie leap out of the portal, followed by another that had tiny black hairs all over his arms and legs. Shadow-crafters of all kinds sprinted out of the portal and ran toward the sea of beacons that were now lit across the mountaintop. They each grabbed a shaft of light and then disappeared into a mist of 1's and 0's, the cloud of numbers sliding up the beacon and disappearing into the mechanism of Minecraft.

Nobody moved. All the warriors were shocked at what they had just seen. Twenty seconds later, light-crafters came running out of the portal, these NPCs clearly pursuing those that had already disappeared. They stopped at the edge of the field of light, looked at each other, then grabbed the closest beacon and also disappeared.

Suddenly, a hissing sound came from the corner of the plateau as a new portal formed. As the purple ring formed, a vile, evil looking shadow-crafter stepped forward. Looking across the now lit plateau, the dark shadow-crafter had a hateful look on his face, and when he glared at Gameknight999, his eyes lit up bright white. Taking three steps forward, he grabbed the shaft of light that led to Crafter's server and disappeared. All of the warriors were shocked at the sight of that shadow-crafter, the glowing eyes being the last thing to disappear as he rode the beacon to Crafter's server, the entire plateau completely silent.

"The war that has been going on for an eternity still rages," Woodbrin said. "The shadow-crafters have escaped to the various server planes, but the light-crafters will find them. We will catch them all, eventually." He then turned to Gameknight and spoke in a low voice. "These NPCs can ride the beams back to their servers just as the shadow-crafters did. Now that Minecraft has been cleansed, they are safe to use."

"What about me . . . how do I get home?" Gameknight asked.

"Ask him," Woodbrin replied, gesturing to Mason.

Gameknight wanted to ask what he meant, but the light-crafter dove into the beam that led to Crafter's server, pursuing the evil looking bright-eyed shadow-crafter. Crafter then stood on one of the diamond blocks that led up to the Source and raised his hands to get their attention.

"I'm not quite sure what that was all about, but apparently we can go home."

A cheer rose up from the army, users patting NPCs on the back. Crafter stepped off the diamond block and moved to his beacon and stood close to the shaft of light, then smiled.

"I can hear the music of my server. This is definitely my server plane. Move through the field until you find your own server."

The NPCs spread out through the field of light, leaving the users where they were. Shawny walked up to Gameknight and patted him on the back, a younger user, Imparfa, standing next to him. Gameknight looked at all the users that had come to help and saw familiar names, famous Minecrafters and YouTubers, some of the best players in the game had come to help. He was touched and a tear slowly seeped from one eye. Maybe he had friends at last.

"Thank you for coming to help," Gameknight said to the users, his voice cracking with emotion, then chuckled. The users laughed, but not at the User-that-is-not-a-user, they laughed *with* him. "Minecraft would have been lost without all of you. You saved Minecraft."

"No!" someone shouted from the back of the group. Everyone instantly became silent as the dissenter came forward. Gameknight could see the name over the user's head; it was the famous AntPoison. "No," he said again. "We didn't save Minecraft . . . you, Gameknight999 saved Minecraft, and by doing that, you saved all of us a little."

He stepped up closer and stood right in front of the User-that-is-not-a-user and sheathed his sword.

"You used to call yourself the King of the Griefers, well, not anymore." He turned to face the other users and then yelled at the top of his voice. "I say that Gameknight999 is no longer the Griefer of Minecraft, but he's the Savior of Minecraft." And then he drew his diamond sword and held it up into the air, cheering at the top of his lungs, the rest of the users doing the same.

"FOR MINECRAFT!!!" they screamed, then slowly, one after another, they disconnected from the server and went back to the physical world, leaving Shawny at his side.

Gameknight smiled at his friend, then turned and looked across the field of beacons. He could see that the NPCs had found their servers and were diving into the shaft of light, their bodies dissolving into 1's ad

0's as they rode the beams back home. Most of the warriors were from the last server, so they crowded around the one block, leaving only a few NPCs standing near Gameknight999.

"What is the User-that-is-not-a-user going to do?" Crafter asked as he stood near his own beacon.

"I don't know, I haven't figured that out, but I will, rest assured. And then I'll be back to visit you again Crafter, my friend."

The young NPC smiled as he grabbed a hold of the shaft of light and faded into a cloud of 1's and 0's, riding the beam back to his own server. Looking about, he saw only a few NPCs left, Hunter and Stitcher, Herder, and Mason.

"What are you going to do, Hunter?" Gameknight asked.

She pulled curly locks of red hair out of her face and turned to look at him.

"Stitcher and I discussed it, and we think we're going to start over on Crafter's server," she said, smiling. "Besides, I think he still needs some looking after."

Stepping forward, she gave Gameknight a bone crushing hug. He then felt Stitcher wrap her small arms around his waist as well, the sisters hesitant to let go. Gameknight helped them to go by releasing the hug first, then stepped back.

"I'm going with them too," Herder said, a gigantic smile on his blocky face. "I think my place will be with my new friends. Goodbye, User-that-is-not-a-user, I will see you soon, I know it."

"You three should be going before another army of monsters decides they want to kill me," Gameknight said, smiling.

This made the sisters laugh, Herder's smile growing even bigger.

"Fare well Gameknight999, the User-that-is-not-a-user. I hope I see you again, in Minecraft," Hunter said as she wiped a tear from her cheek.

Nodding, Gameknight smiled even though blocky tears were now rolling down his face. Stitcher waved, then took her sister's hand and they both stepped into the shaft of light, dissolving into computer bits followed by Herder and his wolves.

Turning, he found Shawny and Mason remaining.

"Well, I guess I'm outa here," Shawny said. "Hopefully, I'll see you soon?"

Gameknight shrugged then watched Shawny disappear. Sighing, he turned and faced Mason.

"What are you going to do after all this chaos?" he asked the big NPC.

"In the midst of chaos, there is always opportunity," Mason said.

I know that saying . . . it's from Sun Tsu's "The Art of War."

"You aren't an NPC . . . you can't be. I've heard that saying before, it's from Sun Tzu. My teacher, Mr. Planck had it up on the wall of his classroom. All of those wise sayings you've been spouting have all been from *The Art of War*. Who are you?"

Mason smiled.

"WHO ARE YOU?!"

Mason closed his eyes for a moment and froze as if he were AFK (away from keyboard), then his skin changed from the big, strong stone cutter to a smaller, bald NPC with a small mustache and beard ringing his mouth. In one hand he had a dark hat that looked something like a fedora, a characteristic hat that only one user wore. And then he noticed the letters floating over his head, the server thread stretching high up into the sky. The name was just five letters, but they formed the name of the greatest

Minecrafter of all time, N . . . O . . . T . . . C . . . H.

CHAPTER 37

RIDING THE SOURCE

You're him . . . I mean you're . . . I mean . . . you're Notch," Gameknight stammered.

"Yeah, I know that."

"But if you're him, why didn't you just stop the war and save everyone?" Gameknight said, and then he started to get mad. "Why did all those NPCs have to die! Why didn't you just make it stop . . . after all, you made all this."

"Well, you see, something happened to Minecraft a while ago. A virus entered the system."

"A virus?" Gameknight asked. "What kind of virus?"

"An artificial intelligence virus."

"What does that mean?"

Notch stroked his dark mustache then turned and looked out across the plateau that was now shining with a thousand shafts of light.

"You see, Minecraft is based on its own artificial intelligence software. That's what it uses to create the landscape and the villages, and the animals, and the . . ."

"The villagers," Gameknight interrupted.

"Correct," Notch answered. "But before Minecraft was released, another artificial intelligence segment was introduced."

"The virus?"

"Yep, the virus. It merged with my AI code and

created something unexpected . . . a glitch in the software. When my AI code tried to compensate, everything went crazy and we started to lose control of the system."

"Why didn't you just delete the software and reboot?" Gameknight asked.

"Because I realized that small segments of the software had become self-aware and sentient."

"What? I don't understand."

Notch stroked his mustache again then took a step closer to Gameknight, then spoke in a low voice.

"They became alive."

"The villagers?"

Notch nodded.

"So I couldn't shut down the system . . . I didn't have the heart to do that. We put in patches and upgrades to try to contain the virus but it kept escaping, causing havoc wherever it went. I tried to put my own AI anti-virus program into Minecraft, but that just made things worse. After a while, I realized that I couldn't completely control the system . . . all I could do was try to help where I could and do as little damage as possible."

"But why didn't you tell the villagers who you were?" Gameknight asked.

"I did once, a long time ago, but they all kinda freaked out and knelt on the ground and treated me like a god. The villagers can't function when they know it's me, their Creator. So instead, I move amongst them as one of them . . . someone from a distant village."

"You mean Mason."

Notch nodded his head again.

"You should know that Minecraft would not have been saved if it were not for you," Notch said in a solemn voice. "I have watched you for a long time within the game, and was very displeased with what I had seen in the past."

Gameknight lowered his head and nodded.

"I know . . . I did terrible things to other people."

"Yes you did, but look how you grew. You put others before yourself. You helped people you didn't even know, and you filled all of the NPCs all across Minecraft with hope."

Gameknight raised his head and looked up into Notch's green eyes.

"The NPCs of Minecraft needed Mason to lead them to the Source, but they needed the unexpected bravery, creativity and problem-solving of Gameknight999. You raised their hopes and made them believe that they could be stronger than they ever realized they could be. Gameknight999, the User-that-is-not-a-user made the NPCs of Minecraft more alive."

Gameknight smiled and looked down again, embarrassed.

Notch reached out and patted him on the shoulder, and for the first time, Gameknight actually felt like he deserved the praise.

Maybe I'm not just a kid . . . maybe I can be something more, he thought, then looked back up at Notch.

"So now I know your story," Gameknight said, "who you really are and what this was all about, but what now . . . what about me . . . how are you going to help me?"

"That is an interesting question," Notch replied, this time moving his thick fingers through his neatly trimmed beard. "But the real question is . . . do you know who you are?"

"What?"

"I can just disconnect and go back to my home in Sweden, but you . . . you are now a part of the game. Look, still no server thread."

Gameknight looked up over Notch and could see the thin line of light that stretched from his head and extended up into the sky. But over him, he saw nothing . . . no server thread.

"You are part of the code that runs Minecraft now, Gameknight999. You could go back to any server here, but will still be stuck in Minecraft."

Gameknight looked across the mountaintop at all the glowing beacons and shook his head.

"I want to go home."

"Then I'll ask you again, do you know who you are?"

"Of course, I'm Gameknight999 and I want to go back home to my parents and my annoying little sister that I miss very much. I just want to go home."

Notch walked up to Gameknight and put a hand on his shoulder.

"Are you sure you want to go home?"

"OF COURSE I DO!"

"You must be confident, because I don't know what will happen when you step into the Source beam. The Minecraft code has changed in ways that I can no longer understand. It has created things that I never intended."

"What do you mean?" Gameknight asked.

"Like the shadow-crafters and light-crafters . . . I didn't create those . . . the Minecraft code did. The AI segments within Minecraft have taken on a life of their own, and are doing unpredictable things. I don't know what the AI will do when you step into the Source. For you to get home, you'll have to hold yourself together when you're in the beam. I suspect the process will test every ounce of courage and confidence you have in yourself. If you have the smallest sliver of doubt in yourself, then I think you will not survive." He paused to let the words sink in, then continued. "I'm sorry all of this happened to you, but it is what it is."

He looked at Gameknight with a curious smile on his face and then quoted Sun Tzu for the last time.

"Know your enemy and know yourself." And then Notch, the Creator of Minecraft disappeared leaving Gameknight alone.

Looking about the plateau of server beams, he turned and faced the Source.

"Know your enemy and know yourself, that's probably the most famous of the Sun Tzu quotes . . . but what did he mean by that?"

Gameknight walked around the Source, then took a step up. The heat of the Source caused small cubes of sweat to instantly form on his forehead, his unibrow keeping them from his eyes. He could feel fear and uncertainty growing within him. When he'd placed the Dragon's egg into the beam, it had only been his arms, but now he needed to put his entire body in the Source.

He climbed up another diamond block, moving closer to the blazing shaft of light.

Know your enemy. He thought about this . . . his enemy, that was Erebus, but no, it was not just Erebus, it was anyone that ever made him feel bad about himself. His enemy was every person that made Gameknight doubt his value or self-worth.

"But I used to doubt my own self-worth . . . I used to be my own enemy."

Know your enemy and know yourself.

"I won't doubt myself," he said as he took another step closer to the Source, the blazing head instantly drying the beads of sweat that were forming on his face. "I know who I am, and I'm the best person that I can be."

Know your enemy and know yourself.

He took another step up. "I won't worry about

what-if. I won't be afraid to try." He went up the last step and stood right next to the Source. "I'm Gameknight999 and I want to go home!"

He closed his eyes and stepped into the beam. Instantly he was overwhelmed with pain as every nerve was ignited. But instead of retreating, he wrapped his arms around himself and held on.

I can do it . . . I believe that I can do this and survive. I'm Gameknight999.

He could feel himself start to dissolve into 1's and 0's as the Source converted his code to something else. Squeezing himself tighter, he let the Source convert him faster and faster. The smallest flicker of fear drifted through his mind, but he pushed it aside.

"I can do this," he said to no one. "I know myself."

"I can survive this," he said louder.

"I am Gameknight999, the USER-THAT-IS-NOT-A-USER."

And then darkness claimed him.

Gameknight felt cold. His arm was slightly numb with pins and needles prickling his nerves as blood flow gradually returned to it. Sitting up, he stretched is aching back, sore from being hunched over for so long. His cheek felt hot and a little numb, like how it usually felt after he had fallen asleep at his desk in history class. Reaching out, he stretched his arms wide, then rubbed his cheek, the feeling slowly flowing back to the side of his face.

It was dark and cold. He felt as if he were underground somewhere and an icy, damp feeling chilled him to the bone. Stretching out his right hand without thinking, Gameknight reached forward, not sure why. His hand bumped into something hard, its sharp edges scratching his fingertips. Reaching for the switch that he'd flipped a thousand times, he turned on the desk lamp, spilling light into the room. Looking at the lamp, Gameknight999 could see that it was made out of old jet engine parts, all of them welded together in a complicated spiral pattern that looked like a mechanical tornado; it was a creation his father had called the CFM56-lamp—he still had no idea what that meant.

The desk lamp . . . his father's desk lamp . . . he was back at home!

Gameknight stood up and moved away from the desk. Spinning, he looked suspiciously at the digitizer. All the lights were off. The angry buzz of hornets was gone and the thing looked dead.

Good!

And then the sounds from some silly carton creatures singing an annoying childish song filtered down into the basement and Gameknight smiled. He was home . . . he was really home.

"Mom, Dad, li'l Sis . . . I'm home!"

Looking about the basement, he saw the corner where he'd hid from Erebus during that terrible dream, the old cracked mirror still leaning against the wall . . . he shuddered, but then smiled.

He was home, he was out of Minecraft, finally.

Taking two steps toward the stairs, he paused and turned to look back at the computer. He could see an image of Minecraft on the screen, his character frozen in place AFK, but surprisingly enough, he could also see images of his friends. Crafter stood next to his character's side, his small hand resting on Gameknight's shoulder. Next to him stood Herder, the lanky boy giving him a huge smile, one arm raised up in a wave. On the other side of Crafter were the sisters, Hunter and Stitcher. Though their vibrant red hair didn't have the same curly look to it, the locks flattened against their Minecraft skin, it still glowed a warm crimson, their smiles warming his heart.

These were his friends, his closest friends. And he'd formed these friendships not by being a griefer, not by trying to be a tough guy, not by bullying someone else, but by just being him. Gameknight smiled and felt a tear roll down his cheek.

"My friends," he said aloud to the empty basement and smiled again. "I'll be back to visit you soon, I promise."

Moving back toward the desk, he reached out with his hand, stretching his arm to touch the monitor. Gently he brushed each of their faces with his now round fingers as more tears trickled down his oval cheeks and smiled again, then turned and headed to the steps and up the stairs.

"Sis', I have something to tell you!" he shouted as he took the steps two at a time.

What Gameknight hadn't noticed on the screen was a figure off in the distance, a dark ominous figure that stood behind an oak tree, the leaves of the tree all turned to ash and lying on the ground in little decaying piles. The figure had a malicious smile on his face, like that of a snake about to strike its next victim. But worse of all were his eyes . . . they glowed bright white and lit up his vile face, filling it with a hatred that seem to be focused directly toward the center of the screen, toward Gameknight999.

And then he moved, and a sound came out of the computer's speakers.

"I'll be waiting for you Gameknight999, waiting right here in Minecraft. And when we meet again, I will exact my revenge and finally escape this prison." And then he laughed a maniacal laugh that would have made the whole world cringe before disappearing, leaving behind the leafless tree as a dreadful omen.

NOTE FROM THE AUTHOR

The Gameknight999 Series has obviously been about something that my son experienced in Minecraft, but it is also about something that I had the misfortune of experiencing all throughout elementary school; bullying. I was bullied as a kid and for me it usually happened at the bus stop. The bigger kids thought it was funny to pick me up and put me in the big trashcans, or take my hat and play keep away or throw it into a tree, or . . .

I hated riding the bus!

But then I met my friend, Dave, who lived up the street. We would walk to school instead of taking the bus, and that solved the problem . . . or so I thought. The bullies were still at school looking to cause mischief, especially at recess. Sometimes I would take a book out to recess, sit under a tree and read, but being alone on the playground just put a massive bully-target on my back.

Staying alone doesn't solve anything! I learned that the hard way. Make some friends and be with them. This might be difficult for some because making new friends can seem scary. Well, then this is the first dragon you must confront. Be brave, focus on *the now*, and ask them what *they* like to do. You'll be surprised at how much people like to talk about themselves, and this can help you to find common things of interest, like Gameknight did with Shawny. In no time, you'll find some new friends to be with.

My parents never knew that I was being bullied when I was younger because I kept them to myself, not wanting them to get involved, but that was wrong. Suffering in silence didn't help to solve the problem.

In fact, it made it last longer and made it feel that much more terrible. You see, when you feel like you are suffering and alone, then all you have are the thoughts within your head for company.

And worry has a way of feeding on itself and getting bigger and bigger.

If you are being bullied . . . staying silent is exactly the wrong thing to do. Tell someone you trust, a friend, a teacher, a minister . . . anyone. If you can't do that, then turn to paper and pen as I did and write about it. Put your feelings on paper. It's surprising how much it will help. Write your own Minecraft story about bullying, or about eating disorders, or about not fitting in . . . or whatever is bothering you.

Silence doesn't help!

You have to confront your own dragon in order to get free, but not with violence directed at someone else, and especially not with violence directed at yourself. Hurting yourself or hurting others accomplishes nothing; it just makes more people suffer. You have to realize that many people feel bullied, or feel inadequate, or out of place, but when people stay silent, it creates the impression that you're the only person going through these challenges, and that's wrong. There are people around you going through the same thing.

You are not alone!

Know your enemy and know yourself—if you are staying silent, then they are the same person.

Be strong, speak out, don't be alone, and watch out for creepers.

Mark Cheverton

CHAPTER I

THE VILLAIN

He materialized onto the lush green blocky landscape with a hateful sneer on his blocky face, his whole being filled with a destructive loathing for the natural beauty that surrounded him. Walking toward a nearby sheep, he grinned as the square fluffy creature bolted away across the blocky hill, a look of terror in its soft square eyes. An evil presence seemed to emanate from him like the heat from a burning house. Even blades of grass wanted to lean away from this sinister creature.

"How can these Overworlders tolerate this place?" the dark creature hissed as he glared at his surroundings.

In the distance, he could see a village, this one not fortified like many were these days. It was the normal collection of houses, each made from individual blocks, as all things were in Minecraft, formed from many cubes of wood. The squat structures were clustered around a central stone building that stretched high up into the air: the watchtower. Nearby, he could see the village well and a field of wheat growing in the distance. Lurking in the alleyways between the buildings, he could see the villagers going about their work, their boxy heads and long rectangular bodies almost blending in with the blocky homes.

These foolish villagers are oblivious to the danger

they're in, the sinister creature thought to himself. He would soon correct their mistake.

Closing his glowing white eyes, he teleported away from the scenic view and materialized in a dark shadowy tunnel. Drawing in a full breath, he let out an abrasive guttural wail that echoed throughout the stone passages and rocky chambers, bouncing off lava pools and reflecting from towering waterfalls until it filled the underground world of Minecraft. In an instant, his call was greeted by the sorrowful wails of zombies.

"I am coming, my children," he yelled to the darkness. "Prepare a Gathering."

The wails changed from sounds of despair and sadness to those of surprise and fear. The dark stranger smiled; he could feel their fear . . . good.

Moving silently through the dark passages, he descended through the tunnels, heading for that secret entrance that only the monsters of the night knew existed. Occasionally he saw giant spiders and creepers hiding in the shadows, hoping to avoid being seen, but none escaped his glowing eyes. He saw them all, their cowering forms veiled in darkness. Normally, these fearful creatures would have been destroyed, for their fear disgusted him, but he had far more important plans to worry about, and didn't have time for these weaklings.

A glow started to fill the tunnel ahead, the soft orange illumination of lava, warm inviting lava. The shadows behind stone pillars and deep crevasses began to grow dark and long as he neared the source of the light. As he turned a corner, he was greeted by a long flow of molten stone that spilled down from high above, forming a broad pool. Nearby, a waterfall gurgled its cool waters from a hole in the wall, the long blue stream flowing into the boiling pool. Where the opposites met, obsidian was formed, the black speckled blocks reflecting the light from the molten stone and casting beams of light throughout the chamber.

This was it.

The entrance to Zombie-town was always near the meeting of water and lava. Casting his glowing gaze across the jagged stone walls, he instantly saw the pattern that masked the secret door: a flat section of stone with a single block sticking out. Moving to the outlier, he placed his hand against the block and pressed. A click sounded, then the wall swung inward revealing a long dark tunnel. Stepping into the passage, the stranger turned and closed the stone door, then sprinted down the rocky corridor. As he ran, he could see the end of the path growing brighter, the walls changing from the stone grey to an inviting orange, like the coming of autumn. More lava: the stranger smiled an eerie smile. He loved lava . . . it always reminded him of home.

When he reached the end of the tunnel, he stopped and looked at his surroundings. Before him stood a massive chamber that stretched upward maybe twenty blocks or more, and at least a hundred blocks across. All across the chamber floor were small homes built out of stone and dirt, each a different size and shape. The blocky structures seemed to be competing with each other, walls pushing against walls in a battle for space that seemed to create a patchwork of geometry that had a strange kind of chaotic beauty to it. Nothing matched, nothing was the same, and yet every Zombie-town looked like every other.

A large clearing could be seen positioned at the center of the chamber, the encroaching buildings kept away by some kind of mystical force. That was his destination. Taking the blocky steps two at a time, the dark stranger ran down to the cavern floor then sprinted through the maze of narrow streets, turning this way and that in a confused serpentine path that wended its way through the town. At some points, he found the walkway blocked by the corners of houses. Drawing his diamond pick, he quickly smashed through the blocks, leaving the damage behind as he streaked for the clearing.

In minutes, he'd traversed the floor of the cavern and reached the edge of the clearing. Near the edge of the open square, strange green sparks seemed to shoot up into an air like the fireworks for some kind of alien celebration. Zombies stood around these sparkling fountains, just standing beneath them, bathing in their flow, their dark eyes closed in blissful contentment. The stranger knew that these were the HP fountains that zombies depended on for life. They did not eat 'brains' as the foolish users thought; that was a silly myth. Zombies fed by standing within the emerald flow of the HP fountains, the green sparks restoring their health and sating their hunger. He knew that if a zombie spent too much time away from a zombie-town, then they would die. As a result, they were forced to always stay nearby, shackled to their underground existence forever...